William U. Desart

Lord and Lady Piccadilly

William U. Desart

Lord and Lady Piccadilly

ISBN/EAN: 9783337122034

Printed in Europe, USA, Canada, Australia, Japan

Cover: Foto ©Andreas Hilbeck / pixelio.de

More available books at **www.hansebooks.com**

LORD AND LADY PICCADILLY

BY

THE EARL OF DESART

AUTHOR OF 'KELVERDALE' ETC.

THIRD   *EDITION*

LONDON

SWAN SONNENSCHEIN & CO.

PATERNOSTER SQUARE

1888

LORD AND LADY PICCADILLY.

CHAPTER I.

' ONLY a tiny drop.'

'Dear me, how pressing you are, Mr. Ballard! And to ask a girl like me to drink such stuff! Why, it will make me cough.'

'How do you know that, Miss Amalia?' asked a blue-eyed youth in his shirt-sleeves, who was seated on the billiard-table. Miss Amalia turned on him with a vivacity almost un-English—if I may be permitted to adopt a word sacred to our magistrates for stabbing cases, and once used in connection with secret voting, now our second Magna Charta.

'You mean—yes, I know, Mr. St. James, you are always so satiric—you mean that I have tried it before.'

'Not a bit of it, Amy,' said the tempter, still holding out his glass towards the fair and hesitating one's lips. 'Not a bit of it; he only means that he is wonderstruck at the ability with which, making use of the enormous powers of inductive ratiocination you possess, you have, reasoning from analogous studies in your father's bar, reached the logical conclusion that brandy-and-water swallowed by a female person un-accustomed to it does and must cause to that person the spasm of the nerves which we call coughing.'

B

But Miss Amalia did not seem much impressed by these fine words; she saw a shade of displeasure in the blue eyes, and—a little reluctantly, perhaps—she pushed away the tempting glass, and said: 'I don't know what you take me for, Mr. Ballard. I believe the serpent used just such words as yours in the Garden of Eden.'

'Evidently not,' replied Mr. Ballard, as he finished the liquor, 'for he conquered and I fail. Are you as particular as your sister, Jane?' And he turned to another girl who was seated on the marker's high stool, and in whose eyes were admiration of the speaker.

'Oh, no! At least, I don't like brandy. But I like to hear you make grand speeches.'

'By Jove, Humphrey, she ought to be in the House of Commons!' cried he of the blue eyes. 'But come on. Old Porty will be kicking up a row if we don't get back by six, and we have only time for one more game. Whose turn is it to mark? Yours, Miss Amalia, I think.'

'I do hope you'll win,' whispered that young lady to him, as she dispossessed her sister of the stool of office and armed herself with the rest.

'No, I shan't; Humphrey is too strong for me, I think. But I'm improving, and I won't take points. I may be inferior, but I don't see why I should acknowledge it in such a practical way. Half-a-crown, Humphrey?'

Then the game began; and while they are thus occupied we may take a look at the characters, or at their outsides; and I may present them in due form to the reader.

Harry St. James, the laughing youth, putting twice too much screw on his ball for a cannon there, is the son of the late Honourable George John St. James, brother to the present Lord Piccadilly. His father having been the third son of the late lord, and having, moreover, spent his patrimony in riotous living,

Harry is not, although born in the purple, very well provided with funds wherewith to keep that purple in good colour, and had it not been for his uncle's generosity, he could scarcely have been sent to that expensive tutor's where he is now completing his education, after a course of Eton and the grand tour of the Continent. He, Harry St. James, is now eighteen years of age, six feet high, has merry blue eyes and well-cut features, broad shoulders, a strong will, a fiery but not bad temper, and an uncommon belief in himself, in the world generally, and in Sentiment—with a capital S. It is sad to think that the usage of the world, the rough and tumble of every-day life, may take the merriness out of the eyes, may misdirect the strong will, may sour the generous temper, and will certainly destroy the belief and the sentiment; but at present, as he stands before us in the billiard-room of the King's Arms Inn at Ilborough, Harry St. James is a good specimen of a well-fed, well-brought-up, refined, and athletic British youth.

His antagonist is a great contrast to him. Humphrey Ballard—who has come down on a visit to his old tutor, Mr. Portleton, of Ilborough Rectory—is a *man*. That is, he has attained the magic age of twenty-one, knows nothing now of Latin verses or algebra, and is revelling in the new and delicious pleasure of independence. True that until the death of his cousin, the well-known Mr. Ballard Erdmore, of Erdmore Castle, in Ireland, he is not of much worldly wealth; but he has enough to go where he will; to dine at his London club; to attend the theatres with praiseworthy regularity; and even to give presents to any young lady on whom his rather roving affections may chance to fall. He is tall and gaunt; handsome according to the dictum of shop-girls and barmaids; with an olive complexion, large unstable dark eyes, a well-pointed black moustache, and just the *soupçon* of

that goat-like growth of hair which used to be termed
'an imperial' upon his chin.   His dress is always perfect; his manner, when judged by a certain not too
refined or knowledgeable standard, perfect also; there
are rings on his fingers; there is pomatum on his well-
brushed hair; and he is versed in the nineteenth-
century edition of the 'nice conduct of a clouded cane.'
But, spoiled by bar-room flirtations and billiard-marker
flattery as he is, Ballard is something of a gentleman
at heart; and Harry St. James, quick to discern good
points, soon found this out when he first arrived at Mr.
Portleton's, and ended by making fast friends with the
'cock' of the tutor's establishment.   True, much
in the man grated on the natural refinement of the
other; but youth is generous, and, after all, Harry
was not quite sure that he was right in his judgment,
nor knew accurately that what seemed vulgar and
swaggering to him might not perhaps be correct and
manly.   As to Ballard himself, he would have been a
paragon of churlishness could he have resisted the
influence of the charm of Harry's manner.   Stern and
unyielding when occasion demanded, he was ordinarily
as caressing and soft as a woman; and, besides (let it
be spoken low), Ballard, whose family—notwithstanding
the Irish castle—was not very grand, liked to think that
by his friendship with Harry he had effected a kind of
foot-hold in the ranks of the true aristocracy.

But it was not love for Harry nor for Mr. Portleton
that brought him back this July to Ilborough, where
the amusements were somewhat limited; back, too,
while Kitty This was dancing her best at the Alhambra
and Jenny That looking lovely in the chorus at another
place of amusement.   Certainly not.   But to explain
what did bring him back it is necessary to introduce
the two young ladies who are looking on at the
billiard match.

Mr. Heckthorpe, owner of the King's Arms at

Ilborough, had two daughters. He had married long ago the governess at the Hall (now in her grave), and the union of intellectual culture with commercial success—for the King's Arms, an old-established inn, brought in a fair income even now that the glories of 'the road' were dead—had been eminently successful. The Misses Heckthorpe, Amalia and Jane, were the undoubted 'belles' of Ilborough.

There was not a farmer within a circuit of twelve miles who was quite heartwhole in their regard, and the young shopkeepers of the little town were reported to propose to one or other of them after closing hours every Saturday. But the young ladies turned up their noses at such mean game. Was not the Rectory, with its twelve young gentlemen of good family, within a short walk of the town? and, notwithstanding the Reverend Portleton's injunctions, did not those young gentlemen make it a practice to spend much of their spare time at the inn? They were young, it is true, and they had a knack of disappearing just as their courtship was becoming practical, but 'hope springs eternal in the human breast,' and there was no knowing what might not some day happen. Mr. Heckthorpe placed implicit reliance in his daughters' prudence, and here he was right. They could take far better care of themselves than he could have taken of them, and their ambition in itself was sufficient to steer them clear of any rocks of youthful folly.

They were twins, and would have been so like each other as to be almost undistinguishable had it not been that Miss Jane—tempted by the solicitations of a hairdresser who loved her—once attempted to add to her beauty by adopting the then fashionably coloured hair of a yellowish or tawny hue; while her sister Amalia adhered to the dark brown tresses of nature. 'Black and Gold' they had been named by a satirical cabinet-maker of the neighbourhood; and even the country gentlemen's wives and daughters, while tossing up their heads when they passed the pair, in their inmost hearts owned that they formed a pleasing contrast, with their neat figures, their well-fitting frocks, their expressive faces, and their cunningly contrasted locks. 'Black and Gold' never perhaps had been quite so contented with their sweet selves as now. Mr. Ballard—the smartest young gentleman they had ever known, even from the Rectory—was undoubtedly in love with Jane. He made no secret of the fact that his visit to the tutor was merely for the purpose of carrying on the flirtation commenced when he was a pupil of Mr. Portleton's; while as to Mr. St. James, well—he was very young, but he certainly was distinguished-looking, and it would be strange if Amalia could not fan the flame she had lit, as she supposed, in his heart, until it reached the desired conflagration. He certainly, as she knew, preferred her society to that of the local attorney's daughters; and there was little danger from the surrounding county aristocracy. Mr. Portleton, though he could not prevent his pupils' visits to the King's Arms, would not permit of such open waste of time as their accepting invitations to lawn-tennis or dinner from the gentry of the neighbourhood.

No wonder that Amalia mistook Harry's manner, for, as I have said, even with a man it had something strangely caressing about it, and with a woman, whatever her class or rank, he could be nothing but courteous and winning. Ballard's arrival had made his visits much more frequent than usual, for the pair were inseparable; and when the two girls retired to the room they occupied jointly, each night they settled all the little details of the double wedding; ticked off the names of the bridesmaids, whom they should ask and whom they should snub, and wherewithal they should be clothed. Amalia knew that

there was a Lord somehow connected with Harry, and
that was pleasant. All the relatives of a Lord must be
rich. And Jane—well, Jane was honestly head over
ears in love with the smart Mr. Ballard, listened to
his flippant converse with intense delight, and never
ceased to admire his young moustache, his embryo
imperial and his jewellery; or 'jewelry,' as the
American 'spellists' have it.

'Make him in love with you, Jenny,' said the wiser
Amalia. 'Don't go and care too much for him. It
don't pay.'

But Jenny, who had something in her character
which her sister knew not of, was content to leave
nature alone with her heart—whatever she may have
done as to her hair—and lived now in the seventh
heaven of maiden ecstasy.

The gossips of Ilborough, who had been wont to
sneer a little at the visit of the 'Rectory boys' to the
King's Arms, sneered not at the courtship of this
emancipated man of the smart garments, and Jane
felt, as she walked down the High Street, that her
importance in the world had trebled since Ballard
had come back, and snubbed the unfortunate young
farmers on market days so unmercifully that —
proud as they knew 'Black and Gold' to be—they
wondered anew that Providence could have im-
planted such overwhelming haughtiness in the human
breast.

The cause of this had no fixed ideas or plans. He
admired beauty, and Jane was decidedly beautiful;
he liked being listened to and flattered, and these
advantages he got from her; and he kept back—with
that resolution often born of irresolution—all awkward
thoughts of what he meant to do with the love he had
gained. He harboured no evil thoughts—no one in
this respect ever does, except the villains of novels or
dramas—he simply let himself drift. Chance had

brought her to him, let Chance get them out of the
hobble as best she might. Fortune or Fate perhaps
he called it, as weak men generally do, and was prepared to hurl the fiercest anathemas at the blind
goddess if she did not save him the trouble of using
his own intellect. At any rate, just at present, there
was no need to make up what he called his mind.
He could prolong his visit to the Rectory for another
fortnight or three weeks, before he went for his usual
visit to the Irish castle; and at twenty-one even a
fortnight's end is a long way off. As to Harry, if
anyone had told him that he was trifling with Miss
Amalia's young affections, he would have laughed in
that person's face. He thought her a jolly, vulgar,
honest girl, who would make a good wife some day
to a farmer or to her father's successor in the public-
house, and he enjoyed their friendly chaffing matches,
their mock quarrels (wound up by a kiss perhaps), and
the pleasant way she had given him of passing an
afternoon, with supreme unconsciousness of difficulty
or danger. Of course, on the other hand, he saw the
state of affairs as regarded his friend.

'Humphrey,' he said to him, as they strolled home,
after their game of billiards, 'ain't you going a little
too far with that girl?'

'How do you mean?' asked Ballard, secretly pleased,
but assuming a gruff air.

'Why, anyone can see she's very fond of you, and—
and perhaps it's not quite fair.'

Ballard 'bridled' to himself, but rejoined still with
a slightly offended manner, 'Not a bit. They all know
how to take care of themselves. And it's natural she
should prefer me to the bumpkins about.'

'Yes, exactly. But when you go away again,
will your coming here and spooning her make her
better like having no one but those bumpkins to
talk to?'

'Come, Harry,' said the other, twisting his moustache and laughing, 'you're a nice one to preach. What are you doing with Amalia, I should like to know?'

'Oh, that's different. I'm only a boy; and, besides, she's not spooney. She'd flirt with you before my eyes if you'd let her. No, you mustn't compare yourself with me. I'm only a pleasant sort of joke to her. To Jane you are an awfully jolly reality.'

'It would be a nuisance,' remarked Ballard, after a pause, during which they neared the entrance gates of the Rectory, 'if the child took it all too seriously. I am very fond of her, Harry, you know; and I believe you are right about her feelings to me. It is a bore in some ways; but she's such a dear little thing—so clinging, you know, and really quite a lady. Don't you think she is quite a lady?'

The contest in Harry's mind between telling a white lie or making an unpleasantly true answer was brought to a termination by the appearance of the Rector, who was weeding some flower-beds in front of his house.

'Oh, here you are. I was just going to put off dinner. Well, Ballard, what do you think of St. James? Has he improved in his acquirements since you left?'

'I scarcely can tell yet, sir. We haven't talked— at least——'

'He has only asked me psychological questions as yet, sir. We were just beginning to touch on logic when we got here.'

'Ah, my dear boy, remembering the exalted sphere you may be called upon to fill, and the absolute necessity of a peer of the realm to be better educated than other persons, it is certainly——'

'But, sir, as my uncle Roger and my cousin George are both alive and kicking, I scarcely see why I should qualify for the House of Lords.

'One never knows,' said the Rector, looking with affection at the merry youth before him. 'There—run in and make yourself tidy. Ballard,' he went on, as Harry disappeared, stopping the other, who was about to follow, 'Ballard, I have just heard what discomposes me somewhat. Mr. Ardle, the grocer, was up here on some household matter, and took occasion to say a few words to Mrs. Portleton about those girls at the King's Arms.'

'Well, sir?'

'Connecting them, or one of them, with our young friend. I am not a lover of gossip, as you are aware, but I confess it would give me great pain if I thought that he grew fond of their society. They may, no doubt, be good girls—in their proper position; but they are not fit company for a St. James.'

'No, sir,' said Ballard, looking a little foolish.

'And remember too,' went on the old gentleman, who loved to prose, as he slowly paced up and down his trim-kept lawn, 'that there are other reasons. These girls—I have often met them in the town, and know them by sight, although they attend the Dissenting Chapel——these girls are well favoured and apparently refined. They may be good and innocent, and they would assuredly be dazzled by a young man like our friend, did he pay either of them what they might construe into attentions. Will you hint to him that he might, albeit innocently, be doing them harm? St. James is a very considerate, generous youth; he would understand this.'

'Yes, sir,' answered Ballard a little gruffly, for he did not see why only Harry should be suspected of Don Juanism, and why there was no anxiety on his account. Although sufficiently acute, he had never guessed that the old-fashioned clergyman had long ago set him down, not as a snob (that word did not come into the Rector's vocabulary), but as a non-aristocrat—as one who had not to be hedged round with all the precautions which should guard a scion of blue blood.

If Mr. Portleton had heard of Ballard's marriage with a tinker's daughter he would have been grieved: but had Harry compromised himself even with the child of a respectable curate, he would have been in despair.

Ballard was hurt by the difference thus evidently made between them, and followed his ex-tutor into the house with a haughty step that Miss Jane Heckthorpe would have thought worthy of a monarch ascending the throne—or the scaffold.

CHAPTER II.

WHEN Joseph St. James succeeded, as a boy, to the title and estates of the family, great things were predicted of him. Tutors, relatives, and toadies all declared in chorus that never was such a fine young man seen. He took first prizes at school; he dazzled examiners at Oxford; he beat truculent bargees both in slang and in fisticuffs. He could run, and jump, and fight like a professional; and, of course, being a Lord (I am speaking of a bygone time), he could swear and drink. When he appeared—the richest young man in Society—women fell in love with him, banks were broken by his reckless gambling, wagers of all kinds—according to the custom of the day—were won by his prowess. He ate twelve dozen of oysters at a sitting, and then ran from the Haymarket to Hounslow and back in some incredible time. He went to a City ball and was accepted by twenty-five damsels thereat, thus winning a bet of a thousand pounds. He rode one horse from London to York,

and beat Dick Turpin in that he shed no tears when
his poor animal gave up the ghost.   Had 'Ouida'
lived then, Joseph, Lord Piccadilly would have lived
with us in a thrilling romance; as it is, we only catch
passing glimpses of him in the chatty and scandalous
annals of his early days.

In those days there was much that was brutal and
debased.   Prize and cock fighting flourished, and
spades were called spades pretty plainly.   Æstheticism
had not come to teach us to live up to our crockery;
nor did the vulgar painters of the time care for unhealthy damsels with thick noses reiterated over and
over again; the gentle art of professional beautyism
had not been invented, nor had the Middlesex magistrates—not to speak of the Salvation Army—made
London moral.   Yet in those brutal days the divorce
between refinement and athleticism had not grown so
complete as now.   A man who aimed at shining before
his compeers would then try to combine the two.   His
horse-racing, or his cock-fighting, or his cricket, or his
boating, would not then be allowed to absorb all his
faculties.   The pleasant, careless effrontery of our own
superior time was not then known.   He doffed his hat
to a lady; he never puffed a cigarette in her face (nay,
he never even smoked in the Park!); and he attempted in some measure to keep up that courtesy
which used to be considered the mark of a gentleman.
A scholar then could fight an impudent plebeian; an
amateur boxer could turn a copy of Latin verses.   No
doubt all this was foolish and unnecessary—at all
events, it has completely disappeared.

It never struck any of the early flatterers of the
handsome and brilliant Lord Piccadilly that his character was wanting in two things, which—let a man be
as beautiful, strong, and clever as you please—are
nevertheless desirable things in a man's nature.   These
two things were heart and principle.   A man without

principle may have heart, and possibly a man without heart may have principle. At all events our Baron had neither, and did marvellously well without them— up to a certain point. For a time his courtliness, his charming way of saying pretty things, and his reputa- tion for gallantry made up with women for sincerity ; while as to principle, the fund is never needed to be drawn upon by a man with more money than he can spend. It is only your poor devil who can scarcely afford a dinner at his own expense who is expected to be a Sir Galahad and a Plato rolled into one.

Lord Piccadilly, naturally enough, never wanted to borrow money, or to obtain signatures on his note of hand, or to steal. So he was writ down honest. Hus- bands of pretty wives for a time hated and feared him, but eventually they generally saw the futility of such emotions, and came to look upon him as a sort of 'act of God' which has to be borne with equanimity, if not cheerfulness. A contentedly-minded parishioner, on seeing his church struck by lightning, is said to have consoled himself by remembering that the storm had, after all, cleared the air. In the same way Lord Piccadilly became a necessary evil, which, if endured with fortitude and good nature, bore some good fruits —such as dinners at Piccadilly House, the loan of the Paris hotel, and the best shooting to be found in Scotland and England. Lord Piccadilly was clever and well-educated ; he spoke several modern lan- guages ; and he could hold his own in most Conti- nental Courts ; but he was something more valuable to himself—he was cunning. Had he been born in the middle-class he would assuredly have made a fortune in company 'promoting,' or he would have gone to the penal settlements as a first-class swindler. And strange to say, of all his accomplishments his cunning was the one on which he secretly most prided himself. To gain a woman's love was to him very little. To

outwit her; to gain all he required with as little expense—of time and money—as possible; to leave her
before he grew tired of her and before she suspected
his purpose—these were the true delights of gallantry
to him.   There was scarcely more sentiment or softness to him in a love affair than in a set-to with a
hackney coachman.   He wanted to win, that was all,
and to win by the fair rules of the game; and he
would no more have dreamed of sparing the hackney
coachman the last knockdown blow between the eyes,
than he would have dreamed of sparing a woman who
cast herself on his generosity.   Poor thing! she threw
herself into a void, and fell very far.

I have said that the man's want of heart and
principle only remained concealed or unnoticed up
to a certain point.   When it became evident that
he would not marry, when the pleasures his money
made procurable by others palled upon him, when
advancing years destroyed his brilliancy, and selfishness, long cherished, did away with his charms of
manner, then people began to cry out upon his
libertinism, his heartlessness, and to wonder and
sneer at his eccentricities.   When there was nothing
to be gained by bearing his haughty humour, proud
Society resolved to bear it no longer.   Lord Piccadilly
soon told Society to go where they could solve the
disputed point as to the 'personality' of a certain
individual, and laid himself out to live without
friends.   He scarcely knew that the reason why he
did not miss them was that he had never had any;
but he found his Bohemian and wholly lawless life
suit him thoroughly well.

I write for a squeamish and desperately moral
public, so—in the usual words of the novelist—a veil
must be drawn over the doings in the pretty Paris
hotel, in the North-country castle, and in the villa
on the Thames.   No doubt these doings were exagge-

rated—such tales as that of his catching the rector
of the parish and forcing him, under pain of im-
mersion in the river, to worship the Goddess of
Reason, set up in the garden, were no doubt wicked
inventions ; but, at any rate, he so managed to sur-
round himself with a halo of darkness—if such a
term be admissible — that his appearance in good
society would have made much the same effect that
the entrance of the Evil One at a meeting in Exeter
Hall would produce.   His relatives, however, although
they never saw him, liked him for several reasons.   In
the first place, he was not supposed to spend more than
his income ; and, in the second, it was pretty well
known that he had ruined his stomach by good living,
and might be soon expected to make way for a new
and more respectable Lord.   Of course there were dark
fears of a possible wife, but as Roger St. James, his
brother and heir, said: 'If Joe had married, he
wouldn't be fool enough to hide the fact till his
death, and deprive himself of the pleasure of my
disappointment.'

Roger knew his brother thoroughly.

At the time when this story opens, the St. James'
family were all anxiously expecting one event—the
demise of their head.

Roger and his son George were awaiting it with
perhaps the greatest keenness, and the news of a
stroke of paralysis had filled their souls with glee,
to be quickly followed by despondency on the receipt
of this characteristic note :—

'The Grange: Richlake.

'My dear Brother Roger,—I know how glad you
will be to hear that I have quite recovered from
my illness.   Sir H. L—— (whom, knowing your
anxiety on my behalf, I sent for from town) gives
me twenty years to live, and strongly advises me

to think of settling down, taking a wife, and doing my duty to the family name.—Yours ever,

'PICCADILLY.'

Whether the fashionable doctor said this or not is doubtful; but he was a courtly man, and would probably have assented to anything proposed by a rich patient. At any rate the letter had the effect of annoying Roger extremely, particularly as he had lately made a mistake as to which horse would first pass the post for the Derby Stakes at Epsom, and as his only son George had already managed to spend his annual allowance in the first two months of his service in the Life Guards Green.

'I rather wish he would marry,' said the unfortunate heir, as he walked up St. James's Street with a friend; 'for either he'd kill his wife and be hanged, or she'd kill him, within a week. But it is hard on a fellow, isn't it, this recovering from a paralytic stroke, and with his constitution gone to blazes, too!'

Poor Roger, who was the smartest elderly gentleman in London, who had instructed his son to call him 'old boy' so as to deceive strangers as to their relationship, and who had long ago made an arrangement with his female friends that he should not be expected to raise his hat to them (for it ruffled his hair), had on one occasion, when anxious to make a little arrangement for raising money, written to his brother proposing an interview at the Richlake villa; but the answer was not encouraging. Thus it ran :—

'My dear Brother Roger,—I should be delighted to see and renew once more those pleasant talks, mostly on money matters, I remember of old. Unfortunately I have given strict orders that all trespassers here shall be turned out or kicked into the

Thames; and I cannot, even for the gratification of enjoying your conversation, alter my rules.—Yours ever,

'PICCADILLY.'

At one time there had been a talk of a commission *de lunatico*, but his Lordship, getting wind of it, wrote so clever, so sensible, and so sane a letter, that Sir John Jorkins, Q.C., to whom it was submitted, at once advised the abandonment of the scheme; adding, as he laid down the letter, that he could scarcely have written a better one himself. Now, as Sir John had at least twenty thousand golden reasons per annum for thinking himself cleverer than the ruck of humanity, this was very high praise; and Roger St. James had to console himself with the certainty that his brother was not mad, but only bad—like the husband of Don Juan's first conquest.

A novelist has the key of every door, and I can therefore ask the reader to accompany me this summer's day through the great iron gates that guard the entrance to the grounds of The Grange at Richlake. The first thing to observe is that Lord Piccadilly has good taste. The gardens are beautifully laid out, as neatly kept as an army of gardeners can keep them, and, though the space is limited, the effects gained by cunning landscape-gardening are wonderful in their variety and in the sense of space they give. The lawn, sloping down to the river, is as smooth as a billiard-table; and the boathouse a cottage of the most picturesque type. A steam-launch lies at the landing-stage, flying the Royal Yacht Squadron burgee; for Lord Piccadilly has been a mighty yachtsman in his time. Passing along the winding carriage-drive, we come upon a mausoleum—in the shape of a Greek temple—in white marble, erected 'by Joseph, Lord Piccadilly, in memory of Griselda,

C

a Cat. She was treacherous and greedy, and died
of a plethora of fish, deeply regretted by the friends
she had scratched, and the foes she had avoided.
Believing and knowing Nothing, her end was that of a
Christian. R. I. P.'

Thus runs the inscription thereon. This mausoleum was indeed one of the principal counts in the
brief handed to Sir John Jorkins; but that astute
man of the world, who had himself lost a wife—
married ere he knew how great he should become,
and how particular about h's and gentility—could not
bring himself to see much madness in the thing.
His inscription to her memory—cut in the marble
slab in the parish church—was decidedly further from
the truth.

Pursuing our way—a little nervously in consequence of the three or four large dogs that come
barking out and smell the calves of our legs curiously
—we come suddenly round a corner upon the house,
which is built of red brick in what is called the Queen
Anne style, and which was originally destined to be
the home of an enterprising inventor of a new soap.
The new soap wouldn't wash, however, and the place
went into the market, and was snapped up by Lord
Piccadilly, just then tired of his various places, and
seeking some residence where there could be no chance
of his being expected to perform duties, either to
tenants or neighbours. Whatever faults there were in
the architecture of The Grange were hidden by the
mass of roses and creepers which reached nearly to the
top of the building, and it certainly looked more like
the nest of a sentimental pair of lovers than the
retreat of a cynical and inhospitable recluse. On the
summer's day when we are supposed to be trespassing
in The Grange grounds there is a visitor in the house
She came—much to the astonishment of the household—by appointment, is now closeted with his Lord-

ship, and is no less than the mother of our hero,
Harry, the widow of the late Colonel St. James, of the
100th Hussars.

Lord Piccadilly is a man who would attract attention anywhere. His figure yet retains the grace of
cultivated strength, and he moves across the room
like a man who had learned how to move. He
neither swaggers, slouches, nor saunters, yet there is
in his motions a little of the pretentiousness of the
first, of the carelessness of the second, and of the
aimlessness of the third. He speaks slowly, not as if
doubtful of his words to come; not so as to give
an idea of pompousness, but as if he knew that what
he says is of value, and is moreover not to be unsaid
or contradicted. He had never found the necessity
of telling a lie—at least to a man—and he looked men
and women in the face with a certain inquiring
sternness that was wont to disconcert them. Those
who believed that he had become a kind of semi-
savage would have wondered at the courteousness of
manner with which he drew down a blind to exclude
the sun from his sister-in-law's eyes, and at the soft
tone of his voice as he addressed her :

‘My dear lady, there is only one thing wanting to
make me accede to your request. I cannot see what
advantage it would be to me.’

‘But surely, Joseph——’

‘One moment. For the sake of argument I am
quite willing to admit that my poor brother threw
away his money, and left you nothing but your jointure. I readily believe that you-- wanting to live
with people with ten times your income—have given
charges on that jointure which leave you very little
to live upon. I daresay you think you are speaking
the truth when you say that you ask this from me as
much for your son as for yourself; though I have my
notions on that head. But you forget one point.

What the—what on earth does it matter to me whether you have to go and live in a lodging somewhere—as you vaguely put it? What on earth does it matter to me whether your son Harry has to leave his tutor and join you in the lodging somewhere? You see you are so good-hearted, that you won't believe me when I tell you—as I told you just after poor Henry's death—that there is only one person in this world for whom I care a brass farthing—namely, myself. What good would helping you do me? Leave the rest of the subject alone, and stick to that. Your only chance of succeeding is to show me that.'

For once Mrs. St. James had an inspiration.

'It would annoy Roger,' she said.

The old Lord looked fixedly and thoughtfully at her with his large grey eyes.

'Would it? If I were sure of that! But I scarcely see why it should. It will not affect him when I am dead; for he knows he will get none of my savings, and he *must* get the entailed property. No. Try again. That is not a good enough argument.'

'It would make me so eternally grateful; and as to Harry——'

He interrupted her with a wave of the hand, and rose with a little impatience.

'My dear sister-in-law, why give yourself trouble and me annoyance? Be practical, or else I fear I shall be forced to put an end to the interview. My only reason for granting it, was a curiosity to see whether you still retain any of the looks I remember. I was too busy at the time to attend to you when you came out, but I remarked your looks. Now I see that Time has treated you just as others are treated, I am satisfied. If you have no more to say——'

'Why not try,' said the poor woman, her hands shaking with anxiety, 'why not try whether it doesn't annoy Roger? He says that you can't live long.'

'Yes, and my living on will be the best annoyance to him.'

'But if you had Harry here occasionally—if you again helped me and him—they would all think he was to come in for your saved money.'

'Yes—they probably would. It might annoy them even more than the idea of the hospitals. It might be tried. But remember, my dear lady, I shall do nothing of the kind; let them think what they will.'

'Oh, of course not.'

'Let me see. Your jointure is 1,500*l.* a year, and you have only left yourself 700*l.* What does Harry cost you now that my allowance is withdrawn?'

'I don't exactly know. His tutor is expensive, and soon he must choose a profession.'

'What will his income be?'

'Five hundred a year.'

'Well, I'll make up your jointure to 3,000*l.*, and I'll go on paying all expenses for Harry—present expenses at least. My solicitor will write to you. Tell the boy to come here next month and stay a week— say the 16th. And now, good-bye. I won't ask you to lunch, because I hate giving my servants trouble for anyone except myself.'

Mrs. St. James, stifling her passion, got into the fly awaiting her, and her brother-in-law repaired to the library, in which, said rumour, there were books that money could not buy—perhaps a lucky thing for morality.

CHAPTER III.

THE end of the season in London. Girls are counting
up their lovers, and fathers their bills. Mothers are
exulting in victory, or are smiling bravely under defeat.
All are making plans, save those few million unfortu-
nates who remain in town when it has been made
'empty' by the departure of a few hundred. Even
those who belong to the despised class of stayers more
or less imagine that they are making some change in
their habits now that August has come. They adopt
something of country manners in town—some don
shooting-jackets—some grow careless as to their boots
—it is whispered that Tommy Beaudresser has been
sitting under a tree in Hyde Park smoking a pipe!
The Straitback family sit out in the square after
dinner, and the Honourable Algernon Videbourse goes to
sleep with his feet in an armchair in the Marlborough
bow window. Gradually the shutters close and the
charwomen creep from their lairs, like those pariah
dogs of Eastern cities whose whereabouts in the daytime
is unknown. West London becomes a desert, which
all are passing through, and in which none but the
Arab of civilisation would linger. Yet Mrs. St. James
—widow of the Honourable Henry—lingered on. She
was sensible enough to prize this dead—or rather mori-
bund —season at its true value to herself. Now came
to her hospitable tea-table many talkers who had not
time in the whirl of mid-season to give her a thought.
To them now she was almost a fashionable woman, for
the greater lights had fled, and '*dans le pays des
aveugles les borgnes sont rois.*' Besides, there was
now so much to talk about. Flirtations of all kinds
—the scandalous as well as the legitimate—come to a
head when mothers and husbands have determined,

hearts or no hearts, to fly away from the common loving-ground; and the lovers grow desperate: which leads in some cases to the Court of Hymen, and in some alas! to the Court of a learned Judge.

The tit-bits of scandal are left to the last, and the gourmands who remain behind can clear the plate without interference.

Mrs. St. James—if the poetical adage anent the proper study for mankind be true—should have been reckoned as a very learned person. She was a species of gentle cannibal, living upon her fellow-creatures. Had she been cast upon a savage island she would have interested herself straightway in the loves of the black chief and the flirtations of the young braves, his sons. She belonged to a class of which it may be said, as of a poet, *nascitur, non fit*, for in her early days of bread and jam she had been the first to detect the keeping company—which resulted in a public-house and felicity —of the butler and housekeeper. The doings of her neighbours were her book, which she read as it only can be read by those with constant practice; and withal there was no intention of ill-nature in her. She simply noted and reasoned, drew inferences and pro-phesied events, and acted altogether after a most legi-timate scientific method.

When one comes to think about it, it is scarcely easy to say what other line she could have taken up with greater satisfaction to herself and less harm to others.

Left a widow early, with a small income, a son, and a love for society, there was not much open to her. She might have turned artistic, but she detested art; or literary, but she couldn't spell; or philanthropic, but she wanted tact and courage. No! Gossip was her oyster, and with her tongue and tea-table she opened it.

She was still a pretty woman—and at a little dis-tance she was a pretty young woman—and she knew perfectly well how to make the most of the charms which forty years had left her. Not that she was vain; all she wished was to look nice enough to allure those middle-aged admirers of beauty who make love between the intervals of telling naughty stories. The love was nothing to her; the naughty stories were everything; so she accepted both, as one eats the bread of a stale sandwich bought at a railway station for the sake of the ham within.

I have said that she had no tact, but she had learned (as who that wishes to please does not learn?) that most men require imperatively three things—first, flattery; secondly, flattery; and thirdly, flattery. And as the most useful kind of it was, she found, affecting interest in what interested them, she, without making any very grave blunders, would talk to a bishop of his diocese, to a politician of the last move of the ministry, to a sporting man of a handicap, and to a poet of the decadence of every school but his own. And she could extract from some most respectable trustee, by half an hour's brilliant flash of silence, the truth about this or that report, which wild horses, or asses braying questions would never have obtained from his roused senses.

Altogether Mrs. St. James was a commonplace sort of person—important only here because she happens to be the mother of her son.

The last visitor had departed, it was not time yet for her tea-dinner (so like dinner in its propriety—so like tea in its expense), so she took up the evening paper and skimmed again over the fashionable intelligence contained in one corner of it, when a ring came at the bell, and she sat up all attention.

'Can it be Lord Todlington? No, it is too late for him. Perhaps Sir Thomas comes to tell the exact facts about Lady Lamobel's affair? Oh, if it is I shall bless him!' But it was none of these things, it was her son, who walked into the room with a smile, and threw his arms round her.

'Harry! Why, what has brought you? Nothing wrong at Ilborough, I hope? Mrs. Portleton——'

'Mrs. Portleton's all right,' said Harry, kissing her and looking affectionately into her eyes. 'Hasn't run away with the curate yet. How well you are looking, mother!'

'Am I, dear?' she replied, pleased, but still puzzled.

'Wonderful. I begin to think there is some mistake in my age; that I am eight instead of eighteen. But you don't seem to expect me. I wrote to tell you I should be here by the 7·30 train to-day. The vacation don't begin till next week, but I wanted to go to my uncle's at the time he asked me, you remember.'

Mrs. St. James produced her gilt-bound velvet bag, and, after much hunting, found her son's letter, unopened.

'Dear me, Harry! Why, I never read it! Oh! I remember; it came just after I had heard that terrible news about Mrs. Ferragus and Lord Babblethorp, and of course I had to go out and find out how much was true; and then it turned out all to be an infamous invention. Such a disappointment! at least I mean so annoying for Mrs. Ferragus.'

'Well, I daresay you can give me a bed and dinner? I shan't bother you much after, for I'm uncommonly sleepy.'

'Oh, yes; ring the bell and I'll tell Thomas. My dear boy, I am so glad to have you back, and you'll stay now.'

'Well, mother, as you yourself settled with my uncle that I should go to-morrow to Richlake——'

'Ah, yes, so I did. Do you know, he was so rude and disagreeable — though his letting me in was wonderful—and he would only consent to help about your——'

'Help! Surely he gives you no money? And about my what?'

'Don't be so sudden, Harry; you startle one. If I choose to take a present from my husband's brother I suppose I may?'

'I suppose so'—this sulkily—'but what about me?'

'Well, Harry, education is an expensive thing, and though I'm sure I'm economical enough, still it is hard to live in London and make both ends meet.'

Harry glanced round the pretty room, listened to his mother's directions to Thomas in silence, and then, when they were alone, said:

'But was nothing left to spend on my education?'

'Oh, yes, a small sum.'

'Not enough for Portleton?'

'Well, scarcely.'

'Then let me leave him at once. I don't see that another half-year will do me much good. But why, mother, if you are in difficulties, should you have educated me all through in such an expensive way?'

'A St. James should be well-educated.'

'If he can afford it.'

'Well, at any rate it can be easily managed. Your uncle has been quite generous, and you must stay the appointed time at Ilborough, unless, indeed, he takes some new fancy into his head.'

'But what if I decline his charity? From all accounts he wasted little enough of it on my father.'

'He never would read your father's letters—sent them back unopened.'

'What a shame!'

'Well, they were ill-spelt. But that does not alter the fact that he is inclined to be kind to you.'

'I hate such kindness. I won't take it.'

'My dear boy, that is nonsense. If you decline, the burden falls on me. His paying the sums he has promised relieves me of a great anxiety, and I do hope you'll be nice and not headstrong and independent and stupid with him at Richlake. On it may depend my being able to afford Homburg and a tour in Italy this winter.'

Harry said nothing, but went upstairs to his room, muttering naughty words that so young a man should not have known.

There was something about this tyrannical eccentric uncle, whom he had never seen, that angered him. It seemed as if Joseph, Lord Piccadilly was setting himself rather too high, trying to single himself out from amongst common humanity. As he reached the landing he made up his mind that, generous or not, his lordship should not impose his will upon him beyond a certain point. There was a certain excitement in this visit to Richlake, too. Wonderful tales were told of what went on within the walls of The Grange, and Harry was the first of the family who had ever been permitted to do more than pay a morning call.

At any rate, anything would be better than London with nothing to do, and a terrible sense of not being wanted when fine gentlemen came to talk of people of whom he knew nothing with his mother. So he set off next day in good spirits for Richlake, and drove through The Grange gates, past the Cat Mausoleum, with a light heart and an expectation of adventure which is always agreeable to the young mind.

CHAPTER IV.

' CAN'T you make ducks and drakes, Joseph ? '

' My dear Nellie, I have all my life been engaged making ducks and drakes of everything that most idiots consider valuable and respectable. I began with youth, then I went on with love, then friendship, and I almost think I have achieved the operation with the only thing that makes life worth having— pleasure.'

' There ! You've broken your promise. You promised me never to talk like that when I came to see you.'

' Dear child, don't you know that the only good that lies in a promise is the breaking of it ? '

' No, I don't, and I never shall,' said the girl, throwing back her dark brown hair, and facing him with all the defiance of youth.

' Perhaps you have never made any ? '

' Yes, I have. I have promised Uncle John to be home by five o'clock, and it's a quarter to now.'

' Any others ? '

' I promised not to wet my feet.'

' And you *have* wetted them,' said Lord Piccadilly, with a grim smile, pointing to the dainty little boots, which had been once or twice too near to the river's bank.

' Oh, I couldn't help that, and uncle won't mind when I tell him how it happened.'

' Teaching me to make ducks and drakes. But that is what we all say. We never can help it, and we always think people ought not to mind when we tell them. Shall I tell you a tale, Nell ? '

' A fairy tale ? '

' Yes, a fairy tale. Once there was a young man,

who had everything in the world, and so he wanted more.'

'How could he when he had all?'

'He did. Facts are superior to logic, Nell. He did, and because he didn't get it, he grew to hate the world, and to despise it.'

'That was unjust.'

'Yes. It seems so to you at sixteen, and it is beginning to seem so to me at sixty-five. But our joint wisdom— of experience and faith—doesn't alter the case. He did. And he kicked the world—like a football.'

'Is the world so soft?'

'Quite. But as he kicked the ball along, he sometimes made bad shots, and he hurt his foot against stones on the ground.'

'That served him right.'

'So the ball said. And then he got tired of kicking, and let the ball alone; and others came and played the game, and said he couldn't play any more because he was too weak, while in reality he only had got tired of so stupid an amusement.'

'Well?'

'Well!' Lord Piccadilly found that his simile had run him into a *cul de sac*. 'Well—no matter. He didn't play any more.'

'And is that all?'

'What more would you have? The young man, now grown old, sat down in the shade and heard the shouts of the football players whom he despised. There was nothing left for him but——'

'To give up sulking and play again?'

'No; to die.'

'I don't quite understand you,' said Nellie Barton, looking at the old Lord, as he sat back in his chair with closed eyes, 'but I fancy you are talking of yourself.'

'I always choose an interesting subject, Nell; and what interests me but myself?'

'*I* interest you.'

'You, you little chit?'

'Yes, I; you said so.'

'Yes, you do—in a way. You are young, and I like youth when it is not foolish, and you are not foolish. You are pretty, and I like beauty when it is not conceited, and you are not conceited. You do interest me. Particularly because you are destined to be the instrument of my vengeance.'

'Your vengeance? I?'

'Yes, my dear. There are certain things called Three per Cents. In all my wildnesses, I always spent less than I had, because I wanted some day to be able to disappoint somebody. So now in these Three per Cents. I have a large sum of money which my relatives expect. They will be delighted to see it all go to Miss Nellie Barton, niece of the Richlake doctor—delighted!'

Nellie Barton's dark eyes flashed fire, flashed scorn, flashed a hundred emotions of her mind at once. She put her little hand on Lord Piccadilly's shoulder to emphasise her words, and said:

'Do you mean you will leave the money—the Three per Cents.—to me?'

'Don't be dull, Nell. I won't let you into the place again if you bore me, and dulness bores me.'

'You do mean that! Then hear what I say, Lord Piccadilly.'

'I told you to call me Joseph.'

'I won't call you Joseph, and I won't touch your nasty money. Do you hear? Rather than that, I'll take it and throw it into the river.'

'It would be paper, and float.'

'Let it float to the sea. It would do more good there than lying idle now to serve your ill-nature.'

'You look nice when you're angry, Nell; almost as nice——Nell!'

'Yes.'

'Don't turn away, I want to tell you another story. We won't say anything more about the Three per Cents.'

'You promise not to leave me them?'

'Yes, I promise.'

'A real promise?'

'One of a superior order. You know that picture in my room?'

'Of that lady with the big blue eyes?'

'Yes. She used to get angry, and look very like you. I was very fond of her, Nell.'

'I don't believe you were ever fond of anyone.'

'That's ungrateful, considering I allow you to spend your afternoons here instead of in your uncle's hot little house.'

'I only come to amuse you, and because uncle wants me to. You are nice sometimes, but generally I——.'

'Well?'

'I hate you!'

'That's right. Sit down there on the grass— never mind the time, I'll make it right with your Uncle John—and listen to me. I was very fond of her, and she was very fond of me.'

'Why didn't you marry her?'

'In our society, my child, we never marry the people we are fond of, because we don't want to see them any more when we have ceased to be fond of them.'

'I should never cease to love anyone I loved,' cried the girl, with enthusiastic unlogic.

'She grew so fond of me that it was inconvenient, so I avoided her, and the next thing I heard of her was that she had married someone else.'

'She couldn't have cared for you.'

'Wait a bit. I was delighted at the news, and I saw as much of her as I could, and in time—it took a whole season—I made her care for me more than ever.'

'And you—how wicked!—but you?'

'I had got sick of her. But she had given me trouble, and the man, her husband, was one of those clever fools whom it is a true pleasure to humiliate. So I—well, it don't much matter exactly what happened—but in the end, he turned her out of his house, and I refused to take her into mine. I believe he never recovered it—not exactly mad, you know, but imbecile. And she died in a very odd way. The coroner's jury said it was accidental. Altogether it was amusing. I like recalling the incident.'

And the old man chuckled to himself.

Nellie Barton's blue eyes opened to their widest, and she looked at him with a horror and aversion that increased his amusement. All of a sudden, however, she broke off into a smile.

'I don't believe a word of it. You are always trying to make me hate you. I *know* it is not true.'

'And how do you know that, wise young woman?'

'Because you keep her picture in your room.'

'A savage keeps in his wigwam the scalps of his slain foes. Besides, the picture is pretty and makes good furniture. I haven't got another that would exactly fit the place over that table. And it reminds me of what I could do once. Come here, sir!'

This was addressed to a Scotch deer-hound that was stealing out into the paddock to amuse himself chasing the young horses in it. The dog stopped and stood irresolute. Lord Piccadilly, with a strength one would scarcely have suspected in him, flung his stick at it.

'Bring that stick here, sir, at once!'

The dog picked up the stick and came slowly to-

wards his master with it in his mouth, adopting, when
close to him, that peculiar wriggle of mingled depre-
cation and affection common to the canine race when
in expectation of a beating.

'Give it to me.   Now I am going to lick you.
Look at Czar, Nell.   That's exactly how the world
behaved to me many years ago.   It licked my hand
and brought me the stick to beat it with.'

'But you sha'n't beat Czar.'

'Sha'n't I?   Who says so?'

'I do.'

'I can't beat you, Nell, or you wouldn't come any
more, and you're useful to read to me.   So I'll give
Czar the extra strokes I should like to give you.
One!'

A howl from Czar.

'It's a shame!' from Nell, who was half crying.

'Two!'

Another howl.   Then the girl made a dart at the
stick, wrested it from his Lordship's hand, and flung it
far into the river.

He scowled, uttered an oath, then let go of his
dog's neck and laughed—not a pleasant laugh.

'Call Edwards, please.   He is in the conservatory.'

Nellie, a little frightened at her temerity, flushing
scarlet, walked off, and came back with the head-
gardener.

'Edwards, take this dog to the back-yard, get your
gun, and shoot him.   At once.'

Edwards, who was drilled to be astonished at
nothing, replied not, and laid hold of the honest
hound's collar.

'At once, Edwards.'

'Yes, my Lord.'

'Stop, Edwards!' cried Nellie, standing before the
man.   'Lord Piccadilly, if you do not retract that
order I will never see you again.'

D

'Wait a moment, Edwards. When there is a quarrel between friends, my dear child, the only remedy is to remove the cause. Czar is the cause of our quarrel. He must be removed.'

'He shall not!'

The child kept back her excitement, restraining her tears, and said steadily, but with an effort to keep her voice from trembling:

'Very well. You may murder your own dog if you please; but you have no power over me. Goodbye! I will *never* come to this wicked place again.'

'Do you mean that?'

'I know I am only a child, but I needn't come here if I don't choose. If Czar dies I will never enter your gate again.'

'Let the dog go, Edwards. He may live. On the whole, I prefer obeying you, Nell, to not having you here to read to me. And, Edwards——'

'Yes, my Lord?'

'You can leave to-day. Your month's salary shall be sent to you.'

The man's face fell.

'My Lord, I——'

'That will do. Go at once.'

'But, Lord Piccadilly,' began Nell.

'Go!' thundered the Lord, and the man shrank away.

'I don't choose,' Lord Piccadilly went on, when he was out of hearing, 'to keep a servant who has seen me change my mind. Don't try me too far, my dear. Your society is pleasant, but I allow no interference with my establishment.'

She held her tongue, and calculated how far the savings of her pocket-money would go towards compensating the poor Edwards for the place she had lost him.

Before this sum in addition was completed, a

servant came from the house and approached his master's chair.

'Mr. St. James has arrived, my Lord.'

'Tell him to wait in the drawing-room.'

'Is that your nephew that you expected?' said Nell.

'Yes. I scarcely know why I asked him. Do you know what a young man of the present day is, Nellie?'

'Yes—no—at least, I——'

'You think you could imagine what he ought to be. I have brought this one here to disenchant you. His father was a thriftless fool who tried to get through the world on good-nature, and failed. And his mother is a painted mummy, whose proper avocation would be to write scandals for a servants'-hall paper. This youth will probably combine their faults. I want you to see young men as they are, my dear.'

'I know one old man as he is,' cried she, with spirit, 'unjust, cruel, and selfish.'

'Why put in the first two adjectives? The last combines them. Injustice means nothing. I have a certain power, and I use it to amuse myself. No one has a right to expect anything. I have signed no agreement to be just with the world. Cruelty—ah! if it were not for those d——d restrictions called laws, what amusement might not be got out of cruelty! But selfishness — your uncle's a religious man, isn't he?'

'Yes.'

'And wants to save his soul. There is the height of selfishness, my dear. Now I only want all I can get in this world. I don't go so far as to make arrangements for my personal comfort in the other.'

'I think you're very wicked.'

'I daresay I am. Now I want to sleep. Put

that cushion behind my chair—so. No, more to the left. How clumsy you are; I hate clumsiness. Run in and tell the young man to amuse himself till the dressing-bell rings, and then to get ready for dinner. And then go home yourself, and be here at three to-morrow to finish that poem—trash it is —but I like the jingle when you read it.'

'Good-bye, Lord Piccadilly.'

'Joseph.'

'No. You are so unkind.'

'To you?'

'No, to Edwards.'

'If you'll call me Joseph, I'll send him a cheque for 100*l*. to-morrow.'

'Good-bye, Joseph, then.'

And she ran into the house.

CHAPTER V.

I AM going to do a very courageous thing—a thing that perhaps only an author writing his first book should dare to do. I am going to write down a love-scene—only an incipient love, truly, but then love none the less, for it is strongest when very young —to write it down word for word, if possible, look for look, and sigh for sigh; and this, moreover, though I can in no way on my unsympathetic paper put down those eloquent pauses which, as all novel-readers should know by this time, mean so much; nor can I find words in the dictionary, and, indeed, I doubt whether Rabelais himself could find them, to express the various meanings which tremble on *her* lips or flash into *his* eyes, or to describe the electric shocks which both do, or ought to, receive from the first contact of their hands, from the first touch of their lips.

Oh, first love! Much as you have been written about, and laughed at, and altogether worried and hackneyed, you stand out in the past of each of us as the brightest spot of life; just as the first dread visit to the dentist stands out as the blackest, not even to be rivalled in its opaqueness by the first twinge of debt, or the first quarrel with the wife of your bosom.

I do not mean in any way to imply that first love necessarily comes to us when we are in our early youth. We may flirt and sentimentalise, and talk rubbish, and kiss ruby lips for ten or fifteen years; nay, we may even marry and produce additions to the cooked-food-devouring portion of the animal kingdom, before we meet the one person whose soul comes out to meet ours, and who produces in us that indefinite, cruel, puzzling, but delightful feeling called ' Love.'

It is not easy to say what its exact symptoms are, but one pretty safe one is a strong desire to make sacrifices for, to immolate oneself at the feet of, the beloved object. Another may be said to be that feeling of intense surprise that one could have lived so long without knowing him or her, and an equally intense conviction that hereafter life without him or her will be a howling void. Loss of appetite is said to be another sign, but as I lately saw a young friend of mine of ardent passions, just engaged to a sweet heiress of fifty-four, with red hair and freckles, whom he loved dearly, as he told me several times—I say, as I saw this young gentleman consume two mutton chops, a lobster claw, and a plate of strawberries, one day at luncheon, I am inclined to put aside this particular test as unsatisfactory.

There is one sensation never absent from first love :

a fear of losing it, an indefinite consciousness that life altogether is short and unsatisfactory, that the operations of nature are altogether ill-arranged.

A lover sitting with his mistress interrupted their billing and cooing to weep, and when asked the reason by the lady, replied that he never could, when gazing on her peach-like skin, avoid remembering that in a few short years—few and short compared with their mighty love—that skin would lose its bloom, and age would trace ugly furrows on its surface.

The gentleman was a philosopher, but, as sometimes happens, the lady was not, and I believe they parted soon after, and there was a returning of several tons of sweet love-letters and a few presents.

But it is unpardonable to keep Harry St. James all this time in the drawing-room of The Grange at Richlake, waiting for a summons from his mysterious uncle, and little knowing that, instead of that awsome personage, little Nellie Barton, in her serge frock, and with a light in her eyes born of her exciting defence of the dog and the gardener, was tripping towards him, assuming, unconsciously to her sweet self, the character of his Fate.

There he stood, idly turning over the leaves of a book that lay on the table, and whistling softly to himself, as heart-whole a young man as any in her Majesty's dominions, looking very little further forward than his next cricket match, or a 'lark' he had projected with some school-friend in town, and not at all despising his dinner. In another moment. *presto!* he is snapped up in the all-devouring maw of the Love-demon, and good-bye to the serene joys of selfish happiness.

I do not mean to say that the moment Miss Nellie stepped into the room he fell in love with her; he only began to do so. The poison had found an inlet; he was doomed. But he liked it; though you

wouldn't have said so had you seen the young people
so awkwardly exchanging commonplaces, both apparently intent on the pattern of Lord Piccadilly's
carpet.

'Yes, very fine; and it is so much nicer at this
time of the year in the country. No; I have never
been here before. My uncle has not asked me.'

'You don't know him, do you?' asked she, stealing
a glance at his handsome face, and blushing as she
found he was doing the same thing as regarded herself.

'No, never saw him, and never expected to,' answered Harry, wondering who this little fairy might
be. He had made up his mind to be surprised at
nothing while at The Grange, but he was surprised,
nevertheless. It was impossible to reconcile this
lovely child with the dark deeds associated with the
place.

'Won't you come out for a stroll? I ought to go
home, and you can walk with me a little way, and I
can show you the grounds,' she found courage to say,
after a short pause, during which he had longed for
some of those high spirits and ready jokes which were
so eminently successful with the innkeeper's daughters
at Ilborough.

'Oh, yes, I should like it; but my uncle?'

'He's asleep by the river, and won't be disturbed
till dinner-time. I wonder how you'll get on with
him,' she continued, as they walked side by side along
the gravel path leading from the front door.

'Not at all, I should say.'

'Why?'

'Because I fancy he's a bit of a tyrant, and I cannot be tyrannised over.'

There was the beginning of a smile in Nellie's eyes
as she glanced at her companion.

'No; but then an uncle——'

'An uncle one has never seen has scarcely much jurisdiction over one.'

'I suppose not. But then Lord Piccadilly is not like other men.'

It was Harry's turn to smile.

'Have you seen many?'

'Yes; at least, I've seen a few. I have an uncle too—the doctor here.'

'Oh!'

What could the Richlake doctor's niece be doing in the wicked Grange?

'And I know several of the neighbours, uncle's patients. They are very kind to me. But altogether no one is quite so kind to me as Lord Piccadilly. I come here nearly every day and read to him—poetry generally. I think he doesn't attend much to the words, you know; but he says the jingle and my voice combined send him to sleep. And he lets me use his canoe, and I have the run of the place. There, under that sycamore—there's my seat. My name is cut on the back, and I believe he would have anyone hanged who used it. He's promised to build me quite as fine a mausoleum as the cat's when I die! Isn't that a grand thing to look forward to?'

She was at her ease now, and rattled on, reassured by the sympathetic look upon the young man's face. He was one with whom women of all ages found it easy to 'get on,' and already Nellie felt as if she knew him.

'And you are not afraid of him?'

'Only sometimes—when he is in his bad temper —and he seldom is with me. He sends me away when he feels it coming on. Do you know, Mr. St. James——'

In her eagerness she nearly put her hand on his arm, stopped and blushed.

'Do I know what, Miss——'

'Barton. Eleanor Barton is my name. Do you know that I sometimes think Lord Piccadilly is a very miserable man!'

'So he ought to be—must be, I mean,' added Harry, remembering he was this man's guest, 'if he shuts himself up in this ridiculous way. Still, perhaps, with a young lady like you to amuse him, he is not far wrong.'

As he spoke, the boy glanced at the erect, slight figure beside him, and felt that his uncle was very far from wrong indeed.

She laughed merrily.

'Amuse him! No, I don't think I quite do that. He says nothing ever did amuse him in his life. But perhaps I prevent his thinking too much, and, at any rate, I can read him to sleep.'

'Shall you come every day now?'

'Yes, I suppose so. Why?'

'Oh, I don't know. Perhaps you will read me to sleep sometimes?'

'Should you like it?'

'Tremendously! I can't imagine anything nicer.'

She stopped.

'Now, Mr. St. James, that's not true. You have hundreds of amusements.'

'No, I haven't. I'm only a schoolboy still, at least,'—this hastily, and with a little pride,—'at a private tutor's, which is not quite the same thing. When I get into the army I daresay I shall amuse myself.'

'I am glad you are going to be a soldier.'

'Why?'

'Because—because you look as if you ought to be one.'

Harry was pleased; this little flattery was so unconscious and so real.

'Don't you think I should make a better clerk?'

'No; you would be wasted,' she answered, gravely. 'People arrange things· very badly, it seems to me. I saw a regiment march through Richlake the other day, and some of the men were so little and looked so weak, while in London I have seen great strong young men measuring out ribbons and standing at doors in servants' liveries.'

'Perhaps they wouldn't care to fight.'

'All men would be ready to fight for their country,' said the girl, as if she were enunciating a self-evident axiom.

Harry laughed.

'You know all about the world, Miss Barton.'

'I haven't seen much of it, but I am very fond of reading, and Uncle John is a very clever man and tells me things.'

'Will you introduce me to Uncle John ? '

'Of course I will—if I may. But here we are at the gate. You had better go back, in case he should wake and want you.'

'He can wait,' said the young man, opening the gate.

'Oh, no! He is not used to waiting.'

'Well, I'm not used to be at anyone's beck and call. Which way do we turn ? '

'Oh, *please*, Mr. St. James, I promised to give you his message, and he'll blame me.'

'Well—if *you'll* ask me.'

'I ? '

'Yes. I'll go back if you ask me—not unless.'

'Then I do ask you. Good-bye.'

'Good-bye.'

But Miss Nellie's diplomacy was thrown away, for when Harry reached the house, he was informed by the butler that his Lordship intended to dine alone ; and Harry ate a solitary dinner in a gaunt dining-room, and found that a pair of large blue eyes and a pouting, smiling mouth perpetually came between him and the French novel he had picked up as a companion.

Gifted as I am with all the rights of a novelist, I have no hesitation in telling the reader that Miss Nellie Barton did not listen that evening with her accustomed attention to the somewhat prosy conversation of her Uncle John.

If, despite this stretch of confidence on my part, the male reader ungratefully exclaims that I have cheated him, that I have given him no love-scene, all I can do in self-defence is to ask him to cast his thoughts back to his first meeting with the excellent lady who is now ascending or descending the hill of life with him, and try to recollect whether there was in that interview anything that would have caused much amusement or excitement to a third person when writ down on paper.

If this plea fail, then I will further urge that a real good love-scene will be given in detail a little further on, with the hand-in-hand and kissing business according to rule. At any rate, this one fact must be here recorded : both Harry and Nellie afterwards declared that the walk through the grounds of The Grange that summer's evening was a real and veritable love-scene.

CHAPTER VI.

It was not likely that there could be much in common between Lord Piccadilly and his high-spirited nephew, yet for a few days they did manage to amuse each other to a degree that surprised both. It was new to Lord Piccadilly to be contradicted and treated as an equal; while his uncle was a deeply-interesting study —not altogether agreeable, but decidedly novel—to the youth. His cynicism filled the air, as it were, with a vague wickedness that was in itself rather exciting, and his tales of bygone days—which he told well and with a relish that added to their piquancy—made the hours they spent together pass rapidly away.

These hours were not many, certainly. His Lordship did not leave his own rooms till three or four in the afternoon, when he was wont to sit in a chair near the river, with many newspapers and a few novels at hand, and at this time Harry was graciously permitted to sit beside him until he grew sleepy, when he was carefully let alone, it being considered by the inhabitants of The Grange that to intrude upon his Lordship at such a time was a crime almost too awful for human punishment.

Then at dinner they met again, and when the old man was in a good humour they sat far into the night, while Harry opened his eyes wider and wider as histories of Society gone by were poured into his credulous ears. For the first two days he was at The Grange there was no mention of Nellie Barton, but on the third day he received a message to say he was not required in the garden, and as he strolled towards the gates, intending to walk down to the village and see whether he could catch a glimpse of her, he did catch the glimpse of that young person seated beside her patron reading to him. The next day the same thing occurred, but Harry could stand it no longer, and went boldly up to the group. Lord Piccadilly turned at his footstep, and the scowl upon his face was not pleasant to see, but he said nothing while the young couple shook hands.

'I was thinking of calling upon you in the village,' said Harry with heightened colour; for he had seen his uncle's expression, and he was angered by the frightened glances of the girl.

'Oh, I am seldom at home; I have so many people about to go and see; and——'

'Go on reading,' said Lord Piccadilly. Harry turned as if he had received a slap in the face. The tone was that you might use in speaking to a wicked dog.

But Nellie obeyed, and her fresh young voice made music of the penny-a-line stuff she was reading from the newspaper.

Harry stood irresolute. He was unaccustomed to being snubbed, and indeed had perhaps a little too good an opinion of himself.

'Lord Piccadilly,' he began.

His uncle looked round, held up one hand to Nellie to stop reading for a moment, and said: 'I can't attend to you now. Whatever you have to say, say it at dinner. Now go! Finish that article, Nellie.'

As Harry walked along the high road he found himself using some naughty words, and he was the more furious because, as he moved away, he fancied that he had discerned something very like a twinkle of amusement in the passing glance Miss Nellie shot at him. However, he was after all consoled for his ill-treatment by meeting that young woman as she came away from The Grange, and receiving from her pretty little hand a rose which she averred she had plucked on purpose for him.

'I say, Miss Barton,' he observed, as they walked along together, 'does he treat *you* like that ever?'

'Generally. You know, he looks upon us not as human beings like himself, but as instruments for his amusement. "A man or woman I don't happen to want to see is like a chair that gets in my way when I have no desire to sit," he said to me one day. And what do you think he said just now? I couldn't help remarking, when you walked away looking so——'

'Foolish?'

'Well, foolish if you like. You did rather, you know. I couldn't help saying that he seemed to think no one had any feelings, and his reply was that it was because they had feelings they amused him, for hurting them would be impossible otherwise. Isn't he an old wretch?'

'Yes, indeed. But why do you go to him? You are not obliged to?'

'Not exactly obliged. But my uncle has an idea that I do him good, and so has Mr. Farquill, the Rector, and I think he *is* a little better when I am with him. I told you about my saving Czar's life and getting that hundred pounds for Edwards. Poor Edwards! I hear that he has been drunk ever since, so perhaps I didn't do him so much good after all.'

So the girl prattled on, wondering within herself a little why she felt so light-hearted when with this young man, and so the young man listened and drank long draughts of an ambrosia that had been hitherto unknown to him, and grew suddenly a MAN—with all a man's responsibilities and cares, and all a man's pleasures too. Harry, notwithstanding some hot scenes with his uncle, notwithstanding countless snubs when he tried to join the reading party on the bank—remained on his full time at The Grange, and was happier than he deemed it possible to be, happier possibly than he ever will be again.

But his dream was rudely shattered one morning by a message from his uncle, sent through the gloomy butler.

'His Lordship wishes to know whether you will go by the 4.20 or the 6 o'clock train, as he will send you to the station, sir.'

Then Harry remembered that the fortnight for which he had been invited ended that day, and he also knew that to leave Nellie would be Death—or what seemed death to his untutored mind.

He hurried down to the village, and found Nellie
at home and alone. To Uncle John he had been
presented, a dignified-looking old man, with old-world
manners, but had only exchanged a few words with the
hard-worked doctor.

Nellie was seated in a rocking-chair under the
verandah at the back of the house, working industriously at the hems of what looked like towels, and,
as she worked, singing under her voice, which latter
fact angered her lover, who thought that in the sky
should have been written the fact that he was going
away.

'Mr. St. James!'

'You don't mind my coming? It is to say
good-bye.'

Did she grow pale, or was it only an effect of light
as she stood up to shake hands with him?

'Are you sorry I am going?'

He ought to have made a pretty speech, but this
was all that would come. It wasn't a bad speech
either, for the reply to it was rather difficult:

'Sorry? Yes, I am very sorry. Must you go?'

'I forgot the exact time I was asked for, but his
Lordship didn't, for the butler came to me just now
to choose my train. It—it has been a very jolly
fortnight, Miss Barton.'

'I thought you would get to like your uncle after
all,' said the little hypocrite.

'I haven't, not a bit. But I have got to like someone else.'

The hypocrisy came to an end. She couldn't
think he liked the gloomy butler, and he had spoken
to no one else. So she said nothing, only went on
working, with her eyes intent upon the towel.

'I don't think I ever was so happy in my life, Miss
Nellie.'

'You must be easily amused.'

'Amused!' The word seemed desecration to him just then. 'I hate being amused.'

'Do you? I like it.'

'Then I'm afraid I must have bored you.'

'No, you haven't. You are very amusing, Mr. St. James.'

'Do you really think so?'

He had sat down beside her, and seemed almost as intent on the hem of the towel as she was.

'Yes—really.'

A pause. You would have thought never was there so interesting a towel. Her little fingers flew to and fro, and his eyes watched them.

At last: 'Will you stop working for a moment?'

She looked up, then down again, then dropped the towel, and then somehow or other (how *do* these things happen?) both her hands were imprisoned in his.

'Nellie!'

'Yes!'

This so low that, although his face was close to hers, he could scarcely hear.

'You won't *quite* forget me?'

'No!'

Again he only just caught her accent.

'And you'll think of me sometimes?'

This was tautological, but tautology is permitted in—nay, is part and parcel of—the science these two foolish persons were just entering upon.

'You won't tell me that you have enjoyed this fortnight, too?'

'You know I have.'

The blue eyes met his for a moment, and then looked down again. But that look has been enough. Harry was the happiest man in the whole wide world that minute.

'Nellie, do you know one thing?'

'What?' in a whisper.

'That I love you.'

Another lightning glance, and her head nestled on his shoulder, while he could just catch a glimpse of the blushes that suffused her cheek.

'Do you—can you—care for me a little?'

'Yes.'

'My darling!'

Her position had to be changed, for the simple reason that, with her head on his shoulder, he could not kiss her lips: and he did kiss her lips.

'Say you love me.'

'I do.'

'Say, "Harry, I love you."'

'Harry, I love you.'

'And I will marry you.'

'And I will marry you.'

'Whatever anybody says.'

'Whatever—— But, Harry, are you sure—are you quite sure? You haven't seen anyone, you know?'

'I never want to see anyone again. But, darling, I am not rich.'

She murmured something unintelligible, but which might be accepted as an expression of utter and entire contempt for pecuniary resources in general; and put her head back upon his shoulder.

'I know what they'll say: that I am too young to marry. But we can wait a little, can't we, my love?'

An onlooker would have thought that she did not reply, but then the onlooker could not have known of the pressure of her hand on her lover's.

'And you'll not like anyone but me?'

An answer conveyed in the same way.

'Give me a kiss to say so.'

She lifted her head; her eyes, with the light

E

of love in them, turned fondly to his, and her lips
met his with a kiss that was pure as the kiss of an
angel.

Remember it, Harry St. James—remember this
moment under the summer sky! In all your after life
you will never again know the bliss that is in your
heart now, as first love takes her heart out to meet it.
Remember it until your dying day! For whatever
may betide—however dark the clouds may lour, however bitter Fate may seem—you cannot complain.
You have known what it is not given to every mortal
to know—one moment of what really distinguishes
us from the other animals—Love!

And in the days to come—the historian of which I
am to be—he did remember, with tears of gratitude
to Heaven, that kiss given him in the little garden
at Richlake.

CHAPTER VII.

THERE was great commotion at the King's Arms at
Ilborough; for Miss Jane Heckthorpe had disappeared,
leaving in her stead a neat little note, wishing a tender
farewell of her father, with a request that he would in
time forgive her and think of her kindly. In vain was
Miss Amalia stormed at and bullied; she declared that
her sister had told her nothing of her plans; and she
didn't even know whether her father's suspicions that
Mr. Ballard was the companion of Jane's flight were
correct.

'I'll soon see as to that,' said the publican; and
off he strode to the Rectory.

As an elder in the Dissenting congregation, he took
little trouble to be courteous to the Rector; and it was

with more than ordinary brusqueness that he demanded, on being shown into the study, where those long sermons were composed, whether or not Mr. Ballard had left Ilborough.

'Certainly, Mr. Heckthorpe,' said Mr. Portleton, mildly. 'Mr. Ballard, having concluded his visit to me, went, I believe, to London yesterday evening.'

'Then he's a d——d scoundrel!' broke out the other.

'Really, such language——'

'Language! What does it matter to me what language I use? Do you think I am going to stand on ceremony now? Where's my daughter Jane, Mr. Portleton—that's what I want to know—where's my daughter Jane?'

The man was beside himself with passion, and shook his fist in the innocent clergyman's face. All Mr. Portleton's dignity was roused.

'If you cannot behave yourself, leave the room, sir! I know nothing, and wish to know nothing, of your daughters.'

'You mean they ain't good enough for you, do you? Damn your impudence! They're twice too good for a twopenny-halfpenny parson such as you, or a barber's block like that Ballard. Oh, if I could only catch him! And to take Jane, too, after all I have done for her, with the extras at school, and the pianner, and the French and German, with the rudiments of Italian. I'll kill 'im, that's what I'll do!'

'Am I to understand,' said the Rector, softened by the man's evident grief, 'that you suspect Mr. Ballard of having taken your daughter away?'

'What else? He's been philandering about these three weeks, making the girl spooney. Who else could she go with?'

'But surely it is not necessary to suspect that he——'

'Do you think that if he meant marriage fair
and square, he wouldn't 'ave come to me? Do you
think a swell, as he thinks himself, would be afraid
of being refused by a publichouse-keeper as a son-
in-law?'

Mr. Portleton at once saw the logic of this, and
was silent.

'But I'll find them—if they 're above ground—
and I'll kill him or he shall marry her.'

'Believe me, Mr. Heckthorpe,' said the Rector
gently, 'that I sympathise with you deeply; and I trust
there may yet be some mistake. Will you take my
advice in one thing?'

'What's the use of advice? Give me a horsewhip!'

'Say nothing about this until you know for
certain; even not then, if possible. Publicity can
scarcely do any good; and it would certainly harm
your other daughter.'

'Damn them both! Cursed hypocrites! I'll lock
her up till she confesses.'

Then he left the house, and—after another course
of bullying Amalia, whom he reduced to a very pitiable
state—he went up to London by the evening train.

Mr. Portleton sat down again, put his sermon on
one side, and proceeded to compose a long letter to his
late pupil, dwelling on the enormity of what he had
done, and urging him to repair his original fault at any
and every cost. 'Family and friends and prejudices of
class must, of course, be considered; but it is too late
(if the story be true) for you now to consider them.
You have a plain duty before you, not only to this girl
and to her parent, but to Heaven. Continuance in
your crime would be doubly wicked; for it would cause
the continuance in crime of another also. Do your
duty, Humphrey Ballard; and know that there is no
shame that comes anywhere near the shame of
wickedness through cowardice.'

The bell on board the Calais steamer was ringing impatiently; passengers were streaming across the narrow bridge on to her deck, in all the misery and anxiety of those taking an unaccustomed pleasure. At the Lord Warden, bags and wraps were being hastily collected, bills paid, and servants tipped. Among those performing the latter function was a tall slim young man with a black moustache, having on his arm a frightened-looking and very pretty girl, who clung to him in a manner which bespoke a tender relationship between them.

'Not much time, sir,' said the Boots; 'the bell's rung. You'll miss the boat if you don't look sharp.'

'Come on, Jenny! It would never do to miss it.'

'But you will miss it, all the same,' said a gruff voice; and a burly form confronted them in the doorway.

Jane Heckthorpe gave a shriek of 'Father!' and Ballard turned ashy pale, and put up one arm as if expecting a blow. It must be allowed that the incensed parent did look sufficiently formidable when you glanced at his broad shoulders and at the thick oak cudgel he grasped in his strong right hand.

'I want a room—anywhere handy,' cried he, driving the guilty couple before him. 'And you'd best get their luggage back, if it's gone. They won't be leaving England just yet, I fancy.' And amid the grins and winks of the bystanders, who understood the position of affairs at a glance, the strange trio proceeded to a room opening out of the hall. Then the door was shut, and was such a thick and well-fitting door that it was impossible to hear what went on on the other side. The interview was very long, and at times during it the voice of the old man was heard raised as if in anger or menace; but eventually they emerged—the father calm and with something like a smile upon his lips, the daughter resigned and certainly with little appearance of un-mitigated misery, and the young gentleman looking very much as a dog looks just before it receives a merited castigation.

The next day the steamer took them, all three, across the Channel to Ostend, and a short time after-wards, Mr. Heckthorpe reappeared at Ilborough, look-ing as if nothing had happened, and dropped in at several of his acquaintances' houses to tell them how Jane had been a little ailing lately, and how glad he had been to take advantage of a chance she had suddenly been offered of a tour on the Continent as companion to a lady.

What the gossips of Ilborough really thought, it is hard exactly to say, for there were many tales about in the little town. One thing only is certain —that no one believed in the companionship and the trip abroad. The favourite story was that Mr. Heck-thorpe had caught the couple at some lonely foreign spot—for Ilborough considered foreign parts sparsely inhabited and wild—and had killed them both; though the other story—that he had confined him-self to killing Ballard, and had shut his daughter up in a convent or a mad-house—had many firm adherents.

Before long, however, the wonder died out;— nothing more was heard of them; and when the dark Amalia took her walks abroad, more beloved than ever of the youth of the town, people forgot that she had ever formed one of the pair called 'Black and Gold.' The Rector called at the King's Arms soon after Mr. Heckthorpe's return, and was much relieved to find that the publican had been utterly mistaken in his suspicions, although the ex-planation of what had really happened was a trifle vague.

'A good girl, Jane, sir; a good girl, but a little

flighty. Took it into her head to take a journey, and then a chance of her using the French I had had her taught turned up. Sorry I troubled you that day. You'll be good enough not to mention it.'

Of course the Rector gave the desired promise, and went away wondering whether his late pupil, on receipt of his letter of exhortation, did not write him (his ex-tutor) down a meddling old ass.

'It's a lesson against interference in the concerns of others,' said he to his wife, who replied:

'Stuff, John! I do not believe a word of it. She's with him somewhere, and that horrid old man has been bought off—that's what it is.'

'Don't be uncharitable, Eliza,' said the Rector, and soon a duet of snores sang the song of triumph of British respectability.

CHAPTER VIII.

NOTHING in all a London season was prettier than to see Roger St. James and his son George (of the Life Guards Green) at church on a Sunday morning. They were both so perfectly dressed, their figures so alike, the flowers in their button-holes so fresh, their gloves so well-fitting, and their little prayer-books so neatly and quietly bound. Then they behaved so devoutly, asking each other the day of the month just before the Psalms, or the number of the hymn in such very devotional whispers; 'smelling their hats' for fully twenty seconds on entering; and moving about and coughing so very little during the sermon. Of the many rich old ladies who attended St. Hezekiah's Church in Mayfair, it has always surprised me that none left their fortunes to one or other of these apt representatives of fashionable piety. The Rector missed them when on rare occasions — the Sunday after Ascot, for instance—they were absent from their pew; and there was, in the hearts of nearly all the young ladies who attended St. Hezekiah's, a feeling of forlorn incompleteness when they were away.

Yet, had you suddenly asked either of them why they went to church, I doubt if they could have replied. I think that in the elder's mind there was a vague feeling that he had to do double duty in the way of piety for the sake of the family, taking his share and his brother's also, while George, who was easily amused, never ceased to appreciate the enormous joke of his father going to church at all. For, unfortunately for the respect due to a parent, Roger shared with his son not only his Sunday goodness, but also his week-day wickedness, sometimes excusing himself by the thought that what a young man does under the parental eye and by the parental authority could not be very wrong after all.

There is a story that on one occasion they had separated and gone to race-meetings in different parts of the country. On the Saturday they simultaneously emerged from two hansom cabs at the door of a well-known money-lender not far from Bond Street.

' Hullo, old chap ! '

' Hullo, George ! '

' Lost, eh ? '

' Yes ; and you ? '

' Clean broke ! '

Then they entered and did a bill together—a very convenient arrangement, as between the two the lender was pretty sure to get his money back out of the princely revenues of the Piccadilly estates.

One more anecdote of them : in the early days

of their brotherly friendship, when George had only just joined his regiment, they attended a theatre together.

'That's a pretty girl,' said George.

'Do you think so?' replied Roger.   'Not very.'

But he never took his opera-glass off the young lady's face, nevertheless.   The play over, they parted, each assuring the other that he had a particular reason for going to his club, but in a few minutes they confronted one another under the gas-lamp at the stage-door.   After this they agreed that, their tastes being thus similar, it would be folly to interfere one with the other, and so, 'Roger and son,' as they were called, became one of the institutions of London life.

Mrs. Roger had succumbed in the supreme effort of supplying the world with the junior partner of the firm, and, having been consistently neglected during her short married life, went without very much regret leaving her husband free to pursue the long heiress-chase which constituted the next fifteen years of his life—a chase the failure of which surprised no one more than himself.   But, somehow or other, the rare and not generally fair damsels blessed with balances at their banker's turned away from the gay lover when he pressed for a practical ending to his courtship. They liked flirting with him and dancing with him, and his conversation was decidedly amusing, but there was an absence of sincerity about him, and a certain cold cunning in his eyes, that could not escape the least observant.   Besides, the tale of his neglect of the lovely girl who had run away with him in defiance of her family was well known: a fact that did not assist him in his efforts to marry again. So poor Roger was fain to subsist on his somewhat narrow income, or occasional bits of good luck or good information in turf matters, and on his expectancies. His acquaintances were wont when meeting him to inquire after his brother's health instead of his own, and his mournful ' Quite well, thank you,' was a standing joke with those (and their name is legion) who find the more amusement in a jest the oftener they have heard it.

There was, by the by, another means by which Roger supplemented his income. He got on directions—that is, he kindly gave his name to divers companies which liked an Honourable among their directors, and was paid wages for attendance at their meetings, when he invariably went fast asleep.

This is the man who called at his sister-in-law's house one morning in October and was promptly shown up to her sitting-room.

' My dear Helen,' he said, taking both her hands, ' how well and fresh you are looking ! When did you come back ?'

' Only two days ago. I wonder we didn't meet in Scotland, and I wish we had, for I wanted to ask you the real truth about the affair at S—— Castle. They said that Lady S—— really——'

Then ensued a long conversation on the newest scandals that the country houses had added to the London season's list, and then Roger said, with a little air of embarrassment :

' And how is Harry ?'

' Oh, I've no patience with him. He has quarrelled with his uncle.'

The suspicion of a smile passed across Roger's face, but he made reply in a concerned tone :

' Dear me ! I am sorry for that. And Joseph seemed to have taken to him so very markedly. What did they quarrel about ?'

' There ! that's so annoying. I am not to be told. But I fancy some woman is at the bottom of it. Anyhow, unless Harry does something or says something

by the end of this month, Joseph is going to do all
manner of dreadful things. It really is too inconsiderate of Harry. He seems to forget others suffer
besides himself.'

Roger had been anxious to know whether his brother
was doing anything for his sister-in-law and her son,
and had indeed paid this visit on purpose to find
out. Of course he knew well enough that none of
the Peer's savings would come to himself, but that
did not prevent his being curious as to where they
would go.

'Harry is an obstinate young fellow, I should say,'
he remarked.

'As obstinate as a mule. I wish you would see him
on the subject. As a man of the world, he might
listen to you.'

'I shall be delighted,' said Roger, and so it was
arranged, and over a bottle of '48 at the Howard Club
a few evenings after, he broached the subject to his
nephew.

'A pity to quarrel with your bread and butter,
Harry.'

'Oh, I've got the bread at least; and I'd rather eat
it dry than pay so dearly for the butter.'

'What does he want you to do?'

'It isn't exactly that. It's what he wants me to
promise not to do.'

'I suppose I mustn't ask who she is?' said the
uncle slily.

Harry blushed scarlet.

'I never said anything about a "she."'

'No. But when ever was there a row without
one? Never mind, my boy, do what is right. I'm
sure, when I was your age I wouldn't have given up
my love for all the uncles and their purses in the
universe.'

'I should like to tell you, Uncle Roger; but the

fact is I promised I wouldn't—and—— Yes, I think you would say I am right if you knew about it. But, you see, my difficulty is that by carrying out my own plans I hurt someone else.'

'Everything must give way to principle,' said Roger, who didn't know what the word meant. 'I sacrificed a great deal because I could not approve of my brother's mode of life, and told him so.'

'Did you?' asked Harry, a little astonished, for his mother had often told him that Roger would have blacked Lord Piccadilly's boots if he had permitted it.

'Yes. I said, "My dear Joseph, there are some things that I, though I am not more squeamish than other men, cannot tolerate. You may have much in your power, but when my conscience tells me to speak, I must speak." And he never forgave me.'

No doubt such conduct would have amused Lord Piccadilly, and certainly would have provoked him far less than the obsequious flattery his heir-presumptive had always showered upon him.

'Let us be outspoken about it, my boy,' went on Roger, filling the other's glass. 'You think yourself bound to a certain course. My brother threatens to stop all assistance to you and to your mother if you take that course. Is that not so?'

'Yes.'

'Then it is a pity; but it seems to me that the fact of your mother's suffering should *not* affect you. That is, if you are sure your determination is the only one you can adopt. *Fais ce que dois*—you know the rest.'

And the old hypocrite leered on his nephew with an approving smile that would have done credit to a saint.

Then a few letters passed.

From Roger St. James to Lord Piccadilly.

'My dear Brother,—I am truly grieved to hear of the ungrateful behaviour of Harry. But I have often remarked that those who most desire to benefit by the generosity of others are unable sufficiently to disguise their real feelings of avarice and impatience of all delay in obtaining the desired result. The affection that is suddenly born of favours given or expected is not very lasting. But I am truly sorry that your experiment should have been so unfortunate. The slight difference that has, probably by my fault, for some time existed between us might, I think, now be allowed to die a natural death. I came upon some very quaint and rare books at a sale the other day, and, not having room for such things, should like very much to bring them down to The Grange and leave them there, if you think them worthy of your collection. I scarcely like to trust them to other hands, so please drop me a line to say what day would suit you.

'By the by, I was talking to old Lady X—— the other night, and she said to me, *à propos* of the dulness of Society just now, "Ah, conversation went out when that wicked, charming brother of yours took into his head to play the hermit." How delightful it will be when you again take your place at the head of Society! and to none more so—whatever my enemies may tell you—than your affectionate brother,

'ROGER ST. JAMES.'

The reply to this was laconic :

'My dear brother Roger,—Harry's little finger is worth the whole of all the other St. James's. I don't want any books, and if I did I know where to get them. As to your coming here, you are at liberty

to do so. I perhaps should, however, mention that
the rule I told you of in my last letter is still in
force, and that there is a flood in the river just now.
Probably, however, you are a good swimmer. Yours
ever,

'PICCADILLY.'

The day after the dinner at the Howard Club,
Harry also wrote a letter to the awsome lord at
Richlake:

'My dear Uncle,—I have made up my mind
finally, and see no reason for waiting until the end of
the month to acquaint you with my determination.
Nothing, except her own wish, shall make me give up
Miss Barton. I asked her to be my wife, and she
consented; that is enough for me. The engagement
is sacred. I do not know what may be your reason
for so disliking the affair, but I feel it is useless to any
longer attempt to combat your prejudice against me.
But I do dare ask you not to make my punishment
fall upon one who is, at any rate, innocent of crossing
your will. You were good enough to say that you
would allow me 1,500*l.* a year and buy me a
commission in the Army. If I forfeit this—as you
say I must—by adhering to my resolve with regard
to Miss Barton, I ask you to continue at least your
allowance to my mother. I will give you my word
of honour not to touch it. I will do more if you
desire it. You expressed—when we last met, just
before you ordered me to be turned out of your house
—a wish that I had no private fortune, that I might
starve or beg, and know what it was to defy your will.
I will not beg, and I hope I shall not starve; but, if
you will not carry out your threat as regards my
mother, I will make any arrangement you may dictate
that the 500*l.* a year which comes to me when I am
of age shall go to you or to her, and I will pro-

mise not to profit, directly or indirectly, by it for two years after I am twenty-one. I will go away and earn my bread for that time, and at its expiration I shall hold myself at liberty to act as I please. Then you can have the pleasure you anticipated, in knowing that for two years I shall have nothing but what I earn. Of course till I am of age I can claim nothing, but, if you accede to my request, you may rely on my word to touch no money from my mother.—I remain, yours sincerely,

'HENRY ST. JAMES.'

In a week's time the answer came :

'My dear Nephew,—I rather like your spirit. Sign the enclosed. It will deprive you of your 500*l.* a year in my favour for the time you mention. The notion of a St. James picking pockets or sweeping a crossing rather tickles me. I will give you no other reason concerning Nellie except that she belongs to me—my goods, my chattels—and she shall not belong to anyone else. On the conditions you state, your word of honour being given to touch no money from her, I will continue my allowance to your mother. At the end of the time you mention I may be dead, or I may have grown tired of Nellie. In any case, I never look forward. Now you may go to the devil. Yours ever,

'PICCADILLY.

'P.S.—I need scarcely remind you that if you desire to carry out your promise it will be necessary to hide this pecuniary arrangement from your mother. The fear of what people would say might lead her to force money on you.'

CHAPTER IX.

HENRY ST. JAMES, who had in him perhaps even more than the usual spirit of adventure pertaining to youth, looked very confidently on the strange arrangement into which he had entered with his uncle, and thought as lightly of entering into the warfare of life (unarmed with the weapon, money), as an ambitious young lady out hunting for the first time thinks of riding with a slack rein a tired horse at a big fence. To think that what he was doing was for Nellie Barton's sake was very sweet to his young mind, and, fond of romance reading as he was, love that ran smooth would only have been half love to him. The scene between him and his uncle had been very stormy. Immediately after his love affair he had demanded an audience, and had at once announced his determination to marry the Doctor's niece. At one moment it looked like turning into a physical struggle between the old man and the boy, for Lord Piccadilly was beside himself with rage; but he soon regained his self-possession, and tried that of his nephew very severely as he slowly brought out all the taunts he was a master of. But Harry was too angry to lose his temper, and the household of The Grange were amused by no riotous proceedings. One parting interview the lovers had.

'You will always be true to me?' said he, and her reply satisfied him. To do and to suffer for her seemed a pleasure in his eyes, and now that the doing and the suffering were also for the sake of his mother, the adventure attained almost heroic proportions. It was agreed with Nellie that, as there was no immediate prospect of success, nothing should be said to anyone on the subject, and that Mr. Barton should be allowed to ignore the troubles that the rascal Cupid had already brought upon the maiden who made his home bright. The carrying out of the plan was very difficult.

'I cannot understand it at all,' said Mrs. St. James. 'You absolutely refuse to return to Mr. Portleton's, and you wish to go away and travel. It is quite ridiculous. You must stay at Ilborough till the end of next term, and then you can come here and I will introduce you in London. I have always looked forward to placing you in a set far superior to that which your cousin George affects. I have nothing to say against racing, for it is fashionable, but I do not think —and I have always said so—that George is in the best racing set, and he knows no one at all in what I call the very best set. No, my dear boy; you must give up your wild projects.'

'But I can't, mother,' said Harry, very gently. 'I really can't. I have good reasons, although I may not tell them to you. If I am happy, surely you need not mind, for old Porty could have taught me no more, and, at any rate, my uncle has promised you what you wished, so you are all right.'

'Dear me, there's another mystery. I do so hate not being told things. First, your uncle threatens all sorts of dreadful things if some unknown occurrence takes place; then, without rhyme or reason, he writes to say he has changed his mind; and then you suddenly go off on a mysterious journey, nowhere particular, for an indefinite time. I really might as well never have had a son.' And the poor lady whimpered.

'Nonsense, mother,' said the son, putting his arm round her waist. 'You can trust me. I shall not get into any mischief, or do anything that will hurt our name. I shall see you from time to time, and I only ask you not to insist on my giving you any reasons, but to believe that the reasons I have are good ones. You will get on without me just as well

F

as you have always done, and you can console yourself by knowing that I am completing my education.'

'Why, what are you going to learn?'

'The ways of the world. Surely there could not be a better finish to a man's education than that.'

'But there's no world worth knowing, except here.'

'I think there is. I think I could learn the world you mean at any time. I don't believe there is much complication in human nature when it is trained and forced in the hot-bed here.'

'Don't you? I wish you knew Lady Tournely!'

'Well, I'll come back and learn Lady Tournely some day. You'll let me go?'

'How can I? Would it be doing my duty as your guardian?'

'If my uncle writes and advises it?'

'That would make a difference, of course—a great difference. But he'd advise anything that he thought might annoy anybody. May I ask Roger?'

'Uncle Roger's opinion is scarcely worth having. Of course he's much pleasanter than his Lordship, and I can get on with him. But—do you care much for his opinion?'

'Well, he's more or less a man of the world; but perhaps one scarcely respects him.'

'How could one? I should think taking lessons in the world of which he is a part would be a waste of time. No. You shall ask the fearful King of Richlake if you like, but no one else. Only, if you ask him you must take his advice.'

So Mrs. St. James duly wrote to her brother-in-law, and received a curt reply to the effect that she had much better, *for her own sake,* let Harry go his own way.

Mrs. St. James was not free from the selfishness that was the chief characteristic of her late husband's family, and the sentence underlined decided her. She gave her consent; and one fine autumn morning Harry St. James, with ten pounds in his pocket, and wearing a thick suit of country clothes, walked out of her little house into the world.

Probably most people have felt and forgotten that exultant sense of being for the first time your own master which comes in somewhere about the moustache-sprouting stage; when, for the first time, you can make plans, and go where you list, and smoke as you will, with no after-taste of reprehension or punishment.

For the first hour Harry wandered through the streets, giving himself wholly up to this feeling, and then he bethought him of a plan of action. He had often read in books of young men left penniless in the streets, and as his ten-pound note was not to be broken in upon except in dire emergency, he was to all intents and purposes a pauper. These young men, he had remarked, generally rescued maidens from drowning, or stopped the runaway horses of benevolent millionaires with no near relatives. But the horses in the carriages that rolled by him seemed to have entered into a conspiracy of docility, and when he sauntered across Waterloo Bridge there was no sign of even so much as a drowning puppy.

As he marched along, beginning to feel a little footsore and wondering how he ought to commence his life of bread-winning, a voice in his ear suddenly exclaimed: 'Ullo, Mr. St. James! The very man I should have liked to meet! Here's Amalia and I with three hours on our 'ands before the train starts and blessed if we know 'ow to get through it!' Then Harry shook hands with Miss and Mr. Heckthorpe, the latter of whom, he saw at a glance, had been devoting himself to the duty of trying whether the ales or the whiskey of London were better than those he retailed at the King's Arms in Ilborough. At most times Harry would have been a little annoyed at

having to escort the innkeeper and his daughter about
the streets of London, for the voice of the former was loud
and his manner to be observed of quiet passengers,
while Miss Amalia had, in a generous spirit, put on all
the finery she possessed.   Now, however, he hailed the
diversion with delight, and it was not until a substantial luncheon at a restaurant had been ordered that he
remembered he should be expected to pay therefor,
and that the sacred ten-pound note must be changed.
However, his spirits rose under the influence of Miss
Amalia's eyes, and he had forgotten all about the
matter, when Mr. Heckthorpe, remembering some
commission, suddenly withdrew and left the young
couple seated together.   At first Harry tried to ignore
that the young lady was unmistakably making fierce
love to him, and parried, with more or less success,
her attempts at sentimentalising, but Amalia was not
to be put off.   Since Harry had left Ilborough, since
she had been so much alone with her thoughts, her
sister being gone, she had, or deemed she had, discovered that her feelings for the handsome boy were
much stronger than mere liking, and it is quite true
that when they tumbled upon him in the Strand her
cheek had flushed and her heart had given several
quite unaccustomed thumps.   I may as well say at
once—to save any wonderment to the sceptical reader
—that very few women could be many minutes in
company with Harry St. James without falling more
or less in love with him.   There are such men, as we
all know, and he was one—men with whom the
hardest flirts discover that there are clefts even in
their armour, looking into whose eyes love seems a
possibility again, and a charming one even to the
hardened child of broken engagements and ruined
hopes.   It was not the boy's fault, it was only that
he did apparently make love to every woman to whom
he spoke.   His civilities had more tender meaning

and passion in them than most men could throw into a declaration of unalterable affection.

'What was it?' asked a mother of her weeping daughter on one occasion (subsequent to this time), 'what was it that made you think he cared for you?'

'It was the way he asked me to pass him the salt at luncheon,' was the reply. And in a corner of that lady's heart, even now that she is the happy mother of someone else's children, there lives the recollection of the day when Harry, with love shining out of his bright eyes and life-long protection sounding in his musical voice, asked her to pass the salt.

'You don't care a bit for me, Mr. St. James,' said Amalia, trying to throw her whole soul into her big black eyes, and putting her hand, which though large was well-formed and white, within tempting reach of his upon the table.

'What makes you think that, Miss Heckthorpe?' asked Harry, gallantly.

'Miss Heckthorpe! Why don't you call me Amalia?'

'Well, Miss Amalia!'

'Why "Miss?" Is that because I am below you in rank?'

He coloured, and the young lady mistaking the cause, which she imagined to be shyness, thought that she had never seen anything so splendid. It must be remembered that she had partaken of two, if not three, glasses of restaurant champagne, and was, moreover, unaccustomed to that beverage.

'No, of course not. Why do you think so, Amalia?'

'Ah! it is so nice to hear you say that! It makes my name sound so pretty! Do you think it is a pretty name, Mr. Harry? May I call you Mr. Harry?'

'Of course you may,' he replied, thanking Heaven that she did not drop her h's.

'Well—Harry——'

She hesitated a moment before she brought out his name without the 'Mr.'

'*Do* you care for me a bit?'

'Who could help it?' said he, wishing Mr. Heckthorpe would return.

'Oh! I am so glad to hear that! I was afraid when you went away and never wrote or anything, that I had offended you in some way, and I have been so unhappy. It is very bad for a girl to be very fond of anyone, isn't it, Harry?'

He was very young, the young girl looking into his eyes was very pretty. But he thought of Nellie, and responded as coldly as he dared, so as not to hurt her feelings.

'It depends, Miss—Amalia.'

'There! you said "Miss" again.' And in the excitement of the moment her hand closed on his, and Harry had not the presence of mind to put an end at once to the awkwardness of the situation. Indeed, sad as it is to record it, he rather lost his head for the moment, put his arm round her slender waist, and imprinted a flying kiss upon her red lips. In another instant he regretted it.

'My darling!' she murmured, and sank into his arms. Then what he had been so impatiently longing for occurred. Mr. Heckthorpe burst into the room, and discovered them in this romantic situation. If Harry had torn himself hurriedly away Amalia would have fallen on the floor. There was nothing to be done but to sit there supporting her and to look foolish.

'Ullo!' exclaimed the innkeeper, whose commission had apparently been accompanied by a friendly glass or so. 'Ullo! here's doings! The old story, eh? But you're a sly dog, young St. James, a sly dog!'

It was intolerable. Harry managed to put the

young woman straight on her chair and to withdraw his arm.

'I assure you, Mr. Heckthorpe——.'

'Oh, don't mind apologising. Lor' bless you, young folk will be young folk. I did a bit of spooning in my young days, I can tell you. And she's a good girl, and is fond of you. I've noticed that, sir—I've noticed that.'

He winked a wink of such extreme familiarity that Harry's anger rose.

'I think you are mistaken,' he said. 'There is nothing between me and your daughter. I—that is, she——.'

The man burst into a boisterous fit of laughter, and quite drowned poor Harry's explanations, which, it must be confessed, were somewhat difficult to frame.

'Ha, ha! Never mind, my boy, never mind; she knows what she's about—and so do I.'

'Papa!' remonstrated the daughter.

'Yes, you do. And so did Jane, eh?'

And again he exploded in noisy merriment.

Harry rang the bell, and ordered the bill. While he was waiting for it the innkeeper continued to laugh, and to pat him and his daughter alternately on the back. Then the ten-pound note was changed, and they all prepared to leave.

'When'll you look us up?' asked Mr. Heckthorpe, as Amalia put on her bonnet and gloves.

'I am afraid not just yet. I have other engagements.'

'Look here, young man,' began the other, with drunken solemnity, putting his heavy hand on Harry's arm, when Amalia interposed.

'Don't be foolish, papa. Mr. St. James—Harry—and I quite understand one another. He'll come and see me soon.'.

Notwithstanding her unbecoming costume, the girl

looked very pretty as she put her hand in his, and, for a moment as Harry watched their progress down the Strand, he rather regretted that he had not had another kiss. Then the absurdity of the thing struck him, and he burst out laughing, surprising an artistic and *tant soit peu* dirty gentleman who happened to meet him. The dirty gentleman stopped short, and addressed him.

'You are merry, sir.'

'I suppose that is allowed here,' said Harry, a little defiantly. He did not like being addressed by strangers.

'Yes, and seldom seen. But I suppose you are rich; only the rich laugh like that.'

Harry was amused by his tone, and looked at him. Poverty was written in every shiny seam of his coat, in the holes of his boots, and still more plainly in the defiant expression of his face.

'But I'm not rich: my whole capital is seven pounds nine shillings and fourpence.'

'Pooh!' said the other, in his turn examining him curiously. 'I can see by your manner and clothes that you are rich. Besides, you are young and strong and have good spirits. Talking of spirits, will you stand me a glass? The Ram and Horns, hard by, is my favourite public. With seven pounds nine shillings and fourpence, you should not be niggardly. It is too small for investment. You couldn't get a one-volume novel printed with it. I don't believe you could buy a plot with it. Such a sum lends itself readily to hospitality. You don't know me, you say. That mistake of Society can be cured. I daresay you have a history. If so, you can tell it me over the brandy-and-water; if not, I can tell you mine if you wish to know it. At any rate I am thirsty, and have not the price of a glass on me. What do you say?'

'Show me the Ram and Horns,' said Harry, who

was amused by the volubility of his new acquaintance, and who thought this a good opportunity for seeing something of the life of a person without money.

So they walked down the Strand together, and people wondered at the companionship of the aristocratic youth and the seedy-looking individual with the long hair.

CHAPTER X

' Two brandies, cold,' said the seedy stranger, and the young lady at the bar, tossing her raven curls when she espied Harry, and sending him one of her well-tried smirks, served them with two glasses of brandy-and-water. As Harry, although accepting the liquor for fear of seeming churlish, nevertheless did not drink it, his companion had every reason to be satisfied with his choice of a host.

' One good turn deserves another,' he said, smacking his lips, ' and I will introduce you to my club. It isn't exactly fashionable, but it's uncommonly pleasant, and it perhaps realises in the fullest degree what the poet meant by " the feast of reason, and the flow of soul." There, every Saturday night, those of us who can manage a pair of boots and a shirt, meet and give reasons for our want of success in art, literature, and the drama, while the way our souls flow, if some discriminating guest will only stand treat, is marvellous.'

' But I thought you said it was a club,' remarked his companion, edging away from a pale-visaged woman who had come in for two-penn'orth of gin.

' So it is. Managed on the strictest rules of Pall Mall establishments. We elect the stranger at once, and then he pays his footing. We shall elect you to-night, and you will feel an honest pride in satisfying

the carnal wants of those whose spiritual writing will
some day keep their memories as green as their coats
are threadbare.'

'Charming! And what is your club?'

'Let us begin at the beginning. Man comes before his club, just as birth comes before barbarism. I
am a self-made man!'

'Are you?' said Harry, glancing at the poverty-
stricken creature before him.

'Yes; I was born well off, with a silver spoon in
my mouth, as they say. But I always hated spoons,
and as to silver, there is, I am sure, something in my
nature that draws me irresistibly to the pawnbroker.
My "Ode to Attenborough" is considered finer than
the "Ode to Death." Well, I spent my money like
what people call a gentleman, and at the age of
twenty-five I found myself a self-made pauper. You
don't think it fine? Well, I don't know. Perhaps it
wasn't. At all events I spent the money entirely on
myself, that is a comfort to look back upon. Not a
sixpence went on others, except so far as their having
it ministered to my pleasure. Besides, you, I feel
from your look, don't care very much for the people
who walk into manufacturing towns with half-a-crown
in their pockets and amass millions. I did the
reverse. I walked into this town with fifteen thousand
pounds in my pocket and amassed debts. So, looking at the thing logically, you ought to like me,
the exact opposite of the other fellow. I was
honest enough, too. The tradesmen and people
charged me so much more than they ought to have
done, that, when my capital was spent, and I had
lived on my credit for three years, at the end of
it they had really—looking on them as a class—received very fair payment. That is a beautiful law of
human nature. First, the tradesmen live upon you;
then, when your wherewithal is done, you live upon

them. Then, when they find you out and the
arrangement ceases, and you become a wild creature,
not very nice to look at, for bad hats and shiny
coat-collars are not things of beauty, but after all as
near an imitation of the primeval wild man as is
possible in these degraded days of civilisation, they
balance their books, write off your debt as bad, and
look out for fresh prey. The cycle of demand and
supply is a marvellously neat arrangement. But I
weary you?'

'Not a bit,' said Harry, 'although I cannot say I
care to stay in this place much longer.'

'Well, I have an appointment—with an editor who
is, I think, getting tired of rejecting my articles, and
who will in a few months accept one in self-defence—
and we will go our separate ways. You will come to
the club, though?'

'Where is it?'

'A stone's throw from here. Let me show it to you,
so that you may easily find it to-night. Be there at
eleven sharp, and I guarantee that you will be amused.
Where are you living?'

'Nowhere.'

'Nowhere! I like that. The man who has a
regular home is a poor creature. I am now using
lodgings that are airy and more or less convenient.
You know the Mall?'

'By Buckingham Palace? Yes. Do you live
near there?'

'I live there. The place is pleasant enough in the
summer months, and the bench I have selected—the
second from the Horse Guards end—is, I think, softer
than the others, and far more free from fleas. As the
cold nights come on I shall move; at present there
is nothing to complain of, and, beyond an occasional
waking up by a policeman who prefers my explanation
of who I am, and defence of my honesty and good

intentions, to solitude, I really can say nothing against my night's rest there.'

'As to the cold, eh?' said Harry, looking at the man with amused interest.

There was no vulgarity in his voluble talk; it was easy to see that, whatever his moral character might be, he had a gentleman's bringing-up, which is the part of birth which makes gentility.

'Cold! Yes. It is cold sometimes. But for those blessed with strong imaginations, as I am (I once imagined an account at a bank, and had a little trouble with a judge and twelve of my countrymen concerning it) such things don't matter up to a certain point. That speech Shakespeare puts into the mouth of one of his characters, "Who can hold fire in his hand," &c., is all nonsense. If you could but stir up my imagination sufficiently about snow and ice, I could easily hold fire in my hand. Once, when my bank— my breeches-pocket—was clean broke, I got drunk on pure water, for I forced myself to think it was mixed with alcohol. And now we part, sir. I will not give my editor the satisfaction of forgetting to call upon him. I send in a new name every day, else I should not get in, and the chaps there enjoy the joke, and vow they don't recognise me. Let me see—I've used up a heap of names—what shall I be to-day?'

'What is your real one?' asked Harry, adding with a little embarrassment, as he remembered the delicate nature of the question to such an individual, 'I mean what name do you go by now?'

My own. A poor thing, sir, but mine own—Lacroix. I never use an *alias*, because I have such an infernal memory. I should forget who I really was, and then the legacy I am expecting (always expect a legacy — it keeps you up) might miss me. I am not dishonest. Once I was accused of obtaining goods upon false pre-tences merely because I wrote a cheque which was not a false pretence ; only the banker wouldn't respect his own paper, and a jury of other tradesmen found me guilty, and hurried away to lunch and to rob those whose cheques were honoured at the moment. I give you my word that on that jury was a man to whom I had once paid ninety guineas for a dressing-bag which I know cost him thirty-six. Never mind. Prison life is eminently respectable, and very inexpensive. Once you have lost your character, you have no idea how little things matter. It's like losing a grand butler who overawes you, and getting your wine out of the cellar yourself. There's the club—that dingy-looking house, second floor. Door on the left. You'll see " Arcadia " on the brass-plate. Knock twice, like a postman, and mention my name. We shall be forced to make you a temporary Arcadian, Mr. —— ? '

' St. James—I mean Jameson.'

' Mr. Jameson. Odd that you should have mentioned the other. Very odd. But things in life are odd. Your face reminds me of some one, too. Your name *is* Jameson ? Never mind—don't answer. The question was indiscreet. Because I have a dislike—arising from my own imperfect memory—to *aliases*, that is no rule for others. Good-day. If you are at all dissatisfied with your present quarters, whatever they are, the bench next to mine is vacant just now. The lady who occupied it during the summer has left for an aquatic excursion—jumped off Waterloo Bridge. Improvident woman, too—actually had two shillings in her pocket. And there was I, always civil and neighbour-like at the next house, or bench, and longing for the price of a drink.'

Mr. Lacroix bowed politely and was about to leave Harry, when he suddenly turned back.

' I want to make sure of your coming to our club to-night, for I like your face. May I do so ? '

'I shall be happy to come, but how can you make sure?'

'The easiest thing in the world. Lend me five shillings, and I'll collect it there and repay you.'

'I don't think I will,' said Harry, laughing. 'I have very little money, as I told you, and I shall want the five shillings if I am to stand treat.'

'But I will repay you.'

'So you say, but——'

'You won't trust me. After all, I don't see why the deuce you should. But I wish you would have done so.' He turned away, when the other, half touched by the disappointed look in his face, stopped him.

'Here are the five shillings. I trust to your honour to repay me, but you must recollect that I never saw you before, and that your own account of yourself is not——'

'Not encouraging,' finished Lacroix, pocketing the silver. 'No. But—do you know, you would never guess it—I am a gentleman, and I would never rob a fellow-gentleman. Usurers and tradesmen are, or were, my prey. *Au revoir.*'

Left to himself, Harry found plenty of food for thought in the strange character of the man he had met; and, being of an adventurous nature, was not afraid to follow up his acquaintance and brave the terrors of this queer club, composed apparently of paupers not very far removed from felons. To see 'life' was his aim, and as there was scarcely time to do much in the way of seeking his fortune that afternoon, he sauntered moodily about the streets and eventually found himself seated on a bench in the Mall where his companion lodged.

He had filled his pockets with cigars before coming out, and as he smoked one of them, and dreamed waking dreams of romance in which Nellie Barton had a prominent place, he looked up and saw a smart phaeton go by with no less a person holding the reins than his friend Humphrey Ballard.

Ballard had lately set up as a smart young man about town, living principally on his expectancies from his cousin, Mr. Ballard-Erdmore. He was looked upon with much reverence by those young men who are wont to frequent stage-doors, and was considered as a very desirable acquaintance by those ladies of the ballet who have an ambition to supplement their strictly professional earnings. Suddenly waking to the imprudence of remaining where he might be recognised, Harry arose, and, conquering a natural inclination to go home to dinner, went to a place he had marked on his walk, where a 'wash and brush-up' could be obtained at the charge of one penny. And thus beautified, after a frugal meal at an eating-house, he found himself at the door of 'Arcadia' as the clock struck eleven.

As he had been told, Lacroix's name served as a sufficient passport, and he was at once admitted, through a small and dark lobby, into a large bare-walled room lit by two or three jets of gas, uncivilised by coverings of glass, and so full of smoke that it took him some time to distinguish the faces of its inhabitants. From the buzz of voices, however, he became at once aware that many were present ; and he was rather relieved when Lacroix's voice sounded in his ear, bidding him welcome to 'Arcadia.'

'Gentlemen,' shouted that person, 'let me introduce to you the guest of the evening, Mr. Jameson!—The Arcadians of London!—The Arcadians of London!—Mr. Jameson! Mr. Jameson will stand drinks all round. Tom, you scoundrel, take the members' orders! Mr. Jameson, take a seat.'

Harry seated himself between his so-called host and a small ill-tempered, looking man, who was dressed in grey tweed and gifted with a pair of sharp small black eyes and an arched back.

'That is Templar; our most distinguished member,' whispered Lacroix.

'Indeed! What has he done?'

'Heavens! To ask what George Mackintosh Templar has done! Why, he has had a play accepted!'

'And acted?'

'No. They didn't pay for it, and they didn't act it. But they did accept it. That was twelve years ago. Probably, before Templar is a very old man it may be produced. Still he has the reward of all great men—at least here. But he fears me. If I eventually get my editor (who was bitter in his wrath to-day when I entered his room) to accept an article, I shall run him close. At present, however, he is our great man.'

'But surely that,' said Harry, indicating a gentleman opposite him, 'is an actor. I seem to have seen his face on the stage.'

'Yes. He is not a member, only a visitor—a very constant visitor. He comes here because we flatter him and give him drinks. Some day he may be able to obtain influence enough to get a play from one of us acted. There, two from him on the left, that is the manager of a publishing firm. He comes here for the same reason. But he doesn't get our books published, though. I sold him the MSS. of seven three-volume novels once for two pounds, to be paid when the first came out. But the first has not come out yet. Here is the liquor—a health to the new member.'

They drank Harry's health with all the honours, and he was relieved when they all began talking again immediately after, as he had feared that a speech might be required of him.

'How do you all live?' asked he, for after some conversation, and after his eyes had become accustomed to the smoke, he had seen that the twenty or twenty-

five men there all bore evidences of poverty as great
as that of his introducer.

'Live! Well; that's rather a problem. I don't
think many of us know how we do it. Dirty work for
editors and publishers, penny-a-lining, social paragraphs. I found out the other day from a footman I
met in the Hare and Hounds that the Duchess of
B—— was—was a little gay, and I got 2*s*. 9*d*. from
the editor of *Belgravian Buzzings* for the " par."
But, as you know, I am on the point of becoming a
political leader-writer.'

'Ah! Which side do you take?'

'Oh! I'm perfectly impartial. When I had
money I was naturally a Conservative. I wanted to
get rid of my goods as I liked, not to have them taken
from me. Now, I suppose, I should like to take other
people's goods from them. But all political feeling
begins at home; and I think I could defend the House
of Lords with the best of them—that is, for a guinea-
and-a-half a column. Do you see that member there
with the clay-pipe—drinking now?'

'Yes.'

'He's our richest man. I fancy he is something
in the Fenian brotherhood, and engaged by Government to report their doings. A desperate patriot
when he's drunk. Weeps over poor Ireland's wrongs,
and goes to the Irish Office next day to show up his
brethren in patriotism. I rather like the man. He is
such an instance of the triumph of self-interest over
general principles.'

'You seem a nice lot,' said Harry, a little seriously.

'We are. A very nice lot, considering. Most
men in our places would be picking pockets. It is sad
to reflect that a hundred years ago we might have
ruffled it on horseback as gentlemen of the road.'

'And been hanged at the end.'

'I doubt whether most natural deaths are preferable

G

to hanging,' said the philosopher; whereupon Harry, disliking the atmosphere and the company, rose to depart, having settled his bill with the waiter and promised Mr. Lacroix to look him up some night at his residence in the Mall.

CHAPTER XI.

HARRY's ten-pound note, as may be supposed, did not hold out very long. At first he paid eighteen-pence for his bed, but Lacroix soon found him one at a quarter that price, and he speedily discovered that poverty, as says the adage, does bring with it most unpleasant bedfellows.

Lacroix also busied himself to find employment for this handsome youth, so evidently a gentleman, who had mysteriously been thrown into the vortex of hand-to-mouth living; and, just as Harry was making a choice between giving up the chance of breakfast on the morrow, or taking advantage of the bench on the Mall that he had been told was unoccupied at night, he actually obtained a subordinate post at the printing-office of a daily paper, which at any rate secured him the certainty of food and lodging.

It may seem strange that Mrs. St. James should have so easily acquiesced in her son's mad and romantic scheme of life; but then it must be remembered that she did not know of all its wildness. She never doubted but that he received money from the awful Lord at Richlake; the idea of anyone voluntarily pauperising himself, whatever might be the object to be attained, could never occur to a mind so comfortable and worldly as hers. Her feeling with regard to her son was indeed one of annoyance. Instead of chiming

in with her wishes and allowing her to push him in
her little world of fashionables, or of those she deemed
fashionables, here he was going off in a mysteriously
disreputable manner, refusing to give his reason, and
leaving no address. That there must be some woman
at the bottom of it she never doubted, that the woman
was of low extraction she felt sure ; and the poor lady
shivered in her dainty boudoir as she pictured to herself
her handsome son, whom she had meant to show off
and be so proud of, seated in some back slum, surrounded by dirty children, and supporting a vulgar
wife. However, there was no help for it—she had let
him go, and not knowing where to direct she could not
write and recall him. A letter she wrote to Lord
Piccadilly about a fortnight after he had gone did no
good ; for his Lordship merely replied that she had
better leave the young man to go his own way—indeed,
he desired that she would do so. Visions of appealing
to the authorities of Scotland Yard and asking the
advice of a magistrate occurred to her ; but Roger,
whom she consulted in her extremity, was quite eager
in dissuading her from this course, and she was not
sorry to relinquish it. Roger had that half-unconscious
dislike for his nephew often felt by a schemer for an
honest man, whose honesty is a perpetual rebuke to
him, and was not sorry that Harry should be out of the
way of his uncle. There was no predicting Lord
Piccadilly's caprices, and it always seemed possible to
Roger that some day the old man might take a sudden
affection for his next brother. So civil letters con
tinued to be indited from time to time from the Sward
or the Feathers Club to Richlake, and were persisted
in, notwithstanding the small effect they produced in
the way of answer. Roger thought his brother read
them, though he could not be sure, and at any rate
they did not give him much trouble. On one occasion
he was finishing one when his friend Colonel Boyler

asked him to come for a stroll in the Park. 'In a moment,' said the old dandy, looking up from his paper; 'I am just finishing a letter to my brother Piccadilly; he insists on my writing to him continually and telling him all the news of the day. Affectionate fellow, Joseph ! And after all, it's well that brothers should be brothers.' Had Colonel Boyler known that the ultimate destiny of the letter he saw stamped and posted was to be thrown unopened into the Richlake waste-paper basket, to be afterwards opened and read with some amusement in the housekeeper's room, he would have been much amused. Not that he believed in the brotherly friendship, or indeed in anything that Roger said.

'He is so false,' observed one of his friends of him on one occasion, 'that if he died and went to heaven, his ghost, could it appear here, would declare it had been damned.'

But a liar more or less in London matters little; and Roger St. James was popular enough as times go, and never had any difficulty in finding a companion at dinner or in the Park. He had good spirits, which are, after all, of more importance than truth telling—at least, in the opinion of busy seekers after passing amusement. It must be confessed that at this period fortune was dealing rather hardly with the man. A horse had lately upset the calculations of its owner and his friends by running away and ignominiously winning a race he was intended to lose; and the gentleman who was wont to befriend 'Roger and Son' when in difficulties had become rather un-amiable, and had begun to hint that the autograph of the firm was losing its value, and that unless some of the floating paper were soon redeemed, affairs would assume a very serious aspect for the said firm. Roger had suggested to the junior partner the advisability of asking Harry to 'jump up behind,' as backing a bill is termed in the slang of impecuniosity; but George, who had the instincts of a gentleman, was very savage about it, and absolutely refused to even discuss the subject.

'He is only a boy.'

'Yes; but Hart would take his name. He'd never disown it when he came of age, and I'm convinced that old fool at Richlake means to leave him money.'

'I don't care a d——! I'm never going to let it be said that I induced a boy of nineteen to do a Stiff for my benefit. He'll probably do them on his own account soon enough—if he's got any of the family habits.'

Roger, with a sigh, gave in to the arguments of his son, but had he happened to meet with the subject of debate, I fancy he would have been so far disloyal to the firm as to try to recruit a new partner without leave of his present one.

In the meanwhile we have left Nellie Barton very love-lorn, but bravely hiding the fact, and going through her task of reading to and amusing the master of The Grange, and of ministering to her uncle's wants with praiseworthy diligence; while before her mind's eye is always the bright eager face of her lover, and in her heart still echo his last words of love and hope. She is no hysterical weeping damsel, and knows that the separation from Harry is not so very great a misfortune. They are both so young, she says to herself, that they surely can wait; and even to know that she has been loved by him is indeed a crown of glory for a humble maid such as she is. That he will come back and claim her, she never doubts; but even if he did not, her life has not been in vain. She has felt his strong arms around her, his kisses on her lips. That is a lifetime of happiness in itself; and she pities the girls she sees about the roads in that they have no Harrys to love them and for whom to wait. Has she not his photograph, too, coloured and enclosed in a little velvet case, and two of his letters—one a note to make an appointment, and one a long, loving, and rather incoherent letter of farewell? What are the riches of the world compared with such possessions as these? It is true that at times she disquieted herself by wondering whether she had not been too easily won, whether she should not have had 'more cunning to be strange;' but, like Juliet, she had little fear that her lover would impute her 'yielding to light love.' As she had told him, he was the first young man to whom she had ever spoken in social intercourse, and, as she jestingly said, it was rather hard that her love for him should deny her in the future the usual experiences of maidens fair and free. Then he had frowned, and told her that perhaps after all she only cared for him for that reason, that she should in very truth be free till she had seen more of the world, and then she had so prettily coaxed him to revoke the words, and reimpose the chains she wished to be irrevocably bound by. 'But you, you know, Harry, you too are young, and you are different, as a man. You ought not to be tied; and, whatever you say, I shall not look upon you as bound to me.' This she repeated at their parting, and was glad of afterwards. To give up even so little as this one-sided agreement meant (for he was loud in his protestations that he was and would be bound by chains of iron) was a pleasure to her.

And she never doubted him, never feared that he would be faithless. The girl was proud, and, moreover, she knew in her heart that she was very fair. A chance word from an artist who passed her in the

road one day had opened her eyes to the fact, and
Lord Piccadilly had one day gravely said to her,
' Nellie, I have been in every capital in Europe, I
have seen all the prettiest women of every class to be
found in them, and I give you my word that I never
saw anything in the way of beauty to come near you.'
Then Nellie had been angry, and had refused to read
to him any more until he apologised; but she had
been pleased, not so much for herself as for Harry.
It was well that what she gave him should be good of
its kind; he was worthy of the best; and she was glad
to know she was of the best.

One day—it was soon after the artist's remark—she
had suddenly turned to her uncle. ' Uncle John,' she
said—and he stopped in his reading of the *Lancet* and
looked up, with his finger marking the place where he
left off—' Uncle John ! '

' What is it, Nell ? '

' Am I pretty ?—very pretty, I mean.'

He put down his paper, took her hand in his, and
as he drew her towards him said, very gravely :

' Why do you want to know? You are not going
to be vain ?'

' No, I hope not. But I have seen so few women,
and I do want to know how I stand with regard to my
sex. Don't be cross, uncle.'

' I am not cross, dear. But, for God's sake, do not
set too high a value on your looks! You are beautiful, my child, and I would to God you were not !'

' Why? It is well to be beautiful, is it not ?'

' It is sometimes—often—a woman's curse. I have
known——'

Then he stopped himself hastily, and turned to his
newspaper, with a sign that he did not wish to be disturbed. And Nellie wondered why she should not
take pleasure in the fact that she was fair, and why the
mere mention of it made her uncle so sad and stern.

In the meanwhile the diminished household at the King's Arms at Ilborough went its way much as usual. The young gentlemen from the Rectory came there and played their games of billiards, made love more or less ardently and with varying success to the fair damsel there, who certainly possessed a power of repartee and of parrying serious courtship that many beauties of 'Society' might have envied; and Mr. Heckthorpe was very proud of her, and made money out of his excellent beer, and chuckled exceedingly whenever the name of his absent daughter was mentioned. Ilborough, however, did not mention her name very often, for there had been new scandals there and new excitements, and Jane Heckthorpe was almost forgotten. Amalia grew handsomer every day, and a certain anxiety concerning the advent of Harry St. James certainly seemed to have little effect either on her spirits or her appetite. To her the embrace meant very little; and her father, having been somewhat bemused during that visit to London, only remembered his discovery of it in a hazy manner, and soon gave up his inquiries as to when 'young St. James was coming to the scratch.' A good many eligible young men had been very near that position, but had not quite reached it; and Mr. Heckthorpe took any little disappointment he might feel like a philosopher, which, seeing so much of the worst and weakest side of human nature, a publican often is.

Amalia herself thought she had been nearer success with Harry than she had ever been before, and, could she only bring him again within the reach of her great black eyes, she thought she could easily do his business for him. The difficulty was the getting him there; but the girl did not despair, and induced one of the pupils at Mr. Portleton's to write to him and invite him to come down and see a cricket match between the Rectory youths and those of a neighbouring tutor's.

This letter, however, for reasons known to the reader, he did not receive.

Of Humphrey Ballard little was known. He had blazed out in London for a short season, and then disappeared. While in the height of his glory many romantic tales were told of the Lothario; but all agreed that he was the happy possessor of an 'establishment' somewhere in the shady groves of St. John's Wood; and he was immensely respected by immature youths who thirsted to do likewise. Then the reports as to his life reached the Irish castle, and Mr. Ballard-Erdmore was very angry and sent for him and put an end to the glory, but not, as some said, to the establishment, which, it was reported, was moved to some less expensive quarters, but which still was kept up.

Humphrey himself, on his return, was observed to be very quiet, and then abjured his usual bottle of champagne at dinner. He even gave up his attendance at theatres and music-halls, and his old associates turned from him with natural contempt. He was duly called to the Bar, and the people said he showed some aptitude for his calling; although it is my belief that he had a stock of novels, as well as his law books, in the little room overlooking the garden in the Inner Temple, and that he knew more of 'Guy Livingstone' and Miss Braddon's and Ouida's novels than he knew of John Doe and Richard Roe, or their modern equivalents.

However this may be, after a time his friends remarked that, although he was known to have a generous allowance, he began to show evident marks of poverty, and that, moreover, he had grown gloomy and taciturn, and altogether changed from the dashing music-hall critic of yore.

CHAPTER XII.

'Sit down, Barton,' said Lord Piccadilly. 'I have sent for you to speak of Nellie.'

Mr. Barton took no notice of the request to be seated, but remained standing. He was a small shrivelled-up old man, with white hair and an amiable expression of countenance; but there was something very like contempt in his eyes now as he looked at his companion in the room.

'I thought as much,' he said, curtly.

'You always were d——d clever. It certainly wasn't very likely that I should want to speak to you of the state of the public health in Richlake.'

'Or of the past.'

The Lord laughed, and the other's face darkened still more.

'Well, I might wish to talk of that. There are many incidents connected with it and with you that amuse me to remember. I think you are the only man alive that has called me a scoundrel to my face. The word was "scoundrel," I think?'

'It was "scoundrel,"' said Mr. Barton, his hand trembling a little as it rested on the back of a chair.

'And you think so still?'

'I think so still.'

'And tell me so. Capital! The Richlake apothecary tells *me* I am a scoundrel!'

There was an amount of amusement in the tone of that *me* which showed the idea of his own importance which this man had, and he glanced at the Doctor with much the same look as you might cast on a three-month-old puppy that attacked your legs.

'I presume, my Lord, that you did not send for me to hear me reiterate my opinion of you?'

'I don't see why you should presume so if the fact of your doing so amuses me.   But in this case you happen to be right.   It is a year since I saw you, and in that time Nellie has grown up.   She is almost a woman now, and infernally pretty!'

The face of the Doctor, as he said these last words, was positively threatening ; his trembling hands were clenched together, and his eyes flashed fire from under his shaggy eyebrows.

'Infernally handsome ! almost more so than her mother—and without her devilish temper, too.'

'Are you a man,' cried Dr. Barton, unable to control himself, 'that you can speak so of her ? '

'Silence, sir ! ' thundered Lord Piccadilly.   ' I sent for you to listen to me.   I have some questions to put.   Answer them briefly and to the point. Your presence bores me.   Does she suspect anything of her parentage ? '

'Nothing.'

'You have kept your word, eh?   Well, I believe you; for it would scarcely be a pleasant tale to tell her. She thinks my having her here is a mere caprice ? '

'Yes.'

'But what do the idiots about say?   You hear the gossip, I suppose ?   Do they imagine anything ? Answer me, can't you ?   Do they couple my name in any way with the child's ? '

'You forget, my Lord, that I pass for her uncle. Whatever they may think, they are not likely to tell their thoughts to me.'

'They probably do,' said Lord Piccadilly, half to himself.   'But after all it matters little.   Look here, Barton !   I have taken a fancy to the child.   Natural affection, I suppose you call it ; but, by God ! if she wearied me, or were ugly, she might die in a ditch for all I cared.   But she does interest me.   Now I suppose her face will attract some young fellows soon unless

she were hidden away, and that is difficult. You probably won't live long, and then the matter will be still
more complicated.'

'I shall leave her all my savings, my Lord.'

'Your savings! Bah! They would not keep her
off the streets.'

Again the Doctor seemed about to lose his self-
control, but he contrived to remain silent. Lord
Piccadilly contemplated his look of rage with
indolent amusement.

'It wouldn't be very strange, with her breeding,' he
said, after a short pause. 'My morals are queerish,
and her mother wasn't far removed from a——'

'My Lord,' said the Doctor, coming close up to the
other's chair, 'I will not hear a bad word of her.
Whatever she was, that you made her.'

'Did I? I fancy it would have occurred in any
case, only I happened to come first. Well, I have
been thinking the thing over, and I have decided that
the best plan is to marry her at once.'

'At once!'

'That is, of course, as soon as I can find a man to
take her—someone who will look upon her face as
compensation for her dubious birth. It's a pity I didn't
make you her father instead of her uncle; but I daresay we can invent a respectable brother for you.'

'Thank you, my Lord.'

'I rather think I have hit upon a man that would
do. My nephew, when he was here the other day——
By the way, did he come to your house often?'

'Once—no, twice, I think.'

'Ah! blind old fool!' (This to himself.) 'Well,
as I was saying, my nephew happened to mention a
young man who was at his tutor's with him, a young
Ballard, and he describes him as a worshipper of pretty
faces. His cousin was a friend of mine, or thought he
was, many years ago, and once asked me to give this

young man a helping hand. I have made inquiries, and I find he is in London—at the Bar—and hard up. I shall ask him down here, and throw him with Nellie. He is a gentleman by birth, and will inherit his cousin's place in Ireland. I shall tell him that your imaginary brother, Nellie's father, has left 20,000*l.* for her if she marries with your consent. What you will have to do will be to give that consent, and to urge Nellie to the match. One of your stipulations will be that he shall take his wife to the Irish place, and live there when he inherits it. I don't want to have her about London. That will be more easy as his cousin has a monomania about a landlord living on his estate. To lose Nellie will be a nuisance to me; but I have had enough of this infernal hole, and shall wander about the Continent again soon. Nellie would be in my way. At any rate, I want her settled in life. I wish her out of danger—perhaps because she is my child, I can't exactly say. Probably I am getting into my dotage. See to this, Barton. I shall write to this Ballard at once. Mind you play your part as I direct. Have you anything to say?'

'Do you place no importance on the girl's own inclinations?'

'Devilish little. If I can't manage a child's imaginary affections it will be surprising. Now you may go.'

The Doctor hesitated, opened his mouth to speak, changed his mind, and left the room; while the other, who was as prompt in carrying out his own wishes as he expected all others to be, wrote the following note:

'Dear Mr. Ballard,—I make no apology for addressing you, although personally unacquainted with you, as years ago I knew very intimately your cousin Erdmore, and he more than once begged me if possible to make your acquaintance when you grew up.

Hearing you are in London, I now write to say I shall be happy to see you whenever it is convenient to you. This place is on the Thames, and I have plenty of boats. You will, I daresay, find a little fresh air from Saturday to Monday, and a row on the river, a pleasant change from the Law Courts.—Believe me, yours truly,

' PICCADILLY.'

'By the way, my nephew Harry has spoken to me of you as his friend at Ilborough. That makes another reason for your coming.'

Ballard was a very proud man the day he received this. It seemed so strange that this haughty, inaccessible Lord should ask him, in such a friendly manner, to see him, that he was at first half inclined to look upon the whole thing as a hoax.

But none of his friends looked conscious or secretly amused when he spoke of the matter, and he eventually wrote off to say that he would take advantage of Lord Piccadilly's kind invitation, and come on Saturday to stay till Monday, naming a date about a fortnight off. He would have liked to go at once and take the ball on the hop—for who knew what the eccentric millionaire might not do with his money?—but he thought that to do so would be to appear too little sought after.

The reasons which made Lord Piccadilly so antagonistic to Harry's suit were manifold. In the first place, he hated and mistrusted his own family, and he honestly desired that Nellie should be happy. He also wanted her well out of the way, where fewest questions would be asked concerning her birth, and this young man, who was pretty certain to be obliged to live in Ireland, seemed the very thing. I don't think the quasi-cousinship that existed between Nellie and Harry had anything to say to his feelings. His first burst of rage had been caused by the idea of losing the girl; of her thinking of anything but his own needs and amusements; but the incident had decided him that it would be impossible to keep so fair a flower unseen by the eyes of greedy young men, and thence his resolve to make use of the first instrument that came to hand to obviate the danger of her coming to ruin through the plucking by unsuitable hands.

It must be confessed that it required all his strength of purpose to enable him to put up with the presence of our friend, Humphrey Ballard. With all his faults, Lord Piccadilly had the one merit of being a gentleman to the ends of his fingers; and the rather insolent self-assertion of the man, barely repressed by a haunting sense of inferiority, which he tried his best to hide, aggravated him to the last degree. Ballard himself never doubted but that he carried himself most properly and bravely in a difficult position. Nellie Barton charmed him, of course—whom would she not have charmed who had eyes to see and blood in his veins? And the many *tête-à-têtes* he was allowed with her were pleasant enough. The girl having seen so few men thought him very agreeable and very handsome, and almost wished her Harry had a pointed black moustache and a large watch-chain covered with trinkets—and all, during those autumn weeks, progressed smoothly enough towards the consummation of Lord Piccadilly's plan. There was at times a reticence or drawing back in the young man's courting which puzzled him. Ballard would suddenly leave Nellie's side and take refuge in the library at The Grange, or would stay away a fortnight at a time, although specially invited. But altogether he was not deficient in lover-like assiduity; and Nellie, in her innocence, and secure, as she supposed, in her love for Harry, unconsciously encouraged him, finding his converse and society a pleasant change from sitting by her sleeping uncle, or reading to the grim and saturnine old peer. This latter person knew well that there would be a pitched battle at the last between him and the damsel, whose high spirit he was aware of ; but he was not accustomed to be beaten, and determined that he would allow no scruples of any kind to stand in the way of winning here. Old Mr. Erdmore was delighted at the civility shown to his cousin, and wrote effusively to the owner of The Grange and also to Humphrey, hinting pretty broadly to the latter that the day would come when Erdmore Castle and the green fields around it would be his property—that is, if he cultivated such fine acquaintances as this Lord, and abjured horse-racing, theatres, and all the other abominations which had nearly brought him to ruin. Barton played well the part assigned to him, and the young man was soon made aware of Nellie's fortune. Strange to say, the day he heard of it he was more moody and gloomy than usual, and had anyone been close enough to him they might have heard a muttered oath escape his lips as he left the little house in Richlake.

CHAPTER XIII.

To earn your living seems a very easy thing. Given health and strength and reasonable intelligence, you would say that it should be feasible enough. And yet how many young gentlemen suddenly turned out into the world penniless, and possessed of such an education as school and college give, could do it? Who will engage a lad to sell pickles because he can construe Homer? or who takes a stable-boy on the assurance that he can ride to hounds?

Harry was astonished at the difficulties he encountered. The newspaper-office work sickened him, and he soon left it. Then he tried to be an author, and went the round of the publishers and editors with an unfortunate manuscript. But the literary market seemed to be absolutely gorged with such things, and his heart sank when one of the few editors who took the trouble to be decently civil to him showed him a pile of paper about five feet high, saying :

'These are all to go in some day. They are provisionally accepted for the magazine. Now you see what chance yours would have.'

'But surely if it has merit, perhaps superior to some of them——' faltered Harry.

The editor interrupted him kindly but decisively :

'Merit is all very well up to a certain point. We must have pretty good grammar and some appearance of originality ; but grammar is as common as dirt now, and half the scribblers have the art of seeming to be original—that is, of stealing with discretion. Great merit as a rule don't pay. You see, people haven't time to detect it nowadays, and it is generally a little wrapped up in something eccentric, which would force the readers to think, and that is what they will not do. The really good things I have published have never taken. What the public likes is trash prettily and smartly dressed. Lots of second-hand moralising—Thackeray and water—and the triumph of Philistine morality in the last chapter. Now, I daresay, in this story of yours you have tried to make your characters talk like real flesh-and-blood people ?'

'Certainly, I have tried that.

'Exactly. A gigantic mistake. Readers don't want flesh-and-blood people ; they want fiction people. You and I know that a Duke, for instance, doesn't wear a coronet on his head in his cabbage garden, and talks as commoners talk, and acts much as they do. But the reading public won't stand that. They want

H

a Duke in fiction to "behave as sich," in the language
of the servants' hall ; and if you depict him in gaiters
going out with a spud, or losing his temper because
his soup is tepid, or quarrelling with the Duchess over
the household expenses, you insult the reading public's
intelligence. It's the same thing all round. Your
heroes—that is, the principal persons in your stories—
must be heroic. They may be devilish, but they
must be strong and handsome, and do all things
grandly. In real life a hero may have a snub nose
and one leg shorter than the other. In fiction he
must have aquiline features and magnificent calves.
In the same way you must make your characters act
up to the first impression you give of them. The ones
labelled "wicked" must never commit good actions,
and those labelled "good" must always retain every
virtue under the sun. Otherwise you confuse easy-
going people, who like to skip without danger. It is,
you must admit, terribly confusing to find that a man
who does a selfish thing in chapter i. does an unselfish
thing in chapter xx. No, no, my dear young man;
leave writing novels to those who have made a trade
of it.'

All this disheartened Harry, and, after some more
failures, he put his manuscript away and went meekly
back to the newspaper office. There he worked
steadily for nearly a year, and gradually rose to be of
service there. It was not a very grand paper, and the
views set forth in it were scarcely those held by our
young assistant ; but, as he said to himself, beggars
cannot be choosers ; and, after all, he might perhaps
benefit his class by learning exactly what the class
beneath thought of them. His chief grievance, and
one that he had to keep to himself, was the absence of
all companionship and friendship that he had to
endure. He was very particular as to his society ;
and, after one or two expeditions with those employed

with him, had come to the conclusion that solitude
was preferable to their company. Cheap debauchery
has something specially revolting in it; and it was
altogether horrible and not to be borne by one who,
like our hero, had no mind for any debauchery at all.
Not that he was by any means of the goody-goody
order of young men, but he had learned, Heaven
only knew how, to respect women too much to obtain
pleasure out of their frailties; and, moreover, was he
not serving out his time of probation, the prize being
Nellie Barton? So he worked steadily on, and was
rewarded by being appointed sub-editor of the chief
daily paper at Porthampton, a seaside town of some
importance on the South Coast, at a rise of salary.
The paper belonged to the same proprietors as did the
one he had served in town, and he gladly accepted
their offer of a change, being wearied by eternal
drudgery in the darksomeness and dreariness of a
London back street.

In Porthampton he had rooms over the office, only
a short distance from the sea, and he amused himself
during his leisure hours, which were now much more
frequent, by sauntering about the port, watching the
loading and unloading of vessels.

The effect of this daily sight on the mind of an adventurous and hardy youth can be easily guessed. He
soon resolved to make a voyage; and for this purpose
he set himself steadily to work to make friends with
the skippers and seafaring people of influence connected with the place, and actually to study the
science of navigation, and to supplement as much as
possible the slight knowledge he had picked up during
his occasional cruises in a small yacht that had once
been lent him by his uncle.

It was some time before an opportunity offered,
but it came at last. A Mr. Marlby of Porthampton
one day informed him that he had been desired by the

owners of a clipper ship, then lying in the docks, to send out by her some one of intelligence and honesty, on whom he could rely, to make some arrangements with them as to a transaction they were anxious to effect, the nature of which would not interest the reader. 'It is essential,' they wrote, 'that he should be of superior class and well educated, and he must be well acquainted with the trade and other affairs of Port-hampton. We might send one of our young men over, but it would be easier to have one from your side, and you have already helped in this way so well that we are willing to trust to you again.'

' What do you think of it ? ' said Mr. Marlby.

' I should like it of all things. But I am afraid the knowing nothing of trade——'

' That's nothing. The *Cordelia* don't sail for two months, and I'll engage you shall know enough for them by that time. You can get away from your present place ? '

' Yes, at a month's notice.'

So it was decided. Harry set to work, whenever he could get away from the office, to study the statistics of the particular trade at Porthampton with which his new employers were connected, and soon had learned enough to see that he could save them a considerable sum when they next sent a ship over. He made the acquaintance of the *Cordelia's* skipper, a bronzed individual with an interminable power of smoking and absorbing whisky-and-water ; and there remained nothing more to do than to go up to London and bid his mother good-bye. He had during the past year written to her several times, but had abstained from giving any address ; and he really felt anxious as for the first time it flashed across him that he might not have heard had anything happened to her. So it was with some little trepidation that, about a fortnight before he was to sail, he knocked at her door.

The servant who opened it was strange to him, and apparently was somewhat offended by this middle-class-looking young man having rung the visitors' bell and knocked with such assurance.

'Mrs. St. James at home?   Yes.   But I don't expect she'll see you.   She's engaged.'

'Well, ask her.'

'Ask her!   Well, I don't think I shall ask her, young man.   And what may your name be, my Lord?'

Harry subdued a rising wish to knock the man down, and replied, as quietly as he could:

'Will you take up this note to her?'

The footman took the note Harry had had the forethought to prepare, as he did not wish to give his name if perchance the servants had been changed —a contingency not unlikely, as his mother was one of those persons with whom servants do not stay long.

'Will I take it up?' said the footman, thoughtfully, as if he were considering some important contingencies.   'Well, yes, I will take it up.   Sit you down', he added, glancing first at the hat-stand and then at Harry's face, and apparently deciding that he could be left safely with the umbrellas.

In another moment mother and son had met. She was truly glad to see him, horribly shocked at what she called his 'common clothes,' and in despair when she heard he had come only to go again.

In vain she pleaded.   He was obstinate, and after a time the poor lady resigned herself to circumstances, after remarking for the twentieth time that she might as well have never had a son.

Then there was a letter, marked 'Private,' and in the handwriting of his uncle, to be given to him. It was short and to the effect that, when he earned his bread for one year more, Lord Piccadilly would consider the arrangement at an end, and Harry would receive his allowance, and Mrs. St. James hers as before.

'Remember, however,' he added, 'I hold you to the strict letter of our agreement until that time has elapsed, and I hold you to your promise not to see or correspond with Nellie Barton.'

The fact is that even Lord Piccadilly had a conscience, and that it had pricked him a little for thus becoming a party to an arrangement which was so likely to turn his nephew, a St. James, into a thief or a beggar. Now, he hated anything unpleasant, and to be pricked by a conscience he thought dead long ago was decidedly unpleasant. Besides, he felt sure of settling the Ballard plan before another year had passed, and so he released his nephew from two years of his penance.

As Harry thought to himself that this would enable him, did he then wish it, to enter the army (a thing he longed for), it was with high spirits that he left the house, and with high spirits that he watched, from the deck of the good ship *Cordelia*, the receding shore of his native land.

That Nellie would be true to him he doubted not, and—let me whisper it low in your ear, reader—the exciting episodes of the last twelve months of his life had just a little dimmed the image of the blue eyes, just a little faded the remembrance of that kiss in the Richlake lane.

I feel rather ashamed of him; but I invite any of my readers who are loud in their blame to try semi-starvation, hard work, and solitude for a year, and then say whether they do not feel just a little less romantic at the end than they were at starting. As the old proverb, quoted by Rabelais, has it, 'Venus takes cold when not accompanied by Ceres and Bacchus.'

Before leaving his mother Harry had heard several items of family news. Lord Piccadilly was said to be breaking. There were rumours of eminent doctors paying visits to The Grange, and it was said that he had for some months taken to his bed, and did nothing but play at chess with his servants, and throw missiles (put handy for the purpose) at them if he lost. That his mind was unhinged also was, according to Roger, evinced by his having written a letter to that gentleman announcing his intention of shortly taking to himself a wife.

Poor Roger professed to laugh at this threat, and to believe that it could portend no danger to him in his position as heir-presumptive; but in his heart of hearts it frightened him horribly; and one evening, when a mutual victory at a race-meeting over a 'real good thing' had drawn father and son together in the bonds of sympathy, he disclosed his terrors to George.

'Pooh!' said the Life Guardsman. 'He's a deal too clever to make himself wretched even to spite us. And, after all, it wouldn't much matter if he did marry.'

'You forget the holders of our paper, my dear boy,' moaned his father. '*They* won't look at things in the proper light. You see, they have such queer ancestors—Methusaleh, and Solomon, and a lot of others; and then, you know, there was the blessed Elizabeth—an awful age. Nothing would seem impossible to them.'

'I never thought of that,' said George, gnawing his moustache. 'But then there are no miracles now.'

CHAPTER XIV.

LORD PICCADILLY was, without doubt, nearing the end of his peculiar journey through life, and the thought angered him. He was not afraid of dying, and regretted not at all leaving the good things of life; but it annoyed him that he should be forced to do anything at a time and in a manner not chosen by himself. He had made plans for a journey through Europe, picking up pictures and statues as he went, and refreshing his memory by a sight of the beauties of foreign galleries, and he did not like this impertinent Death to set his plans at defiance.

'A year at most,' he said to himself, repeating the words he had with difficulty extracted from the doctor, 'and perhaps pain, which I dislike, towards the end. No. If I cannot choose any date after the time named, I can at least choose one before it.' The thought pleased him, and he immediately began to put his things in order, and to make every possible arrangement for the due annoyance of Roger, whose letters of sympathy and condolence were numerous now.

He broached the subject of marriage with Nellie to Ballard about a month after Harry had set sail and Lord Piccadilly had his letter thanking him for shortening the time of penance.

'You ought to be thinking of marrying, Ballard. Your cousin, whose health is not good, is anxious to see you settled, he tells me, and a little money with your wife wouldn't displease him. Now, Nellie Barton will have 20,000*l*. if she marries with her uncle's consent. Old Barton has taken a fancy to you.'

'I have the greatest admiration for Miss Barton,' faltered Ballard, 'but——'

' Then why the devil don't you marry her?'
thundered the old Lord from his bed, where he was
lying, with a chessboard by his side.

' I am not sure she'd have me.'

' Pooh! a girl will always marry the first man that
asks. Mind, I don't say that she will be true to you
afterwards ; you're not the kind of man to keep a
woman true ; but I daresay she'll have the wit to keep
you comfortably in the dark, and, as Othello remarked,
the whole camp, pioneers and all, don't matter as long
as you know nothing.'

This was not very encouraging, but Ballard secretly
flattered himself that he had produced an impression
on the girl, and, moreover, the sound of 20,000*l.* was
very pleasant.

' Well, I'll take my chance.'

' Do ; but not till next week There she is, outside: I hear her step. Send her in to play chess with
me, and go back to London yourself. I've had enough
of you, and your chess is damnable! Come back
on Saturday next, and have some pretty speeches
ready.'

Ballard was accustomed to the tyrant's ways, and
did as he was bid meekly enough.

Then, as the game proceeded, the tyrant broached
the subject of his plan to Miss Nellie.

' Check. You should have moved your bishop.
There, that's better. What should you say to a
husband, Nellie ? '

' Say to a husband ? ' she repeated, deeply considering her next move. ' Oh—I—it would depend on
what he said to me. Was that move right ? '

' Infernal folly. Check. We'll stop a moment,
for I want to talk. Don't you want to marry, young
'un ? '

' Me ? No ! '

' Me ? No ! I suppose that is what all girls think

it necessary to say. But I am serious. I am near death, and I want to see you married. Your uncle won't live long, and you mustn't be left alone to go to the bad. You must marry at once. You can guess whom ? '

' Marry at once ! You don't mean Mr. Ballard ? '

' Yes, I mean Mr. Ballard. If you don't obey me your uncle will starve; you can't suppose he earns much, doctoring. He will starve because I shall give him no more. I know all about that young scoundrel, Harry ' (she started and blushed violently), ' and I have a bit of news for you about him. He has just sailed for Australia, and has written to me to say that he sees the folly of his conduct, and bids me to tell you to give up, as he has, a silly childish dream. Here's his letter.'

So saying, his lordship just showed the letter, taking good care that Nellie didn't read any of it.

' He said that ? ' she asked, turning very white. ' He said that ? '

' Yes. He's a sensible young man, and dependent on me. More than that, he's a poor man, and will always be so, unless I choose to make him rich. I can give him a grand career. But it will be only on condition that he does as I wish. So you see, my dear, you have it in your power to starve your uncle and to ruin the prospects of the man you pretend to be fond of. Of course, you will decide on his ruin, and call it being faithful—like any other woman. Now go and think it over, and don't bother me until you have definitively made up your mind. As you know, I never argue.'

' But——'

' Go ; ring the bell first for Andrews.'

The poor child left the room in a state of absolute bewilderment. In one second all the brightness of life seemed to have been blotted out.

Give up Harry—ruin him! Could it indeed be that these were the alternatives? She knew Lord Piccadilly well enough to be certain that he would never change, and also knew that Harry was dependent on him for the things that make success in life.

To doubt the story of the letter never occurred to her. To do Lord Piccadilly justice, he seldom lied, and therefore—like a glass of brandy to an abstainer—a lie from him had great effect, and did yeoman's service.

'Never waste your lies,' he remarked on one occasion to a peculating servant, 'it destroys their value. A reserve fund of them is of infinite service, but then they must be believed. A lie not believed in is worse than a disadvantageous truth.'

So Nellie never doubted but that her young lover had been brought to give her up; and the poor child cried herself to sleep that night in despair, and prayed that the sun for her might never rise again. But she didn't die, and the sun went on rising till the Saturday came round, and with it came Ballard, agitated and uneasy, but primed with loving words and pretty conceits. She liked the man. She liked everything, having little capability of dislike in her bright nature. Even now, when he was put forward as part of her torture, she owned to herself that he was very pleasant, very soft, and—she saw that very plainly too—very fond of her.

There was a slight air of gloomy mystery about him that interested her; he spoke vaguely of some desperate misfortune he had encountered, and of being to some extent to be looked upon as a Blighted Being; and it had pleased her to console him, to bring back the smile to his face, to hear from him that with her he forgot all his miseries. That she had flirted with **him** I will not exactly assert; but in her innocence and happiness she had certainly met his advances half-way, and was scarcely able to assume an air of very great astonishment or indignation when he, after some careful preliminary hints, plainly asked her to be his wife.

'I will try to make your life very happy, Nellie. I shall have money enough, and we shall be comfortable, and——'

'But, oh, Mr. Ballard! I never imagined that you could want such a thing.'

'Couldn't you?' he said, smiling. 'But you see I do want it, and I want it very badly. Will you whisper " Yes ? " '

But she wouldn't whisper anything. She would do nothing but weep, and eventually, having spoken no other word, she escaped from him and reached her home.

But her uncle was of no assistance to her when she went to him for advice.

'If you love the young man, marry him.'

'I do like him, but——'

'Don't be in a hurry. He is a nice young man, and you might do worse.'

'But supposing I—I was fond of someone else?' she whispered, putting her arms round the old man's neck.

'Is the someone else fond of you?' asked the Doctor.

'Oh, yes—at least—I don't know;' and she, remembering the terrible letter, burst anew into tears.

The Doctor, usually so kind and fond, said nothing; he watched her gloomily as she sobbed, with her fair head between her hands, and when the violence of her grief had abated, he asked other questions.

'Could you marry him? Could he marry you? Is he free?'

Nellie said nothing for some minutes. Then she dried her eyes and came and stood close to him, holding his hands in hers.

'Tell me the truth, uncle. Are you very poor?'

'Not very.'

'But do you earn much?'

'Here? Is it likely? No, and now the new man from town has settled here I shall make less. Seventy pounds this year. Probably fifty pounds next year. They say I am past work.'

Then I think it was that the girl decided. The tyrant Lord with his money was too strong for her. But she did not at once capitulate. Ballard had to wait three weeks longer for his answer; but when the tyrant heard from him that a prompt 'No' had not been said to his first advance, he knew that the citadel was carried.

And this is how she avowed her defeat. Ballard had just arrived, and was seated in the now unused drawing-room, awaiting a summons to the sick-room upstairs. He was turning over the leaves of a book, and humming softly to himself the refrain of some half-forgotten music-hall ditty, when Nellie entered. Her eyes were red with crying, and her face pale, but she still looked, he thought, the prettiest picture he had ever seen. She held out her hand to him.

'I have been a long time in answering your question, and I ought to apologise to you; but I had to decide what was best for both of us. If you still want me I will marry you'—here he took her in his arms, but she extricated herself, and went on with the air of one repeating words learned by heart—'but you must know the whole truth. I do not love you as one should love the man one marries. I cannot—yet. Perhaps it may come. I have been—I still am very, very fond of someone, but it is impossible that he and

I can be anything to one another. If you take me,' she said, with a little hysterical laugh she could not repress, 'you must take me as—as it were a second-hand article. But I will try to be a good and faithful wife to you. Are you content?'

'My darling,' cried Humphrey, 'I will teach you to love me!'

CHAPTER XV.

'HULLO, Roger!' cried a young gentleman sitting in the bay window of the Sward Club; 'what news? You look mean. Has Bubble-and-Squeak broken down, or Jenny de Courcey bolted with a scene-shifter, or can it be—the idea is terrible—that all the Pommery of '74 are finished at last? Let us know the truth quickly.'

Roger St. James, faultlessly dressed, his wig and his false teeth glistening moderately in the dim London sun, came up to the group of young men with a kind of tempered jauntiness that was rather taking. It was as if Bacchus were for the moment enacting the part of Adonis with a very *exigeante* Venus, or, to make a closer simile, as if the Archbishop of Canterbury were to pay a visit of inspection to the Trocadero in semi-state.

'My dear boys, none of these misfortunes have occurred, though, 'pon my honour, I don't think those '74 Pommery will hold out much longer. No; I'm a little anxious, that's all. Bad news about my poor brother; I fear he's very ill.'

Mawworm, Chadband, Tartuffe, Pecksniff—none of these could have managed a glance to rival that which accompanied these words.

' Poor old Roger ! ' said one of the young men, who never would have dared to speak so contemptuously to Roger's son ; ' poor old man ! It will be terrible for it to have to pay its debts and give up the sixty per centers, and write cheques and be rich ! Poor thing ! '

' There are some things,' said Roger, pensively looking out into the street, and wondering whether he will start a coach like that Fitzpurse is trying to steer yonder, ' which affect a fellow. My brother——'

' Why, you old hypocrite, you know you hate him and haven't seen him for the last five years ! '

' Piccadilly is a queer fellow,' said Roger. If his brother was indeed on the point of death he needn't go to much trouble to keep up the fiction of their friendship.

Then the party in the window broke up, and Roger remained alone to write several letters to disagreeable purveyors, all hinting that the time of universal payment, the creditors' millennium, was at hand.

One thing disquieted Roger. He could not ascertain who was the doctor in attendance at The Grange. He knew nothing of Dr. Barton, and he had ascertained that Sir William Gubble had not been sent for. This was puzzling. That his brother would live as long as he could, if only to spite him, Roger, he never doubted ; and how better could a man cling on to life than by the help of a recognised and knighted physician ?

So, hovering on the brink of greatness, the poor old gentleman was spending a far from comfortable afternoon, when a telegram was put into his hand :

' From Mrs. Richards, Richlake, to the Hon. Roger St. James, Sward Club. Lord Piccadilly died suddenly last night. You had better come at once.'

A mist came over his eyes as he put down the paper, and for a moment he was very near the feminine expedient of a fainting fit. It had come at last! He had waited so patiently for it all these weary years. He had seen his youth go, his middle-age disappear, and, just as he had been obliged to owe for his cigars and bouquets in youth, so he had up till lately to owe for his false teeth, his wigs, and his cosmetics. And now the trifling intervention of the destroying angel had suddenly made him Lord Piccadilly, with a princely income, with endless possibilities of amusement, tempered only by limits imposed by the hard facts of years. He rose and looked out of the window. Pooh! That brougham of Jack Wallet's was not half so neat (the neatness of knowledge and riches) as his should be. As to Fitzpurse's team, they were cheap and nasty. The letters he had just written were torn up. Who was he now to apologise or write civil letters to dirty tradesmen? It seemed to him as he left the club that the hall-porter looked at him in far too insolent a manner (for he forgot that he had owed him a small account for many months), and that the waiter who held open the swing doors for him gave quite a Radical sneer when he tripped over the mat. The people in the street, too, why did they not make way for the rich Lord Piccadilly? He might have been quite a common person, he thought, as a heavy solicitor's clerk trod on his toe; but the idea of how he could astonish them by throwing off his *incognito* and revealing himself, gave him pleasure; and he chuckled at the incivility of the porter at Waterloo, who had many a time been disappointed of his expected shilling by the smart old gentleman in those days when he voyaged Thameswise, and not alone, in quest of pleasure.

Not all the sports with Amaryllis in the shade, nor all the toyings with the tangles of Neæra's hair, could have made Mr. Roger St. James forget that it was bad economy to pay away money which you were not obliged to pay.

Arrived at Richlake, he took a fly, having a vivid recollection of the dogs at The Grange when once he had tried to force an entrance; and as he drove past the celebrated mausoleum he made up his mind that he would at once pull down that memorial of folly, and that he would also give himself, by hanging all the dogs, a pleasing revenge for the expense he was now put to and for the alarm he had once felt.

Mrs. Richards, the housekeeper, a handsome, dark-eyed, firm-jawed woman of forty, received him, and with all becoming reverence and solemnity ushered him into the drawing-room. Then she turned and faced him, and Roger quailed under the contemptuous glance of her big eyes.

'It must have been very sudden,' he faltered.

'It was.'

Roger thought she might have added 'My Lord,' but refrained from remarking the omission as yet. He inwardly resolved, however, that this lady should pack up her box within a few hours.

'And did my brother suffer much?'

'Yes.'

'You were quite right to telegraph to me.'

She smiled—a disagreeable smile, he thought.

'I was.'

'And—and—perhaps I had better see him. Show me to his room.'

He gave this latter order somewhat imperatively. It seemed absurd, but the position of the two was decidedly wrong. She was far the more at ease, and she even assumed a kind of superiority, which he resented, but did not know how to destroy.

'That will do afterwards. I want to speak to you first.'

'You! What have you to say, Mrs. Richards?'

'Mrs. Richards! Yes, I suppose that's my legal name; but morally I am Lady Piccadilly.'

I

'Really, my good woman——'

'I'm not a good woman. Listen to me, sir. His Lordship died without carrying out his instructions concerning me. He meant to leave me a large sum of money. I have tended him for years; I have borne with his caprices and whims; I have borne his abuse, his blows, his ill-usage; I have played chess with him till I have almost prayed for death; I have been his slave, his more than wife; I have my rights. What will you do for me?'

She said this without excitement, with her arms folded, her eyes fixed on Roger's face, and a sort of odd smile upon her lips.

'Really, this is very strange. I shall be guided, of course, by my brother's will.'

'I tell you I am not mentioned in it. What shall you do for me?'

Then Roger plucked up a spirit.

'I am afraid I can do nothing. I had heard enough of the dreadful life my poor brother led; and—and I cannot lend it any countenance, even in a post-mortem and indirect manner. To acknowledge any claim of yours beyond those of any other head servant would be—would be—immoral.'

'Very well—you will do nothing for me, even though I proved to you that for years I have been more than any wife could be to him?'

She still spoke very calmly, and a satirical inflection in her voice angered Roger.

He answered her promptly and decidedly. 'I will do nothing. Show me to his room!'

'Wait a minute, sir'—why *would* she not give him the title he longed to hear?—'shall you require me to leave to-day?'

The woman bothered him. Her tone was humble, but her eyes mocked him.

'Yes.'

'Very well.'

'And mark me, Mrs. Richards, I daresay you think you know particulars, secrets of my brother's life which I shall buy the suppression of. If so, you are mistaken. I have always disapproved of his mode of life, and the world has always known of it. I do not care what may come out.'

'You wouldn't pay a five-pound note to save his memory from dishonour?'

He wondered how it was she managed thus to put his very thoughts into words, as he replied:

'Not a farthing.'

'I am glad to know that. I may go and tell anything I know?'

'Certainly.'

'And—I was to ask you—about the dogs? His Lordship wanted them all kept.'

'Such a wish is childish. They will be destroyed or sent away.'

'You won't pull down the mausoleum, too, sir?'

'Really, my good woman,' began Roger, exasperated.

'I was told to ask, sir.'

'Were you? Well, I may as well answer all your questions at once. I shall clear all the servants and dogs out of this at once. You yourself will go this day. The mausoleum will be pulled down. Probably the place itself will be sold.'

'His Lordship wanted certain sums—I have the list written by himself—to be given to the servants and people in the village. But they are not in the will. Shall you carry out his instructions?'

'Show me the paper.'

It certainly was in the dead man's writing, and Roger's brow darkened as he read it.

'Decidedly not. It must have been a conspiracy. The sums are preposterous. Certainly not.'

'You will then carry out none of his wishes, except those that you are legally obliged to carry out ?'

'I cannot submit to this cross-examination,' cried the poor man, miserable before the calm contempt of the black eyes, and a little frightened by the firm mouth and the resolute lady-like manner.

'You may as well answer, once for all!'

'Well, then, once and for all, I will consent to no impositions of this kind. What is legally obligatory on me I will perform—not an iota more.'

'Very well, sir. Now we will go to his room.'

There was something very like a smile on her face as she turned to lead the way; and he followed, wondering to himself how it was that he could not assert himself in the presence of this housekeeper. They went down the passage, and she faced him for a moment, and her hand on the door handle. Yes, she certainly smiled. It seemed indecent in the presence of death. Like most elderly persons, Roger St. James had a wholesome fear of death. To a young man death is like a war at the Antipodes, too far off to care about, as he thinks.

Then Mrs. Richards turned the handle and they entered the room.

CHAPTER XVI.

'Ah, Roger! I'm delighted to see you,' said Lord Piccadilly, who was sitting up in bed, propped up by pillows, and with a chessboard on his knees.

Roger held on to the back of the chair and said nothing. The amusement in Mrs. Richards' face was grim; that in the Lord's was that of a child that has been given a new toy.

'False alarm, eh? I knew you were fond of practical jokes—or, at least, George is, and you run in couples. I wish you'd brought the young 'un with you. But you don't look pleased. Ain't you glad to find your dear brother is not dead?'

'But that telegram?' faltered the other, still almost unable to articulate.

'I sent it,' said his Lordship, rubbing his hands, 'just for fun, to pass away the afternoon. Besides, I wanted to see you, and I knew you'd come by the next train.'

The chuckle that accompanied this speech was positively fiendish. Roger shivered, and did not dare to meet his brother's glance.

'You were very sorry, Roger, eh? Didn't he seem very sorry, Moll?'

'Very,' said Mrs. Richards, with gravity.

'And you told him of my last wishes?'

'I told him of them.'

'Well, d—— it, go on! He of course acceded to them all?'

'He told me to leave the house; he said he would not give a farthing to save your memory from dishonour, that the dogs should be destroyed or sent away, that the servants' annuities should not be paid, and that the mausoleum should be pulled down.'

'Is this true, Roger dear? Oh, yes, I see by your face it is true. Capital!' And the old man burst into a fit of laughing that made him cough and necessitated some attention on the part of Mrs. Richards.

'You're consistent, Roger,' spluttered he, drinking off his mixture. 'You're a true St. James.'

Then Roger found his voice.

'I think, Joseph, your practical joke was—wicked—and cruel.'

'Do you? But then, you know, I don't much care

for your opinion. How like a flogged hound he looks, eh, Moll? No, Roger, you won't turn her out yet. And that will will be signed after all. You were right, Moll—he is worse than I thought him. But, Moll, I'm d——d if you know how to make the most of your bishop. Do you know of any good chess-players who'd come here at so much an hour, Roger?'

He asked the question as if nothing had occurred, as if his brother was paying him an ordinary morning call.

'I'm afraid I don't,' stammered Roger.

'No; you never do know anything. Confound it, there's that pain again. That'll do now—go away, both of you. I like being alone when I'm in pain.'

'But, Joseph——'

'Go!' roared the tyrant pointing to the door and raising himself in bed—'go!'

People generally did obey Lord Piccadilly when he was in earnest, and Roger was no exception. In the passage he found himself face to face with Mrs. Richards. Her calmness was all gone now, and her peals of laughter echoed through the house.

'Ha! ha! You'll turn me out to-day, will you? But it's you, my poor old gentleman, that's turned out. Ha! ha!'

And she snapped her fingers once, twice, under Roger's aristocratic nose.

There was one gleam of satisfaction in his mind as he journeyed back to town—at least he had told no one of the delusive telegram, at least there would be none to laugh at his discomfiture. Had the news arrived half an hour before, when the young men were in the club, he shuddered to think what the consequences might have been. For Roger—who had become accustomed, as all would-be young men must be accustomed, to be the butt of the youths he lived with—shrank from any ridicule save that which his position necessitated. When later in the evening he met his son he invented a plausible excuse for his absence, and by the time he had got well into his second rubber he had almost forgotten the diabolical laughter of his brother and the snapping fingers of the black-eyed housekeeper.

CHAPTER XVII.

It was all very well for the old Lord at Richlake to play at dying; the grim reality was approaching him with sure if not rapid steps, and as his pain grew more severe, the more did he rebel against being obliged, for the first time, to take a step against his will. His faith was firm and fixed. He believed in nothing; and his fear of death was simply a kind of amazed consciousness that there was a power stronger than he—a power that could make him give up his whims and amusements (such as they were) before he had thoroughly tired of them. Besides, the idea that Roger, whom he despised and detested, would dance over his grave was gall and wormwood to him. Of one thing, however, he was assured. The angel that, in that nursery rhyme we have been taught to call poetry, visited the green earth and took the flowers away, should not visit him, Lord Piccadilly, at his own angelic time. His Lordship would choose for himself. And lest there should be any miscarriage in this matter, he one day observed to Mrs. Richards, as she arranged the small table on which his dinner was to be placed:

'Moll, where have you put my revolver?'

'What do you want your revolver for?' asked she, looking up, with a knife and fork in one hand.

'Never answer a question with a question. Where the devil is it?'

'I put it away.'

Then his Lordship foamed at the mouth and raved, and threw the chessboard at Mrs. Richards, but just missed her head, for she ducked skilfully.

'When you've quite done,' she remarked, 'I'll tell you. But first'—this as he lay back exhausted with his vehemence—'but first you will tell me one thing.'

'I know, you infernal old harpy!' he said feebly, between his coughs, 'you want to be assured I have signed that will. Well, then, you harridan, you wild cat, you female Shylock, I have. That scoundrelly attorney, Tomkinson, was here to-day and brought a witness.'

'I should like to see Mr. Tomkinson,' said Mrs. Richards, putting on the table the soup tureen which had been handed her at the door.

Again an explosion of rage, less violent than the previous one; and then Lord Piccadilly gave Mrs. Richards a letter to his solicitor, and had to wait till next evening, when she had returned from London, for his revolver.

'You have kept your word, Joseph,' she said, handing him the pistol-case.

'Fool! trebly distilled fool!' he cried, as he clutched the box in his strong nervous hands. 'What object could I have in telling a lie to such as you?'

For a moment his old sarcastic spirit showed itself, and then, with the petulance of age and disease, he began to whimper about some alleged want of attention on the part of his body-servant during Mrs. Richards' absence. All the time, however, he kept a firm grip of the pistol-case.

'Yes, you want me,' said the black-eyed house-keeper, in answer to his complaints. 'I have kept you alive when you wanted to live, and I let you die when you want to die. When shall you do it?' There was a ring of something very like horror in her voice as she asked the question, but her face was calm and resolute.

'Do it! D—— you! You talk as if it were the drowning of a new-born puppy.'

'No; it's something far better. It's ridding the world of a troublesome, malicious old man.'

He laughed and tenderly looked over the locks of the revolver.

'You're a good 'un, Moll—no cursed soft sawder about you. If I were only a few years younger I'd go into society, as they call it, again, and take you with me. By G—d, you'd give it 'em! Ladies! There isn't one of 'em who'd know how to take all situations as you do. Now'—he had slipped a cartridge into the revolver whilst he was speaking, and he now held it up, pointed at the woman—'now I'll wager you'll behave like a born lady—dirt from the streets as you are— when I tell you I'm going to shoot you through the head, through one of those d——d black eyes of yours, and then blow my own brains out.'

She faced him steadily enough, but her hand on the chair-back behind her trembled. 'Don't miss, though: if you do, I'll strangle you before you can fire another shot.' This time his Lordship roared with laughter, and let the pistol fall upon the bed.

'No, no, Moll! You shall live! You are too good a pest upon society. I wouldn't deprive the world, the beautiful world, of your services. I think you are one of the Furies, my Moll. You quite come up to the idea of them I had when I was at Eton.'

'Do I? Well, what I want to know is, do you mean to do it before or after dinner?'

'Why so curious, my pretty Moll?'

'Because in the former case I'll tell the cook not to be bothered with the cooking.'

'Admirable!' and again the old man chuckled with delight. 'Admirable! Here am I, as books say, about to go out into the great unknown, &c. &c., and you ask me whether I'll dine first or not. But the question's foolish, my beauty. Did I ever travel on an empty stomach? No; dinner first, eternity afterwards. What are the lines?

'Fate cannot harm me—I have dined to-day!

'Fate! Luck! Chance! Bosh! No, my Moll, go and tell the cook. By the way, what was it that fool of a doctor said I must on no account touch?'

'Port.'

'Bring up two bottles of the '20. You know it —green seal. Give me the food my soul loveth. Leave me alone now—I want to write. I will dine at seven. Let it be a dinner fit for the gods. I am going to them, you know, and I'll take the bill of fare in my soul. Go!'

But Mrs. Richards did not go at once, she hesitated.

'Why don't you go?' he asked, surprised.

'Must you do this to-day?' she said, standing by the door with her hand on the handle.

'Must? No. I do it of my own free will. There is no must. I live or die as I choose. Why do you ask?'

'I heard this morning,' she said, slowly, 'that your brother Roger was ill—very ill. Why not wait a little? You would like to know that he never will step into your shoes?'

'Yes,' said Lord Piccadilly, thoughtfully; 'I think I should. But I haven't much time to spare. I'll be d——d if I die at the will of nature. Nature that I have defied living, I will defy dying. I haven't much time; but I might see him out. By G—d, I might! A fine race, eh? Shall I beat him on the

post? Moll, you're right. Send for the doctor again—
Sir William, if you like. I'll try and live a bit.
No, thank you'—this as she attempted to take the
revolver from him—'I'll keep that under my pillow.
And, look here, Moll, if I am suddenly taken worse,
remember this: dress me in my usual clothes, and put
me—don't mind how much I am pained by moving—
put me in the armchair, with the revolver in my
hand, mind. Do you hear?'

'Yes, Joseph.'

'Now go.'

This time she went; and before long the great
doctor from London was driving down to see how
long he could keep the worn-out machine in working
order.

For two days Lord Piccadilly submitted to be
treated like any other invalid. Then he sent for
Mrs. Richards.

'I can stand no more of this,' he said. 'The
remedies are worse than the disease, and the medical
knight's boots creak into my brain. 'Gad! if he
knew how tempted I have been to blow out his, as
he has smirked and hopped opposite me! No, I have
had enough. Roger wins—wins in a walk.'

'I think not,' said Mrs. Richards, smiling, and
she put a letter in the old man's hand.

'D——n you! Why did you open this?' he asked
in one of his sudden paroxysms of fury.

'I wanted to see what was in it,' she simply said,
and he laughed.

'You'll win yet,' she added, as he read it.

The letter was scrawled by George St. James, and
was to the effect that his father had been attacked by
typhoid fever, and that the doctors had but little hope
of his recovery.

'I did not write to you before,' added the youth,
'because I did not think it was very serious, and

because I did not think you were on very good terms with my father. He has, however, now asked me to tell you that he forgives you everything, and only hopes that you and he may meet in a better land.'

Lord Piccadilly flung the letter from him with a gesture of ineffable contempt.

'Canting hound!' he cried. 'Meet in a better land! Why, by G—d, this cursed earth was too good for Roger! And he expects to go to a better! I only wish there were a hell, if for him alone. Do you believe there is a hell, Moll?'

But Mrs. Richards knew better than to be drawn into an argument, and only said :

'You were right to wait, eh?'

'Yes ; but by Jove it is a near thing! I'll have one more dose of that beastliness, and then let it be fair play between us. I have the stronger will of the two, and I think I would back myself to see him out. Telegraph to George to send word here continually.'

It was a little before midnight that the house-keeper entered her master's room, bearing a message which had been sent down by horse, conveying the intelligence that 'he died, quite quietly, at ten minutes past ten o'clock.' The old man was sitting up in bed as high as his strength would allow him, and to her astonished view seemed to be kissing a miniature he held in his hand. She was accustomed to move without any noise, and for a moment he did not hear her enter. Then he looked up, saw her, and hurriedly placed the miniature with the revolver, which had been on his knees, under the pillow.

'Is he dead?' he asked.

She handed him the bit of paper without speaking. He put it down with a sigh, and the woman, seeing an unwonted moisture in the eyes which were absolutely undimmed by age, thought that the news of his brother's death had touched him. But the words undeceived her.

'Dead! I always hated him—I hate him still! But he has never been able to exult over my bones.'

Then there was a pause, after which he said, 'Now I'll get up and sit in the chair.' She dressed him as if he had been a child, for he was helplessly weak, and at last he was placed, propped up, in the large chair in the room adjoining his bedroom, the revolver and the miniature by his side. Then he spoke again.

'Moll, my brother Roger was a sort of man to make us wonder why Swift's fable is not the truth. There was more of what we call human nature in one claw of my old cat buried yonder than in all his body. And he's gone. Well, now at least, there is no obstacle. Let me see. I have no further instructions to give you. You know what to do—Mr. Tomkinson has the will, as you know; you'd better go to him. Don't trouble yourself about an inquest. Let them find any verdict they like—it won't hurt me or you, and it may hurt the "family" as much as it likes. A peer buried at the meeting of four roads, with a stake through his stomach, would be quite interesting to the newspaper readers. Good-bye, Moll.'

He held out his hand to her with a touch of that courteous grace that had once made him a distinguished gentleman in every capital in Europe.

As she took it her lips quivered and whitened, but she shook it as if she were parting for the night, with an assumption of carelessness almost rivalling his own, which was real.

He chuckled as he noted her trembling lips.

'Ah, Moll, you're a good plucked one, a rare plucked one; but it frightens you, this does. Own that it frightens you.'

'Good-bye,' she said, wrenching her hand from his, and turning away.

'You won't go and make a fool of yourself with my money?' said he, carelessly, arranging himself on his pillow. 'I don't think you're likely to be made a fool of by any man; but we never know; you're all so d——d vain. Here, settle me up in the pillows. Let me see—yes—sitting up would be best. No! no! not like that. Don't you see I might shoot right through and spoil that Vandervelde—my sweet little Vandervelde? Thanks. That is the position, I think. Now go.'

'Good-bye,' she said again, and went swiftly from the room.

Left to himself, he took up the revolver and looked at it with eyes in which could almost have been discerned a kind of affection, then laid it down on the small table beside him, and again opened the miniature case and looked long upon the portrait.

'My Nell,' he muttered, 'you after all were almost worth living for. And I ruined you and left you to starve. Well, well, it's all the same to you now; and I have made some reparation. Your child is safe from harm—married—well off. And I saved her—remember that, Nell, before you curse me again, as you did that night when you came to me and I laughed at you and bid you go. I saved your child from an alliance with a St. James.'

He addressed the portrait as if it were capable of hearing and answering him; and, after pressing it once more to his lips, he flung it into the fire which was burning in the grate, and watched it gradually shrivel up.

Is there no angel now that can step between the man and his evil destiny, that can take advantage of his first weakness, of his first sense of sorrow and remorse, and save him from the fate on which he is about to rush? Not one! The clock ticked on, counting the last moments of a life. The wind outside moaned as it passed through the trees around the house : all else was silence.

Silence, until a sharp report rang out, and in a few moments the passage was full of terrified servants.

' It was in his room,' said Mrs. Richards, and she led the way there.

. . . . . .

' Temporary insanity,' said the coroner ; ' temporary insanity,' echoed the jurymen ; and then they went away to talk the terrible affair over anew, and to take all the advantages possible out of having been, as it were, behind the scenes of the great tragedy. But the coroner, in his admiration for the aristocracy and his utter inability to associate for a moment one of their number with a verdict of *felo de se,* had in his pocket a letter which, read aloud at the inquest, would have somewhat shocked the jury, and which would have been assuredly of infinite service to newspaper editors hard up for ' copy.' It was in the deceased's handwriting, and thus it ran :

' To the Coroner and Jury who shall sit on my body.

' Don't let there be any d——d humbug about the thing. I, of perfectly sound mind, shoot myself in the head because I am tired of living. Don't call me insane. I should be so did I bear any more of this pain.'

He showed it to his wife before committing it to the flames.

' Poor man !' said she. ' He must have been very mad.' Then the coroner thought of his long struggle for bread before he had attained to his present eminent position, and the coroner was not quite certain that Joseph Baron Piccadilly was so very mad after all.

' I fear he was a bad 'un, my dear Eliza,' said he, evading the point at issue.

'Ah, John,' said that lady, holding up little Johnnie's frock to the light, and speaking with difficulty, in consequence of a profusion of pins in her mouth, 'ah, John, we must remember what temptations he had. Always pray, Edward'—this to her first-born—'that you may never have such temptations as he had.' Then Edward, who was to begin the world shortly on 100*l.* a year and what he could earn in practice, thought to himself that he would willingly take on himself such of the temptations of the defunct as consisted in his wealth and his title.

But Mrs. Coroner—one of those sweet Tories of Nature who think that a little wickedness is necessary in high places—sorrowed much more for the wicked Lord whom she had never known than she had sorrowed the week before for poor Jones, the baker, whom she *had* known to be an honest, hardworking tradesman.

I, reader, have seen a fair lady weep on hearing of the death of a German Princess, who could dry-eyed and firm-voiced read to her family circle the account of a railway or mining accident in which dozens of common folk were killed or mutilated.

Regardless of the directions in the will, which decreed burial with the cat in the white marble mausoleum, the remains of the dead Lord were buried in the family vault at Mall Castle, in the county of Slumberland : and he slept with his fathers, a set of decent, selfish, money-saving gentlefolk, who had invariably taken the winning side in civil wars, and who must have been a little scandalised by his presence.

The nine days' wonder of his death faded. The will was proved, and for another nine days people talked of its absurdities—of the enormous sum left to servants, and other points which struck them.

Mrs. St. James wrote to her son to implore him

to return, sending the letter to an address at Port-hampton which he had given her; and one of her strongest arguments was that he, by the late Lord's will, came into possession of a pretty little fortune of no less than five thousand a year. But for many months the poor lady remained without reply, for Harry was at the other side of the world, up to his eyes in business, and learning how money can be made.

Mrs. St. James's income had also greatly benefited by the will, and she now moved, as became her en-hanced dignity, into a house in Belgrave Square.

To live in Belgrave Square was to her only second to taking possession of one of the heavenly mansions we are told of on certain Sundays.

CHAPTER XVIII.

Harry received the news of the death of his two uncles by the same mail. He was at Sydney, and he at once made arrangements to return home, and wrote to tell his mother he would come to her with all possible speed. He had, however, to finish the negotiations in which he was engaged—for Harry was nothing if not conscientious—and was delayed nearly three months at Sydney. Just before he sailed (again in the *Cordelia*) he received a letter found among the late Lord's papers, addressed to him, and enclosed with one from the St. James family solicitor, which he read with a good deal of surprise and some pain. It does not much concern the story I am telling, and therefore the reader is at liberty to skip all he chooses. I give it because I think that Joseph, Lord Piccadilly, was in many ways a remarkable man, and as a rule (as some

K

clever deceased person has remarked) the world knows nothing of its greatest men.

Thus it ran :

'If you could explain to a newly-born babe what life is, honestly and without exaggeration, giving the lights and shadows fairly, do you suppose there is any babe that would not claim the right of the puppy of doubtful parentage—to be drowned before its eyes are opened ? Not one. Some men (to parody a quotation from Shakespeare that always appeared to me to have nothing in it except that it was written by Shakespeare) can make their lives, others can take the chance life gives them, and others dare not rebel and yet cannot bear their haphazard destiny. The first become sometimes great, sometimes happy, men, according as their taste takes them. The second are as dependent on chance as the dice in the box. They do sometimes turn up sixes, but there is no credit to themselves about it. The third kind *go under.* They are full of " vague yearnings," of " unsatisfied desires," &c., and they beat against the bars till they die— die generally disliked and unremembered. Now and then they flare up and do big things ; but it is only a flash in the pan. They are not stayers ; and if their race is over a longer distance than the T.Y.C. they get behind, and either break down or come in with the crowd, and are despised as selling platers ever after. I was one of the latter class, Harry ; and it is because I fancy you have in you the makings of the first sort of men I have mentioned that I take the trouble to write you these lines. My life has been from the first a gigantic mistake. I thought till lately that the mistake lay with the world I despised, or with the errors of my birth, which gave me no ambition, for how could one who knew 'who was behind the scenes' care for political renown ? But I have discovered that the fault has always been with me.

As Rochefoucauld said—or he said something very like
it—one may be cleverer and stronger than many, but
one cannot be cleverer and stronger than all. I was
too sweeping in my contempt; and I omitted one
great consideration—happiness. Despising your associates, your amusements, your world, may be
pleasant and productive of agreeable private thoughts,
but it is not amusement; it don't make you happy.
Cultivate credulity. The only thing in this life worth
clinging to is belief in something and somebody. The
greatest happiness of the greatest number, says some
idiot, is or should be the aim of a statesman. But
what does he mean? It might be, for instance, that
an English politician was convinced that the world
would be the better for the annihilation of England.
But this a thing, invented by geographical or
ethnological philosophic word-coiners, called Patriotism, would step in to prevent. So then he turns to
the greatest happiness of the greatest number of his
own countrymen. Well and good. But if this is
logical and right, why should he not go on? Why
should his country be his care? Why not his county?
If his county, why not his village? If his village,
why not his own family? If his family, why not himself? The object therefore, logically following the
exact reasoning of patriotic statesmen, to be attained
is the greatest happiness of oneself. The nearest
approach to the carrying of this out that I have ever
heard of was a case I read of somewhere, where a
youth, after hearing from his preceptor of the dangers
he must undergo in this life, incontinently took poison.
The game of living did not seem worth the candle to
him. But he was a very high philosopher, although I
don't know his name, and if I did, and told you, you
wouldn't find it in the biographical dictionaries.
When I began life, with everything in my favour, I
determined to be as philosophical as I could, and I

took great pains to please myself. But the pains were greater than the results they brought. Seeing people cringe palled after a time. Most women became like overripe fruit to me. They fell almost before I shook the tree. The unripe or difficult ones only annoyed me, and therefore, being a member of the Fox Club, I decided, on philosophical grounds, that they were sour. I was too fond of myself to care much for anyone else; and I had, even at college, weighed the respective merits and demerits of what people call " Love," and found the former to kick the beam. I have, I think, tasted of every pleasure to be found in the world. I have never denied myself anything. I have made others happy, and it has bored me; I have made others miserable, and it has bored me too, in a rather less degree. I have courted danger, but it has not made my pulse beat faster; for if you are not afraid danger does not excite. And now, living alone, and having given up the hopeless search after happiness, I have actually come upon the reason of my failure. I have never tried *goodness*. Only within the last two years a small atom of humanity, for whose presence in the world I am in some measure responsible, has actually made me feel a new sensation—that of shame. That I have a conscience I doubt; for even if there were such a thing, it could scarcely work now after so many years' disuse; but certainly there is something in me better than I ever imagined. You, Harry, with your boyish truth and frankness, had something to do with my discovery. But I did not like you, because you seemed to show me what I might have been had I been strong enough to shape my destiny, and to defy the Fate that decreed I should go wandering through life after happiness. Therefore it is that I—in the intervals of reading French novels that profess to dissect human nature and that only dissect the diseased bits of it—scribble down these lines to go to

you after my death.   Therefore it is that I have left
you a few thousands a year (although I have not
signed that will, and may not do so); therefore it is,
at least partly, that I have prevented your taking a
step at the outset of your career which might possibly
prevent your ever succeeding better than I did.'

'Does he mean Nellie?' thought Harry.

'To do what you wish now would be to allow Fate
to make your life.   I want you, after learning the
world, to make it for yourself.   I want you to be wisely
selfish; the selfishness of early youth and passion is
apt to turn to ashes in the mouth of after-time.   Of
course I don't know what you may have already
become.   You may be a thief, for all I can tell.   If so,
be a large one.   Don't pick pockets.   I hate anything
mean; anything like your uncle Roger or your cousin
George, or your mother either.   The atom I mentioned just now would die like a heroine for her con-
victions; your mother would tell a lie to save her little
finger from aching; your uncle and cousin would tell a
thousand lies rather than run the outside risk of their
fingers aching.   Looking through history, it strikes
me that Jack Sheppard was a greater man than Napo-
leon.   The latter robbed and murdered to be great;
the former scarcely could have expected any end but the
gallows.   He disliked Society, and I dislike it.   Only
he dared to give vehement and active expression to his
dislike.   I could only snarl and sneer, and kick people
who liked being kicked, and almost assisted me in the
operation.   No.   To come back to my point.   Goodness,
the only thing I never tried, is possibly the only thing
that leads to that grand desideratum, happiness.   And
I strongly recommend you to try it.   The other is a
mistake.   There was a woman once, dead now, who
might have been alive and at my side, had I come to
this conclusion earlier.   But I was consistent to my
creed in those days; and she died.   Yet, Harry, I—I

who supposed I had no feelings, think of her in the long nights when I lay awake in pain, and I know that she pities me. If you knew me better you would know how I like pity!'

·   ·   ·   ·   ·

'Let me see, there is one thing I wanted to say to you. Nellie possibly may some day want assistance. It is not likely, but it is just possible. Give it her to the best of your power.'

Harry smiled when he read this, and his heart leaped as he thought of how he would assist her.

Then the letter went on, with vague, half-remorse-ful, half-scornful sentences, revealing how often during his existence of pride and contempt for others the man's real nature had yearned for companionship, even for love.

'There was something fine in him,' said Harry, putting down the paper, his mind full of that direction concerning Nellie; 'but his life certainly was, as he says, a sad mistake. That advice to be good, as he calls it, from selfish calculation is charming. Oh, my dear uncle Joseph, you hadn't got to the very ABC of the knowledge of how to be happy!'

And the young man, strong in that youth which can triumph over most ills, locked the letter up in his desk and sallied forth to look after the last preparations for the start of the *Cordelia*.

CHAPTER XIX.

'BARRY,' said Mr. Erdmore of Castle Erdmore, in the county of Tipperkerry, Ireland; 'Barry, I like her.'

Mr. Barry Delancey, agent, factotum, and ruler of

the Irish laird, took no notice whatever of the remark.

Again said Mr. Erdmore : ' I like her, Barry. She is pretty and looks like a lady.'

Then Mr. Barry looked up from the accounts he was going through, and observed in a sullen voice, and with a strong brogue :

' Sure, and why wouldn't you? You'd like anyone that boy brought here. And you'll fritter away your money, leaving it him just because she's a pretty face. I'd engage to find you a dozen prettier in Ballymorty any afternoon.'

' You know, Barry,' said the old gentleman, apologetically, ' that you are well provided for.'

' Do I know it? Well, I know your will, as I wrote it myself, by heart, and I know the codicil by heart, too : " The remainder to go to my cousin, Humphrey Ballard, and his children after him, on condition that he take the name of Erdmore in addition to, or in lieu of, the name of Ballard ; and in default of such issue, then, on his death, my remaining property, as aforesaid, I will and bequeath to Barry Delancey, Esquire, of Erdmore Lodge, and to his heirs after him." Do I know it? I do.'

' Well,' said Mr. Erdmore, nervously, looking at his tyrant, who was scowling under his shaggy eyebrows, ' well, but there's the Clonane property. That's yours, anyhow.'

' The Clonane property ! A dirty three thousand a year ! '

' But you haven't that now, my dear Barry.'

' Haven't I? Well, perhaps not,' said the agent, smiling ; ' but then I've the handling of the lot.'

Mr. Erdmore was so pleased to see his agent smile that he forbore to question how the ' handling of the lot ' benefited him, and the conversation turned upon farm improvements, tenants' requirements, squaring

of holdings, and the thousand and one things that
occupy the time of those ravening wolves, Irish
landed proprietors.

Mr. Barry Delancey had been seriously put out by
the arrival at Castle Erdmore of young Ballard and
his bride. It had been understood that Humphrey
was to inherit the property at the death of its owner;
but Barry had always reckoned on being able to upset
this arrangement by making a quarrel between the two
men. The arrival of Nellie, Mrs. Ballard, had however altogether upset his plans. She charmed the old
gentleman, and she kept her husband's temper in check.
Under ordinary circumstances there could have been
little doubt that Humphrey would, before he had been
a week at the Castle, have ruffled in some manner
the temper of his cousin, who only stood opposition
from those of whom he was afraid (as he was of his
agent), and that the will, which was always at hand,
would have been altered. But Nellie's influence
already nearly equalled Barry's, and the codicil had
been added, after a hard struggle, on the off chance,
as the agent looked at the matter, that there might
be no children of the marriage. The last time
Humphrey had been there Barry had contrived to
make him drunk, and had shown him to his cousin, in
the same manner as the Spartans exhibited the drunken
Helots to their children, and with the result desired in
both instances. But old Erdmore's sense of justice
had proved stronger even than his fear of Barry, and
he refused to alter his will, saying he would give the
youth one more chance. And now here he was, and
with him a young woman who spoiled all prospect of
another scene, of another quarrel! It was certainly
very annoying, and as Barry Delancey thought over the
delights of seven thousand a year, he felt much
inclined to pay a few bold peasants to greet Mr.
Humphrey some dark night in the way in which

Irish tenants are often urged to greet their landlords
—with 'an ounce of lead.'

However, he had the Clonane estate, and as he
had commenced life as a cow-boy to the late owner
of the property, three thousand pounds a year and a
good square house, which he mentally decided should
be renamed Castle Clonane, was not to be absolutely
despised.

Besides, like most Irishmen, Barry was far from
insensible to the charms of female beauty, and he
could scarcely withstand Mrs. Humphrey's witching
manner and frank honesty, that had captivated everyone who got to know her.

Poor Nellie was not happy, though. The thought
of her first lover and her first love lived ever in her
mind, and although she honestly believed he had
forgotten her, Harry's image was always in her heart.
Good and true as she was, this alone made a daily
pain and trouble to her; for she wished to love her
husband as a husband should be loved, and she failed.
The showy qualities that had taken the girl's admiration vanished soon after the honeymoon. Blind herself as she might, she could not quite conceal from
herself the fact that he was weak, vain, ill-tempered,
and not too honest. His outspoken (to her) wish for
his cousin's death sickened, while his curious moods of
depression and savage gloom puzzled and saddened
her. Could it be, she thought, that he had divined
the secret of her life—that he knew that she never
could love him above all others? And poor little
Nellie brooded over this till she was often tempted to
solve her doubt by telling him the whole story, and
asking him to forgive her and to send her back to her
uncle. From that uncle, who had gone to live in
London, she heard occasionally; but he wrote as if
he intended henceforward to be entirely apart from
her new and grander life, and steadily refused the

invitation to Castle Erdmore that she persuaded her husband to send him. She had grieved for the curious old Lord too—perhaps was the only human being who had done so—and altogether it seemed to her as if life, as she had pictured it in her young dreams, were already ended, and that nothing remained now but the wearisome round of duty, but the terrible waste of solitude. She did not 'take to' religion, for she was, and always had been, naturally devout. She did not 'take to' flirting, for the excellent reasons, first, there wasn't a male living within twenty miles of Castle Erdmore with whom she could conduct that operation; and, secondly, she had a natural and instinctive horror for that kind of sham love-making which goes by the name.

And it was hard for her to take much interest in the place and people she had come to. Barry Delancey would suffer no interference with his plans; and the *employés* and people about looked with extreme disfavour on the young English lady who asked questions and tried to make herself agreeable. Barry had sedulously spread a report that Humphrey's first act on coming into his kingdom would be to collect arrears of rent and perform other atrocities, and there was a general feeling that Barry was a martyr, and that she and her husband were cruel Saxon invaders and interlopers. So she soon gave up her attempt at visiting the cottages, and perforce gave herself up to reading, which—the Castle Erdmore library being principally composed of theological treatises of the fiercest order, with a sprinkling of old biographical and geographical dictionaries—was not, perhaps, a very lively occupation.

She learned, however, to see that one theologian that differed from another was a hound and a rascal, and that all who happened to hold views that didn't work square with the views of the especial book she happened to be perusing were without doubt heretics or atheists, and doomed to everlasting perdition; and after several months' course of study it is to be hoped that she was properly imbued with the splendid qualities of Christian charity.

Humphrey hated the place, disliked his cousin, and loathed Mr. Barry Delancey. As he vented all his grievances upon his wife, this perhaps did not tend to make life pleasanter. He drank too, although his cousin and the crafty agent knew it not. Nellie was aware of a certain cupboard in which a full bottle was so often placed, and had not yet plucked up courage to try and stop the thing. Drinking and its fearful results she had often heard of from her uncle, for even in orderly Richlake there were drunkards. And sometimes, when she saw Humphrey's shaking hands and lack-lustre eyes, she felt that she might, by her cowardice, be throwing away an opportunity of saving him from a ghastly doom.

She had once made a little attempt:

'Humphrey dear, don't you think you would be better if you didn't drink any whisky for a few days?'

'Do you mean to say I get drunk? Say it, please, if you do,' he replied, starting up in a rage.

'Oh, no, dear; but——'

'Then leave me to do as I choose. Do you think I will allow anyone to regulate what I do? If you were as sick of this d——d hole as I am, you'd——' He stopped, feeling that his intended conclusion would scarcely be logical, and substituted therefor, 'you'd hate it as much as I do.'

'I'm not very fond of it, Humphrey,' she said, quietly, alarmed by his vehemence, and feeling confident that at any rate now was not the time to speak.

'Oh, you women can always amuse yourselves. I only wish I could get to London for one day.'

'Why shouldn't we go?'

'We!' he exclaimed, his face growing pale, and his eyes nearly starting out of his head. 'Go to London with you!'

'I didn't mean anything wrong, Humphrey,' said the poor child, 'I only thought——'

'Put it out of your head once for all. London, indeed! No. Here we stay, until——'

She put her little hand on his mouth. 'You *shall* not say that. It is horrid of you.'

Humphrey Ballard laughed uneasily.

'Remember one thing, Nellie. You married me to live where I choose. Never think of London—or of England.'

'Very well,' said she, with a sigh. And as the man before her mixed himself a glass of whisky-and-water, she thought—she could not help it—of what life with Harry might have been. She was very near hating her lawful husband at that moment.

CHAPTER XX.

IT will surprise no student of human nature (and who does not think himself one of this band?) to be told that George St. James, the new peer, at once renounced his former extravagant habits, and became what his disappointed friends called mean. The oil seemed unaccountably to have deserted his once shining hat; his boots became broad at the toe, and reflected the sunbeams no longer, and his umbrella swelled almost as his income had swelled. His argument was simple and should have convinced, if it did not, those of his old 'pals' who ventured to remonstrate, 'You see, old chap, when I had nothing, or

less than I spent—which is about the same thing—it
didn't much matter what I did. You can't have less
than nothing, you know, and all you get on tick is
clear profit if you know you can't pay for it. But, by
Jove! it's different when you have something. I
didn't care for money before, because I hadn't it to
care for; I got all else I could—I was a miser, if you
like, in buying all I could induce the beggars to let
me have on credit. But now, don't you see, I have
money instead of horses, and goods, and opera-boxes,
and—ladies; and, by Jupiter! I like money best, and
I always did. You used to call me extravagant; but
I never chucked money away, because I hadn't any—
over and above what I was obliged to spend as a
gentleman—to chuck away. You try it, some of you
fellows, and you'll find it devilish jolly to go into your
bank and see the old Johnnies in the back parlour bow
to you, and treat you as if your account kept the shop
going.'

'We don't mind trying it,' sighed his auditors.

'Yes; and the same chaps used scarcely to nod
to me when I came in to ask to be allowed to over-
draw; and never respected me a bit when I paid in a
cheque from Moses, or Abraham, or Hart, because,
you see, they knew it wasn't respectable money.
Damme! there's nothing so pleasant as being respectable. I've tried the other thing, you know.'

'You have indeed,' sadly said a friend.

'But only because I couldn't be respectable. You
can't—by Jove! you can't—be respectable on less
than twenty thousand a year.'

'How disreputable we must all be!' from the
chorus.

'Well, no offence to you fellows,' said the respectable man, standing before the club smoking-room fire
with his tails raised; 'but it was infernally low form
at last, that hunt after money, and I got very sick of

having to seem not to care when I had got the knock
over a handicap.'

'What, shan't you bet any more?' asked the horri-
fied chorus.

'Bet! What's the good of betting when you don't
want to win and would hate to lose? You see, when
I betted there was always the off chance of my not
being able to pay. That made it devilish exciting.
Now,' he continued, rather mournfully, 'I could not
even get a week's law, and I might possibly get paid
in stumers.'

'But you might win,' said chorus.

'Yes, I might win,' he said, thoughtfully, rattling
some sovereigns in his trousers' pockets, 'but it would
be devilish difficult. How could I go touting about
for news of " dead 'uns " now? And besides, how could
I win enough to make much difference to me, unless
I risked what it would be a d——d bore to lose?'

'That is one of the difficulties of betting to us
all,' said a sarcastic member, 'and an escape from
that difficulty is one of the problems set to us
laughing philosophers of the nineteenth century
school.'

'I don't know anything about schools,' returned
the Lord, didactically; 'but I know that I'm not
going to fool away my money any longer. And look
here, Tom '—here he addressed an impecunious young
man who was, big cigar in his mouth, gazing at him
with an expression of mixed incredulity and awe—
'look here. I backed that bill of yours, you know,
because I thought I might want your name to one of
mine before long; but since the governor and the old
lunatic went off things have altered. I can't do any
of that humbug of renewing, remember that. You
must take up that bill when it's due—'pon my soul,
you must.'

'You said you'd sign a renewal,' said poor Tom,

removing his cigar, and quickly putting it back, as if the orifice required instant stopping up.

'Yes; but then I was in a different position. You must get someone else, some other idiot, to back the renewal; and mind you send me the old bill.'

'I'm afraid Shadrach won't see that, as he's got your name.'

'Well, upon my word, that's too bad,' said George indignantly; 'I never heard anything like it. Because a fellow comes into his property everyone expects him to pay up for them. Why, paying that 360*l.* would be intensely inconvenient to me. I have my accounts arranged exactly to——'

But even the respect due to a rich man broke down here, and the chorus gave vent to a shout of laughter.

'Accounts! Fancy George St. James keeping accounts!'

His Lordship reddened with anger.

'George St. James didn't; but that's no reason why Lord Piccadilly should not,' he said, and left the room.

He had not been talking at random. He wished at once to make it plain to his ex-boon companions that, like the English king who had a little trouble in early youth with the police, he intended to reform now that he had come to his kingdom, and, finding several of them together, he had taken the occasion by the hand. What they thought of him or said behind his back he cared little. He had in him that kind of independence which is often born of stupidity and thick-skinnedness, and even in his most apparently careless and most jovial days shrewd observers had remarked that George St. James always insisted on getting a good pound's worth of amusement for twenty shillings. He did not go quite as far as the great Marquis of W——, who, we are told, kept a journal, in which such items occur as, 'Upset a

Charlie, paid him 5s. He wanted 8s.' But he assuredly took as much advantage of the high spirits of his companions as was possible, and no one had ever known him very quick with his change when it was a question of paying a cab fare. That he had been able to retain his popularity was because those with whom he lived were seldom calm enough to analyse things, and because meanness or cleverness was the very last crime with which they thought anyone of themselves could possibly be charged. But it had nevertheless been remarked that the amount of favours, in the shape of regimental duty done for him, bills of exchange backed by friends, &c., he generally received was out of all proportion to the amount that he did for others.

During his days of jollity and battling with creditors and impecuniosity he had not always quite successfully, but still to a great extent had subdued one vice which had been a terrible temptation to him, that of drinking. At his tutor's there had been troubles on this account, and after every fourth of June and Election Saturday poor St. James, ma., was flogged and turned down for his too grateful appreciation of the champagne the ' sitter ' of the boat provided, until at length he was removed suddenly from the classic groves of Eton—for incorrigible idleness, it was permitted to be called. But after a few unpleasant experiences—in one of which a metropolitan magistrate figured, and figured to the amount of five shillings—George, who could scarcely be called weak, pulled himself together, as he phrased it, and few of his friends knew how very nearly being a drunkard the smart Life Guardsman had been. Once or twice the old devil had broken out in him; but he always retained his faculties sufficiently on these occasions to hide from the gaze of men : and his illnesses, at rare intervals, were set down to anything but the real cause.

Now that he had become entirely his own master—for a Lord Piccadilly might get as drunk as he chose without offence—he rather relaxed the bonds he had imposed upon himself; and during the time that the *convenances* obliged him to keep more or less aloof from society and wear a broad band of black upon his hat, he had, with a few choice spirits, indulged in orgies in the villa by the river which would have scarcely met with the approval of Sir Wilfrid Lawson.

It was not very long after the club scene I have sketched that he again gave one of these little parties. The cronies consisted only of four, besides the host; and they were all men who, had they lived in the days of our grandfathers, would have risen to the distinction of three-bottle men. As it was they could only truthfully have been described as 'ten B.-and-S. and magnum men,' to say nothing of 'nips' to steady their nerves after breakfast, and glasses of dry sherry to while away the afternoon hours; when the wit engendered by a heavy lunch had died out, and the wines of a still heavier dinner had not come in.

It was autumn, and although our genial climate had not yet put forth all its horrors in the shape of fog and sleet and east wind, it was scarcely weather in which most people would choose to go out boating at night upon the Thames.

But after about two bottles of various wines apiece, our revellers were anxious for some opportunity of letting off their spurious energy. There was no place of easy amusement within eight miles; nor could the most ingenious dissipator find anything to excite him in the decorous streets of sleepy Richlake; so when one of the wildest spirits suddenly suggested the river, the idea was received with unanimous applause.

George, who had been what was termed in his set 'on the nip' all day, was sober enough to dislike the idea of having his own boats knocked about; but the

L

others were not sober enough to respect his economic ideas, and utterly rejected his notion of going half a mile down to the boat-builder's and purloining one of his tubs.

It did not take long to force the doors of the boat-house—the key, of course, being forgotten; and soon two canoes and one pair-oar were flying down stream, the pace being good if the course was not very strictly straight.

The exercise was fast sobering the men, who were all good performers with oars and paddles, when his evil genius prompted one of the most thoughtless to shout out from the pair-oar, just as they were approaching Kingsley Weir:

'You don't shoot it for a fiver!'

'Done!' shouted George from his canoe. 'There's plenty of water.'

'No! no!' said one, who had kept his wits about him. 'It's beastly dark, and the river's not very full. It isn't safe.'

'Then it's a fiver in my pocket!' said the first speaker. 'George, you owe me a fiver.'

'I'm hanged if I do. It's as safe as a church. Do you think I'd risk my canoe if it wasn't?'

'Or your life, eh?'

'Life! I've shot it twenty times. Come on, Jack'

'No, old chap,' said the man addressed; 'I don't much like it in broad daylight, and I wouldn't think of it in the dark.'

'But I've got a fiver on,' said the millionaire Lord.

'Oh, he'll let you off. You'll let him off, Tibbs?'

'Of course I will. Don't do it if it's not safe, George. The bet's off.'

'No, it isn't,' said George, who was determined to go home richer by five pounds. 'Not a bit of it. I hold you to it. Go on a bit, you chaps, and I'll just shoot it, and if I can't get back through the lock—and the old beggar sleeps like a top—I'll just carry the canoe over and come back to you.'

'Don't be a fool, George!' cried the originator of the bet. 'Let the bet be off.'

'You want to get out of it, do you? No, I mean to have your fiver. You are a great deal too ready to bet, and not ready enough to stand to your bets.'

And with this sneer the great man paddled off, while his friends waited. They could just see him steer himself straight down to where the water tumbled over the artificial barricade, and then the darkness hid him. There was no shout of triumph; but then George was not demonstrative, and so they still waited, expecting every moment to hear his voice raised to rouse the lock-keeper.

'Oh, he's going to carry his canoe over,' said one of them.

But no one appeared. And at last a feeling of anxiety began to take possession of the gay young men. They did not own it to each other, but as they landed and ran up to the lock, saying that of course George had gone on for a paddle farther down, the same thought was in the mind of each. With difficulty they roused the old man in the lock-house and obtained a lantern, whose feeble light showed them but little. Oh, he must have gone on. 'George!' they shouted with all their lung-power. But the answer was silence.

Then they got their boat and canoe through the lock, and went down the river.

The rest of the story had better be told by a cutting from a newspaper of three days after:

'THE FATAL CANOE ACCIDENT.

'Thomas Perry, a waterman of Mornington on the Thames, found this morning a dead body in a creek

about half a mile from that village, which has now been
identified as that of Lord Piccadilly, who was upset on
Tuesday night when shooting the Kingsley Weir in his
canoe.   The canoe, as our readers will remember, was
found next day bottom upwards, about two hundred
yards down the river.   The last hope for his Lordship's
safety has thus vanished, and the gloom which the
rumour of his loss had already cast over the West-end
of London will be confirmed.   It is curious that there
will have been four different Barons Piccadilly within
the last three months, as the uncle and father of the
deceased Lord died in July, within a few hours of one
another.   The new peer is the son of the late Lord
Piccadilly's uncle, and consequently was cousin to the
deceased and nephew to the two previous bearers of
the title.   It is said that he is abroad, and has been
seeing the world in a very inferior capacity.   The
rental of the St. James estates is set down at not less
than 130,000*l.* per annum.'

*   *   *   *   *

'The *Cordelia* is in?' said Mr. Marlby, starting up
from his office-chair as a messenger entered, and not
waiting for the answer in the affirmative that he saw
in the man's face.   'That's all right!   By Jove!   The
news ought to take away his breath.   The Right
Honourable Lord Piccadilly!'   And the worthy man
hurried along the streets of Porthampton, feeling
more important than he had done since his little
daughter had presented the Princess with a bouquet at
the opening of the new graving-dock.   He soon
reached the steps where he was accustomed to take a
boat, and within half an hour was shaking hands with
our friend Harry, who, bronzed and happy, was looking
with all a seaman's fondness at the dry land, and
longing, with all a seaman's enthusiasm, to get
upon it.

But there was much to do in the way of business

yet, as ne assured Mr. Marlby, that would have to be finished ere he could go up to London.

'I want to see my mother,' said Harry, 'and although you may think me weak, I mean to give up this business. I'm not ungrateful to you, Mr. Marlby, but——'

'Don't say another word, Mr. Jameson—I mean St. James—that is, my Lord.'

'My Lord! No, no,' said Harry, laughing. 'I have come into a little money, and you seem to have found out my name. I suppose a man with even five thousand a year may not be *incognito* in these prying days. But five thousand a year don't make a man a Lord, Mr. Marlby. I believe the Prime Minister puts it at twenty thousand.'

'And you've over a 'undred,' gasped Mr. Marlby, dropping an *h* in his excitement.

'What do you mean?' said Harry, staring. 'How many bales is that, Jack?' he asked of the second mate.

'Ninety-two, sir.'

'That will do for to-day, then. Now, Mr. Marlby, I can come ashore. Where's my wealth come from, eh?' He spoke jestingly, and turned, as they went together towards the gangway, to give some directions about the next day's unloading.

'Read that,' said Mr. Marlby, overcome by his emotion, and entirely giving up the dramatic situation he had promised himself—one to be something after the fashion of the discovery of the long lost heir to the vast estates in a Victoria or a Surrey Theatre play.

'Good God!' cried Harry, standing up in the shore boat that was bearing him to his native land, 'is this true?'

'As true as—as—as Hansard,' said Mr. Marlby, who was a great reader of debates.

'Both my uncles—and George—dead! Poor George, poor chap! Then—why—then I am——'

'Baron Piccadilly of the Mall, in the Peerage of England, and a Baronet,' put in the shipbroker, with whom for the last few days Burke had jostled the parliamentary reports.

Harry sat down in the stern of the boat, and did not speak. At last his friend grew impatient and nudged him with his elbow:

'Well, you're a great man. Are you pleased?'

'I don't know,' said Harry simply. 'I only hope I shall be able to do my duty.'

CHAPTER XXI.

WHATEVER may be said of London society, it can never be averred with truth that it is slow to recognise merit —that is, when the merit consists of high rank, youth, a state of promising bachelorhood, and an enormous fortune. At any rate, in the case of Henry, Lord Piccadilly, those persons with bankers' books who reside westward of The Griffin, and who call themselves the aristocracy of England, were quick enough to take him by the right hand of friendship—nay, to place him on a pedestal, as if he were a brewer or a royal personage.

The flattery he met with on all sides pleased Harry. He had not a sufficiently mean opinion of human nature to believe that it could all be false, that it would cease to-morrow if a claimant came forward and successfully asserted his right to the St. James title and estates.

He had not, for instance, seen any little bit of true everyday comedy like this:

Scene at a Club. To BROWN *enter* JONES.

Jones. Heard of the FitzCrown smash ?

Brown. Yes. Sad thing. Poor Fitz loses his
title. Scamp, his father. But he's got 10,000*l.* left--
the Basland estate. Poor chap! I'll ask him to dine
with me next week.

Jones. No. You're wrong about the Basland
property. That goes with the title. I have just seen
B——, who is arranging the affair. Poor Fitz is a
pauper.

Brown. By Jove! Well, he always was rather a
swaggering chap—and—and—no, I won't ask him to
dinner next week.

Harry was not fool enough to think that he was
liked for himself alone by all ; for instance, by old Lady
Molygold, who pelted him, until he was morally sore
and bruised, with notes of invitation, compliments, and
daughters, nor by Colonel Mouther, who asked him for
the loan of a 'monkey' five minutes after introducing
himself to him on the club steps. But he did find it
very pleasant to be greeted everywhere with bright
smiles of welcome, and to know that there was not a
house in London where his entrance would not give—
or, at least, seem to give—pleasure. The thing did
not turn his head, as the phrase goes, but it filled his
head with very pleasant thoughts, and, with one exception, he had nothing in his life just now to give
him anything but unmitigated satisfaction. His
mother, now a wealthy dinner-giver of Belgrave Square,
had improved under the influence of prosperity. Although still eager about the scandals of the day, she no
longer searched for them with the eagerness and asperity of yore. To use a hunting metaphor, she did
not dig up her foxes when she ran them to ground.
They were given another chance of life, till the tittle-

tattle dogs—the character-hounds—drew the covert
another time, and then who knows?--there might be
other foxes afoot with a stronger scent than they. No
woman was ever prouder of her son than Mrs. St. James.
To see him doing the honours at the head of her table
gave her as much pleasure as half-a-dozen of the newest
stories of friends' delinquencies, and she, by some
mysterious logical and inductive process—known alone
to the female mind—had quite persuaded herself
that Harry's success was entirely owing to her own
unparalleled sagacity and foresight.

The one thorn of Harry's rose, the one exception
to the rule of his happiness, was that, search as he
might, he could find no trace of his early love. Nellie
Barton had entirely disappeared. The house in Richlake where they had lived had been pulled down, and a
new house had been erected in its place. None of the
village inhabitants could tell him more than that, first,
Nellie had gone away, to London they believed, and
that, some months after, Mr. Barton, whose medical
practice had died away almost to nothing—a new and
more popular physician having set up in opposition—
had gone too. As everyone who left Richlake did go to
London this intelligence was not worth much, and yet
it was all he could obtain. The servants who had been
with the old Lord at The Grange had disappeared
long ago, taking with them their handsome legacies ;
and though Harry did manage to hunt up Mrs. Richards
and the butler—who had joined forces and taken a
corner public-house in East London—from them he
could gather no more than a vague idea that Nellie had
married a young gentleman who used to visit at The
Grange, and that Mr. Barton was dead 'for sure'—he
was 'that old,' and besides, very unhealthy.

Although at first this unsuccess made Harry very
miserable, it was scarcely possible for him, in the
active bright life he now led, to keep his first love

always in his thoughts, and gradually he ceased to remember the early romance and reconciled himself to the fact that one page—a pleasant one—of his life had been read, turned over, and done with.

Absence often makes the heart grow fonder of those who are not absent, and he was surrounded now by so many pairs of bright eyes that would sparkle at his humour or damp at his sentiment so very—so extraordinarily—easily.

To give my readers a notion of the position that he occupied in the world at present, I think it would scarcely be safe to trust to my own unaided power of description, and I am relieved to turn to an account of him which appeared in one of the 'Society' papers of the day, which, under the heading of 'Great Ones *Chez Eux*,' had been indulging its readers for some time with sketches of those persons who filled the public eye :

'Great Ones *Chez Eux*.   No. XXI.

'HENRY, BARON PICCADILLY.

'The young nobleman who has lately appeared upon the horizon of society is much to be envied. From a position of comparative obscurity he has suddenly sprung into the zenith of fame and grandeur. The St. James family, which can scarcely be said to go back into the mists of time, has always been noted for its loyalty to that entity known to us slangy nineteenth-century folk as "the main chance," and the result is apparent now in the person of the subject of our sketch. Many a petty German prince of the good old days before Bismarck and Moltke put their heads together and evolved a German Empire might have envied him, for without the cares of Government he is a petty king, and without exigencies of state etiquette he may be said to preside over a court.

'Let us see what he has, this young princeling, who

only the other day led the Four-in-Hand Club their drive to the Crystal Palace, with a Royal Highness on the box-seat, and a coach load of beauties that no other capital in Europe could match.

'There is Mall Castle in Slumberland, a splendid edifice in cut stone, with something like five thousand acres of wild picturesque park undulating around it, and placed in the centre of an estate estimated to bring in some 70,000*l.* a year.

'Then there is the old Manor House in Kent, built when the Tudors were kings, and a miracle of ornamental architecture.

'Shut up for years—as had also been the Castle in Slumberland—the old walls must have been startled to hear the sound of gay voices the other day, when a galaxy of beauty and fashion congregated there for the Canterbury Week, and desecrated (as no doubt the old housekeeper thought) that gloomy room where Geoffrey, Lord Piccadilly, was murdered, by playing battledore and shuttlecock in it on a Sunday morning. Then we have the Scotch forest, with the lodge of Ellancruich nestling among the heather-covered hills, and the stags only awaiting the advent of their new owner, with his friends and his rifles, to do the thinning that has so long been wanting.

'Besides these, is there not a lovely cottage in the Isle of Wight, with, close to it, a perfect little natural harbour, where two or three yachts can lie in any wind? The Villa Moresca, in the outskirts of Naples, a paradise of Italian art and English comfort? The little house in the Rue Scribe, in Paris? The palazzo in Rome? The curious shooting-box, built by Joseph, Lord Piccadilly, in Albania? Then who in London does not know Piccadilly House with it garden of six acres enclosed with a high wall, and its stately if somewhat gloomy façade looking over the park? Or who that has gone a-pleasuring to Richlake has not seen that rose-embowered cottage, with its trim lawn sloping down to the river ?

'Lord Piccadilly lives, when in town, at his chambers in the Albany, disliking the space and emptiness of the family mansion ; but it is said that he does not intend the latter to be wasted, but has sent invitations to such of his county neighbours as find a stay in town expensive to come up for various periods and take advantage of the French cook and household he has placed there.

'But we have not got half through our young Crœsus' possessions.   He has about the nicest house near Melton, and quite the best stud in Leicestershire ; he owns a little place not two miles from Newmarket, which is said to be a miracle of comfort, where he is gradually getting together a string of race-horses under the experienced guidance of Colonel Ditchin, and much helped by his trainer, Jack Knight.

'He has a place in the west of Ireland which those few brave persons who dare venture in that country describe as something quite magnificent, with some miles of shrubbery walks, and with splendid fishing at hand ; he has twelve thousand acres of the best shooting in Norfolk ; he has a rental of something like 80,000*l.* a year in London property ; and he inherited the sum of over two millions in the Funds.

'Then rumour has it that his Lordship, anxious, like so many of his class, to promote the interests of the drama, has taken a lease of the Quip Theatre, and that, cherishing the same feeling as regards art, he has bought a large hall, not far from Piccadilly, where young artists will be encouraged to give the public a view of their early efforts to achieve fame.

'Nothing, perhaps, in the naval architecture of pleasure can come near the *Banshee*, a three-masted schooner, with auxiliary screw, of seven hundred and eighty tons, just completed for him by Mr. Black, of Porthampton; and all know of the powers of his racing cutter of one hundred tons, the *Katinka*. To sum up, this Dives of the modern time is said—and we believe correctly said—to enjoy an income of three hundred thousand a year, and, judging from what he has already done, it may be predicted that he will spend it like a gentleman.'

Thus far the Society paper. It is scarcely worth while to correct the blunders and exaggerations of the article, for in the main the picture is correct.

Harry was unquestionably a great man, as we measure greatness, and it is for this veracious history to describe not so much his greatness as what he did with it.

If there should be found lurking a moral in my story I protest that it is not my fault. Morals will get in where they are not wanted, even as a Radical flea has been known to invade the sanctity of a princess's bed.

CHAPTER XXII.

WHEN John Heckthorpe was observed by his cronies to take seven glasses of grog at night instead of his customary eight, all agreed that something had gone wrong with his affairs. What that something was he told nobody, and it was some time before he even confided to his daughter Amalia the cause of his trouble. But at length it came out. One morning he was more than ordinarily loquacious, and he felt a sudden need for human sympathy.

'Maly, my girl,' he said, sitting in the armchair that took up a large part of the back parlour; 'Maly, the child's dead.'

' What child, pa ? '

' Why, Jenny's, of course ! '

' You never told me she had one.'

' Where's the good of my telling you ?   When young
'Umphrey had come into his property then 'ud been the
time to talk about the heir, Maly.   And, damme, the
young beggar's gone off.   I heard from 'er a month ago.'

' She hasn't written home for nearly a year,' cried
Amalia, with a *tremblement* of half anger, half affection
in her voice.

' No.   You see, he were ashamed of us.   And besides,
he daren't own to his marriage till the cousin goes off
the hooks.   When that's come off I'll precious soon see
that he owns us.   But it's too dangerous now.'

' But where is Jenny ? '

' Where ?   Why, at Brussels ; in a lodging.   He's
'ad to go to his cousin's.   But he sends her money
pretty reg'lar ; and I suppose it's all right.   The only
thing is that she writes that she's ill too.   Now, if *she*
were to go off——'

' Oh, papa, she can't be as bad as that ! '

' Can't she ? ' he sneered, taking his pipe out of
his mouth with a trembling hand.   ' 'Ow the devil do
you know that, miss ?   I say if she were to go off too
we lose all hold over the feller ! '

' Oh, mayn't I go to her ? ' cried Amalia, who
really was fond of her sister.   ' Let me go and nurse
her if she's ill ! '

But Mr. Heckthorpe went on, without taking any
notice of the remark :

' And I've bin speculating on it all the time—not
to speak of your pianers, and masters, and things.   I've
been a-going it a little bit too fast on my own account ;
and what's come to my luck I don't know—I haven't
spotted a winning 'orse these six months.   D—— them !
they allus run second when I'm on, and win when
they're supposed not to be trying.   I tell you that

if I lose my hold over that feller I'm about in Queer
Street.   Do you know what that means?'

'You mean in difficulties about money?'

'Yes, my girl. B-A-N-K, bank—R-U-P, rup;
that's about what I mean. Read that.'

He handed her a letter which she glanced over.   It
commenced abruptly:

'I really have no power of doing any more for you
now. You must be patient, and trust to me when the
time arrives. It cannot be far off. I send J. all I
can spare. Do not make any inquiries or do *anything*;
and write and tell J. to be most careful. A discovery
would be ruin to us all. I must stay on here. To
leave here just now might be disastrous.

'H. B.'

'What's the postmark—"Ballydrum?"'

'It's somewhere in Ireland. If I thought he was
playing me any trick——But I believe he's on the square;
and I daresay, what with Jenny and one thing and
another, 'asn't much spare cash. But 'e'll have to stump
up pretty smart when this blessed cousin cuts it.'

'And Jenny's all alone and ill at Brussels,' said
Amalia, her thoughts reverting to her sister. 'It is
dreadful! You told me she was well and happy!'

'Did I? I daresay. If you'd a-asked no questions
you'd a-heard no lies. Now go and draw me a glass
of bitter, and then leave me alone. I've got to look
through that 'andicap. If Joe Waite comes in, tell
him I want him.'

'You'll let me hear any more news, father?' said
the girl, as she put a glass before him; but his only
answer was an impatient order for her to be gone.
And with a sigh she went back to her household
duties.

Amalia Heckthorpe had in her some of the elements
of a fine character.   Intelligent she was, and possessed

of immense courage and determination. Her affections were rather of the animal kind, but she clung by them very fiercely, and a certain grocer's wife's ears tingled still when she remembered having dropped an insinuation against Jane Heckthorpe's fair fame before her sister. It was said, indeed, that those ears had more than moral cause for this tingling, and that it had taken all Mr. Heckthorpe's strength to drag his daughter away from the culprit; and those who knew Amalia's ungovernable temper believed in the tale. At any rate, people were afterwards very careful as to what they said concerning the absent young lady. Amalia was, for one in her position, very well educated. She had read a good deal in a desultory haphazard way; she had learned to play upon the piano; and she possessed a rich voice, which only required teaching to develop into a most melodious one. The science of dress she had not yet mastered, being still a little addicted to brilliant colours and not too harmonious a disposition of them; but Nature had instructed her in the art of moving; she carried herself erect and put her small feet down as so few Englishwomen can; while there was not in her an ounce of that shyness that often produces awkwardness in a young woman. Proud of her looks, and imagining herself to be a good many cuts above those with whom she mixed, her demeanour in Ilborough society might have been studied with advantage by many a London would-be-fine lady. Vulgar enough at heart, she had learned enough to show but little of it on the surface, and her dark eyes, fine bust, and bewitching smile played sad havoc with the Ilborough young men, and with the hearts of the commercial gentlemen who came from time to time to the King's Arms.

The Reverend Portleton had some time since gone to sleep with his fathers, and the rectory had passed to a pastor who did not require to eke out his income by taking pupils, so that one source of innocent enjoyment to the publican's daughter had been removed. Still, she had grown rather weary of the incessant chaff and useless sham love-making with which the gay pupils had favoured her. Besides, there lurked always in her mind the beautiful youth of high lineage who had held her in his arms in the London restaurant, and never a day passed that she did not expect to see his handsome face and stalwart form at the door of the King's Arms, and to hear that her fate had found her out. For it need scarcely be said that Amalia was ambitious, and fully intended some day to be ' a lady.'

True, there was in her mind an alternative possibility—the stage—but her ideas as to this were as yet crude and unshaped. She only knew that her face and figure would surely attract, and that she was troubled with no scruples as to that thing people call 'morality.' Success with respectability if possible, but at all events success. *Si possis, recte; si non, quocumque modo, rem !* '

Harry was her Victory, the photograph-shop windows her Westminster Abbey. You see, she was so unsophisticated as not to be aware that nowadays our beauties amass all the glories of respectability as well as those of its opposite.

Things went on getting worse for some time at the King's Arms. Mr. Heckthorpe betted more and more, and a row in his house, commenced, it is said, by himself, made people whisper a doubt as to his obtaining a renewal of his license. An enterprising rival started a club, with singing twice a week and political debates on Saturdays, which took away a good many of his customers; and he began doubling his once modest bets upon horseraces, in the vain hope of winning back the money he had lost.

Then worse accounts of Jane came from abroad,

and at length Amalia obtained his permission to go to her sister.

'I am so lonely,' she wrote, 'and I do not think I can live long. I cannot breathe when I lie down, and have to sit in a chair all night. And H. says he can't come to me. He scarcely ever writes now; but he does send me money enough. But I want *him*. I think he is in London again. Can't you persuade him to come ? I know I worried him before; but I'll be better now, and it isn't for long.'

'I *must* go to her!' cried Amalia, when she had read this letter; and her father, after some use of bad language, had at length consented, and was much relieved to find that Amalia had saved enough out of her allowance to defray the expenses of the journey.

Amalia's progress to Brussels was a series of triumphs. Young male passengers vied with each other in attentions; Belgian guards put her tenderly into *coupés*; and even haughty gendarmes twisted their moustaches less fiercely when they looked upon her graceful figure, and smiled with infinite condescension when she asked questions in British French. But her thoughts were too much set upon her sister's woes to care much for these things. She only experienced a comfortable feeling that she had not over-estimated her powers of pleasing outside the narrow limits of Ilborough, where her rivals were so far behind her in attractions; and it was with a beating heart that she ascended the stairs of the lodgings where Jane lay.

I need not dwell upon the meeting of the sisters, or the weary weeks while the life of the one ebbed slowly but unmistakably away, nor on the grief of the one that was left when Jane's sweet face, beautiful in death, lay upon the pillow surrounded by its masses of fair hair. The Belgian doctor always avowed that he had never seen anything more beautiful than the sight of the dark beauty clasping to her the inanimate form of her dead sister, while their tresses, dark and fair, mingled together. 'Black and gold' were at length to be dissevered for ever.

It was on November 24 that poor Jane passed away.

She had gone, while at Brussels, by the name of Mrs. Humphreys, and it was under this name that the certificate of death was given. Amalia was so furious at the desertion of her sister by her husband—for practically he had deserted her for the last five months— that she was more than half inclined to leave him in the dark as to her death; for she scarcely knew in what terms to address him. Jane had given her the name of a London club at which to direct to him, but the letter remained unwritten. Mr. Heckthorpe, to whom she had telegraphed, sent an unintelligible answer, by which however she made out that he did not intend to come to Brussels; and on Amalia, therefore, devolved all the arrangements as to the funeral. On the day after this ceremony she left the town, and having, owing to an accident to the engine, missed the steamer at Ostend by which she intended to cross, she was obliged to go to the inn there and wait until next day.

The bedroom she had taken being uncomfortable, and there being many people in the *salon*, she was about to go out and kill an hour in walking through the streets, when her ear was caught, as she passed the open door of a room where servants of travellers took their meals, by the sound of a familiar name; and not being troubled by scruples, she stopped and listened. The speakers were of opposite sexes. The man's voice was raised now:

'Yes, Miss Jones, as I tell you, it was a rum sort of wedding. There was young Ballard—Humphrey Ballard is his name, a regular young swell—a-looking more like death than a bridegroom at the altar; and the bride—a pretty young woman she were—not much more happy like. They say she had a fortune of ever so many thousands, though goodness knows who from, as she lived in the village with the doctor; but I has my suspicions; and then there was the old Lord a-cussing and a-swearing as usual in his chair, and the parson as frightened as twopence, nearly dropping the book.'

'Weren't it in church, Mr. Perker?' asked the female voice.

'Church! Do you think my Lord 'ud go into a church? He were a rare old heathen, he were. Oh no! They had a special license from the Harchbishop of Canterbury, and done it in the drawing-room.'

'And where did the young couple go?'

'They went to Ireland, I 'eard say, where Ballard has an uncle or cousin or something with a castle.'

'Well, I don't envy 'em Ireland,' said the lady. 'But how come you to have left so sudden?'

'Oh, my Lord got in one of his rages after the wedding, and packed a lot of us off at a moment's notice; and I happened in the nick of time to catch Sir Thomas—as I was with before—in London. He wanted a travelling-servant in a hurry, and I came on with him the very same night, and we're a-going to tower on the Continent all the winter. I'm blessed glad to get away from that old tiger at Richlake, I can tell you, Miss Jones.'

At this point Amalia pushed the door open, and addressing the man, said, with great politeness:

'Excuse me, Mr. Perker, but I accidentally heard the name of a person in whom I am much interested. Mr. Humphrey Ballard, I think you said?'

'Yes, miss,' said Perker, a little taken aback.

'He was married, I think you said,' went on Amalia, steadying her voice with difficulty, 'the other day? Could you tell me the date of the marriage?'

'Why, yes—it was—let me see—to-day's Thursday—it was Tuesday.'

'That would be the 25th, I think—November the 25th?'

'Exactly, miss.'

'Thank you. And—could I speak to you a moment? I am much interested in Mr. Humphrey Ballard.'

'Oh, lor! Don't mind me,' said Miss Jones, rising, with some asperity. 'I know when I'm not wanted. Good day, Mr. Perker.'

Then, by the aid of some money which luckily remained in her purse, Amalia obtained all information as to the wedding at Richlake.

'The 25th—the 25th!' she repeated over and over again to herself, as she walked rapidly up and down the esplanade that evening, with an expression on her face that boded ill to someone. 'The day after! One day after! But he did not know it! The scoundrel!'

CHAPTER XXIII.

'It is so good of you to call,' said Mrs. Maintenong, rising picturesquely from her sofa and holding out the prettiest hand in London to Harry. 'I never thought you would.'

'I always keep my promises, Mrs. Maintenong,' said he, keeping the hand perhaps the fraction of a second longer than was absolutely necessary for the customary salutation of our latter-day barbarism.

'*Do* you?' she said, italicising the first word with a sigh that spoke volumes. 'I hope so. People so seldom do. My husband promised to love, honour, and obey me, you know, and he doesn't.'

'I thought you promised that?' observed Harry, smiling.

'Ah, by the way, so I did! But he promised to help me in sickness and sorrow, in poverty and riches, until death do us part. And he refused to buy me the prettiest bay horse to-day. But I don't mind so much, for Lord Passaye is going to get the creature and give it to me.'

'What does Mr. Maintenong say to that?'

'Why, what can he say to it? If he won't give me the necessaries of life, somebody must. I am told it is the law.'

'Perhaps he can't.

'Perhaps not. I do believe Tom is head over ears in debt. But that's *his* fault. He must have known when he knew me first that I wanted things.'

'Not so many things as you do want, though,' said Harry, glancing round the room, crammed with objects which, if not particularly adornful, were very expensive, and then looking back into the liquid wonderful eyes of his hostess, and at her perfect figure in its perfect covering. She sighed as she poured him out a cup of tea.

'Ah, Lord Piccadilly, how do we know what we want? I want to be good. I do so want to be good.'

'And you are.'

She gave him a side glance which would have spoken volumes had he not at that moment been engaged in admiring her hand as she held the teapot.

'Ye—es, I am good. But I am not good from right motives.'

'How is that?' said he, coming back to her eyes, which were fixed on his with a look of perplexity and confidence which was entirely charming.

'Well, you see—sugar—yes?—you see, when I came to London from Cornwall, I had fully determined to be always very, very, very fond of Tom. And I am very fond of him—ain't you?'

Harry had only seen Tom once, and that was as he escaped downstairs when Harry was announced. However, he grunted a kind of acquiescence, and she went on :

'But, you see, husbands are so very different to—friends—and I scarcely knew I was pretty then. By the way, do you think me pretty?'

'Yes, Mrs. Maintenong.'

'I am so glad. I wanted you to. You are so different to most of them. But what was I saying? Oh, about my feelings when I came to London! You know, I wanted to be good from really good motives—those things you read about; but I couldn't.'

'Couldn't you?' said Harry, a little startled, and wondering what revelation was coming.

'No. I found ever so many men that could make love ever so much better than Tom ; and there's no knowing what might not have happened if I had not looked at things in a philosophical spirit.'

'Ah! you took that line?' said the puzzled young man.

'Yes. I saw that all the others—I mean the pretty married women—did the same thing; so I determined to be more or less original. And for very practical ungood motives I determined to be good. You don't think me very horrid, do you?'

He would have thought her very horrid if she had not been so exquisitely lovely, and if she had not looked at him in that pleading way that would have touched an American. So he said nothing ; but he in his turn must have looked a great deal, for Mrs. Maintenong brought him his tea, and allowed her hand to rest a moment on his as she gave it to him.

'Do you know, Mrs. Maintenong,' said he, after a few remarks that were rather at random, for the touch set his blood on fire, 'do you know, it offends me to see your pictures all about the streets.'

'Does it?' she said, opening her big eyes. 'Not really? But Tom don't mind. And after all they generally put me between a bishop and a statesman. I especially asked them always to put me in respectable society in the shop windows.'

He laughed. 'After all it is a kind of fame,' he said.

Mrs. Maintenong was very nearly offended, and he little knew that she said to herself the word ' booby.'

' Isn't it? About as much fame as a woman gets nowadays. You wouldn't like me to make speeches about woman's wrongs, would you?'

'I don't think you have many wrongs.'

'Not now, because I am young and pretty. But when I grow old and ugly, what shall I have except what I get now to keep—and Tom?'

'Yes, you'll always have Tom.'

'But even he, who would kiss the ground I tread upon now, will get just like the husbands of ugly women when I cease to be the fashion. "Make hay while the sun shines" is my motto, and when I have no more flattery I shall still have those pearls the Duke of St. Ablative gave me, and the diamond tiara of Prince Punskofoukis.'

'But—but what do they—the St. Ablatives and the Punskofoukis—get in exchange?'

'Oh, they get my reflected glory; they get the credit of my liking them, though I don't; and they have a sort of right to monopolise me now and then in public. And then, you know, the people who write in papers say, "There was the Cornish Beauty, with Prince P—— as usual in attendance;" or, "The reigning beauty attended with her chief favourite, the Duke of St. A——." That's what they get, and it's quite enough. Besides, poor dear Tom is fond of shooting, and the Duke has plenty; and he and I are both fond of Paris, and the Prince has a charming hotel there.'

'You're queer people,' said Harry, rather disgusted, and wishing he could tear himself away from the fascination of her eyes.

'Are we, do you think? No; we're only what the world makes us. And we have hearts, Lord Piccadilly, though we hide them.'

'Have you a heart?' said he. It was a dangerous question for anyone to put to Florence Maintenong; but the eye-spell ruled him.

'No—yes! I thought I had not, but I have.'

They were sitting very close together, and the mad feeling we all of us (excepting Lord Castlereagh of historic memory and a few others) have known in sentimental youth came to him and made his senses reel.

'When did you find it out?' he said, in that husky voice which so often ruins pretty speeches when a man is half out of his mind.

'When? When did we meet?'

'Three weeks ago.'

'Yes, at Lady Coyster's; and you got introduced to me only just as I was going away.'

'Because—because you were so engaged.'

'But I saw you looking at me long before. You admired me that night?'

'Who can help it?'

'But you did not like me. You thought me fast.'

'I don't know what I thought, Mrs. Maintenong.'

'I hate that name. Call me Flossie.'

'I thought, Flossie, that you were the most beautiful, the most dangerous creature I had ever seen.'

'And you think now——?'

'The same.'

'Nothing else—Harry?'

He thought his name had never sounded so sweet, but he did not answer. He was fighting with himself and could not speak. She read him easily enough. At twenty she had the wisdom of forty years, and Harry had only been in London for a few months.

'Nothing else?'

Then he rose with a mighty effort.

'Mrs. Maintenong—Flossie, why do you tempt me? Let me go!'

'Harry!' she cried, catching his hand; 'why will you not be my friend?'

'Your friend?'

'Yes, I want a friend. Among all my lovers I have none; and Tom—Tom is so stupid. I want someone to confide in; to get advice from; to come to when I am unhappy; to rejoice with me when I am happy; to know me as I am, and not only as I seem to be when I'm in my best frock and looking out for admiration. I'm not as bad as you think, Harry— really not.'

They formed a pretty group as he stood over her, and she, still holding his hand, pleaded with such sweet humble petulance. I do not know what most young men would have done under the circumstances, I only know what this one did. He sat down again; and the arrangement of hand-clasping was rendered more likely to be permanent by his putting his other hand over hers.

What they said to each other matters little. They did not make love. That was decided. They had instituted a friendship after the true principles taught by that impostor Plato; and they were—or at least one of them was—uncommonly happy for the best part of an hour. Then the front door was heard to bang.

'Ah, there's Tom!' cried Mrs. Maintenong. 'I'm so glad, for I'm afraid I've been boring you! But you'll come again? When?'

'To-morrow.'

'Yes, and very often afterwards. And we shall

meet to-night at Lady Beeswing's; and I'll tell Laura
Loopline to ask you to her party at the Chambord on
Saturday; and—— Oh, Tom, where have you been?
Come and tell us the news. This is Lord Piccadilly.
I thought you had met before. But Tom is so absurdly
shy. He always hides behind a door when I want to
introduce him to some of my admirers; and then when
they come here they take him for a waiter, or something
of the kind. You must go? Well, good-bye. Don't
come to Lady Beeswing's very late. You might let
me take you on to Mrs. Green's of Glengorgon. I
promised to look in there for a moment. Young
Green is devoted and gave me—— What did he give
me, Tom?'

'The furniture of my dressing-room, Flossie,' said
Mr. Maintenong, in a subdued manner, standing up as
if awaiting orders from his wife.

'Oh, yes; very nice—walnut. But I thought his
was the stair carpet. Oh, no; that was Lord Tolly-
boy's. All our furniture is a present, Lord Piccadilly.
We could just afford to take the house, and no more.
So I wrote a kind of circular asking for different
things, and the result was charming.'

'Yes, I had no idea it was so easy to be popular
in London society,' said Mr. Maintenong. 'As a
bachelor no one ever gave me anything.'

'But you have so improved, Tom,' said his wife,
with a half smile at Harry, who did not like it.

'What was I saying?' pursued the beauty, who
saw his frown. 'Oh, about the Greens. I'll take you
on there. Tom will be sleepy by that time.'

'But I'm not asked.'

'Dear me, as if that mattered! No one who is anyone waits to be asked to Mrs. Green's. When I've introduced you, she'd black your boots if you wanted her to;
and she'll probably make young Green give me a magnificent present on the strength of your coming. I've

already provided her with several Highnesses, and
when a woman has been, not so very long ago, a
housekeeper, those sort of things affect her, you see.
Good-bye, Lord Piccadilly.'

Then Harry got away, and as he stepped into his
buggy did not know whether he was in love with or
in hate with the talkative, unscrupulous, but lovely
little woman he had left.

Had he seen the very pronounced flirtation that she
carried on at and after dinner that night with Jack
Vancouver of the 120th Hussars, I fancy he would
have made up his mind.   However, at Lady Beeswing's
and at Mrs. Green's that night, at the Chambord Club
on the Sunday, and at many places afterwards, she so
thoroughly allowed him to devote himself to her,
to the dismay and wrath of all the Jack Vancouvers
and other admirers, that no wonder Harry got a little
confused, and began to think that, after all, to look
into Florence Maintenong's eyes was about as much
pleasure as could be vouchsafed in this planet to a
monkey-evolved biped.

Mrs. St. James was delighted at what she called
the *liaison*.   In the first place, it made the chance of
her son's dashing into sudden matrimony remote ; and,
secondly, it placed him at one bound in the position
which his fond mother expected and desired him to
take.

As his historian, I may say that this friendship—for
it was nothing more—with the unconventional beauty
did not do Harry much harm, and possibly it did her
some good.   She grew fond of the honest, true-hearted
boy, and ashamed sometimes of the pettiness with
which her nature was plentifully supplied.   As she
described the thing to a woman friend :

'It's like being in church, my dear, rather ; but
then it's like being in church when you're very fond of
the parson and they sing beautifully.   If I'd married

Harry instead of Tom I'd be the best woman in England.'

People—people are so ill-natured, at least so other people ill-naturedly say—declared that Harry wrote cheques for thousands at Flossie's dictation, and perhaps he did. It is no business of a novelist to scrutinise the bank-books of his heroes, especially when such heroes happen to be as rich as mine. That the Maintenong household flourished exceedingly about this time cannot be denied, nor can it be gainsaid the disused frocks handed over to Louise the maid would have set up a second-rate society beauty in trade. But this is no business of ours. Harry was happy, Mrs. Maintenong was happy, Tom was happy, and Louise was radiant. If Mrs. Grundy, when she came home and bedecked her frowsy old head with curl papers, did grumble and growl, and say atrocious things, Mrs. Grundy in her diamonds and rouge was very glad to meet her dear ' Flower of Cornwall,' and indeed would do a great many undignified and humiliating things to have the chance of so meeting her.

CHAPTER XXIV.

As Harry's first London season was drawing badly, like a cheap cigar, and asking to be thrown away and done with, it became necessary to choose which of his numerous country places he would honour with a visit. A cruise with a few choice spirits in the *Alexine* tempted him ; but Mrs. Maintenong clamoured for a party in the big house at Slumberland, and declared she was tired of Cowes, and detested sailing—even to Ryde for shopping and back for dinner. Besides this, the agent of the Slumberland estates wrote that a visit from the new owner was very desirable. So eventually Mall Castle was selected as the place in which to spend the dying days of the summer.

Harry—who had become rather lazy—left the asking of the guests very much to Mrs. Maintenong, and it was not probable she would invite anyone he did not like; for the little woman was gifted with much tact, and was actuated, moreover, by a genuine wish to be a useful friend to our hero. 'The world' had by this time grown tired of talking of the two; even the mysterious paragraphs in the journals had ceased to appear; indeed, old Colonel Jabers, C.B. (who was currently said to have photographed himself into society, and who now kept there by dint of saying ill-natured things with a genial smile), declared that Mrs. Maintenong's being alone with Mr. Maintenong and without Harry to chaperon them was absolutely improper.

'Whom shall I ask for Tom, Harry?' asked Mrs. Maintenong one day, as he lounged by her side in her pretty boudoir. She said 'Who,' but we are Lindley Murrayites.

'How do you mean—for Tom?'

'Why, for him to flirt with. I'm not so selfish as you may suppose, and don't keep all the flirting of the establishment in my own hands.'

'As if a man with you for a wife *could* flirt with anyone else.'

'My dear boy, that only shows how very little you know of human nature. After a time—a few months —wives almost cease to be human beings in their husbands' eyes.'

'Pooh! Tom's as much in love with you as ever he was.'

'I think I could make him,' she observed with a smile.

'Don't!' said he, half seriously.

'It would not be acting well to you, would it? No, you need not be afraid. I am not quite without principle.'

'You're a——'

'What, sir?'

'A careless, lazy little woman. You were to have this blessed little party cut and dried a week ago, and I don't believe you've asked a soul. It'll fall through —everyone will be engaged—and we shall be a party of three in the marble halls, which halls I rather dread, by the way.'

'Engaged, will they?' said Mrs. Maintenong, with more sweet heedlessness of grammar, and then, with a mock tone of triumph:

'Not come! Catch one of them allowing anything to stop them! I've asked the Cannibal.'

'What—the Duke?'

'Yes, the Duke. And he'll come; and so, of course, Lady Burlington comes too, and her sisters-in-law, the Ladies Arcade——'

'*Arcades ambo*,' put in Harry.

'I don't know about that,' said the 'Flower of Cornwall,' looking as wise as people do when they hear what they don't understand, 'but I'll see. Then Tom Grigson, of course, comes where Jane Arcade comes, and Harry Tufter where Emily Arcade comes; and Lady Arloff is not likely to refuse to meet Harry Tufter, while old Quilpington would go a million miles, gout and all, to speak two words to Lady Arloff. And then——'

'Oh, stop!' cried he, laughing. 'Your plan is like the house that Jack built, which always confused my boyish senses. But it strikes me that we ought to have some lively scenes at Mall if everyone is making up to the wrong someone else.'

'Oh, they'll shake down. Besides, the Cannibal there will make them agreeable, as they'll all be scheming to go to Gloribargh.'

' I rather wish you hadn't asked him.'

' Why ? '

' Well, I don't like him.'

' Hush ! You mustn't say that.'

' I think—I know it sounds very wicked—but I really do think his Grace of Ulster and Dorsetshire is a sno——'

He could not finish the word, as she put her little hand upon his mouth.

' I will not hear such things, Harry ! ' she cried, half in earnest. ' He is my dearest friend—next to you. Indeed, if he didn't prefer dear Georgiana Burlington to me, I'm not sure he wouldn't come first of all in my list.'

> ' Souvent femme varie,
> Fol est qui s'y fie,'

quoted Harry, not much perturbed by her speech.

' Ah ! you don't think I'm in earnest. Wait till you see me trying to cut Georgiana out ! '

' I shall await the issue of the game with equanimity, and take the loser.'

So they talked on, perfectly happy in their easy familiarity ; and soon he took his leave and sauntered as far as the Park, stopped about every ten yards by an eager friend who had something particular to say to the hero of the hour. Harry's manner was very nearly perfect. He had not learned to swagger, and everyone seemed so glad to see him that it was but natural he should appear, and be, glad to see everyone. He little guessed how many of those who grasped his hand and smiled in his face secretly hated him for his good fortune ; nay, hated him for that same genial manner, in which they managed to discover something of condescension. And here let me make a digressive confession. Good fortune had not materially improved my hero. The high aims and aspirations that had at first filled his heart when he landed in England had gradually faded, just as the recollection of Nellie Barton had faded. He had made a short struggle, but wealth, and luxury, and flattery, and some constitutional laziness, had, all combined, proved too strong for him, and he had at last allowed himself to drift with the stream, and accept the good things of life so plentifully showered upon him, without asking whence or why they came, or whether they could be turned to higher uses than amusement.

Even occasional attendance at his London agent's office became irksome, and he was content to leave the charitable duties which he had added to the purely business ones of his agent entirely to that gentleman. Now and then some case came under his especial cognisance, and he would feverishly take it up and never rest until some lavish and probably highly injudicious arrangement had been come to. But in the long run the imposture and whining wearied him, and he was glad to shut out by forgetfulness the consciousness of all the misery and sin there was round, and nearly touching, his own bright life. If time is money, he argued, the converse must be true ; and by giving his money he gave all that was required of him.

He had walked up the Row once, and had grown tired of taking his hat off and of exchanging soft nothings with people he should probably meet at least once again that day, and certainly the next, when he suddenly came upon a man standing under a tree, with his hands in his pockets, surveying the procession of well-dressed people with a face indicative of the highest contempt and aversion.

For a moment he thought he knew the face, but the man did not appear to recognise him, and he was passing close to him, when he heard him utter the following remarkable words:

'Thank the Lord! they've all got to die like me.'

Then Harry turned——

'Mr. Lacroix, I think.'

'My name, sir,' said the shabby man, haughtily; 'but I have no acquaintance here. I am not of this society; I am only a spectator. These dolls are trotted out for my diversion. But diversion is difficult on an empty stomach.'

There was something touching in the attempt at a jaunty air which failed before he reached the end of his sentence.

'Don't you remember Mr. Jameson, whom you took to the Arcadians, and——'

'And borrowed five shillings of—which I repaid! That, sir, is a fact that stands out like a pyramid in the vast desert of my impecunious life. I do remember you, sir. How are you getting on?'

'Very well, Mr. Lacroix—and you?'

The man glanced significantly at his boots, in which fissures were too apparent, and then at his black coat, shining with sad radiance in the sun.

'Rather of the ventilating order, my garments, as you observe, sir. It is the fashion in my set. And we have given up shirts,' he added, turning his threadbare collar up a little higher, more effectually to conceal the fact that he was in this latter fashion.

'I am afraid——' began Harry, and hesitated. He scarcely knew how the other would take a direct offer of money.

But Mr. Lacroix interrupted him. 'I observe, Mr. Jameson, that you happen to belong to a different society to that which I affect at present. Under these circumstances I think our being seen talking together might attract attention. Good-day, sir.' He was turning away, when Harry stopped him.

'Stay, Mr. Lacroix. I should like to have a short conversation with you. Can you not call upon me this evening, say seven o'clock, at the Albany?'

N

'I doubt my getting past the porter's lodge,' said he. 'No, sir. I am not *very* haughty, but I have a little pride left. I only visit in my own—the ventilatingly clothed—set.'

'Nonsense,' said Harry, somewhat impatiently, for he saw approaching some young gentlemen with an intention of chaff on their faces. 'Let me ask you to accept a loan—a five pound-note—and to come this evening. I'll leave word at the lodge if you like—ask for me.'

The sight of the note was too much for Mr. Lacroix's pride. He accepted it with a graceful bow, and stuffed it with somewhat ostentatious indifference into his trousers pocket.

'I am to ask for Mr. Jameson, I presume?'

'No, no; ask for Lord Piccadilly!'

The man started, and his face changed. He drew the five-pound note quickly out of his pocket and tendered it to Harry, but Harry had turned away, and was engaged in quieting the noisy tongues of his friends, who were anxious to know what he was doing with the dog-stealer. Then Mr. Lacroix looked again at the money, muttered an oath, replaced it in his pocket—this time with more care, for his philosophy went so far as to imagine holes in pockets—and walked away slowly, with a curious look of mingled hatred and irresolution upon his haggard face.

Of course Harry forgot all about the appointment, and arrived at his chambers at ten minutes to eight, engaged to dine in Grosvenor Square at the hour. He calculated, however, that he could give Lacroix five minutes, and then be only half-an-hour late. But the Grosvenor Square hosts had that night to do without the chief attraction of their feast, and were very cross in consequence; one elderly lady, who had come with a daughter who had been a beauty for six or seven seasons, being indeed so insulting to her neighbours

after dinner as to send one of them away in a cab—her
carriage not having come—weeping on the mouldy
cushions ; while the beauty declared that she had
always considered Lord Piccadilly to be the very worst
kind of young man, with no manners or breeding, and
betraying in every word the fact that he had been a
common sailor.

For at nine o'clock Harry and his strange visitor
were still in close conversation, and it was not until the
clock on the mantelpiece struck that hour that the
former woke up to the fact of the rudeness he had
committed. However, young men who are pestered
with invitations, and whose lightest whims are borne
with, scarcely think much of such things as an engagement forgotten.

'She must be found, Lacroix—she shall be found.
If only in reparation of the wrong my uncle did, I
must find her. Of course every word you have told
me is true ? '

'True! My Lord, since the day when I turned that
woman out of doors, and left her and her child to
starve, I have never had a happy moment. I could
not lie when her name is on my lips. When—on that
terrible night—I learned what I believed to be the
truth, and what was partly the truth, and I left her and
her child to starve, and went abroad, I was mad with
rage. But I was an honest man. *Then* I had not so
fallen as to accept money as the price of my shame.
But poverty will work wonders. It made me a
scoundrel. When I came back in rags, desperate, and
found that when she was left she had, for the sake of
food, for her—for our—child, accepted his terms—the
villain !—forgive me, my Lord, but I cannot help it,
though he is your uncle——'

'Go on,' said Harry, sadly; 'you have the right.'

'When I found the story I had so quickly believed
was only an artful plot of his to get her into his power ;

N 2

that he had worked on my jealousy and violence, and had calculated on her yielding when alone and penniless; and that he had succeeded only because of Nellie —my child!—I say, when I came home to find all this out, I meant to kill him. As I told you, I went to his house, I managed to obtain access to him, only to be baffled by his revolver, and in the end to be conquered by his gold. Yes, I took his money,—his;—till she died, and then he bought me off from claiming my child with a sum down; and when, having spent that, I went to him and threatened him, he defied me. He told me to prove that the child was mine. Her father —my wife's father—was against me. He hated me, for he knew I was unprincipled, and a gambler and a drunkard, and he feared for Nellie in my power. All the people down there believed that she was his child—your uncle's. They baffled me, gave me some money, and sent me away. Once again—only last year—I went there, just to ask to be allowed to look upon her face; but she had gone—gone no one knew where.'

'But she shall be found!' cried Harry, jumping up. 'If it cost me every penny I have in the world, she shall be found! Good God! to think what may have become of her!'

'They tell me the old Lord—d—— him!—was fond of her.'

'Yes,' said Harry, more calmly. 'Yes. I don't think he would willingly have hurt her; but yet—— Are you sure that Mr. Barton died?'

'Yes. He went to Liverpool, his native town, and died there not long after I saw him. I was very near strangling him when he refused to tell me where my child was.'

Soon after this Lacroix left the Albany, and slunk off to the garret in a back street where he hid himself at night; while Harry—whose appetite was that of youth—thoughtfully and slowly changed his clothes, and went to his Club for dinner.

The next day he met Lacroix at Richlake, and proceeded to The Grange.

' There,' said he, taking the man into the room where the old Lord had always sat, and pointing to a portrait over the fireplace—a portrait of a sad-eyed, pale, but exquisitely lovely woman—' is that she ? '

But Lacroix made no reply. It was not necessary. He had fallen on his knees before the picture, and his body shook with sobs of remorse he could not express. Harry gently left the room, and soon after Lacroix rejoined him in the garden.

' Listen to me,' he said kindly, but with an air of authority that had of late become habitual to him. ' I will not reproach you with the past. You were the victim of a foul conspiracy, and she—poor woman—was more sinned against than sinning. But Nellie, your daughter, has not sinned at all, and we do not know how she may be even now suffering. I am much to blame myself, for I have been false to a vow I made some years ago. A solemn duty falls upon us now—on you as her father, and on me as one who loves her—to leave no stone unturned in our search. Promise me that you will give up all your energies to this. As to money, you shall not be stinted.'

' I promise, my Lord,' said Lacroix, in a husky voice ; ' and if you could see into my heart you would believe me, ruffian as I am.'

' I do believe you,' said Harry, holding out his hand, and as the other grasped it his lips quivered and he turned away his head.

   .   .   .   .   .   .

But fashionable parties, especially when there are mighty dukes included in them, give way to nothing, and, despite his new-born anxiety, Harry found himself some weeks later entertaining his guests at Mall Castle, and in the intervals of this labour sending frequent telegrams to and receiving answers from Lacroix, who had gone to France on a false scent, but with a firm conviction that he had hit off the trail. Mrs. Maintenong could make nothing of Harry at this time. She almost began to doubt whether he was in love with her, and in consequence she began to fall very much in love with him.

Otherwise the party was most successful. There were practical jokes of an infantile order, and 'hunt the slipper' and bolstering matches to please the Duke of Ulster and Dorsetshire, K.G., K.P., &c., and there was a deal of quiet flirtation, and a grand county lawn-tennis party, of which Slumberland talked afterwards for months; and a grander ball in the great banqueting-hall, of which all Slumberland and some of Blunderland (the adjoining county) are still talking; and altogether much festivity and rejoicing. But when the last joke had been made at night (or rather in the morning), and the ladies and gentlemen of the Castle party, in their peignoirs and smoking suits, had taken themselves to their much-needed repose, there were two of them who tossed restlessly upon their pillows. One was the master of the house, thinking of his early and now his lost love : and the other was the reigning beauty, thinking of the master of the house.

CHAPTER XXV.

To give the Duke of Ulster and Dorsetshire, K.G., K.P., mere passing mention would be as gross a breach of etiquette, as awful a social solecism, as to eat peas with your knife. Although he had for some years lived in

England, all his early life had been passed at different foreign Courts, where his enormous wealth and his illustrious descent had always made him a prominent figure. Although possessor of vast estates in England and Scotland, as well as many thousands of acres in the far West,—and although his wife, the Princess Maria of Bonderburg-Gerolstein-Booberei, now dead, had brought him a principality, or rather the income of one until the eldest son came of age and succeeded to the Grand Dukedom, even all this scarcely accounted for the astonishing amount of ready money he seemed always master of. Nor would his luck at cards, and his rule of never waiting a day for moneys won by him while he often deferred for months the settlement of an account that was against him, quite account for it. Be this as it might, however, he was immensely popular. He liked everything that was nice, so people called him affable and good-natured. The same quality of mind that made him never forget an injury enabled him also never to forget a face; so people called him tactful and free from *hauteur*. Even the husbands whose wives he affected could not but be disarmed by the pleasing smile with which he would greet them on the staircase of their own houses as he ascended, and they slunk away to their back rooms below or to their clubs outside.

There was something especially taking about the smile. It knocked people over like a chilled shot, reporters at charitable dinners were sent into fits of admiration by it; and aldermen gasped with wondering delight as it was turned on to them. And the best of it was that the turning it on was no trouble whatever to his Grace. He assumed it just as he assumed his Garter when he went out; and while he was meditating an attack on some new friend's household, or scheming a revenge on some lady who had dared prefer virtue to the Duke of Ulster and Dorsetshire, K.G., K.P., he was able to extract from a room full of hard-headed men (even in the cynical mood brought on by a bad and long public dinner, with cold food and hot champagne) rounds of applause for his affability and geniality. Then his dignity was one of his strong points. He would toss one of his hangers-on in a blanket with such engaging frankness, or throw a guest out of a window with grace and ease, while he would not for a moment endure that a frown of irritation at the temporary inconvenience should rest on the faces of those thus honoured. One day, when out shooting, he had playfully pushed a friend into a ditch full of very muddy water, and when, on emerging, that friend had shaken himself so as to splash the Duke, his Grace had at once sent him home in disgrace and given out the terrible verdict of ostracism, which Society of course at once accepted and complied with. And ostracised he was accordingly. He is now driving a mail-waggon in Australia, and they say that he has repented.

Need I say that a born leader of men, such as I hope I have shown the Duke to be, was of course a king among women? He went through Society, as it were, throwing his handkerchief about, and matrons and maidens, marchionesses and the wives of opulent new men, brides of a fortnight and virtuous wives of forty, all scrambled in the mud to pick up the coronetted, be-scented rag. Its possession meant the *entrée* to Granderly House, and what was there to be sought for in the whole range of their poor lives to be compared with that? Heaven might or might not exist in the future. Since the clergy had taken to disbelieving in Adam and Eve, and the personality of the Devil, things had got a little mixed as to that; but at any rate there was Granderly House as a blessed certainty in the present; and its price!—only to love a handsome man (they all agreed he was handsome) with a genial smile. It was true that a few bitter husbands and a few still more bitter wives (whose husbands were not bitter, by the way) called him 'the Cannibal,' and said ill-natured things about a few of his well-known and trivial peculiarities, such as his inability to tell the exact truth, and a certain want of physical bravery that characterised him; but after all he was only a little uncivilised; and, if he did like his meat nearly raw, and would look oddly at a fat baby, he probably would not have eaten his friends any more than you or I; while as to the other matters, any common person can tell the truth, and brute beasts and private sentinels can show courage.

Perhaps the Duke's most valuable trait was his inability to accept defeat. Your commonplace Lothario will, when he finds he has made a mistake, retire as gracefully as may be, and fly to fresh woods and pastures new. Not so his Grace. On the few occasions when, for some extraordinary reason—virtue, or husband love, or want of appreciation of Granderly House—he had been repulsed, he had at once, with an industry that in itself showed a grandeur of character, set himself to ruin the person who had thus done violence to the higher instincts of Society. All his toadies were at once commissioned to declare war against her; her friends were commanded, at the peril of losing the Duke's acquaintance, to cease being her friends; her name was removed from as many visiting-lists as he had the handling of, and, of course, for ever blotted out from the book of names kept at Granderly House. And Society said, 'Serve her right.' There are moments when, to adapt the words of Burke, virtue itself loses all its goodness in losing all its respect for rank.

In the same way the Duke would, with sportsman-like instinct, hunt to death any unfortunate male being that should offend him by word or look or rivalry in the jousts of Venus, until such wights almost envied the scoundrel of the ditch-water episode: in that he might perhaps, jolting over the corduroy roads of the Antipodes, forget the displeasure of the mighty Duke.

One word more as to his affability, and I have done enough to allow any intelligent reader to conjure up before him the image of this truly great man. He would get drunk with the meanest persons, even with those persons who are so disliked by our wise rulers in the metropolis that they are obliged to walk up and down the thoroughfares at night to keep themselves warm, instead of dancing as in the bad old days ; and even in his most drunken moments he never so far forgot that economy of resources which is the secret of success in this world as to give one of them a farthing. His rank paid for all ; and if he forgot to acknowledge next morning the bow of a friend who had given him supper the night before, it was that he knew where to draw the line : an art in which many great men are sadly deficient.

Poor Pimpernel (the Hon. Octavius, fourteenth son of the Earl of Splitlick, K.T., Hereditary Procurator-General of Scotland) declared that his friend the Duke had but one fault—that he would insist on everyone about him playing pony points at whist, and they were at once dismissed from friendship when they were cleaned out ; but then no one much minded what the Hon. Octavius said, and no one had, indeed, discovered that young man's good qualities until his usefulness and density of cuticle had endeared him to the owner of Granderly House. Pimpernel, who had lived for some years on the social fees given him for introductions to his great friend, was being superseded by a more adroit social manager, too, and that accounted for the spiteful and ungrateful accusation, not to speak of his having been lamed for life from a broken leg, the result of a practical joke at Gloriburgh one evening after dinner, when the Duke had been dull and wanted diversion.

It may well be imagined that, with such a man as this for guest, Harry could not dream of putting off or curtailing the duration of the party at Mall Castle, and he had to endure the week unto the bitter end, and join with the appearance of enjoyment in the infantile amusements which were—at the Duke's desire—introduced to lighten the hours 'twixt tea and dinner, and in the more serious occupations of nap and baccarat which succeeded the meal of the day.　However, everything ends at last—except Irish discontent—and Harry, wearied and depressed, stood one afternoon on the steps in front of his house, watching the carriage in which the Duke of Ulster and others were proceeding to meet the special train that was to take them to London. The last to leave were the Maintenongs, and Mrs. Maintenong contrived to gain a few moments' *tête-à-tête* in which to say good-bye to her host.　She looked very pretty in her coquettish travelling-dress, with its ridiculous little assumption of masculinarity (lexicographers beware!), and the trace of melancholy in her eyes became those orbs uncommonly well.

'Good-bye, Harry,' said she, holding out a little *peau de Suède* hand.

'Good-bye,' said he, absently, not keeping the hand a moment.

'Haven't you anything to say to me?'

'Say!　Well—what shall I say?　I hope you have enjoyed your visit.'

She stamped on the ground, showing the tip of the prettiest boot in England.

'Enjoyed my visit!　You know I haven't.'

'Dear me!　I am very sorry.'

'No; you're not a bit sorry, and you know perfectly well that I couldn't have enjoyed it.'

'Do I?　Well, I thought you got on capitally in your flirtation with the Duke; and if I were Tom I should be much alarmed.'

'I hate you! Or at least I should like to be able to hate you.'

Very few men could have heard the last whisper—so prettily spoken—unmoved; but Harry was full of his remorse as to Nellie just then, and said nothing.

'That's very unkind of you, Flossie,' he said, with as much concern as if they were talking of the weather. 'What have I done?'

'It's not what you have done—it's what you haven't done. Here have I been snubbing poor Algy Alanmore for weeks—and he worships the ground I tread upon (he gave me that lovely carpet in my drawing-room, you know)—and all—for—for nothing.'

There was something like a tear in the little woman's eyes as she spoke. No one except Harry had ever seen her so near a moment of real emotion. But when a man is in love—even though it be but with a recollection—other women are alike to him. He did not mean to be cruel, but he thought he had pretty accurately gauged the depth of this woman's feelings; and it never occurred to him that he had aroused something that the owner herself did not before suspect the existence of.

'So we part like this!' she said again, after a pause during which Harry had stared rather foolishly out of the window, and the beauty had looked at his face, and given two little gulps.

'We shall meet before long, somewhere,' he said cheerily, wishing Tom would only come in and end an awkward scene.

'Not in the same way. It's all over—I see that,' she said, rather huskily. 'But you won't quite put me out of your life, Harry? I know I'm not a good woman—I don't come up to your standard; but you do know I'm a little better than they'—with a wave of the hand, intended to designate the rest of the world—

'think me. You'll come and see me sometimes and we can be friends—a little—always—Harry?'

She was not to be resisted in her plaintive pleading, and he took the hand that was ready enough to nestle in his. With the other she hastily dragged up her veil, as at that moment a step was heard in the hall.

'Give me a kiss to say good-bye!'

He touched her cheek with his lips, tenderly, but as a brother with a sister. If Tom had come in one moment sooner and seen it, he should not have minded.

Then they went off, with much arranging of parcels and maids, and Harry went back to the office, for he was to spend the day in going through the accounts with his land-agent; and poor Flossie Maintenong cried nearly all the way to Slumberborough Station, with her head on her husband's shoulder; and, just as they were approaching the town, turned round to him, and putting her red lips close to his, whispered to him in tones that thrilled him, 'You'll never desert your poor little Flossie, will you, Tom? You're not unkind like the others—say you are not, quickly!' And she stamped with semi-comical, semi-hysterical vehemence, and then fell to crying afresh. Then Tom Maintenong took her to his sturdy breast, and kissed and soothed her, and vowed that he would always love and cherish her as he had vowed at the altar, while there was all the time a pain at his honest heart, and on his lips a silent prayer that the day might come when his selfless love and devotion would be rewarded.

Lady Burlington and the Ladies Arcade, who were already at the station, detected Mrs. Maintenong's redness of eyes even through her veil, and, as they settled themselves in their carriage, Lady Burlington thus gave tongue:

'I always knew he was not so long-suffering as they said. Did you see her eyes? He's been giving it to her about her shameful conduct with the Duke. The poor man! He absolutely couldn't get away from her.'

'Yes, indeed,' said Lady Jane Arcade, moistening her handkerchief at her delicate mouth and applying it to a tiny black spot that had settled on her nose—of which she had just been informed by her sister, who added that it had been there for the last two hours. 'Is it off? Yes, indeed. I think the affair with Lord Piccadilly is quite over. But anyhow, I expect she's getting near the end of her tether. Poor Mr. Maintenong hates her, I know, and when he leaves her of course she'll be done for. Won't she be done for then, mamma? Isn't it the rule?'

'Yes, my dear,' said Lady Burlington, with severity. 'She is now tolerated because her husband tolerates her, and that can't last much longer. The man's life is a burden to him, as anyone can see.'

Meanwhile, a few yards from them, the wretched husband was wrapping his wife up, and soothing her, and delighting in the bit of affection she was giving him, the unaccustomed pleasure of seeing her eyes soften when they met his: stifling the while his suspicion of what the cause of all this might be.

'Oh, Tom, how good you are!' she exclaimed, once more laying her head on his broad shoulder; 'much gooder than anyone else. Dear me! I believe you are the best of them after all. You can give me one more kiss. There! Now stay quite quiet, as I think I can go to sleep.'

At the next station people looked into their carriage, and smiled at the lover-like picture they saw; but Tom Maintenong cared not a jot. He would have sat hand-in-hand with his wife—if she allowed it—in front of the window of the Sward Club, or in the centre hall of the Law Courts; he would have kissed her on the top of an omnibus in Piccadilly. But the poor man's dream of happiness was of short duration, for Flossie

woke up cold and cross; and when they arrived in London
she sent off one of those mysterious notes which he hated
so, and which always eventuated in the sudden appearance of some smart young gentleman with a scheme
for the evening's amusement—a scheme the upshot of
which was invariably that Tom should find himself at
about eleven o'clock at his club. On this occasion they
had not been home many hours before Algy Alanmore
('Dandy' Alanmore, as he was called by his friends)
called with a box at the theatre he had suddenly
become possessed of, which, he thought, it might suit
Mrs. Maintenong to make use of.

'There's only Bob Fatherton and Lady Dole coming,
and you like them both, I know.'

'I want to see the piece they are acting there, particularly,' cried Tom, with an assumption of confidence
he was far from feeling.

'Nonsense, Tom,' said his wife, with some asperity.
'You know that the boxes there won't hold more than
four, and we are four without you.   I'll dine at seven;
you can come, Algy, if you like; and if you don't care
to dine so early, Tom, go to your Club. You know you
delight in grumbling about the food there, and then
playing whist for shilling points with a lot of antedi-
luvians.'

And so it was settled. After the play was over a
gay little supper-party of four were enjoying their
oysters and champagne (horrible mixture!) in Lady
Dole's pretty house in Curzon Street, while poor Tom,
in the dimly-lit and empty library of the Fossil Club,
was trying in vain to concentrate his mind on the
last article in the *Bi-Monthly Review*, the object of
which was to prove that the plays of Shakespeare were
written by a Limited Company, of which Bacon was
managing director and Ben Jonson secretary, and that
the original share list was now in the possession of an
eminent American citizen; who, indeed, was the author

of the article, and was willing to treat for his priceless treasure.

But the unfortunate man could think of nothing but Dandy Alanmore's straight classic features and reputation for successful gallantry, and threw down the brilliant essay with a groan. It might have astonished him to know that, even while Dandy was throwing at her eyes his most killing glances, while Lady Dole and her cavalier chatted discreetly in another part of the room, and a musical-box of gigantic proportions was playing as a further aid to, or screen of, pleasant converse, Flossie Maintenong was only wishing she was at home, longing once more to put her head on her honest Tom's shoulder and to cry herself to sleep.

But it is no wonder that he could not guess this, for not a soul in all that great, clever society in which they moved would have believed it, had Flossie Maintenong maintained it on oath. Strange, and yet not so very strange, that Harry's coldness should have given Tom about the best opportunity he had ever had for gaining his wife's heart!

Had he only known it, had he only at that moment, when the weariness of empty compliment and half-simulated affection was upon her, taken her by force away, asserted—sternly if necessary—those rights so long in abeyance, the chances are that he might once for all have won a victory. But he did not know.

The woman only wanted a strong, firm hand held out to her. She was drifting out to sea, half-frightened for the first time at the danger she had been so long courting. To drop metaphor, she had but now woke to the knowledge that she had a heart. Folly and thoughtlessness there had been plenty in her life; now the choice lay, as it lies for us all once in our lives, between good and evil. If Nellie had not existed, I do not know what might not have happened at this crisis; all I do know is, that if she had not existed this history would never have been written.

CHAPTER XXVI

WHEN Harry went to London—too restless to remain in his great house with only his agent for companion, and too engrossed in the subject of his search to ask any friends down there—he received a telegram, which had just missed him at Mall and followed him to town, from Lacroix, to the effect that he had provokingly for a time lost sight of the party with which he believed Nellie to be, but that he had every hope of catching them at Naples, whither he had now discovered them to have gone. Harry had a repugnance to having his old love's name bandied about by detectives and police inspectors, so checked his impulse to go to Scotland Yard. There was nothing to do but to wait; and as London was what the do-nothings call empty just then, it struck him that he might as well take the opportunity of crossing the Irish Channel and having a look at the broad acres he owned in the Isle of Saints. Happening to mention his plan at the Club one evening, it was eagerly caught up by several men who had not yet been invited elsewhere to kill their time; and the next evening saw him, Jock Tarleythorpe, a jovial young gentleman, engaged in eating, as the French say, a respectable inheritance of some hundred thousand pounds; Harry Kelt, a more or less fashionable author and critic and story-teller at dinner-parties; and Lord Adolphus Canway, a rising politician, who asked questions—speeding along some fifty miles an hour in the Irish express. They were all young, particularly Mr. Kelt, who had lived so long with young men that he remained a permanent twenty-five; and their high spirits were infectious.

Harry found himself soon roaring with laughter at the somewhat broad stories that were told, and only

O

when the last cigar of the evening had been smoked,
and in attitudes indicative of a determination to be
comfortable at all hazards the others slept profoundly,
did he again give himself up to the remorseful and
gloomy thoughts which the sudden recollection of
Nellie Barton had given rise to. It was very terrible
to him to reflect that, while he had been feasting and
enjoying himself, she might have been in trouble—in
want perhaps. Rumours of her having succeeded to
money he had heard, but they were too vague to be de-
pended upon; and, knowing how very small her circle
of acquaintance had been, it seemed certain to him that
she must, after the death of his uncle and of her own
reputed one, have been left very lonely and uncared for.

When he recalled her innocent face, with its sensi-
tive lips and laughing eyes, her gentle admission of
love, her first kiss, he looked back with almost loathing
to his recent flirtation with Mrs. Maintenong; and for
the first time he thought of that lady's husband, and of
what he—Harry—would think if he were married to
Nellie and she looked at anyone as Mrs. Maintenong
had looked at himself.

'In those weary days of work,' he said to himself,
'I used to think of Nellie as my good angel, and now
again it seems to me that she was meant so to be.'

In spite of himself, the thought of her birth and of
Lacroix's not too probable story came into his mind;
but Harry's training had not been of the sort to make
him a great stickler for the sanctity of blue blood, and
he put away the scruples that had forced themselves
upon him as altogether unworthy.

She might be married. That thought intruded
over and over again. If she were—well, he deserved it;
and then, with a jumble of half-pleasant, half-sad
memories in his brain, he fell asleep.

   .   .   .   .   .   .

A man of Lord Piccadilly's position does not visit

his property for the first time without a fuss. At
Ballydrum station there was a crowd of knee-breeched,
tail-coated peasants, all cheering lustily for the young
Lord. At intervals along the road as he drove towards
his house, groups of them dashed out and saluted him
with true Celtic ardour. Arrived at the lodge there was
a triumphal arch and more cheering, on the steps of the
Hall an address was read by the parish priest, and a
short poem, of doubtful metre but charming sentiment,
by the schoolmaster of the Kilhorty National School.
The whisky (thoughtfully provided by the land agent)
that was consumed that day was said to have been
sufficient in quantity to have floated the mail steamer
that had brought him over ; and Harry thankfully saw
the last of his welcoming tenantry off, somewhat un-
steady in their gait, but wild in their expressions of
undying affection for him and his, with a feeling that
the tales he had heard of the unpopularity of absentee
landlords were scarcely consistent with facts. He expressed this idea to Mr. Murphy, the agent, who replied,
' It isn't the absentees they don't like, it's the system '—
an answer that sounded correct, but on analysis scarcely
seemed a very lucid explanation.

There are some things connected with Ireland,
however, that few people can understand very clearly,
and Jock Tarleythorpe's professed solution, namely—
that they never hated an absentee landlord till he came
to live in the country—did not do much towards the
elucidation of the problem.

Mr. Kelt said that the whole joy of the neighbourhood came from the people's love of sport. They had
a new landlord for stalking purposes, the cynical author
explained ; while Lord Adolphus determined to bring
the incidents of that day into his next oration, as prov-
ing decisively the immense influence for harm the
doctrines of the Free Traders had in Ireland. Lord
Adolphus could generally make any one fact explain

any other fact, and there was but little doubt that he would some day form a part of that clique called a Cabinet which kindly usurps the trouble of governing the Empire.

Harry and his friends found plenty of amusement in exploring Kilborty Hall—a rambling, ugly house, built about one hundred years ago—and the vast shrubberies, park, and woods that surrounded it; but after a time, there being no partridges to shoot, the three visitors began to weary of a non-slaying existence, and all (oddly enough) received letters the same morning requiring their presence elsewhere. 'The dear Duchess!' said Mr. Kelt, with admirably assumed mournfulness; 'she says she cannot do without me. I always arrange her *tableaux*, you know; and this year she has all the beauties coming to her, and wishes to make the thing as perfect as possible.'

'Mrs. Maintenong 'll be there?' asked Jock Tarleythorpe, from the sideboard, where he was piling up his plate with kedgeree, glancing round at Harry.

'Oh dear, yes! She will appear in two *tableaux*; one, Venus rising from the sea——'

'Oh dear! Who'll do the sea?' put in the irrepressible Jock.

'And the other, Beauty and the Beast. Tom Maintenong to be the Beast.'

'What a shame!' said Harry, a little absently. He had received a letter from Lacroix which announced no further progress in the search.

'Oh, no! He is delighted in being allowed to be alone with his wife so long. The Duchess didn't want to ask him, but Mrs. M. would have it. They say she has got quite fond of him lately.'

'Yes,' said the host, 'people do say such ill-natured things.' He had not listened to the first part of the other's sentence, and was surprised at the burst of laughter with which his remark was greeted.

'Well,' said Lord Adolphus, looking up from his pile of correspondence, 'I am very glad to have come here for this week. It is a great thing to understand a subject thoroughly, and now I think I may say I know exactly what remedy is necessary to put Ireland right.'

'Found it out in a week, Dolly?' asked Jock, who believed in his friend firmly.

'Certainly,' replied the politician with some asperity.

'And here have all what we call our leading men been trying for centuries to discover it!' remarked Harry. But Lord Adolphus thought it better to take no notice of the remark. There are occasions when silence is indeed golden, as instinct, rather than experience, had already taught him.

When his guests had gone, Harry spent a few days riding about the country, visiting tenants and planning improvements and alterations that took good Mr. Murphy's breath away; and rather enjoying himself. One evening, as the two were returning after a long ride, it struck him to inquire as to neighbours.

'Neighbours, is it?' said the agent. 'Well, there isn't much of that about here. There's the rector, but he's only sober on Sundays, and then he's about just fit to do the service and then gets drunk again; and the parish priest, but he won't speak to a Protestant; and the doctor, but he's never to be found, what with his shooting and hunting and coursing and horse-racing— there were four deaths last week in the hospital and divil a doctor the craturs had; and then there's O'Donovanahan, of Castle Bally-O'Donovanahan, but he's hiding from his creditors generally in the wine-cellar, and don't allow the front-door bell to be answered; and there's Mr. Smither, the resident magistrate, but I wouldn't advise your Lordship to go to him—he'd quarrel with Job and Mark Tapley rolled into one; and then—but that's a good ten miles off— there's Castle Erdmore.'

'Castle Erdmore ! I seem to know the name. Whose
is that ?'

'Old Mr. Erdmore's it's supposed to be, but in reality
it belongs to a Barry Delancy—a scoundrelly agent,
who don't let his employers have a say in the management of the estate. He left a card on your Lordship
the other day, by the by, and so did Barry—the idea of
the man having a visiting card! I knew his father—a
decent body, who hoed potatoes mighty lazily, and got
drunk every Sunday with praiseworthy regularity.'

'A self-made man, Mr. Delancy, eh?' asked Harry,
smiling at the other's disgust.

'Self-made, is it? He only makes himself by un-
making old Mr. Erdmore. Though I hear now that
there's a nephew, or a cousin, or something come to
stay, who may put the fine fellow's nose out of joint
yet.'

A day or two after this conversation Harry mounted
his horse, and, armed with profuse instructions, proceeded
to find his way to Castle Erdmore ; a fine place wretch-
edly kept, and with the air of gloom which neglect
always brings with it. It was some time before his
ring at the bell was answered, but at last a youth—
smelling strongly of the stables—appeared, putting on
his coat hastily as he approached the door. Mr.
Erdmore was out, but the young gentleman was in the
grounds somewhere ; and Harry accepted the servant's
invitation to seek him.

It was one of those lovely autumn days that come
to us in our foggy island now and then, as if to show
what we might have in the way of weather did we only
deserve it ; and as he walked over the springy turf,
amid the ill-kept flower-beds, and marked the wild
stretch of landscape before him, with its background of
purple hills, on which the light played fitfully, as masses
of fleecy cloud rolled across the sun ; and heard the
countless birds singing in their delight from every bush

and tree around, and felt in his veins the glow of youth and strength and hope ; the exhilaration of that moment should surely have told him that he was on the eve of a crisis in his life. But he walked on, unconscious, humming to himself a favourite operatic air, and never dreaming that only a few yards of grass and a shrub or two intervened between him and destiny. He turned the corner of a thick privet hedge, and on a bench close by he saw a lady—a lady reading, with her face averted.

'Mrs. Erdmore?' he thought. 'No ; she looks too young. Probably the wife of the young man Murphy mentioned. Erdmore! Strange that the name seems familiar to me!'

Then he advanced, and at the sound of his steps on the gravel path the occupant of the bench turned, started, and then rose suddenly up and confronted him.

'Nellie!'

That was all he could say for the moment; he was literally paralysed with surprise. She was the first to recover herself, though she was deadly pale and her lips trembled.

'Mr. St. James—I mean, Lord Piccadilly.'

'You here—Nellie? I thought——'

'You didn't know that I had married Humphrey Ballard? He has taken the name of Erdmore.'

'Humphrey Ballard! You are his wife?'

'Yes, I am his wife.' She answered this question firmly enough, for the reproach in his tone put her on her guard.

Harry said nothing. He stood and looked in her face with an expression in his own that hurt her.

'Lord Piccadilly—your uncle—wished it, and—and —you know how much I owed him—how kind he was to me.'

Still Harry remained silent. He did not dare to speak yet.

'And—and—of course old follies had to be put away when one grew older and more sensible—and——Why do you look at me like that, Harry?' she cried at length, all her calmness vanishing before his despairing gaze. 'Why don't you speak to me?'

'I can't!' he replied, in so low a tone that she but just heard him. 'I can't speak! What can I say?'

'That you—that you are glad to see me again.'

'No; I am not glad. I suppose it is right—other things were follies, as you say. But I cannot be glad, Mrs. Erdmore.'

'And you think me to blame?'

'I did not speak of blame. I have no right.'

'No!' she cried, her cheek flushing, and an almost angry look coming into her eyes. 'You have no right! When you wrote to give me up——'

'I write to give you up! Never!'

'You did not do that?'

'Nellie, who made you think it?'

'Your uncle. He showed me the letter.'

'Then he forged it. Even now I have been seeking you with only one wish, one hope.'

'Oh, Harry!'

That was all she said; but the despair in her eyes, that spoke of the possibilities of happiness she saw destroyed, of the world of love they two might have lived, but now had lost, was enough for him.

'And we meet at last like this!' he said, with a groan.

At that moment steps were heard approaching. 'It is Humphrey, my husband,' she said, hastily. 'He knows nothing of this; he need never know. And we must forget.'

'How can I?'

'If not, we must never meet again!'

'My dear fellow,' cried Humphrey, hastening up to

him, 'I only just heard you were here. How are you? By Jove, you are looking well, but a little pale. So I see you have made Nellie's acquaintance. We don't stand on ceremony in Ireland. Come in. Mr. Erdmore has come back and wants to receive you with all proper formality. He's one of the old school, you know. I'm so glad you should know Harry, my dear; he's one of my oldest friends.'

And so talking with a volubility which—so unusual to him—surprised his wife, he led the way to the house. Harry followed as if he were in a dream. And old Mr. Erdmore's verdict was that either he took opium or was the stupidest young man he had ever seen.

It was lucky that his horse's instinct led him to select the right turn home, or he would have taken some time to get there. Although he had sometimes contemplated the possibility of Nellie's having married, its reality stunned him. He felt that he loved her more than ever; and he registered a vow that night that the moment he had finished some necessary arrangements connected with improvements of his estate, he would put the Channel between himself and temptation.

'Man proposes,' says the proverb; but one is sometimes almost forced to alter the latter part thereof.

CHAPTER XXVII.

'WHAT do you think of him?' asked Humphrey of his wife soon after their visitor had departed.

'I like him—I knew him a little at Richlake, you know,' she said, her face turning suddenly crimson. Humphrey, however, was too much absorbed in his own thoughts to observe it; and, after a pause, she continued, 'You knew him at—at that place where you were at a tutor's, did you not?'

'How do you know anything about Ilborough?' cried he, starting up, with an oath. Nellie looked at him in surprise.

'How do you know, I say?

'He—Lord Piccadilly—mentioned your name once when speaking of the place.'

'Idiot!' ejaculated Humphrey; then, sitting down in front of her and putting on an air of carelessness that would scarcely have deceived a child of ten, 'Did he ever mention any of the people about there?'

'Oh, yes! Let me see; there was your tutor, Mr. Portleton, and a Mr. Gregson, a farmer, I think, and the innkeeper in the town—I forget his name—and——

'Yes—yes—and—anyone else?'

'No.'

'Are you quite sure?'

'Yes, though I may have forgotten,' she answered, astonished by his apparently meaningless curiosity. 'Yes, by the by, there were two young ladies—where you used to play billiards—Heckthorpe was their name, wasn't it?—and they were called Black and Gold.'

'He told you of them?' stammered Humphrey.

'Yes; but he never told me much about them. I think he said they were handsome and rather fast; and——'

'Well—well?'

'And that you admired one of them.'

'That's a lie! I never did. Never!'

'Well, my dear,' said Nellie, a little mischievously, 'it doesn't much matter now.'

'No,' he replied, sulkily, and wondering whether she had remarked his agitation. 'Not now—or then; and I don't want ever to hear their name again.'

But Humphrey Erdmore was destined to hear the

name again before very long. Only a few days after
this conversation he was rather astonished to receive a
second visit from Harry, who asked only for him, and
was shown into the untidy den where Humphrey was
allowed to smoke and to muddle away his wits with
potheen at night.

Harry, looking very serious as he came into the
room, did not sit down, and the other, glancing at his
face, remained standing also. Without any preface
Harry began :

'Humphrey Erdmore, you and I were friends in
old days. I always thought you an honourable man.'

'Well?' asked Humphrey, with rather an abortive
attempt at self-assertion.

'Well, I have just been told—nay, I have been
given what looks like proof of your being a scoundrel.'

'My Lord!'

'Hear me first and then do as you please. But, by
Heaven, I *will* speak! When you married Ne——
your wife—were you free to do so? Yes or no?'

'Really, my Lord, I fail to see what right you have
to make such inquiries.'

'I have the right of every honest man to detect
and to obtain the punishment of fraud and crime.
Answer my question.'

'It is a strange one—that even our old friendship
does not excuse. What do you mean?'

'I mean that I will know. Surely it is better for
you to answer to me than to the nearest magistrate.'

'Magistrate!'

'Yes. Do you suppose that, if the horrible tale is
true, you will go scot free? You have a child, have
you not?'

'Yes.' Humphrey had turned ghastly pale, and
was clinging for support to the back of a chair.

Harry went on, his manner growing sterner as he
marked the confession of guilt in the other's face :

'You have a child—a son. Do you look upon him
with pride—with pleasure—as the heir to your name
and fortune? Your cousin's estate is entailed beyond
you, is it not?'

'Yes—upon my boy. But what does this cross-
examination mean?'

'It means that I have—only yesterday—seen
Amalia Heckthorpe.'

'Amalia Heckthorpe?'

'Yes. And I have seen the certificate of your
marriage with her sister.'

For a moment Humphrey did not speak, and then,
unable to meet the other's accusing eyes, he muttered,
without looking up:

'Jane's dead.'

'Is she? Are you sure of that? Was she dead
when you married Nellie? Is your wife—your boy—
good God, man, how could you be such a blackguard!'

'I don't know the exact date of her death, but ——'

'But you deserted her. And when you married
again—for the sake of the 20,000*l.* my uncle bribed
you with—you did not know anything of her. I tell
you that Amalia Heckthorpe is here to expose you;
that it is only at my request that she has consented to
put off for a few days that exposition. And I would
save you if I could—not for your own sake, you hound!
but for your wife's sake. D—— you! to take Nellie
from me, and then to ruin her!'

The violence of his emotion for a moment choked
him, and Humphrey was too much alarmed to notice
what otherwise would have filled him with jealous fury;
for, like all weak men, he was jealous.

'But you will stop her!' he cried; 'for Nellie's
sake—and the boy's! It would kill her—it would,
indeed! Tell Amalia I will pay anything she likes—
when I can. Not now—I can borrow little now—but
when my cousin dies. She shall have any sum she

wants, only to say nothing. There could be no good in stirring up the thing. She can only have come to extort money. Oh, Harry! we were good friends once, and I am not so bad as you think me. You are very rich—will you not help me to buy the woman off?'

'I have tried already,' said Harry, sternly, and with an accent of contempt in his voice; 'but I have hitherto failed. I shall see her again to-morrow, and——'

'Does anyone but she know it?' interrupted Humphrey, eagerly.

'She says not. I don't quite understand what her father thinks; but I fancy he is almost half-witted now. Now I shall go. No; I had rather not take your hand. There are some things that are unpardonable—some crimes that can never be forgiven. Look here, Humphrey Erdmore; I knew and loved Nellie before she had ever heard your name. I hoped to win her for my own some day. But you stepped in between us, and, with a lie on your lips, you took her from me for ever. Would it do any good to her, poor child, I could kill you where you stand. As it is, your exposure and punishment mean her ruin—her shame—and the shame and ruin of her innocent child. So I must try and spare you the consequences of your crime. But I warn you that I have little hope of success. Amalia Heckthorpe seems to be animated by a spirit of revenge. She says you neglected and ill-treated her sister; and I doubt whether any money can buy her off. I will come back to-morrow or next day. Promise me that you will await my coming.'

The other hesitated. The idea of flight was before him, and also the vision of a felon's fate.

'Unless you promise, I will do nothing. At least, Nellie shall not be deserted.'

'I promise.'

Then Harry rode away. In two days he returned,

and was almost touched to see the haggard face of the man who had spent forty-eight hours of mortal terror.

'Nothing is definitely settled. The woman has her terms, but they are very hard—they are almost impossible,' he said.

'Oh, Harry—oh, my Lord!' cried Humphrey in desperation; 'if it's half—more than half—my fortune, I will pay it—when I can. Anything is better than exposure.'

'Anything,' repeated Harry, a little absently; and then, suddenly, 'I want to speak to your wife alone.'

'You will not tell her?'

'Tell her? No! Ask her to come here; or better, show me the way to where she is.'

'She is in the nursery.'

'Very well; take me there.'

They went upstairs in silence.

'Nellie,' said Humphrey, opening the nursery door, 'Lord Piccadilly wants to see you, and I thought you would not mind his coming here.'

Nellie was engaged in playing with bricks on the floor with a flaxen-haired young gentleman of some three years old, and looked up with a bright blush which became her well.

'Oh!' she exclaimed, rising, 'I am so glad you should come to cheer Humphrey up. He has been quite ill with depression lately, and wanted some one to talk to besides his wife and child.'

'He is a very pretty child,' said Harry, taking the little boy upon his knee.

'Do you think so? He is such a duck!' And the mother's love could be plainly seen in her eyes.

Harry sighed.

'I wanted to ask you a question, Mrs. Erdmore,' he said, as the door closed behind Humphrey; 'and you must not think it rude of me, or inquisitive. I have a reason. You are very fond of the child?'

'He is all I have in the world to love,' she said, simply; and the sentence told volumes concerning her lonely, useless life.

'And rather than misfortune came upon him you would——'

'I would gladly die.'

'If it were possible to avert from him some terrible catastrophe only in one way, and that way sacrificed your whole life, made your future a certain misery, you would do it?'

'I would—indeed I would.'

She had taken the child into her lap, and looked very pretty as she sat, her eyes opening wide with astonishment at Harry's questions, and the blush caused by his entrance still upon her soft cheeks.

He looked at her in silence for a minute or two. Then he rose and took her hand.

'Nellie,' he said, and his voice was so tender and so melancholy that tears which seemed to her to have no meaning or reason sprang into her eyes; 'Nellie, we were very fond of each other once. Some day, perhaps —who knows?—you may find out how much I loved you. Good-bye!'

He pressed his lips upon her hand, and in a few minutes she heard the noise of his dog-cart wheels as he drove away.

CHAPTER XXVIII.

IT had been known for some time in the town of Ilborough, which had not much to talk about, that Mr. Heckthorpe had started on the first stage of that journey which, oddly enough, we others, who have all to take it in our turn, never make any preparation for. Death, with a curious irony of his own, has seized upon the very least valuable of the publican's personal effects, his mind, to work first upon; and, amid flashes of the old brutality, the new idiocy quickly gained upon him. A philosopher might have found food for cynical reflection; for certainly, if the thinking powers are the only attributes that distinguish us men from the brutes that perish, then it is lucky in some cases that there is the distinction. John Heckthorpe *sans* mind was very many degrees a greater brute than the veriest cur that cringed outside the butcher's shop and ran contentedly away with any offal that might fall from the counter.

It was a hard time for Amalia; and her devotion to his bedside won the admiration and astonishment of the neighbours, who had never deemed she was very fond of her father. Many, too, inquired why he was left with only one daughter to tend his dying hours, and one young lady belonging to the milliner's establishment, and therefore of the town aristocracy, had the boldness, meeting Amalia one day when she was taking a hasty walk, to make an inquiry on the subject.

'I wonder you don't send for Jane,' she said.

Amalia flushed a little, and then replied abruptly: 'Jane is abroad.'

'Oh!' said the other; and then, with ill-affected carelessness:

'She has not been home for a long time, has she? Do you know, we are all so curious about her. If she is married there can be no reason for keeping it a secret.'

Then Amalia turned on the young lady, and the latter wished the ground would open and swallow her; for the black eyes could be dreadfully fierce.

'Mind your own business, Miss Jones, and you'll get on better. My sister is what none of you tattling idiots will ever be—a lady. Good-day.'

That Jane had somehow become 'a lady' had long been one of the Ilborough tales, and when this rude speech (with a few embellishments) was reported that evening at Mr. Jones's little party (to meet the charming commercial gentlemen and a new veterinary surgeon who had settled in the town) it was pretty well decided that she had married a French marquis or a German count, and was living on frogs or sauer-kraut in luxury and foreign parts.

One day when Mr. Heckthorpe was a little more sensible than usual he turned to his daughter, who was sitting in the room reading, and said : ' Where did they bury her ? I should have liked to see my Jenny again. So pretty, and so well married too! She did better than you, with all your pianer-playing and Frenchified airs, Amy. Where did they bury her, eh ? '

'Bury whom ? ' asked Amalia, sharply. ' Mrs. Edwards, you can go out for a walk. I'll look after my father this afternoon. Whom do you mean ? '

' Why, Jenny. Where did they put her ? '

'You're dreaming, father ! Jenny is alive.'

'Alive ? then I must have dreamed it. But didn't you go away, somewhere abroad—the place where the sprouts come from—and see her die, and have her buried, and did it so cheap too ? You was always a careful girl, Amy, but not so loving-like as Jenny. D—— it, girl, can't you speak ? Did I dream all on it ? '

' She was very ill,' said Amalia, coming close to him, and speaking slowly and distinctly ; ' very ill, and I went to Brussels to her, and she recovered ; she got well, and is alive.'

' Then why did I think you told me she was dead ? '

' I didn't. If she had died shouldn't we have gone into mourning ? '

' Yes, my girl, I s'pose we should.'

' And did we ? '

P

'There's something in that,' said the man, overcome by the logic of the argument; 'there's something in that. But I'll swear I remember you telling me she died.'

'I tell you now that she is alive, and I tell you that you imagined the other thing,' said Amalia, decisively; and then she turned the conversation by pouring something into a glass, which Heckthorpe drank off and then fell asleep.

For weeks he lingered on 'twixt sleeping and waking, and patiently his daughter watched by his side, until her face grew thin and pale, and dark lines formed under her flashing eyes. But the end came at last, and the black horses came to the door to take the owner of the King's Arms out for his last drive. When it became known that he had left next to nothing behind, many of his old friends and neighbours came forward with offers of assistance to his almost penniless daughter; but she refused all aid, packed up her few things, and departed quietly no one knew whither, though it was shrewdly suspected that she had gone to live with her titled sister. Then an enterprising butler who had married a cook took the premises, started a new signboard and a couple of lively barmaids, and in a few months the very name of Heckthorpe died out of the memories of the Ilborough folk.

Amalia, as we know, did not go to any titled sister for several reasons; the only one necessary to state here being that she had no titled sister to go to. She took a ticket from Euston Square to Dublin. Arrived in that city of smells and soldiers, she went to a solicitor, and, after being closeted with him for a good two hours, she proceeded by one of those delightful Irish express trains that go about the same pace that a one-legged blind man could kick a heavy hat, to a station called Ballydrum.

Not wishing to incur more expense than necessary,

she, on arriving here, set out on foot to walk, and had
not proceeded more than a couple of miles or so when
she perceived a man on horseback approaching her.

As he came nearer she stopped, and for a moment
her breath went and came quickly. Then the horseman
pulled up with a jerk, and the recognition was mutual.

'Mr. St. James!'

'Amalia Heckthorpe! Here!'

'Yes, I have come to do a terrible duty. You can
direct me, no doubt, to the place I am going to find.
Perhaps you are staying there—you were a friend of his.'

'Where are you going?'

'To Castle Erdmore.'

'What—to see Humphrey?'

'Yes, Humphrey Erdmore—Humphrey Ballard that
was. He is a scoundrel. I am going to obtain justice
from or get justice done upon him.'

When Amalia first recognised Harry, she had had
no time to form any very clear plans as to her conduct
in his regard; and indeed the sight of his handsome
face set her heart beating so violently that she had
almost to force herself to remember the reason of her
journey. Now, however, as she stood opposite to him
in the road, her ready brain conceived a plan worthy of
a Macchiavelli or a Russian diplomatist.

'You speak in parables,' said Harry, jumping off his
horse and standing beside her.

'Yes—but—I think it could do no harm—I think
I should like to speak to you about what I have come
to do. Not here, but at the Ballydrum inn.'

'I will come there whenever you please.'

'You are friends with Humphrey now?'

'Yes.'

'And with—his wife?'

'Yes.'

'Did you know her before? But of course you
did—she was always with your uncle.'

'I did know her,' said Harry.

He knew not how to conceal his emotions, and Amalia noticed the momentary look of softness in his eyes as he spoke of Mrs. Erdmore.

Then her half-made plan was decided upon.

'Will you come to the inn with me, or better, will you come there to-morrow? I shall call myself Mrs. Harper, and say that I am looking out for workers in lace for a London shop. You can, no doubt, make some plausible excuse for coming to see me. And now let us part. I see some people coming, and our talking together here looks odd. Good-bye. By the by, you are Lord Piccadilly now; I should have congratulated you on your accession, my Lord.'

Harry watched her graceful figure till it was hidden by a turn in the road, and then got on his hack and trotted slowly home, utterly mystified. Amalia Heckthorpe alone, and so fierce-looking, at Ballydrum and seeking vengeance on Humphrey Erdmore! It certainly was a funny combination of circumstances, and would have puzzled a cleverer man than our young Lord.

The next day, affecting to have some plan of placing a work-mistress of his national school in business in London, which he confided to the Ballydrum innkeeper in a careless way, he was shown into a private room, where he found Amalia awaiting him. She was looking fagged and worn, but wonderfully handsome, and her sobered, saddened manner became her, he thought, better than her rather noisy merriment of old days; while her being in mourning precluded any of those wonderful effects in the way of dress that used to shock his æsthetic instincts.

After a few words as to the cause of this mourning and a few inquiries as to old friends at Ilborough, they came to the point.

As Harry listened to the tale of his friend's crime,

and knew what that crime meant to the woman he loved best on earth, his cheek turned pale, and a smothered ejaculation of fury against Humphrey let the clever woman at once into the secret of his thoughts.

She took him at a disadvantage, woman-like.

' You love her ? ' she said.

He did not answer ; he indeed affected not to hear, and walked to the window ; but his eyes had spoken. Amalia felt like a jockey when he sees his rival's whip go up, and he knows he has only to sit still and win.

' And she has a child ? '

Again no answer ; but again the silence was enough for her purpose.

After a pause he spoke :

' And what do you mean to do ? '

' To avenge my sister's wrong—to expose him ! '

' Your sister ? Where is she ? '

' She is abroad. She is ill. I am empowered to act for her.'

' And why has she remained silent so long ? '

' He left her like a scoundrel—left her alone to die, as he thought, sending her a pittance from time to time ; and then he was married so quietly—almost secretly— at Richlake, that it was long before she knew of it; and then she was ill and alone, and she was fond of him, and did not wish for exposure. But all that has passed now. She left the place she was at in despair when she heard of it, and left no address. His letters and remittances were returned ; and when he made inquiries he found that a woman answering her description more or less accurately had died at about the time when his letters ceased to be answered, and at the very boarding-house where she had been. But, mark this, my Lord, he no less committed wilful bigamy, for he married the woman he lives with now as his wife '—she paused to see Harry wince under these cruel words—' before the date at which he was told this other woman died.

Had Jane really died when he thought she did, the woman now with him would no less be his mistress and her child a bastard.'

'Does he know she is alive now?'

'He should know it. I wrote to him some time ago to tell him so, and he wrote back a whining, lying letter, offering money—or rather promising money—when his cousin dies. And my sister urged me to say no more for a time, and I consented; so no doubt he thinks we accepted his promises. But it can go on no longer. I am fully authorised by my sister to claim her just rights and to demand his punishment.'

'And your terms?'

'My terms! Lord Piccadilly, you may be a great rich lord, and I only an innkeeper's daughter, but you insult me none the less when you talk to me of bargaining my sister's honour.'

'Is there not another woman, as innocent as your sister, to be considered?'

'No. Why should I consider her? I never knew her. She has been all the time enjoying the money, the position, that belongs of right to Jane. No, I will not consider her.'

'But if I offered to pay——'

'Your money, my Lord, is no better than his.'

Harry paused for a moment. He was at his wits' end, yet he could not see Nellie's life ruined. Then he said:

'But the proofs of this extraordinary story?—extraordinary because of your sister's long silence. How do I know she is alive?'

'If you will come to London I will take you to her. She is very ill, but she will see you at my request.'

After this there was little to be said, and, soon after Harry left, having obtained a promise from Amalia to do nothing until he had seen her again. Then he went to Castle Erdmore, and had the interview with the husband and wife that we have seen; and a few days after he hurried away to London. The day before he left Amalia had also gone as quietly as she came, leaving her vengeance unfulfilled; and Humphrey Erdmore received a letter from Harry enjoining him to hold his tongue and to do nothing until he heard again.

'There is just a chance of the thing being a plot,' the letter said, 'and I am going to probe it thoroughly. Therefore do nothing. Trust me to warn you in time to save you from the consequences of your crime, as, at any rate in the sight of Heaven, it was.'

Perhaps throughout the length of that island which is rendered melancholy, a high authority has told us, by the proximity of the melancholy ocean, there was not a more melancholy man than Humphrey Erdmore as he sat late into the night, pipe in mouth, thinking of the blow about to fall upon him and his; for, to do him justice, he did sometimes remember his wife and child and the gross injury he had done to them, innocent.

CHAPTER XXIX.

Mrs. St. James did not get much comfort out of her son when he came to town. He was *distrait*, and seemed perpetually on the point of making to her some confidence which he yet at the last moment withheld. When she tried to interest him in the charms of London life, in the glories that yet awaited him in that world of which he was a chief ornament, he only sighed. When she told him choice anecdotes of her friends, even Mr. Kelt's last *bonmot*, he still did not smile. And when at last he rose to take his leave of

her, she was not sorry ; for Mrs. St. James hated gloom
of this kind as much as she hated too much light on
her face in the morning.

'Good-bye, mother,' said Harry, stooping down to
kiss her cheek ; 'I shall go back to Kilhorty
to-night.'

'Back to Ireland !' screamed his mother. 'Surely,
Harry, you have had enough of that dreadful country?'

'I have business, very important business, there,'
he said, abruptly.

'But it can wait—or you can write. I did so want
you to see little Mrs. Wassell, the new beauty, who
dines with me to-morrow.'

'Mrs. Wassell must wait, for my business won't;
and I can't do it by letter. Good-bye again.'

Then Mrs. St. James made up her mind that he
was in love, and pictured to herself his return with a
young lady who would jump the railings in Hyde Park,
and in a rich brogue chaff the mounted policeman
on duty.

Harry took a cab and drove far away into Camden
Town, stopping at the end of a small dreary street,
and walking down it until he came to the number set
down on the paper he held in his hand.

The door was opened by a middle-aged woman, with
fierce dark eyes, whose face seemed familiar to him,
though where he had seen her before he could not
tell.

He glanced at the paper.

'Does Mrs.—Mrs. Ballard—live here?'

'Yes. You are Lord Piccadilly?'

He nodded.

'Mrs. Harper told me you were coming. You
must be careful. Mrs. Ballard is very ill—an
affection of the eyes, besides other things, that have
made her too weak for any excitement. You will not
excite her, my Lord.'

'I only wish to see her for a moment,' answered he impatiently; 'and my time is limited.'

In a few moments he was ushered into a darkened room. The woman with him proceeded very quietly to open one of the shutters, saying as she did so :

'Now don't take on, deary. It's only a doctor come to look at you. Turn this way for a moment, that's a dear, and let the gentleman see your face. You see, sir,' she added, turning to Harry, as she let in a ray of light upon the patient's white face, 'you see her beautiful hair hasn't lost its colour. "Black and gold," I have heard say, she and her dark sister used to be called: and gold she is, indeed.'

Harry looked for a moment at the face he remembered well, so singularly like that of her sister, save for the golden aureole of wavy hair, and now altered by its excessive pallor and the black lines under the weary and half-closed eyes.

The girl moaned as if in pain.

'The light hurts her,' said the woman who had brought him upstairs. 'May I close the shutter, sir?'

'Yes, yes!' said Harry, and something like a groan escaped him. It was true, then. Here was the man's lawfully-wedded wife, while that poor woman and child in Ireland were—— He clenched his fist as he thought of the foul wrong that had been done, as he reflected that there could be no redress.

About two hours afterwards a veiled woman was shown into his chambers by a somewhat shocked valet —for Harry was not given to intrigue—and Amalia Heckthorpe stood before him.

'Are you satisfied?' she asked, with a touch of triumph in her tone.

'I am satisfied,' he answered, his eyes fixed upon the ground.

'And have you chosen?'

'Amalia!' he exclaimed, looking on her set face and gleaming eyes with a shudder. 'Amalia, I will pay anything, do anything you wish, to avert this blow from——'

'From the woman you love. Is not that so?'

'My God, yes!'

'But you have not reflected, my Lord, that the blow, as you call it, would free her—would make her yours? Your money would buy sympathy; your money and position would avert shame. Do you not see this?'

'It would kill her,' he said, half to himself.

'And at what price, then, do you estimate her life?'

'Name any sum.'

'How proud you are of your money! But I want something else, Harry—I want your position, and—you.'

She approached close to his chair as she spoke, and in her handsome face was an expression of love which was fierce in its intensity.

'Explain yourself,' he said, coldly.

'Oh, there is no necessity. My terms I told you the other day at Ballydrum.'

'You could not have been serious?'

'Why not?' she exclaimed, angrily. 'Why not? In what am I inferior to this woman, who is at present no better than a——'

'Silence!' he thundered, 'or I shall forget you are a woman.'

'Forget what you like, but remember one thing I have made up my mind. The terms I have mentioned are all that I will accept.'

'That is your last word?'

'That is my last word. See, Harry'—he shuddered as she pronounced his Christian name, and she saw and resented the action—'I have written them down that there may be no mistake. Of course I must trust in your honour, as in the matter of secrecy you must in mine.'

She handed him a paper, which he took, but did not open. There was a pause, and then he spoke.

'And how long will you give me to make up my mind?'

'A month—two if you like; but you must give me money, for I am penniless now.'

'You shall have what you want,' he said, wearily, taking a cheque-book from his pocket.

'Two hundred will do now.'

He filled up the cheque and then rose.

'I will take the two months. If at the end of that time I refuse your terms——'

'I shall at once, on my sister's behalf, apply for a summons against that man for bigamy.'

'Then we understand one another.'

'I hope so,' said the young lady, going towards the door. Then, turning suddenly back, she came to him with outstretched hands. 'Oh, Harry, say you do not hate me. I am not doing this for position. You will believe that I love you?'

'What does it matter about my belief? Ours is a purely business transaction.'

'No, no! Because I am doing this to get you, there can be no reason why you should not learn to be fond of me. You were fond of me once.'

He did not answer; but the reply in his looks was not reassuring.

'At least that day in London when you took me in your arms you cared for me a little?'

Again no reply. Had Amalia Heckthorpe been a shy woman it would have been embarrassing; but shyness was not one of her weak points.

'You will give me your hand?' she said; and then possessing herself of it, she covered it with kisses and dashed out of the room, nearly knocking down in so doing genteel Gibbins, the valet, who was hovering about the door, anxious to ascertain what the veiled lady could have to do with his master.

'She was a grand one,' he afterwards said when detailing the incident, without reference to his equivocal position outside the door, 'with eyes like bits of cannel coal alight and a step like a hempress. My word, couldn't she dust a fellow's jacket for him if he contraried or cheeked her!'

That evening Harry again crossed the Channel.

CHAPTER XXX.

BEFORE leaving town, however, Harry saw Lacroix, whom he had recalled from his now useless search, and informed of his discovery of Nellie. The man was naturally delighted to think that she was what he called 'so well settled in life,' and put down Harry's depression and absence of all enthusiasm on the subject to his chagrin at finding himself too late in the field.

'Do you think I might take a look at her, my Lord?' he asked.

'Well—you'd have to go there. Yes, I don't see why you shouldn't, if you wish it. You are a good penman?'

Lacroix smiled.

'I was fond of writing my own name across oblong pieces of paper once. Yes, I *can* write pretty well —more's the pity.'

'And you've no objection to some honest work?'

'Certainly not. I am fond of novelty.'

'If you can get your things packed in half an hour, and meet me at Euston, you can come over with me,

and you can take the place of a sub-agent whom I am
pensioning off. Not permanently, you know, as he
wasn't wanted, but just while I look into my projected
improvements at Kilhorty.'

'My baggage does not take long to pack. I will
not fail at the station,' said Lacroix ; and he swaggered
out of the Albany, with his hat on one side of his head,
and with the air of a man who has come into a fortune.
And indeed to him the knowledge of where he might
assuredly find food and shelter for the next few weeks
was boundless bliss —sweeter from its rarity than his
daily calipash to an alderman.

When they reached Ballydrum next evening, Harry
was somewhat astonished to find Humphrey Erdmore
on the platform, in an evident state of ill-suppressed
excitement.

'Well?' he said in a hoarse whisper, as he stood by
the open carriage door.

'All right for the present,' replied Harry in the
same tone; 'but I will come over and explain to-
morrow. At any rate, you have two months.'

Two months! Humphrey gave a sigh of relief.
When you expect immediate sentence two months
seem almost as long as do the three mentioned for
payment of the young spendthrift's first note of hand.

'When shall I find you?' asked Harry; while
Lacroix bustled about the station, and tried to usurp
the valet's duties with regard to the luggage, much to
that functionary's indignation.

'Oh, at the hotel here—any time.'

'The hotel?'

'Yes, haven't you heard? Castle Erdmore caught
fire the other night, and we have had to turn out.
The damage isn't very great; but the right wing,
where my cousin lived, suffered most, and so we thought
it best to come into town. It will be nearer to you.'

Then the men parted; but Humphrey noted, half

with shame and half with anger, that Harry never offered him his hand, nor addressed him in other than tones of the most frigid politeness.

It was not to be wondered at; Humphrey himself admitted that. But a man's crime never seems so very heinous to himself. He perceives all the extenuating circumstances so clearly that in the end they prevent him from seeing the damning circumstances at all.

And Humphrey Erdmore was one of those men who believe in only one commandment—the eleventh. There was no shame to him but in exposure. He had one of those easy-going consciences that are so convenient, unless they betray the owners into stepping beyond moral into legal wrong-doing.

'To hang me for killing him may be law, but it isn't equity,' cried a murderer once. 'How can the judge and jury know how much I hated the brute?'

Harry's agent was the first to put into words an idea that crossed his mind when he heard of the fire at Castle Erdmore, namely, that his being the only neighbour's house within decent distance of that place, and the Ballydrum inn being very wretched, he should invite the whole party to take up their temporary abode at Kilborty. He did not like the notion. The idea of having Nellie and her husband under his roof together was especially repugnant to him; but it did seem the right thing to do, while it would give poor Lacroix the opportunity he so desired of seeing her, which would have been rather difficult else.

So when next day he called at the Ballydrum inn he mooted the plan. Old Mr. Erdmore received it with enthusiasm.

'Now I call that very kind of you, my Lord—very kind. I am being slowly poisoned in this barbarous place, and my cook says she can make nothing of the kitchen appliances, and flatly refuses to come to my aid. I'll accept your invitation with pleasure. It's ages since I've been at Kilborty—a grand demesne! Why, it must be thirty years and more since the old Lord had me turned out of the house for playing some trick on the agent. Let me see—what was it? Oh, yes; I let off a squib under his horse as he started away one night after dinner. And the man only broke his leg, after all. But your uncle was a very hasty man—very hasty. I'd like to see the old place again.'

'Well, then, Mr. Erdmore, I shall expect you to-morrow. I hope the arrangement suits you?' he went on, turning to Nellie.

'I think it will be very nice, and it is very kind of you,' she said, in a low voice, angry with herself for blushing; and more angry because she knew she had not turned away from him quick enough to hide it.

And so it came to pass that he found himself under the same roof with the girl he loved, while over her head hung the terrible sword of ruin and disgrace, the falling of which he, and he alone, had the power to avert.

Lacroix's behaviour when the Castle Erdmore party arrived was diverting to witness. He literally could not keep away from Nellie, but kept popping in and out of any room where she might be, with excuses so lame and far-fetched that at length she looked upon him as an amiable lunatic whom Harry was harbouring for philanthropic reasons.

At first—for the first few days—Harry and Nellie met seldom, and then only in the presence of others; but then Mr. Erdmore was confined to his room by an attack of gout, and Humphrey was forced to go to Castle Erdmore for a few days to attend some urgent business.

After a time they drifted into that dangerous current, the recollections of old days.

The enchantment of distance throws such glamour over the smallest occurrence of times gone by; there is such a sad sweetness in the recollection of happy moments never to be recalled. And so they edged round that day in the garden at Richlake, nearer and nearer, until each knew that the other's heart was beating fast; each knew that the same thought was in both their minds.

Then Nellie rose with an effort. ' Good-night. I am very early in my habits, you know. I must go and see my boy, too; he is not quite well, and I promised to kiss him before I went to bed, if he is not asleep.'

Harry just touched the little hand held out to him, and they parted. A bystander would have said that they disliked each other, and would assuredly have voted them both guilty of bad taste.

O Propinquity! monstrous tempter of innocence, breaker-down of nice moral barriers! 'Absence makes the heart grow fonder!' Go to school, Mr. Poet; go back to school again! Give me a decent-looking woman under forty, and a passable man of no more years; let me put them together for a fortnight in a dull country house in damp weather, and if they don't strike up a flirtation I will eschew all literature but American analytical novels, and give up all gaiety save Social Science congresses!

The next day they did not meet at all. Nellie had a headache, and did not come down to dinner, which meal Harry ate in an ill-humour, not sending for Lacroix for fear that he might be unable to put up with that gentleman's somewhat vulgar pleasantries, which a few glasses of wine did not tend to improve.

But at breakfast the day after Nellie appeared,

looking so radiant, so soft, so lovable, that Harry could scarcely restrain himself from taking her in his arms then and there. He luckily did not know what a struggle it had been to her to keep up her fiction of a headache the previous day, and what a wild delight it was to her to see the face she loved.

They got on better this day. He showed her about the place, and played with little Jack, her boy; and at times they were quite merry, and forgot the cloud that hung over them.

The danger—in Nellie's eyes—seemed to be passing away. It was the first step that had been so difficult, so dangerous. Now she felt that possibly they might be friends—only friends, but very dear ones.

O Plato! Plato!

The child, too, was such a safeguard, such a topic of conversation, such a splendid chaperon! When, after an hour's ramble, they re-entered the house, Harry carrying Jack, who was tired, in his arms, they both felt that if the present state of things could only go on they would ask nothing more of Providence.

And, indeed, it would have required a very sharp-sighted observer to have detected any danger in the thing. Lacroix, who was no fool, and who was naturally suspicious and a profound disbeliever in Plato, saw none. Indeed, when he went back to his own room after dining with them, his mental comment was that, if he had been a young man like Harry, who had once loved a young woman like Nellie, and who was thus thrown in contact with her—her husband away—he would scarcely have kept to the formalities which were rigidly observed between them. He did not understand that the keeping up of these formalities was their great safeguard. Every time Harry called her Mrs. Erdmore it reminded him of their position, of their danger. Had the sweet name 'Nellie' once passed his lips, the words he longed to say to the Nellie

Q

he had loved, and might no longer love, would have followed.

At length, in about a fortnight, Humphrey returned from Castle Erdmore, and though they both breathed more freely when he had arrived, they both felt that one very delicious page of their lives had been turned over.

CHAPTER XXXI.

WHEN Harry abruptly quitted London without so much as calling to say good-bye to Mrs. Maintenong, it may well be imagined that the little lady was scarcely pleased. Her anger was mentioned by her confidentially to several of her intimates; and the Duke of Ulster, who made it his business to know everything, was at once informed of it. So he sent Octavius Pimpernel to tell her he—the Duke—would come to tea. So Tom Maintenong was told to go to his club —he had been allowed to stay at home a good deal lately—and the servants were warned to admit no one but the Duke.

'The "Cannibal" is coming to tea,' observed Mrs. Maintenong, coming down to her husband's den, where he smoked half the day away; 'so you must be off.'

'I'll be very quiet here, dear,' pleaded Tom, glancing at the comfortable slippers upon his feet.

'Nonsense! You know the first question he always asks is whether *he* '—*he* always means the husband in these cases—'is in the house, and he's furious if he *is* in it. So evacuate!'

'It's too bad that a man should be turned out of his house like this—I'm hanged if it isn't!'

'A man's house is his club, sir; a woman's house, is her boudoir. The castle idea is exploded.'

'But I say, Flossie, how long will the—will he stay?'

'Oh, I don't know. It depends how nice to him I am; and I've had such a lot of you lately that I feel inclined to be very nice indeed.'

'I wish you wouldn't say such things!'

'Dear jealous old chap!' said Mrs. Maintenong, patting the top of his head with an affectionate gesture, and marking the glow of pleasure the simple act brought into his face. 'Well, oo shall give oo Flossie just one little kiss before you go. There—only one! They're much too valuable to waste on you. I say!'

'What, darling?'

He had his arm round her waist and was looking into her 'eyes with an expression of love that nearly touched her through all her levity.

'Fancy, if Harry Kelt, or little Froggie, or the great Octavius had seen that! What would they have said? Or if it was reported to Teddy Dirtell, of *The Spy*? He'd have a flaming paragraph—"Outrage in high life! A lady kissed by her own husband!! Vigilance Committee started at Bachelors' Club!!! *Emeute* at Granderly House. Dismay among the photographers. Suicide of three editors of Society journals!!!!"' And the girl, for she was little more, laughed merrily, and pinched her husband's ear.

'You're a naughty little woman,' he said, with a smile and a sigh; 'and I suppose I must obey orders. Just ring for my boots, Floss.'

'I'll get them for you,' she said; and scuttled upstairs, singing as she went, as light-hearted and childish as if her picture were not in every shop window and her name—not too pleasantly—on every tongue.

But the discussion in the den had taken longer than they thought, and, as she darted downstairs, a pair of boots in one hand and a button-hook in the other, she

ran full tilt against no less a person than the Duke
himself, nearly knocking his Grace down again into
the hall, where the butler stood, the picture of dismay
and confusion.

'How are you, Duke?' she said, shaking his hand
with that of hers which carried the button-hook. 'I'm
just taking Tom's boots to him. Come in; he'll be
delighted to see you. Tom,' she went on, opening the
door, 'here's the Duke come to help me to button your
boots. Blobbs!'

'Yes, ma'am,' said the butler, red with shame.

'Bring me another button-hook; quick—run;
Duke, are you a good buttoner?'

'Really, Flo—really, Mrs. Maintenong, I scarcely
know. I——'

'You never tried. Ah! you've no idea how much
harder it is to button someone else's boots than one's
own.'

'If you will send for me when next you require
that operation, I shall fly to perform it,' said the Duke,
gallantly; while Tom looked on, tongue-tied, somewhat shy, and decidedly sulky. Then Blobbs appeared
with the button-hook.

'Perhaps I'll let you another time,' said Flossie,
with a mischievous smile; 'but just now it's a question
of buttoning Tom's boots. We'll have a race. Give
his Grace the button-hook, Blobbs, and stay here as
umpire. Kneel down, all three of us, because then
Blobbs can detect any cheating. Sit down, Tom.'

'Really, my dear.'

'Did you ever see such a thing?' cried Flossie,
stamping her foot. 'Am I not to be obeyed in my own
house?'

It was here that the Duke's grandeur of character
came out. He was flushed, there was the little con-
traction of his brows that usually presaged a storm;
but he turned to poor Tom, and said, quite pleasantly,

'You had better sit down, Mr. Maintenong—we are
waiting.'

Then Tom sat down. 'I bet you a sovereign I'll
have finished first!' cried Flossie.

'Done!' said the Duke, and they set to work. I
think both of them more than once caught a bit of the
husband's skin, for he winced several times during the
operation, but he bore it manfully. Naturally Flossie's
slight fingers triumphed, and she threw down her
button-hook and clapped her hands exultingly, while
his Grace was yet two buttons behind.

'Won by two lengths!' she cried. 'Haven't I,
Blobbs? You're umpire. Haven't I won?'

'Yes, your Grace—I mean, ma'am'—stammered
the respectable servitor, hot all over.

The Duke threw away his button-hook with some
petulance. Stooping did not agree with his habit of
body, and he was as red in the face as the butler.

Mrs. Maintenong burst into an uncontrollable fit
of laughter, which prevented her from speaking for
some moments, during which the two men—for
Blobbs had fled—stood looking at each other with no
great love in their expression. At last she found her
voice.

'A grand race, wasn't it? But you want practice,
Duke. What fun it will be when Teddy Dirtell puts it
in *The Spy*! Of course I shall tell him. Now you
shall have some tea to reward you. Come upstairs;
don't be late for dinner, Tom; we have some people,
you know.'

Whether she succeeded in consoling the Duke
during the afternoon for having been made to look as
nearly like a fool as such a man can look, history
deponeth not. All we do know is that from that day
the names of his Grace and of Mrs. Maintenong began
to be seriously coupled together; and that a diamond
tiara which, at a hint from the Duke, young Silvergilt

presented to her, was universally considered to have been the gift of that great man. If Lord Silvergilt thought this hard luck, he was wise enough not to say anything about it, for to him (his father had been a manure merchant, and he was only the second of the ennobled race of De Wurzel) the *entrée* to Granderly House and Gloriburgh was worth a great many diamond tiaras.

CHAPTER XXXII.

MONOTONOUS as was the life at Kilhorty, it was probably the pleasantest time that either Nellie Erdmore or Harry had ever spent. Love when it scarcely knows of its own existence is in its heyday. There is something so delicate about love that its very confession rubs the bloom off; the ignorance as to whether a kiss will be resented is often far more delightful than the kiss itself not resented. ' Heaven were not heaven if we knew what it were,' says the poet, with somewhat peculiar grammar ; and the only heaven, or taste of it, vouchsafed to us here is the feeling that enters into the minds of two persons of different sexes, and makes fools of them for the time.

‘ When do you mean to go to London ? ’ she asked one evening as they sat out in the garden in the gloaming and watched the gathering darkness, and heard in the still air the distant barking of those countless dogs without which the down-trodden Irish peasants cannot exist, and which no tyrant Saxon Government can tax them into parting with, perhaps for the simple reason that, when tax time comes, the dogs belong to no one in particular.

‘ When do you mean to go to London ? ’ she

repeated, softly; for Harry did not reply at first. He was wondering how he *could* return to London; how he could ever tear himself away from the woman beside him.

'How can I tell?' he answered, almost roughly; and then, seeing her surprised air, 'I mean that I have made no plans. As long as I can keep you—you all— here I shall stay; and I suppose when you go back to Castle Erdmore I shall go back to town.'

He sighed; and there was a dangerous pause. Then she spoke. After a pause it is always the woman who speaks.

'Fancy its being three weeks since we came! It seems like three days; it is so pleasant here.'

'Three weeks! Nearly a month!'

She turned surprised at his tone.

'Nearly a month!' he repeated, half to himself. 'And I have but two!'

'You do not seem to like the idea of going back to London?' she asked, with that tender playfulness the best woman cannot at times help assuming to the man she loves, although she knows it to be fatal to that man.

'Like it! I hate and abhor the idea that we cannot be always as we are now. If you only knew——'

'I do know one thing,' she said quickly, her colour rising: 'and that is, that if I don't soon fetch Jack he'll never forgive me. You forget that he was to make his first attempt in the swing to-day, Lord Piccadilly.'

He winced as she pronounced his name so calmly, as he thought so coldly; for he never dreamed what the effort to be calm just then caused her. She too was thinking of what life would be to her when they were parted. Just then the nurse appeared with the little boy, who came toddling over the grass as fast as his mottled fat legs would carry him, to be made much of by his mother, and to be 'jumped' by the tall gentleman who was so much kinder to him than his own father. Humphrey hated children; and indeed I sometimes think the love for them is an acquired taste, although when there is a young and lovely mother in the case it is wonderful how far less slobbering and eye-poking the sweet cherubs seem. Harry looked at the mother and child as they romped with merry laughter on the lawn, and his heart leaped to think that it was in his power by a sacrifice far greater than that of life to save them both from ruin; but it seemed hard, very hard, and when, flushed with the exercise, Nellie turned to him with a smile to ask him to take his turn at amusing the insatiable Jack, she was astonished to see the scowl upon his face.

It vanished quickly enough, though, and soon Jack was screaming with delight as he flew up and down, impelled by Harry's strong arms. Soon after, ere the child was tired of the fun, Humphrey was seen approaching them, and Harry, who could scarcely bear his presence, gave the child to his mother, and taking up a newspaper he had brought out with him, threw himself down upon the grass some few yards away and read in a determined manner, which showed Humphrey that he did not wish to be disturbed.

It so happened that Humphrey, whose temper had not been improved by recent events, was in one of his worst humours that morning; in which, indeed, few but his wife had ever seen him, for he had the sense to seek solitude when he felt them coming on, and for a time he had hidden them even from Nellie.

He now came striding up to her chair, never casting a glance towards Harry.

'Put down that brat,' he said, roughly, 'and listen to me. D—— it! do you hear? Put down the brat!'

'He will be quieter in my arms,' said Nellie, quietly.

Humphrey burst out into a string of imprecations that caused Harry to look up from his paper, and then Nellie put down the child, who promptly commenced an uproar.

'Curse the child!' cried Humphrey; 'take it up again, then. If you give one more yell I'll whip you. Do you hear?'

Jack, thoroughly alarmed, and seeing something dangerous in his father's eyes, managed to moderate his grief to an occasional sob, and Humphrey proceeded.

'What do you think the old scoundrel wants now?'

'Oh, Humphrey!' said Nellie, gently. 'You don't mean your cousin?'

'Of course I mean him. The infernal old miser! the miserable old villain! Keeping me waiting for his shoes under false pretences! Here have I been slaving for him and kow-towing to him for all these years, and now he wants to leave a thousand a year to that infernal nephew of his out at the Cape.'

'Well, surely he has as much right as you have.'

'Right as I have! Oh, yes!—you say that to annoy me—when you know that he as good as promised me every shilling—every shilling!—and that it was on that understanding that I married you.'

Nellie glanced significantly at Harry, but her husband was too excited to heed.

'Yes. Do you think I'd have married to be a pauper? Do you think I wanted to tie myself for life to this infernal country to get nothing? And then, when I see myself about to be robbed, and come and ask you to help me, you turn round on me! By God! it's enough to drive a man mad!'

Nellie's reply came in wonderfully clear tones.

'I thought that you had twenty thousand pounds when you married me, invested at four per cent.—exactly eight hundred a year, is it not?'

'Oh, you taunt me with that, do you? You want to take that and make me a pauper in reality, madam, eh?'

'I taunt you with nothing, Humphrey; and I have no power to take it from you, as you know.'

'That's true enough,' he said sullenly.

'Then what is it you want of me now?'

'I want you to go and tell him that to leave this money to the scamp in Africa will be unfair to us and to our child; that you, as well as I, would look upon it as no less than a fraud.'

'But I cannot say that, Humphrey.'

'Cannot! I am master here, and I say you shall!' His tone was violent, and a fire very like that of madness—to which passion is so near akin—was in his eyes as he advanced a step towards her. But Nellie was not easily frightened, and her voice was steady enough as she replied:

'You are master in many things, but you cannot make me do what would be wrong.'

'Wrong! D—— you! do you care for your child?'

'Yes, as you know. But there is enough for us all. Don't be very angry with me, Humphrey—perhaps I ought to have told you before—but I never thought my words would have so much effect. I told your cousin that I thought he ought to leave this money to the only other relation he has, and let bygones be bygones.'

'You told him—you suggested it?'

'Yes.'

'You dared!' shouted Humphrey, fairly beside himself with rage. 'You—Do you know what you are—what that boy is? You come in between me and the money that is mine by every right, you who are no better than——'

'Stop, Erdmore,' said a low voice at his elbow. 'Take care how you finish that sentence.'

Humphrey turned—to find Harry standing by his side.

' By what right——' he began, but the bluster was already out of him ; he was one of those men who can only bully when there is no fear of reprisals.

' Do I interfere ? ' asked Harry.   ' By the right of a gentleman.'

' By which you infer that I am not one.'

' Infer what you please,' said the other, haughtily, ' but be thankful that I did interfere.   It is getting chilly and Jack will catch cold.   Shall I carry him in for you, Mrs. Erdmore ? '

Nellie was ashy white and trembling in every limb. She could face her husband's passion calmly enough, but the comparison between the two men standing before her that forced itself into her mind made her a very coward.

As she and Harry, he carrying the child, walked slowly towards the house, not a word was exchanged between them ; neither dared speak.

Only as they reached the drawing-room windows, and he turned to give her Jack, their eyes met, and each knew what the other thought.

Over Jack's cot that evening the woman knelt and prayed a heartfelt prayer to be saved from the horrible temptation that assailed her, and to be made strong to live her life as it was given her.

And the man ?   He thought he was past praying, poor fellow—he could only think, think—and the more he thought the more hopeless the future seemed.

They were all so dull at dinner that night that old Mr. Erdmore, recovered from his gout and able to attend that meal, vowed that he would hasten the repairs at Castle Erdmore as much as possible and get back to the congenial companionship of Mr. Barry Delancy.

CHAPTER XXXIII.

AFTER the episode on the lawn the chief thing in Nellie's mind was a desire to get away as quickly as might be, ere there was an explosion between the two men. Of course she put down Harry's evident dislike of her husband to his affection for herself, and, woman-like, she was secretly pleased that it should be so. Of her sufferings she had told him nothing, and since she had seen his look when he came up to Humphrey and touched him on the shoulder in the garden, she congratulated herself on her reticence. Not that it was at any time likely that she would have complained to another man of her husband. The *femme incomprise* dodge, which is so common among young married women in search of flirtation, was unknown to her; and she would have bitten her tongue off rather than have breathed a word of what she had at times to undergo.

Humphrey was not a bad man at bottom, but a naturally uncertain temper had been soured by diffi-culties and dangers, which were not lessened by the fact of his having brought them upon himself; and his conceited nature was not one which could accommodate itself to any other nature that would not entirely sub-ordinate itself to his, and be content to remain in a state of unreasoning and unquestioning admiration. This he had found in his first wife. Jane Heckthorpe looked upon him as one of the proudest and most noble of God's creatures. She never forgot the immense con-descension he had shown in marrying herself—he, a smart, high-born 'gentleman'—and looked upon it as only natural that he should neglect and occasionally ill-treat her. To him the change from her to Nellie was not at all agreeable; that is, after he had got over the so-called love which the latter's beauty and charms had evoked. Nellie was, he knew well, his superior, and he chafed under the knowledge. Not only did she excel him in education, in refinement, and in a kind of instinctive knowledge of the world, of men, and of manners; but she also—and this was gall and wormwood—excelled him in those very attributes on which men—meaning male creatures—are apt to pride themselves.

On one occasion—the memory of which never left Humphrey—he had bought a new dog, and gone next day to the kennel to see it. The keeper happened to be away, and the dog refused to come out of the far corner of the little yard.

Nellie opened the gate.

'Go in, Humphrey, and pat it; it's only shy, and wants encouragement.'

Humphrey advanced a few steps; but the dog's eyes did not look reassuring, and he fancied he heard a low growl; so he retired, carelessly remarking as he reached the gate :

'Oh, the brute's sulky; we'll wait till O'Leary comes back and then have it out.'

'I don't believe it's a bit sulky,' said Nellie; and opening the gate, which her husband had closed, she walked up to the dog and put her hand on its head.

'Poor old fellow! poor boy!'

The big black tail described a semicircle on the stone floor, and the intelligent eyes turned up to hers with an expression of thanks for her sympathy.

'You see, Humphrey!' she cried. 'Come in and make friends with him. He has such a dear face!'

But Humphrey, who thought—as it happened quite unjustly, for a woman does not easily suspect a man she at all likes of cowardice—that she despised him, only grunted in return, and sauntered away in the direction of the piggeries, whither Nellie, after a final pat of the retriever, followed him, and wondered during the remainder of their walk what could have occurred to spoil the good humour in which he had started.

I have given this little incident as to some extent showing the frame of mind in which the man was in as regarded his wife. It was a grinding sense of inferiority with occasional outbursts of determination to assert himself; which outbursts only put him in the wrong, and proved more clearly than ever that his estimate of their relative positions was the right one. He had intelligence enough to recognise this, and it maddened him—sometimes almost to the degree of crushing her with the awful weapon he possessed, although that weapon would descend equally upon himself.

Since he had discovered that Jane Heckthorpe was not content to remain hidden, a pensioner on his bounty, or at least on his promise of bounty, but had the will as well as the power to ruin him, he had lost all that pride in his son which had stood in the place of affection. By a strange inversion of ideas, he despised the child as a bastard, and met his infant glances with dislike, feeling that they reproached him, and reproached him unjustly.

When he left his wife on the Continent, he did not think she had long to live, and any delay would—or at least he thought it would—have lost him Nellie and her 20,000*l*. That Jane should have lived beyond the two months allowed her at the furthest by the doctor was wonderful; but how could he be held accountable for that? If, by an awkward accident, his second marriage had turned out to be before her death, that surely could have been hushed up, particularly now that old Heckthorpe was dead; but for the present contingency how could he, or anyone else, have been prepared? It was characteristic of the man that he never dreamed of going to Brussels to make certain of the facts, not even before Harry came back with the news that he had actually seen Jane. Now, of course, the thing was placed beyond doubt. All he knew was that, first, Jane was very ill, and should surely die soon ; and, secondly, that Harry had some plan in his head for averting danger.

It was a desperately uncomfortable position, and Humphrey felt very sorry for himself. Self-pity was indeed the strongest of his possible emotions, and in these he was indulgent and soft-hearted to a fault. In the meantime, the dulness of his life, together with the ever-present terror that overshadowed it, made it in-cumbent upon him to forget his trouble as much as possible ; and a constant application to bottles of various kinds—sherry at luncheon, champagne at dinner, and whisky in the evening—was only a natural and wise course of action. Since they had met Harry he had observed a certain change in Nellie's demeanour which puzzled and annoyed him ; for, like a few other people, Humphrey Erdmore hated anything he could not comprehend.

Before, she had been tolerant, if somewhat con-temptuously so, of his fits of petulance and unreason-able ill-humour ; but now at times her colour rose and her eyes flashed, and in vulgar but expressive language 'she gave him as good as he brought.' The comparison between him and Harry which her heart was always making was sometimes too much for her ; and her growing dislike and contempt for the man with whom it was decreed she should pass her life broke out in speech and look. Deeply repentant she was after she had said bitter things to him ; and then came his triumph, when he would slowly recapitulate all the things he had said which had raised her wrath, secure that this time he could say them without fear of repartee or retaliation.

Money was a frequent source of trouble to them. Always fond of it, Humphrey had now conceived the idea that by money only could he be saved from the disaster impending, and he watched every shilling spent by his cousin with growing anger, becoming furious when he learned Mr. Erdmore's intention of leaving a substantial legacy to a nephew with whom he had quarrelled some time before. As to Mr. Barry Delancy, he loudly declared that the moment his cousin was dead he should bring an action against that gentleman and force him to disgorge all that he had swallowed during his years of management ; and he watched the present accounts of the estate with lynx eyes.

Humphrey, when not muddled with drink or its effects, was not a bad man of business, and, to tell the truth, Mr. Delancy did not feel very comfortable, and was quietly putting back many little plums he had, when it seemed safe so to do, abstracted from the Castle Erdmore pudding.

About one month of the two of grace allowed to Harry had elapsed when the Erdmores took their departure from Kilhorty.

They were about to start before luncheon time, and soon after breakfast Nellie and he met in a bow window of the long gallery. Both their hearts were full, and for a moment they did not speak. As they stood there, Lacroix—whose odd manner of gazing at her, and constant in-coming and out-going, Nellie had become accustomed to—came up to them ; and they noticed— one with some surprise—that he was very pale, and that his lips quivered as he spoke.

'Good-bye, Mrs. Erdmore—good-bye. You will allow me to come and see you sometimes—will you not ?'

'Certainly, Mr. Lacroix, certainly,' said Nellie, holding out her hand. 'The ride will do you good, and we shall all be glad of so pleasant a visitor.' She spoke carelessly, for her mind was too occupied by other things to give much thought to the old man before her.

But though he took her hand and pressed it, he did not go.

'May I—you see I am an old man, Mrs. Erdmore—a very old man—may I——?'

She looked at him in astonishment as he hesitated and came to a dead stop.

'What, Mr. Lacroix?'

'Oh, nothing,' said he, turning away.

Then Harry came to his rescue.

'He's a foolish old fellow, Mrs. Erdmore, and takes wonderfully strong likes and dislikes. The former he has taken for you, as you can see; and I think he wants to know whether he may kiss you. You see,' Harry went on, noting the raising of the arched eyebrows, 'that he is an affectionate old boy, and has lost his only daughter, and—you might humour him,' he wound up in a whisper.

'Oh, yes!' cried Lacroix, in an eager, trembling voice. 'Humour an old man who has lost—yes, lost —the daughter he loved.'

Then Nellie advanced towards him and held out her cheek; and, after pressing his lips to it, Lacroix burst into tears and hurried towards the door. He recovered himself as he reached it, however, and turned round.

'Mrs. Erdmore,' he said, solemnly, 'the man who stands beside you is your true friend — remember that; and I am another—a humble but a true one. If trouble or danger ever come to you, remember that old Lacroix would die to serve you; remember that some-one may even now be sacrificing more than life for your sake.'

'What does he mean?' asked Nellie, when the door had closed on him. 'Is he not a little——' And she touched her forehead significantly.

'No; at least, not altogether. He has had great misfortunes. Nellie.'

R

She started at the familiar name. He had never called her so since the first day.

'Yes, Harry,' she said almost in a whisper.

'Nellie, I am driven mad by all this.'

She did not affect to misunderstand him. There was a feeling in both their minds that they were parting for a long time—perhaps for ever—and all play-acting was past.

'And I—I am almost mad too.'

'Nellie,' he said again, lingering on the name, and possessing himself of one of her trembling hands, which was as cold as ice; 'there are times when the truth is best. Can we bear it?'

Their eyes met for a moment. His—pleading, beseeching; hers—frightened but loving.

'We *must* bear it, Harry.'

'And part now—for ever?'

'For ever!'

The words sounded so horrible that she could not help echoing them.

'Yes, for ever. Do you think this could go on much longer? We are not made of stone, Nellie. We both know—it must come out, I must say it once—that we love each other. We both know that we were parted by an unworthy trick. We both know that our lives apart will be only so many years of wretchedness. Is not this true? Answer me as if I were on my deathbed, Nellie—is not this all true?'

'Yes. But, Harry'—both her hands were in his now, and his eyes were fixed upon her face—'we have something to think of above Love—duty.'

There was a pause, during which they still stood hand in hand.

Then Nellie spoke again:

'You will never know, my Harry, how I have struggled with temptation. Perhaps you will never quite know how much I have loved, I still love you;

but—hear me out, dear, while I can speak—but fate seems to have willed that we should not have the desire of our hearts. During the long nights when I have lain awake and thought—thought till my brain reeled —I have sought strength, and I have found it. Even if it were not for the duty I owe the man who has given me his name, remember what is due to my child. Could I bear—could you bear, Harry—that in days to come, when he grew up to knowledge, he should be told things of his mother which would make him curse her name ? I was oddly brought up, as you know ; but the uncle who was so good to me all the earlier part of my life taught me one thing above all others—to love honour, to hold fast to virtue. "All else may go, my child," he used to say ; " but, that kept, you have an abiding comfort." I scarcely know—do not reproach me, Harry, it was for your sake I have had the wrong thoughts—I scarcely know what would have happened had my Jack not been born ; but now—remember that I am the defender of his honour in my own, that that innocent child's future may depend on my love, on my protection. Yes, Harry—my own Harry—I may say that once—yes, duty must come first.'

' So be it,' said he, hoarsely ; ' so be it. You are right, Nellie, and I was wrong in thought. But breaking hearts are hard to keep in order. I, too, have always held that a man, equally with a woman, should be pure and without reproach. Half for your sake, perhaps, but half for that, I could, had Fate willed it, have come to you worthy of your innocent love—aye, and I could have so come any time during my life. But now, answer me one thing, Nellie. If you could save the one you loved best on earth from disgrace and utter ruin, by a sacrifice of your future, would you not do it ? '

She looked at him inquiringly.

'I think I would, if I could without disgrace to myself.'

'Disgrace! I hardly know. There is the carriage. Good-bye, Nellie; good-bye. If you hear things said of me; if even circumstances themselves seem to say things of me not consonant with what you yourself know of me, disbelieve those tales—disbelieve even those circumstances.'

'What are you going to do?'

'You will know soon enough.'

'Oh, Harry! you are not reckless—not——'

'Not reckless!' he laughed, bitterly; and then, changing his tone, he drew her towards him and murmured, his face close to hers, 'Good-bye, my own love; good-bye.'

Their lips just touched, and then she sprang from him, and Mr. Erdmore appeared, in high spirits and well wrapped up, to bid farewell to his host, and hie him back to his beloved barrack and still more beloved agent and master.

That evening Harry received a short missive, written in bold but not inelegant handwriting, on paper that exhaled a strong smell of patchouli, to this effect:

'Dearest,—One month has gone. I shall hope to hear from you punctually, and am a little disappointed at not having had a line. But no doubt you are under *other influences*. Remember what the person who uses those influences may have to bear. Jane is still very ill, but I hope she will yet recover. She is absolutely determined to do nothing *but what I wish*.—Your most loving

'AMALIA.

CHAPTER XXXIV.

MRS. ST. JAMES had many happy moments now in the pretty drawing-room of her Belgrave Square house, but perhaps the happiest of all were when she could persuade Lord Scobell to come and see her, and could extract from him so much news of the political world behind the scenes as was known by that veteran 'whip' and party manager. When he went away she always felt that her part should be indeed that of a political great lady, and that it would be easy for her to make her *salon* the scene of many a conspiracy; the place of meeting of embryo cabinets: the battleground of splitting coalitions. But, like the farmer with the old claret, she seemed to get 'no forrarder' in this her pet project; perhaps because the news Lord Scobell brought was scarcely of a kind from which much political knowledge could be gathered. He told her, indeed, how the Lord Chancellor refused to have his corns cut and was cross in consequence of them; how the Prime Minister had once for all given up muffins, and so on. Sometimes, indeed, he rose to still higher flights, and she heard all about the quarrel between Mr. A. and Mr. B. as to which of them was to be sent down to contest Briborough; and how Mr. C.—who had shown signs of mutiny—was to be quieted with a Fisheries Commissionership; or how it was well known the young Marquis of D. would take his seat on the Opposition benches, although his father had sat on those occupied by the party now in power for forty years. But even these stern and important facts scarcely helped her much. Still, to get Lord Scobell to come and talk was something; he might act as a decoy duck for them; and he had, moreover, been something of a lover in his salad days, and tender reminiscences of the past came in between scandal and personal politics as pleasantly as comes the dainty sugar-lump into the expectant tea.

'My dear lady,' said he one day, after some compliments as to her looks, 'I hope you have spoken seriously to your son on the subject we talked of the other evening at the Foreign Office party?'

'Well, I haven't, for the simple reason that he has been in Ireland, and I thought it better not to write.'

'But I hear he has come back; indeed, I think I saw the announcement of his return in the papers.'

'Yes,' replied she, with some acerbity. 'He has come back, I believe. I have also seen it announced; but I only know it in that way.'

'Dear me,' said Lord Scobell, sniffing, as was his habit when anxious to express emotion. 'Very undutiful, but the old story, I suppose; depend upon it, all his eccentricities come from the usual cause. Do you know who she is?'

His look of archness was rather spoiled by the sniff that accompanied it, although that sniff was intensely interrogative. In this manner he could express most kinds of feeling, and it is said that his sniff on hearing of the death of a great light of his party actually moved those present to tears. By many, however, his sniff of dignity was considered the *chef-d'œuvre*.

'No, I haven't a notion. He was very much taken by Mrs. Maintenong for a time, and I rather hoped that would last. A thing of that kind keeps a young man so out of mischief.'

'Yes, yes; a pretty woman is a liberal education. But surely he has not tired of our best beauty?'

'Well, he doesn't seem able to keep away from Ireland, and yet I don't believe there is anyone there. Dear Mrs. Maintenong talked to me about him the other day with tears in her eyes; and I don't believe

there is any truth in those stories about the Duke of
Ulster. At any rate, the tiring was not on his side.'

' With a mother like you,' said Lord Scobell, with a
sniff, half of rumination, half of admiration, ' he ought
to do great things. It isn't as if he was wild, or
wanted to sow oats——'

' No,' put in Mrs. St. James, ' he hates farming.'

' And I should have thought politics would have
been the very thing to suit him. I met him in the
winter at Babbleton Royal—when the Royalties were
there—and I ventured after dinner one night to introduce the subject, when, I'm sorry to say, he wasn't too
civil.'

' Oh, dear! I'm sorry for that.'

' I don't mean to say he was exactly rude to me, but
he was rude to my profession—which is almost the
same thing to an earnest man. He said politics were
all infernal humbug. Yes, those were his words '—a
slow portentous sniff of memory—' and he went on to
explain that he hated the idea of a lot of mediocre
men hoodwinking the country merely for the sake of
getting places and notoriety.'

' Dear me! I am afraid he has got some low
friends.'

' Yes ; and then I remember he declared that his
opinion was that there scarcely had ever been a Prime
Minister who didn't deserve impeachment and behead-
ing for treason to his country at some time or other.'

' Why, he's a Radical! ' cried the mother.

' No ; only unformed opinions, and a liking for so-
called original notions,' replied the statesman. ' But
we mustn't be hard on him. Let me see what
can be done. Why shouldn't we make a few little
parties for him ? Men like Dashleigh would make an
impression on him, and so would Lord Babbleton, and
where could he meet them more pleasantly than in his
mother's house ? '

' But men like that are so hard to get.'

' Oh no—not if there be an object. I was talking to Dashleigh only the other day about it, and he agreed with me that a young man in Piccadilly's position must take up politics. It should come as natural to him as to drive a coach, or build a yacht, or go out hunting. And it's not a bit more trouble or less amusing than any of those things. I don't know what I should do without politics.'

' It would be very nice,' said Mrs. St. James, thinking of the dinners, and wondering if she were at last in very truth on the eve of realising her ambitious dream. ' Of course I just know Mr. Dashleigh and Lord Babbleton ; but Cabinet Ministers are always so engaged and preoccupied that——'

' Wait till I've arranged it all,' he interrupted, gaily. ' Fish like your son are not always catchable. Why, you know he sits on the cross-benches now.'

' Does he ?' exclaimed his mother, not knowing whether to do this were a good or an evil thing.

' And for a young man to do so is preposterous. They are only meant for Royalties and peers who have grown sour by being neglected by both parties. Even Ulster doesn't do that.'

' He is with you, is he not ?'

' Oh yes, very much ; and he's really getting quite keen.'

' Is he ?'

' Quite. I got him to stay for a division only last week, though he had to miss two acts of the new burlesque for it. It is true he made a mistake and voted the wrong way after all, but the staying showed keenness. I wish Piccadilly was a friend of his.'

' Yes—so do I. He is too charming.'

' Quite one of the best sort. I don't know when I have ever met a young fellow with pleasanter manners.

By the way, I dined at Granderly House last night,
and we spoke of your son.'

'Did you?' cried she, her eyes sparkling.

'Yes. Mrs. Maintenong brought in his name, and
the Duke declared he liked him very much, and
wondered why he was so little in town now. I shouldn't
be surprised if the Duke would say a word to him
about his social duties. There's no one understands
social duties better than the Duke.'

'No, indeed. When does he give another ball?'

'There's a dance—not a ball—on the 15th of next
month. Very few people to be asked. The great
Octavius told me that he thought there couldn't be
more than sixty couples.'

'Old women like me are not asked to those things,'
said she, mournfully.

'Clever—and beautiful—women are always wanted
and never old,' he returned, gallantly. 'But seriously,
Mrs. St. James, I do think that—if you care for that
kind of thing—a good deal depends on your son.'

'How is that?'

Lord Scobell leaned forward, sniffed mysteriously,
and then went on in a low tone :

'Of course this is confidential. The Duke of
Ulster sometimes wants money, and even for him
money is not always easy to get. You know Chartwick
—the man with the rich daughters?'

'Yes; and how he got into the Granderly House
set beats me.'

'Well, his daughters are pretty and he is very rich.
Not a bad fellow either, when you get accustomed to
his little peculiarities—the want of *h*'s, and the putting his knife in his mouth. He has often a few
thousands to spare that are handy for the "Cannibal"
after a bad race week; and in return he has his own
way a good deal as to who shall be asked to Granderly
House and Gloriburgh.'

'Yes; but I don't see——'

'Well, as you, I daresay, know, the friendship of a leading statesman is at times invaluable to a great financier. Dashleigh can do almost anything with Chartwick. Do you understand now?'

'Not exactly.'

'I thought you would,' said the Whip, with a sniff of impatience at her density. 'Dashleigh wishes to get hold of Piccadilly, and thinks you can very much help him in the laudable project. If he is right—if you can and will—he will take care that Chartwick uses *his* influence with the "Cannibal" to do anything you wish in the way of invitation to Granderly House. Now am I plain?'

'Quite,' said Mrs. St. James, enchanted, thinking him perfectly lovely, though indeed he was a beauty that it required a peculiarly educated taste to admire.

'Your son has a queer idea of duty, and he is very fond of you. If you put it as a personal favour to yourself he would, I know, do all we wish. Now, for instance, before the end of the session Dashleigh intends to bring in a measure which will meet with very serious opposition on our own side in the Upper House when it gets there. It will be said to be aimed at the rights of property in land, and the old Duke of Foozlebore declares that he will oppose it tooth and nail. Just fancy what additional strength the support of a great proprietor like Piccadilly would give us! It would be worth twenty votes at least.'

'But will this measure really do harm to property?' asked she, wishing to keep up her character as a clever politician.

'Oh no, I suppose not; I haven't studied the question. But we can trust Dashleigh, particularly with Lord Babbleton in the Cabinet. Besides, it is absolutely necessary to dish the other side; and the measure, I am told, goes much further than the one they brought in last session, on which we beat them and turned them out. Dashy's a splendid fellow—a splendid fellow!'

And Lord Scobell walked up and down the room, sniffing loudly in his admiration of his great leader.

'It's like the house that Jack built,' said the lady. 'But I think I understand. Quite a plot, isn't it?'

'Yes, yes; and mind you are very quiet. Don't say a word about the Bill—the Bill as to land. That is to come as a surprise. I'll find out when Dashleigh has a spare evening, and then you must ask him to dinner. Have some pretty people; he likes that. Mrs. Maintenong, of course; a dinner is nothing without her now, and one or two clever men who don't want to do all the talking; and little Teddy Dirtell, if you can get him to come. He amuses the Premier after dinner. Now, Mrs. St. James, I'll just have one more cup of tea, and then I must run down to the House.'

While he was drinking his tea Harry came in, looking, as his mother thought, very handsome and sunburnt, but with a seriousness in his face which seemed new to her.

The pleasant smile was there to greet her, as always, but it faded quickly, and gave way to a gravity that was almost mournfulness.

'We were talking of you,' said Lord Scobell, sniffing over a bit of bread and butter.

'Sorry to hear that a busy man like you, Lord Scobell, should so waste his time,' said Harry, sitting down on the sofa by his mother.

'It is you who waste your time, you naughty boy,' said she, pinching his ear. 'Staying away making love to pretty Irish girls when you ought to be making speeches in the House of Lords.'

'Speeches!' echoed Harry, with some scorn. 'I

cannot see the use of speeches, or at least of most of them.   Indeed, I'm not sure I see the use of the House of Lords!'

'Harry!'

'He is going to show us the use of it before long, I hope,' said the older Lord, smiling and sniffing with arch courtesy; 'namely, to bring out himself as a statesman.'

'It's a selfish game,' said Harry, throwing himself back on the sofa, and wishing Lord Scobell, who bored him, would depart.

'I shouldn't call it selfish, dear,' said his mother, with gentle disapproval.

'No,' said the Whip, gravely, for the young man hurt him; as he said, what he called politics were part of himself now.

'No, indeed.   Where men of birth, position, and wealth give themselves up—their time and amusements sacrificed—to working, for no salary, for their country, they can scarcely be called selfish.'

'You might as well say that amateur actors are unselfish to do it gratis; and very badly they generally do it.   It strikes me that a good many things are selfish which we are accustomed to think the reverse. Ask the unpaid magistrates if they want to give up the privilege of doing judge's work for no salary, or the colonels of volunteers, or the fellows who do coachman's work, driving four horses up and down the same roads day after day without any pay or any fees.   I'm not sure, indeed, that what we call patriotism isn't selfishness.   If you—-But, good heavens, mother!' he exclaimed, checking himself, 'here am I giving you a regular lecture.   Please forgive me, Lord Scobell; I am not often taken like this.'

'I like a young man to hold strong opinions,' said Lord Scobell, who had none whatever of his own, unless knowing which side his bread was buttered can be called an opinion; 'because he has something to hold by and to change.'

'That's a pretty sentiment!' said Harry, laughing, and wondering whether the man was a fool or thought he (Harry) was one. 'Are you busy in the House just now? I declare I haven't read the parliamentary reports for the last week.'

The Whip looked at Mrs. St. James with raised eyebrows, as who should say, 'Nothing but a woman could keep a man for a week from the parliamentary reports,' and then took his leave.

'He's a nuisance. I hate your professional politician,' remarked the young man, as soon as he was out of earshot.

'Just now you said the amateur ones were no good.'

'By Jove, you have me there, mother!' he cried, bending down to her and kissing her cheek, which was not wholly innocent of artificial colouring. 'The fact is I don't know what I think, or whether I do think or mean to think anything of these matters. I can't help to govern the country; I can't govern myself yet. Why I don't even know which side of the House I shall sit on when I do go in for it seriously—if I ever do.'

'Oh, Harry! it is your duty.'

'I'm not sure of that. But why are we so political all of a sudden? I declare Lord Scobell leaves a sort of bureaucratic scent behind him. I feel all bound up in red tape and official pomposity and humbug when I see him.'

'He's a very important man—to his party, dear.'

'I'm glad you added the last words. Party and country are very different things.'

'And very clever in politics.'

'I don't believe he knows as much English history as would pass him into fifth form at Eton. I feel pretty sure that if you asked him suddenly what Magna Charta was about he would take time to think it over.'

' He wants you to take some interest in the debates,'
said she, with mild persistence.

' Does he?   Of course every fresh fool magnifies his
office of whipper-in of the fools.   The bigger the pack
the greater man he.'

' And I want it too, dear.'

' Do you?   Well, we'll see about it.   I suppose I
shall have to do something.   Do you know, I often wish
I had to earn my own living.   I never was meant to
be a rich man.   I feel ashamed of being so comfortable
when others are working for their dinners; and I hate
being able to indulge my laziness and do nothing.'

' Yes ; you want an interest.   You must become a
great statesman, and you must marry.'

He started as she said the last word, and she
noticed it.

' You don't like the idea of marrying yet?' she
asked, wondering to herself what girl could possibly be
good enough for this son of hers.

' I—for Heaven's sake let us get off these solemn
subjects, mother.   Tell me all the news.   Have the
Carandoles come together again, and where has the
wicked one flown to ?'

His stratagem succeeded easily enough.   Soon Mrs.
St. James was deep in the iniquities of the world in
which she lived, and politics and marriage were both
for the time forgotten.   Only for the time, though.
Independently of her ambition for her son, her ambition
for herself would suffice to make her strain every nerve
to deserve the good offices of Mr. Dashleigh with the
Duke of Ulster, *viâ* Mr. Chartwick.

We will now go back a few hours, and see what it
was that kept Harry from at once waiting on his
mother after arrival, as had always been his wont.

CHAPTER XXXV.

AMALIA HECKTHORPE did not live in the same house
where Harry had seen her sister Jane; she had lately
rented for a time a curious little place at the end of a
narrow passage—which also led to a mews—in one of
the innumerable small streets in that debateable land
which lies between Pimlico proper (or improper, if you
like) and South Belgravia. It was a funny, tumble-
down cottage, but not without its charm; for it
was unlike any other London house: it had well-shaped
and not too small, though very low rooms; and its position gave it an air of privacy that had not always been
undesirable to its various tenants.

Her retinue consisted at present only of one woman
and the woman's daughter—a ' slip of a girl ' who did
most of the real work of the establishment.

And the retinue certainly worshipped its mistress
—if the worship was mingled with just a little fear.
There was something about the handsome, fearless,
clever, and unscrupulous woman that had much effect
upon her equals; and joined to her other qualities was
a *bonhomie*—if one may use the phrase in connection
with a woman—that always gained her the unquestioning obedience and respect of her inferiors. On the
morning of the day when Harry was expected in
London, let us imagine ourselves in her largest room,
which went by the name of drawing-room. Amalia had
given strict orders that the term ' parlour ' was never to
be used.

' Please, miss,' said the housekeeper, or maid-of-all
work, coming suddenly in, ' here's Mrs. Fitz-Jones.'

' Show Mrs. Fitz-Jones in,' said Amalia, who was
very neatly clad, and who appeared altogether to have

improved in her notions of dress and deportment within the last few weeks.

Then Mrs. Fitz-Jones, an elderly but well-preserved lady, tripped into the room, and the moment the door was closed by the housekeeper was received by her hostess with an exaggerated curtsey worthy of a Queen's Drawing-Room.

'Was that right?' asked Amalia, rising with some slight awkwardness.

'Not quite,' said Mrs. Fitz-Jones, in languid but very carefully pronounced accents; 'there was a little deficiency of *finesse* about the arm during the curtsey, and a want of absolute harmony in the motions of the legs and head in rising.'

Down went Amalia again, and this time a faint smile took the place of the critical frown that had hitherto been on the visitor's face.

'Much better; very good, indeed; but there was— I think there was—excuse the expression, but at the moment I can find no better—a slight wobble even then in the rise.'

A third attempt was more successful; and Mrs. Fitz-Jones proceeded, in a most leisurely and lady-like manner, to divest herself of her wraps and bonnet.

'Is it to be an hour?' she asked, in a business-like tone.

'Yes,' said Amalia.

'And the usual price?' This still sharper.

'I think ten shillings ought to do.'

Mrs. Fitz-Jones took up her bonnet, and, compressing her thin lips, began to put it on.

'Although,' she said, as she tied the ribbon under her chin, 'I have fallen from the position that I once occupied, and am obliged to sell my knowledge of good-breeding and aristocratic manners for my bread, still, Miss Heckthorpe, I have not fallen so low as to bargain for shillings.'

'Very well,' said Amalia, coming up to her and putting her hand on her shoulder; 'very well, fifteen bo—I mean shillings, as usual. I am afraid I shall not be able to take many more lessons.'

'And you are so far from perfect still,' murmured the other, removing her bonnet.

'All the more reason for wasting no time. Now sit down.'

Mrs. Fitz-Jones took her seat, arranging the folds of her gown with haughty care, upon an armchair at the end of the room, and Amalia retreated to the door.

'The door is thrown open by a footman,' said the lady in the chair, in solemn tones, 'and he announces to the Countess of A. the visit of the Viscountess of B. The Viscountess of B. follows him up the stairs—not too slowly, for that would imply indifference or rudeness; not too quickly, for that might mean over-eagerness—and enters the room. She advances towards the Countess, who rises to receive her, and comes forward about five steps from her chair, wearing on her face the appearance of glad welcome.'

Mrs. Fitz-Jones had suited the action to the word, and was standing exactly five steps from her chair with extended hand, as Amalia advanced with dignified demeanour towards her and grasped it.

'A little too hard, that squeeze,' murmured Mrs. Fitz-Jones, in an aside. Then—'My dear Lady B——'

'My dear Lady A., I am delighted to see you—looking so well too! I hope Lord A——'

'No, no;' again came an aside from the instructress. 'Never ask about the husband. They may have just quarrelled, or a thousand things. Besides, no one cares to talk of their husbands. Now we both sit as simultaneously as possible.'

'I really haven't seen you for an age,' said Mrs. Fitz-Jones, in her *rôle* of Countess.

'No, indeed,' said Amalia, languidly, in a voice and manner singularly unlike her usual one. 'But one has quite a lot to do in the season. I hoped to have seen you at the Duchess's last night.'

'The dear Duchess! But I could not manage it. Was it a good ball?'

'Delicious! All the best people; very few girls. And the Prince was good enough to say that he liked my diamond tiara.'

'Which means that he liked its wearer,' said the Countess (Mrs. Fitz-Jones) archly.

The Viscountess (Amalia) laughed an affected little laugh of depreciation.

'How silly! But he did dance with me nine times, and he took me in to supper. After him it is very hard to care for other men.'

'No,' said Mrs. Fitz-Jones, resuming her own character for a moment; 'I wouldn't have said that, under the circumstances; you see, it has a *soupçon* of—of flattery. You see, you elected to be a Viscountess, and therefore you are not dependent on even a Prince's favour for your position. No, I think you should rather laugh at him; very gently and genteelly, of course, but a little banter of any peculiarities he might have would not be out of place.'

'I see,' said Amalia. Then quoth the Viscountess, 'Do you know, my dear, that he twaddles a little?'

'Ah!'—again intense Countessian archness—'ah! but men do twaddle when they are in love.'

'And he talks of himself so much.'

'Because it is *the* subject he wants you to think of.'

'But Lord B——'

Here Mrs. Fitz-Jones gave a scream.

'No, no! You must never mention *him* in a conversation of this kind.'

'Oh, I forgot. I'll go on. But you see, it is so difficult when the people are all imaginary.'

'Never mind. It will come. To me they all seem real. I remember once when the Duke of——'

'Let's go on with the lesson,' interrupted Amalia, rather rudely. 'I think we'll drop the talk; that must come when I want it. I can generally say what I mean; and I know I can amuse people. But I want to know exactly the way to *do* things. Now let us go to dinner.'

Mrs. Fitz-Jones was hurt; but she recognised the professional nature of the interview, and acceded.

An imaginary butler announced that 'Dinner is on the table, my Lady;' and Amalia, under the supervision of the other, went round the room and confidentially told the furniture whom they were to take in, occasionally introducing a table to a chair where they were not previously acquainted, and finally taking the proffered arm of Mrs. Fitz-Jones, and walking, making pleasant remarks about the weather the while, to the door.

'That is nearly perfect,' said Mrs. Fitz-Jones when they reached it. 'It is one of the most difficult duties of Society; and how seldom one sees it even passably done! I believe there are more solecisms in etiquette made in sending guests down to dinner than in any kind of social duty. And the conversation on the way was right too. You should never say anything that requires any answer until after soup. Before then the conversation should be just enough to prevent a dismal silence, but no more. What shall we do next?'

'I should like to cut you,' said Amalia.

Mrs. Fitz-Jones looked astonished.

'Imagine me,' said the publican's daughter, 'a great lady at a party, and you somebody who has got an invitation there, but whom I think ought not to be received. Here am I talking to a lot of people 'ere—*here*, I mean—*here* are you coming along alone; you bow to me; I look you straight in the face in a loud kind of way—I mean so as everyone sees it.'

Mrs. Fitz-Jones looked at the girl in admiration.

'With twenty more of my lessons, Miss Heckthorpe, you would hold your own with anyone,' she said.

'And I mean to,' remarked Amalia, quietly.

They went through the programme as arranged two or three times, and then they did a little shopping in Bond Street, Mrs. Fitz-Jones doubling the parts of shop-keeper and footman, with an occasional performance of the character of a friend encountered in the shop, and Amalia bought little articles at the counter (her writing-table) and stepped into her brougham (the sofa) until she was perfect in both.

'Should one show one's ankles in getting in?' she asked at the second rehearsal.

'It depends on two things,' replied Mrs. Fitz-Jones didactically: 'whether you have good ones, and whether there is any one to see them. You don't want the shopman who is bringing your purchases out to see them?'

'Of course not,' said Amalia, remembering the time when she had shown them, without the excuse of a brougham to get into, to the admiring eyes of young Ilborough shop youths.

'We have yet a quarter of an hour,' remarked Mrs. Fitz-Jones, glancing at the clock; 'I suppose we had better finish in the usual way.'

'Yes;' and Amalia rang the bell.

'My train,' she said to the 'slip of a girl,' who answered it.

Then a long bit of stuff was pinned on to her waist and swept the ground as she advanced very slowly towards her companion, bearing in her hand a card which she presented to a chair about four feet from that lady, who was standing, uncommonly proud-looking, on a footstool in front of the fireplace.

But when Amalia reached the footstool there was a little difference between the professor of etiquette and the pupil.

'You kiss my hand,' said the former.

'No, you kiss my cheek,' contended the latter.

'My dear Miss Heckthorpe,' remarked Mrs. Fitz-Jones with supreme scorn, 'only peeresses or the daughters of peers receive that honour. I really think you might trust to my knowledge of such things!'

'But I am playing at being a peeress,' cried Amalia, 'and I want to be so.'

'It certainly seems to me almost—almost irreverent; but if you insist——'

'I do. I am a peeress. Do as the Queen would do.'

Then Mrs. Fitz-Jones's thin and bloodless lips touched the soft white and red cheek that was offered her, and the ceremony was completed without further mishap, the train being given to Amalia to put over her arm by the whilom Queen, who had nimbly slipped from her footstool to become an equerry for the nonce.

Then from a very smart purse on which a gigantic A standing on its feet embraced another gigantic A standing on its head, in solid ormolu, was extracted the stipulated sum of fifteen shillings, and Mrs. Fitz-Jones departed, giving her pupil a final lesson as she went on the proper way to leave a room and take yourself out of the house.

Amalia imitated this twice after she had gone, having her maid-of-all-work and the girl to stand on either side of the door in the mews, and sending a stableman who happened to be outside cleaning a carriage into an ecstasy of mingled wonder and ad-miration.

Just as she had come to the conclusion that come what might she at least knew how to gracefully go, a knock and a ring were heard at the door that had wit-

nessed so much deportment, and in another minute
Amalia was holding Harry's unwilling hand, and, looking
into his eyes, was trying to read there something beside
shame and dislike.

Shame and dislike.   Shame that he should be thus
in her power; that he with all his firmness, his force of
will, his position and his wealth, should be thus at the
mercy of old John Heckthorpe's daughter; and dislike
of the woman who, even though it might partly be for
the love of him, could so humiliate him—could purchase
him, as it were, at the price of his honour and his freedom.   Looking into his face Amalia honestly forgot
the position for which she had schemed, for which she
had just now been fitting herself, as she deemed, and
remembered only how goodly his face was, how sweet a
thing a smile on those now compressed and stern lips
would be; how much, in her gross animal way, she
loved the man himself.   And doubtless, had Harry been
a plebeian in a goodish line of business with a sufficient
income to keep a wife well, Amalia would for him have
relinquished her ambitious schemes.   Whatever she
had of heart had gone out to him, and beat down a
certain pride she had which would otherwise have taken
umbrage at his manner—his evident dislike—and thus
have, as she inwardly termed it, ' upset the whole
blessed coach.'

The blessed coach was not upset on this occasion,
however, for she bore his coldness and his short replies
to her numerous queries with a good-natured unconsciousness that nothing could rebuff; and after half an
hour's conversation he began to own to himself that she
had improved wonderfully in every way.   Her dress
was perfect, and her manners really far better than
those of some fine ladies that he knew, while her face
and figure were quite undeniable.   As he looked at her
while she prattled gaily on of her doings of late, and her
difficulties, and her household, and her hopes and fears

for the future, he could not but acknowledge that, turned into a ballroom in smart clothes, she would unquestionably make a sensation, and despite himself a smile came over his face as he thought of the coarse innkeeper's daughter as a possible 'leader of Society.'

The smile gave her encouragement, and she touched upon a topic that speedily drove it away again.

But Amalia had a marvellous capacity for coming to the point.

'I suppose, dear, that you have come to settle about it all definitely ?'

'About what ?'

'About our marriage.'

There was a determination in her voice as she said these words which did not escape him.

He rose and stood facing her, with his back to the chimney-piece.

'You are determined on that ?'

'You know I am.'

'Will nothing else suffice ?'

'That is cruel, Harry.'

As she said this she also rose and stood beside him.

'Cruel! Good God! the cruelty does not seem to be on my side.'

'Do you hate me so much ?'

Few men could have looked into those lustrous eyes, now dimmed by rising tears, and told her they hated her ; but Harry looked steadily at the carpet, and answered coldly enough : 'It is not a question of love or hatred, it is a bargain.'

'You insist on treating it as a bargain ?'

He inclined his head.

'Very well. A bargain be it, and we will be business-like. Yes, I adhere to my terms, which I have told you several times.'

'And will make no change. Any sum——'

She stopped him with an imperious gesture that was only half play-acting.

'Stop! Your whole fortune would not do. Oh, Harry! don't you see—don't you see—I want *you*, not your fortune? If you were as poor as—as Job—I would choose you out of the whole world for my husband!'

He looked up at her. Was any of this real? Certainly there was pathos in her voice, and tears were in her eyes as they met his.

'But,' he began, and seemingly the sentence was difficult to him to finish—'But you can scarcely expect I can look upon a thing forced upon me as this is with any other feelings than those of aversion. You must forgive me if I say that all our tastes and habits are dissimilar. It is absolutely impossible that I——'

'Stop a minute!' she exclaimed, putting her hand on his arm; 'stop a minute! Tell me one thing—are you wanting to marry anyone else? Tell me on your honour as a gentleman.'

'No.'

'Then you *shall* be fond of me! You shall! I will educate myself so as to be worthy to be your wife. You shall never have cause to blush for me. More, Harry; the day shall come when you'll say to yourself that the best thing you ever did was to marry John Heckthorpe's daughter.'

The semi-sentimental turn the conversation had taken was eminently distasteful to Harry, who had come with a vague idea of buying himself free at any cost. This love or pretended love for himself he had scarcely taken into account, and he only half believed in it. As he had listened to the girl's conversation, more than once his mind had reverted to the consequences of defying her. They could not be less than the ruin of Nellie and her boy. True, public sympathy would be

with the betrayed woman; but the fact that she had
been betrayed would rest, the sympathy would die out,
and nothing could alter the facts as regarded the innocent child.   In talking with Nellie he had once made
allusion to a case of bigamy reported in the newspaper,
and had elicited from her a strong opinion of sympathy
with the wife that was no wife, but also an expression
of opinion that she was utterly ruined.

'And suppose there had been a child?' he had
asked.

'Then—oh, it would be very horrible—but the best
thing she could do would be to kill herself and it.'

'You exaggerate things: neither man nor woman
can forfeit their honour and self-respect through no act
of their own.'

And Nellie had replied, 'I don't know.   A singer,
for instance, loses his voice through no fault of his own.
It is all he has, and people may be sorry for him, but
he is not engaged any the more for that to sing again
in operas or concerts.   His *raison d'être* is gone.'

Then the conversation had changed, leaving on
Harry's mind a profound impression that the exposure
of Humphrey's crime would be the death of the woman
he loved.   He would give his life for her, he said to
himself; and now he was called upon to do it.

'Take any shape but that,' he exclaimed with
Macbeth and with so many others to whom the actual ill
is always the worst possible ill; yet, when he looked
upon the comely woman beside him, who was so relentless in the use of her power to gain him, the idea did
come into his mind that the situation might have
been worse, and he shuddered as he thought of what
the daughter of John Heckthorpe might have been.

Before he left Amalia's house he had consented
within a week to arrange all the details of their projected
marriage, to take place in a month's time; and she on
her part had agreed not to insist on the making of it

public for another three months, stipulating, however, that she was not thereby to forfeit any of the rights and glories of his wedded wife, and that moreover he was, as she put it, after that time to make the best of his bargain and not to show any shame on her account before his world.

One question she put just as he was leaving :

'Tell me, Harry, you do this thing for the sake entirely of—of Mrs. Erdmore ? '

'Yes.'

'You love her ? '

'You have no right to ask that.'

'I think I have ; but I don't ask it as a right.   Do you ? '

'I think I am giving good proof of it,' he said bitterly, and departed.   It galled him to hear Nellie alluded to by the woman who in a short month was to be his own wife !

CHAPTER XXXVI.

Telling a story by taking the liberty of reading the correspondence of one's characters is generally, I think, a clumsy fashion, and is apt to weary the reader if persisted in.   Even that infamous yet delightful French novel which we have all read, but only speak of with bated breath in smoking-room or other wicked place, loses greatly by the form in which its plot is revealed, while some of the old-fashioned English romances are rendered absolutely unreadable by the same cause.   After these prefatory remarks, no one will be surprised at my giving the following letters.

The first is from Harry, written, a few weeks after leaving Ireland, to Nellie Erdmore.   Its constrained tone may be accounted for by the fact that it was as likely as not to be perused by that lady's husband.

'My dear Mrs. Erdmore,—When an important thing is about to happen to anyone—one of the most important things in his life—he naturally feels an inclination to tell his friends of it, and as I think I may be permitted to look upon you as one of my closest friends, I write to tell you that I am going to be married.

'There are circumstances connected with this marriage that render it advisable to keep the fact private for the time, but before long the world will know the fact, and—I may as well tell you at once—all the world will blame me for what I shall have done. I don't want you to join in that blame, Mrs. Erdmore. One day, I remember, you sketched out to me the sort of woman you thought a man should look for as a partner in life. She should, you said, be capable of sharing his ambitions, of understanding his schemes and desires of the higher kind, of sympathising fully with him even when his trouble was of that sort that refuses to be defined in words—that world-sickness all those with imagination know at times. She should bear a stainless name, and be proud of it and of the one she takes, with the responsibility of shielding both from dishonour. She should know much, for knowledge gives refinement, and she should be beautiful, for true beauty (that of expression as well as of feature) is an outward sign of inward nobility. Well, the woman I have chosen is not one of these. I scarcely know why I am writing this to you—why I recall your words; but I long for someone who can sympathise with me, without understanding clearly why I want that sympathy. Probably no human being will ever know the reason for what I am about to do, and I shall never attempt to defend or excuse myself for that act—only to you. I wish you to know beforehand that I do it with my eyes open—that I do it without shame—that I am acting as I think most honourable men would act in like circumstances. And there is no shame in the past either. Do not misread my words, and do not strive to guess my reason. That would be impossible. Even in your far-off place rumours and talk of the world here do come at times, and you will hear many explanations of what may be called my folly, my madness—my disgrace, perhaps. Believe me, none will be near the truth. I do not ask for any mercy from what is called " Society," but I do want you to know that I am only worthy of pity; and I would only accept pity from one person. Whatever my future may have in store, I shall always look back with a pleasure that no future's grief can destroy to the memory of those happy days at Kilhorty, and I think the memory will not be unpleasing to you either. Good-bye, Mrs. Erdmore. I do not know when we may meet again. If I go abroad for any length of time—which is what I want to do—I must run over to Ireland for a few days' business first, and in that case I shall come over to Castle Erdmore, and say good-bye in person.—Yours ever, 'P.'

By the same post was despatched another letter—to Humphrey Erdmore—which had no beginning—that is, of the usual kind supposed to be necessary for courtesy's sake—and ran thus :

'The person we know of has, I am credibly informed, gone abroad. I have arranged about money matters. There will be no chance of anything disagreeable happening; but you must be very careful as to what you say. Enough of that subject—now to another. I remarked, when at home, your manner to your wife was scarcely what it should be. Considering the circumstances of the case, I have the right to demand of you that you shall treat her with all the respect and courtesy due to a woman such as she is. If you cannot do so from affection, do so from fear of me, for I warn you that her happiness and safety are my only objects in what I am now doing; and that, if I find that happiness and that safety are not secured by my action, I shall have no hesitation in permitting you to receive the punishment you merit.

'If we meet it will be best we should not meet as strangers, but I beg you to understand clearly that our friendship, or even our real acquaintanceship, are at an end.   'P.'

To go on with the objectionable practice—bad habits are so very pleasant—I will now put before the unfortunate reader Nellie's answer to Harry's somewhat clumsy and vague letter. Poor fellow! he scarcely knew what he intended to write, and the result is not surprising. I have noticed the same result with regard to eminent novelists of our day, and even —*mutatis mutandis*—in the speeches of Cabinet Ministers.

'What are you going to do? Oh, Harry, pause before you sacrifice your life. I can imagine no circumstance that can oblige a man to perjure himself at the altar; nor do I think, in your position, you have the right to ruin a career that might be so useful and so great. I cannot guess what the cause may be, but I *know* that it *must* be inadequate. By the friendship between us, of which you speak, I implore you to pause. Surely there must be some way of avoiding the fate you dimly foreshadow!

'You say so little of her—save that she is *not* what your wife should be—that I find it difficult to speak of her. But how can I give my sympathy to you when you want it for an act so hurtful to your own self? No. The very affection that I have for you, dear Harry —the affection of a sister, and of which I am not

ashamed—forbids me to give you the sympathy you
ask.   If a man told me he intended to cut his throat,
and asked beforehand for my pity, could I give it?   I
might pity his madness, but my only thought would be
to prevent the effects of that madness—to take away
his razor.   Cannot I persuade you to put away your
razor?   But I am only a woman—a woman who has
seen nothing of the world.   Have you not consulted
someone else—some man friend, on whose judgment
you might rely, as well for what the "world" *would*
say as for what the just part of it *ought* to say?   That
always seems to me to be the real true object; to act
so as "Society" (meaning the best educated of our
acquaintance) *ought* to praise, although they may not
do as they ought.   Write again, dear Harry, and tell
me you have reconsidered your resolve.   There can be
no reason strong enough to dictate your lying to
Providence in His church.   Forgive me for venturing
to say all this.   You know you asked for my sympathy,
and I *must* tell why I cannot give it.—Yours ever,

'NELLIE.'

This letter caused its writer almost as much difficulty as that to which it was the reply.   And, indeed,
few persons would have found it easy to write about a
subject so very ill-explained as was that mentioned in
Harry's epistle.

That the man she loved best on earth was in dire
difficulty, in imminent danger, and that she had no
power to save him was all she realised; and her despair
at receiving no reply to her impassioned appeal to him
to save himself was extreme.   This despair was not
lessened when one morning, about a month later, old
Mr. Erdmore came down to breakfast bearing in his
hand a copy of *The Spy* (a very amusing journal of
gossip), and asked whom she considered to be pointed
at in the following passage:

'What an extraordinary family it is! One committing suicide by pistol, the next by canoe, and now a third killing himself socially by wedding a publican's daughter! Can it be that wealth, when beyond a certain point, deranges the intellect? Could not his Lordship's family have taken steps to lock him up? The idea of some hundreds of thousands of pounds a year being in the possession of a fair lady whose ambition has been hitherto confined to serving commercial gents with goes of whisky-and-water really comes up to a grave social scandal. I wonder whether the ancestors hanging on the walls of M—— Castle will leap from their frames when Lord P—— brings home his blushing bride. The days of the Upper House appear to be numbered. How can young gentlemen be allowed to make laws for us when they cannot even arrange their domestic affairs with decency?'

A publican's daughter! What could it mean? As Nellie put down the paper, saying that she hated these scandalous stories, and believed they were invented to fill up a column, she almost turned sick at the thought of her noble Harry, who in her estimation was scarcely of common clay, having laid himself open to such vulgar attacks as these.

. . . . .

The soul of Mrs. St. James was glad within her. The windows of No. 53, Belgrave Square shone with unaccustomed brilliancy; the linkman and the policeman with difficulty kept back the little mob that impeded traffic on the pavement, as they stood at the door to watch the great ones of the land descend from their chariots and pass in to partake of rich viands, washed down with generous wines. What a great business it was! To get the Prime Minister was much, but to get the Duke of Ulster on the same night was more than falls to the lot of many hostesses. Then there

was, too, Mrs. Maintenong, whose presence was as hard
to ensure as that of Royalty ; and Octavius Pimpernel;
and Lord Babbleton, the great Whig minister, the secret
pride of the Radicals, the secret hope of the Tories;
and there was Mr. Chartwick, the millionaire, with his
two heiresses, for whom every impecunious youth in
the town was sighing, but who were destined, as was
publicly announced, for first-class coronets only ; and
there was Lord Scobell, pushing and amusing, impart-
ing bits of parliamentary backstairs gossip with an air
that invested them with the importance of Cabinet
secrets ; and Teddy Dirtell, of *The Spy*, the literary
bravo of the day, so clever with those stabs in the back,
so bold in personal defiance on paper, so callous as to
personal chastisement, so feared and fêted in consequence.   And there too—this being not the least of
Mrs. St. James's triumphs—was her son—the *parti* of
the day (for the Duke of Ulster was supposed to have
a legally wedded wife, either in Germany or St. John's
Wood), the social enigma of the day, of whom his
friends said, 'He could do anything if he chose,' and
his enemies, 'Gone in the head, will be in a strait-
waistcoat within the year,' but whom all fawned upon
and courted.   And there were gathered together many
other great ones, to enumerate whom would be tedious,
but who, my readers will kindly take my word for it,
were all of the bluest blood, highest rank, and most
irreproachable fashion, even including Harry Kelt and
Lord Adolphus Canway, the latter of whom hurried
away directly after dinner to 'the House,' not because
he had anything to do there that night, but because it
came into his part as a tremendously rising politician.
Lord Adolphus, I may mention by the way, went on
the principle that if you only spoke often enough, the
odds were in favour of your sometimes speaking well,
which is nice logic, though some illogical listeners
refused to see it.

The dinner was a decided success. Mr. Dashleigh was a great man in reality, and therefore was not obliged to keep up any dignity; the Duke of Ulster always unbent after the fifth glass of champagne; Harry Kelt had a flow of anecdote that was practically inexhaustible; and Teddy Dirtell kept the table in a roar when the ladies had left. He generally communed gloomily with himself when in the presence of what he called 'ladies,' in contradistinction to those fair creatures to whom his full-flavoured repartee and wit was a thing of beauty and a joy for ever.

Mrs. Maintenong looked lovely in —— (but that was fully reported; see Society papers *passim*), and distributed her smiles with delightful impartiality. After dinner she managed so that the Duke of Ulster should be monopolised by one of the Ladies Arcade (who was a true daughter of Lady Burlington—*the* Lady Burlington), and that our hero should somehow find himself obliged to sit beside her.

'I never see you now,' she said, plaintively.

'You would have had to see across the Irish Channel,' remarked Harry, wondering at the smallness of the foot that peeped out underneath her dress, and remembering the funny story of the button-hook he had read in *The Spy*.

'Yes, you must have had a great attraction there. Is she married or single?'

'Dark or fair, young or old, and has she had the measles? You ought to send me a form to fill up.'

'I will, if you promise to fill it up truthfully. You know I am very much interested in you. And so you are going in for politics in earnest at last?'

'Am I? I didn't know it.'

'Oh, yes. Mrs. St. James—what a pretty woman she is for her age!—told me so just now; and I asked Mr. Dashleigh, and he said he considered you likely to make a great success.'

T

Mr. Dashleigh had said nothing of the kind, but flattery rarely descends to the details of fact.

'That's very kind of him,' said Harry, a little absently. 'I believe my mother does want me to, and old Scobell is always bothering about it. But I don't care about the thing. Besides, I'm in the wrong House.'

'It's only the wrong House,' said Mr. Dashleigh, who happened to come up and to overhear this sentence, 'because there isn't enough energy in it. I see no reason whatever for the idea that has lately sprung up that a man is shelved when he enters it. It's that idea—which is false—that has done so much to paralyse its energies. A vicious circle.'

'That's what they call my tea-parties!' cried Mrs. Maintenong, who didn't mean the conversation to take a serious tone, and who wished Mr. Dashleigh at the bottom of the sea.

'Do they?' said the Duke of Ulster, who had escaped, with difficulty, from Lady Grace Arcade. 'What a libel! Why, I go there!'

'Oh, but you go to square it,' said Harry, who was not over fond of his Grace.

The latter, not understanding, looked sulky, and leaning over Mrs. Maintenong, whispered in her ear. He was, you see, too great to have good manners, as lesser people understand them.

But Mrs. Maintenong would have her way, though the White Czar himself forbade.

'You're not to go away!' she cried, as Harry moved off. 'Come back and sit down. I haven't seen him for a thousand years, and I declare he won't talk to me for a moment.'

Mr. Dashleigh, with a smile, moved away, and the Duke was obliged to enter into conversation with Mrs. St. James, who at that moment addressed him.

'Ah!' said the Prime Minister to Lord Scobell a little later, as they were walking together towards Westminster, 'I sometimes think that youth and a woman's smile are better things than ambition and power.'

'Do you?' was the Whip's astonished answer; and he mentally settled that, for once in his life, Mr. Dashleigh had drunk a glass too much wine.

But to return to our beauty and Harry, who were now left together.

'You have quite given me up,' said she.

'It hasn't afflicted you much,' he retorted.

'How do you know?' This with some energy, and a little quick movement of her hands that was rather French and quite pretty. 'Do you think a woman nowadays is to sit sighing and singing "He cometh not"? And yet many of us are very, very weary.'

She was in her most dangerous mood; and, despite himself, Harry felt a tingle in his veins. She looked so soft, so pleading, and so very fond of him!

'I don't know,' he answered, with outward calmness. 'Most women would, I fancy, change places with you pretty readily. The Cannibal——'

'Stop! Don't talk of him. I hate the sound of his name, particularly as it is always being mixed up with mine. I suppose that's what you were going to talk about?'

'Yes. One can't shut one's eyes and ears.'

'I should like to cut off most people's ears and to burn out their eyes.'

'That's a kind wish.'

'I thought you, at least, were above common, ill-natured tittle-tattle.'

'Is it only that? Can you tell me so, Mrs. Maintenong?'

'Flossie.'

'Flossie, then. Can you?'

She looked down at the tip of her shoe for a moment, and then up into his eyes; and hers were suffused with tears.

'Harry,' she said, in a gentle voice, whose tremble made it dangerously sweet, 'I don't set up to be better than my neighbours. But I will tell you one thing— if you won't look so cross.'

'Am I looking cross?'

'You were. Well, here's my confession, though you haven't got a bit of right to it. I think—I like you best in the world of any one—and—and Tom next. The rest might just as well be tailors' blocks for all I care.'

This was a difficult speech to answer, and he was rather relieved when his mother swept down to summon him to bid adieu to Lady Burlington, whose magnificent coach stopped the way.

Soon after the party broke up—most of them to meet again once or twice that evening; but before Mr. Dashleigh went he said a word to Harry on the stairs.

'Will you read some papers about the forthcoming Land Bill if I send them to you? I should like to interest you in the most important measure it has ever been my lot to bring forward.'

Harry was flattered, as any man of his age would have been, by the request, and readily promised his greatest attention to the subject.

'We shall have him,' whispered Lord Scobell to his hostess as he took his leave. 'Have you got your card for the dance at Granderly House? Chartwick spoke about it, I know.'

'I got it yesterday,' replied the beaming lady. 'Good-night, *my dear* Lord Scobell.'

CHAPTER XXXVII.

POLITICS in real life are bad enough, but politics in a novel are generally worse. They interrupt the flow of the story, and they entail upon the reader, who has no time to waste, the trouble of performing that not too easy operation of skipping—I mean that *judicious* skipping which requires practice. The gentleman from the Far West who read 'Hamlet,' leaving out the speeches of the Prince of Denmark because they seemed dull, and then complained that the plot of the play was hazy, does not present an example to be followed.

So we shall have little in these pages of Mr. Dashleigh's Land Bill, which was creating such excitement at the moment of which I write, and which, while pleasing many enemies of the party which that gentleman led, offended grievously many of that party's friends. Harry was as good as his word, notwithstanding the peculiar position he was in, and the many things which took up his time, and did read most carefully the papers sent to him by the Prime Minister's secretary. Being clear-sighted and just, he at once recognised that these concessions to the Have-nothings contained in the proposed measure ought to be made, and also that these concessions would be a severe blow to the 'landed interest,' as it is called. Singularly clear from class prejudices as he was—having been, as it were, a working man himself—he winced a little as he considered what the beginning of a change in the direction to which this measure of Mr. Dashleigh's pointed might mean to the land-holding aristocracy. But he was, against his wishes, convinced; and before long he wrote to Mr. Dashleigh in this wise :—

'Dear Mr. Dashleigh,—I have read with care and

attention the papers you were good enough to send me. I think they prove the justice—the inherent justice—of your measure; and if I have hesitated in making up my mind as to the advisability of that measure, it is because I am not always sure that in this world justice should not be sometimes tempered with expediency. It may be that a man has a right to a certain thing, although he knows not of that right, but that it is well to keep it from him till he has learned how to use it when he gets it. But such arguments as these—not dealing with actual facts, concerning which we all have the privilege of an opinion—are scarcely for me to bring forward when such experience as yours and Lord Babbleton's goes the other way. If I see a thing is just, and you say the time has come for it, how can I—whose knowledge of the world and of politics is so limited—say "No" to you? I will gladly support the measure you are about to bring forward—at any rate with my vote. As to my voice I cannot answer for that. I don't think a bad speech would do the Bill any good, and I am sure I should hate to make a bad one. If I feel like saying anything that is not wholly useless, I shall ask Lord Scobell to put me on the list for the second reading debate. I need scarcely tell you how flattered I feel at your taking the trouble to show me the rights of this question, nor how I shall attempt to merit the kind opinion of my intelligence which, it seems, you expressed to my mother the other night. Of course you knew that a mother could not keep such pleasing news from her son. Believe me, my dear Mr. Dashleigh,

'Yours very truly,
'PICCADILLY.'

Mr. Dashleigh's secretary was not altogether pleased when he read this letter. There was, he thought, too much self-assertion and a dash of levity in it that

should not be in a letter addressed to a Cabinet
Minister, especially a Cabinet Minister of whom he,
Mr. Loddy, was private secretary. But Harry had
not exactly been in a good temper when he wrote it.
In the first place he rather resented the way in which
the plot had been laid to drag him into politics against
his will; and, besides that, he had so many important
things to think about at the time, that whether English
tenant-farmers got advantages and concessions seemed
to him almost unimportant. Let a man take as much
interest in public affairs as he may, he will always, or
nearly always, put domestic matters first. He will care
more in his heart for his child's mumps than the
'Abolition of the Drinking of Wine by Landlords
(Ireland) Bill,' although the latter may mean the salvation of a teetotal Celtic peasantry's morals. And
Harry's domestic affairs just now were, it must be
admitted, a little 'mixed.' Despite himself, the idea
of his lofty position had crept into his mind, and he
was continually being shocked at the idea of Lord
Piccadilly marrying so far beneath him. He only
wished that he had a brother and the power of abdicat-
ing in his favour, and then hiding himself away in
some remote spot with the woman he was obliged to
tie himself to for life. To bear the double burden
seemed almost impossible; and when he thought of
what would be the inevitable results of that fierce light
which beat upon his place in Society, and of the natural
anger of all that Society at his defection from the
ranks of 'rich men to marry,' he shuddered. If I have
at all succeeded in shadowing forth his character, it
will have been seen that he was not a man who cared
unduly for the verdict of his fellow-men. He had
always been of Nellie Erdmore's creed, that as long as
you merit their good opinion you are right; but he
might well pause before he flung down the gauntlet of
defiance of *les convenances* by marrying a publican's

daughter. If you do a thing that seems outrageous to the world, and decline to explain your reasons for so doing, the world has a perfect right to blame; for the fact of being born puts each of us in a more or less public position of responsibility. And in this case he could offer no reasons, no explanations. He had just to bear the blame, if possible without too much brazenness, but certainly with no appearance of shame or apology. And then, to make it all the more bitter, the woman for whose sake alone he did this thing herself blamed him; refused to sympathise with him in his trouble! It certainly seemed very hard, and when he walked down to the House of Commons one evening to hear the provisions of the great Bill explained by Mr. Dashleigh in his gracefully lucid style, it is to be feared that thoughts of Nellie and Amalia Heckthorpe often obtruded themselves in the midst of the figures and arguments so skilfully marshalled by that politician.

'D——d humbug!' remarked a young nobleman who sat next him in the gallery, when the Prime Minister had sat down amid the ringing cheers of his partisans. 'It'll never pass our House, eh, Harry?'

'Never,' echoed Harry, absently; wondering what his companion would say if he knew his own story.

'Why, you are going to speak in favour of it!' exclaimed the noble Lord on his other hand.

'Who said so?'

'Scobell. He says that Dashy looks upon your support as its best hope with us.'

'Does he?' said poor Harry, feebly. 'Then he must indeed be hard up for help there.'

'Why, surely, old chap,' said the young man who had first spoken, eyeing a Radical member below, just risen, with supreme contempt, 'you can't go in for Communism?'

'It isn't Communism; but I really can't argue

about it now. If you'd listened to Dashleigh's speech
you'd know it wasn't Communism.'

'Oh, Dashy can prove anything. They say he
once proved to a starving beggar in the street that he
had had a good dinner, and sent the man home quite
cheery. If you go against your order—a man like you
—I declare—well—'pon my soul—I don't know what'll
happen next.'

'That's a state I should say you were often in, my
dear boy. To know what will happen next is *the* great
secret of success in life.'

'Well; d—— it!—I've succeeded pretty well. If
winning the Derby the third year you're on the Turf
isn't success, I don't know what is.'

'Who do you think won the Derby—your horse,
your trainer, your jockey, or yourself?'

'Why, the whole boiling of us. If I hadn't bought
the horse, and engaged the trainer and the jockey——'

'Someone else would have; and the fact of his
being able to gallop faster than the other horses he
met would have had the same result.'

'Well, I call that rather hard on a chap. But
you've got quite queer lately, Harry—you used to be
such a cheery fellow.'

'Hush!' said Harry, leaning over the rail. 'I want
to hear what Mr. Dilblain is saying.'

'Good Lord! If you want to listen to a d——d
Radical!' exclaimed the young peer; and he rose
and proceeded to Spratt's, where he announced over a
glass of whisky-and-water that Harry Piccadilly had
been 'got hold of' by that brute Dashy, and that in
consequence the speedy deterioration of his character
might be looked for.

In the meantime this victim sat on in the Peers'
Gallery of the House of Commons, wondering at the
animation there, which contrasted so strangely with the
gravity, not to say dulness, of his own gilded chamber,

and also wondering a little at the patience with which the faithful Commons listened to speeches which in the Lords would have been met with a gentleman-like inattention, chilling enough to strike silence into the heart of the most fiery Irish member. After about an hour of this amusement he was tapped on the shoulder, and looking round was surprised to see Mr. Dashleigh behind him.

'We shall not divide to-night,' said the great man, 'and I am going home. I think our ways lie some distance together; will you walk with me? I always walk home from the House if possible. We servants of the nation do not get much time for exercise.'

Of course the young man consented, and was soon arm-in-arm with the Premier, listening to his flow of conversation, and wondering what would happen if one of those cabs that dashed past them at a crossing were to put an end to the life of such a man.

'There is nothing very fine in politics, perhaps,' he said, in reply to a remark of Harry's as to his want of belief in that occupation; 'but next to religion it certainly comes first in human occupations. I was myself brought up for the Church, and had I felt a vocation for it I daresay I might have done more good as a clergyman than I have ever done as a politician. But I should have done harm to myself. The first thing to learn in my profession is to look ahead. There are many little things that have to be done and borne that jar terribly at first against our conscientiousness. It is only by keeping the grand object—the good of one's country—always before one that they can be accepted. I don't mean for a moment to adopt the so-called Jesuits' motto, that it is allowable to do evil that good may come; but I do say that in dealing with human elements you must adopt human means. If I want a man to help me to pass a measure that will do good to millions, am I to risk the loss of that good because I cannot consent to approach that man in the only way—perhaps an ignoble, or even a hypocritical way—in which he can be approached? Supposing (I take an extreme case) a vote is all-important at a crisis (of course presupposing that my object is one that I am convinced is good), and that vote can only be obtained by purchase—not of money, of course, but of honours of some sort—am I to lose the battle because I am too high-minded to make that purchase which I know all the time statesmen on the other side as high-minded in general affairs as myself will willingly make without a single qualm of conscience? Diplomacy has been defined as lying abroad for the good of your country. Statesmanship is managing men for the same purpose at home. Some require a curb, others go in the snaffle; and your business is to discriminate—to know the light mouths from the hard, the free-goers from the slugs. But behind all this management there is always the sustaining and invigorating consciousness of a grand, a glorious purpose. Yes, a politician's life, with all its petty worries and mortifications, is a fine thing. Here is where we diverge, if you, as I suppose, are going Pall-Mall-ward. Good-night. Don't look at the petty part of the subject, but at the main purpose and meaning of it all.'

'Good-night, Mr. Dashleigh,' said Harry, as he turned down Pall Mall and walked home to bed.

CHAPTER XXXVIII.

A CHEERY knot of men sat far into the grey morning in Spratt's kitchen, and talked of all things under the sun—which was just making London look as if it had never known what gloom and fog mean—and reasoned high over their glasses and cigars. Enter to them a pale and wearied senator fresh from the debate, and thirsting horribly.

'You've heard of Harry's speech?' he said, when his immediate wants had been supplied.

'No! Did he speak? Wonders will never cease! Was it good?'

'Magnificent! He spoke just after Lord Fitzbooble, and the contrast was refreshing. It really was grand. He tumbled over all the arguments of the fine old crusted Tories just as if they were ninepins, and then he turned on the Government and warned them—so impressively that you quite forgot how young he is— that this must not be considered as an instalment of anything, or as the beginning of a warfare against the rights of property. If that was what they meant he would never have taken up the thing; and he ended with what the summary writers call a "glowing eulogium" upon Dashy, saying that his character was sufficient guarantee that this was simply meant as an act of justice and equity, and was not a sop to Revolutionists, Communists, or even Radicals. By Jove! I never saw such enthusiasm in the House of Lords before. All the front bench ran across and shook hands with him; and Lord Turberville got up next and said he had come into the House intending to oppose the Bill, but that Harry's arguments had convinced him, and he should vote for the second reading. And I believe it was true, too.'

'Bravo! Well, I'm deuced glad of it. He's a rattling good fellow.'

All agreed to this, and soon afterwards the conversation changed; and we will leave the gallant murderers of the night to discuss the weighty point as to whether Miss Colly-wobble can give Tom-up-a-Gumtree (horses are so wittily named nowadays) three pounds over a mile and a half, and will follow the successful orator as he drives home from Westminster.

It certainly had been a triumph. After the first few moments, when his intellect seemed to evaporate, his tongue to strike work, and even his legs to be about to give way under him, he had become suddenly aware that he possessed that gift that no art, no teaching can quite supply. Words came as they were wanted, without effort of will or memory, and his thoughts, hampered by no searching for an expression, marshalled themselves readily into clear sequence and logical order. An interruption had shown that his speech was not merely one prepared and learned by heart, for he had taken advantage of the contradiction of a statement of his to turn and rend the interrupter until that noble and didactic Peer wished that he had never spoken. Humour and pathos he had shown too, and the peroration in which, as our friend at Spratt's has told us, he said that he relied on the Premier's character for his belief that the measure he was supporting was no trick to catch Radical votes, brought down a storm of applause such as is seldom heard within the solemn Chamber of Peers. Yet, with the recollection of this triumph fresh in his mind, the expression of his face as he drove towards the Albany was gloomy in the extreme.

Leaving his carriage at the lower end, he walked up the passage of the Albany and entered his chambers. A couple of lamps were alight, and, to his astonishment, in the large armchair before the fireplace and fast asleep, reclined Amalia, looking very handsome in her *abandon* of pose. She had removed her hat and cloak, and had evidently done her best to be comfortable; for an empty teacup lay on the small table at her elbow, and on her lap was a novel, the reading-lamp having been arranged just behind her.

With something very like a groan Harry surveyed her for a few moments, and then took up some letters lying on another table and turned them over absently. The handwriting of one envelope caught his eye, and he chose it to open first. We will read, as usual, over his shoulder :—

'Brussels, July—, 18—

'My dear Lord,—You have been tricked. There is no doubt of it. You have been somehow duped by that woman. She must——'

At this moment Amalia woke with a start.

'Oh, Harry, you have come back at last! Where have you been?'

'At the House,' he answered, shortly. 'But why have you come here? Did you not agree——'

'Oh, yes,' she said, impatiently sitting up in her, chair and arranging her somewhat dishevelled locks. 'I know I wasn't to be seen, or come to you until a certain date ; but I got tired of my own company, and I thought I would look in, only just for an hour or two. Don't be angry, dear,' she went on, seeing the frown upon his face; 'I'll go directly. I only just wanted to see you for a minute, and then you were out, and I thought you wouldn't be late, and I fell asleep. No one saw me but your servant.'

'Very well,' said he, turning away, and proceeding with his letter :

'She must have dressed someone up to represent her sister. You *cannot* have seen her; for I have proof—proof absolute—that Jane Ballard (*née* Heckthorpe) died in No. —, Rue D——, on November 24, 18—, and, as you know, Humphrey Ballard was married to his present wife on the 25th, the very next day. Evidently he thought he was committing bigamy, and I fancy the idea of hiding the fact of her sister's death must have occurred to Amalia directly she heard of Humphrey's marriage. She knew he could not know of Jane's death, and the power over him she got was tremendous. That trick of showing you someone resembling Jane, and thus convincing us and preventing our making inquiries here in Brussels, was wonderfully clever. It was lucky it occurred to me to try this last chance to save you from her clutches. All you have to do now is to snap your fingers at her. I enclose a copy of the certificate of death. You see the date is clear enough. I shall be home in a week or so.—Yours very faithfully,

'C. LACROIX.'

Harry read the letter over twice very slowly. Then he looked at the woman in the chair, who was watching him with lazy curiosity.

'That seems to be a very interesting letter,' she said, as their eyes met. He was in the shade, and she scarcely could distinguish his expression.

He did not reply.

'And when people have only been married a week they ought to prefer each other to any letter, however interesting.'

Again no answer.

'What is the matter? Are you dumb, Harry?'

Then he walked up to her chair, and she shrank from the expression of his eyes.

'When did your sister die?' he asked, almost in a whisper.

CHAPTER XXXIX.

'WHAT do you mean?' asked Amalia, starting out of her chair and retreating before him.

He took hold of her arm, unconsciously hurting her with his grip; and he repeated, still in a low voice:

'When did Jane die?'

'Who told you she is dead at all?' said Amalia, setting her teeth and boldly meeting his look of fury.

'This,' he replied, holding up Lacroix's letter.

'Then it is a lie!'

'It is no lie. My informant has seen the certificate, and mentions the date.'

'Then if you know it, why ask me?'

'Because I will have an answer.'

'Will you let me go? You are bruising my arm.'

He flung her from him with an action of loathing, but she did not shrink now before him. Amalia was one of those women who can rise to an emergency; who can shriek and become helpless if confronted with a mouse, but who can face shipwreck with calm presence of mind. And there are many of such women.

'Jane died before Erdmore married,' said Harry slowly pausing before each word, as if trying to clearly understand the meaning of his own sentence.

'Well?'

'And you dare look me in the face?—you dare exist in my presence?'

'There are few things I would not dare!'

'You knew this all the time?'

'What if I did know it?'

'You tricked me.'

'If you like to call it so—yes.'

'And that woman you showed me was——'

'Do you want the whole story? Well, as you know so much, you may as well have all. I always cared for you—yes, I did, though you shudder now when I say so. I cared for you in the old days at Ilborough; I cared for you that time we met in London; and I have never forgotten the kiss you gave me then. My sister was ill, abandoned by that mean hound, who had persuaded her to do and say nothing, and who sent her a pittance from time to time. She was ill, and sent for me, and

I went to Brussels to see her die. Then, by accident, I found out that the very day after her death the scoundrel married another woman. I determined to be revenged on him, to hide Jane's death, and to work on his fears as a bigamist, which he morally was. Then I met you in Ireland, and I at once saw the state of things between you and Mrs. Erdmore, and that you would do anything to save her from the exposure and disgrace you thought I had the power to bring about. I tell you I cared for you—the idea of your loving this woman drove me mad—and then this plan came into my head. You should think you were saving her, and should belong to me. I was afraid of your making too close inquiries at Brussels, and so I bought a wig like poor Jane's hair—you remember how pretty it was, light brown with gleams of auburn—and got up my face to look ill. We were so alike in features that it could hardly fail. Now, tell me what spying brute has been to Brussels to find it all out !'

He turned away from her with a groan, and leaned up against the mantelpiece, and Amalia heard the muttered words :

'Too late !'

'Yes,' she exclaimed, angrily, 'it is too late. I have won—we are married ! It *is* too late !'

Harry looked at her and shuddered. There was something in her strange beauty, as she stood there, with the light of anger in her eyes, that struck terror into his heart.

This unscrupulous woman—this almost fiend in human shape—was his wife. Her name was Lady Piccadilly !

He tried to speak, but his lips refused to shape the words ; he could only point to the door.

'You want me to go ? Oh, Harry !' and she held out her arms to him with a sudden tenderness that was very pretty and naturally graceful. 'Won't you forgive me ?

U

I did it all to get you. We are man and wife now—
that cannot be undone; and she—the other—could
never have been anything to you. Will you not make
the best of a bad bargain? I will work so hard to be
worthy of my position; I will never give you reason to
blush for me. I learn easily, and can imitate what I
see very quickly. And I have one quality which must
go a long way: I am very, very fond of you. Won't
you forgive me?'

She was kneeling at his feet now, having caught
one of his hands in both hers; and, whether by accident
or design, her hair had come down, and was all about
her in its darkly lustrous beauty.

My friend Dabchick, R.A., who paints sacred
subjects so genteelly, would have given anything to
have her as she was then for a model Madonna. But
it did not move Harry. All he said was one word:

'No.'

'Oh, yes, you will—you must! I will be so good
a wife to you, my darling—better than most of these
fine ladies. I will always think of nothing but you and
your happiness. I have done very wrong—committed
a crime, if you will have it so—but I have done it
only because I love you. I would have done more—
I would have stuck at nothing—to gain you. You
cannot utterly condemn me for a weakness which is
your own fault. Why, if you hate me so much, did
you come so often to our house at Ilborough? Why did
you single me especially out to talk to? Why did you
take me in your arms that day in London and kiss me?
Why are you so clever, so handsome, so all the world
to me? Oh, Harry, you cannot hate and detest me,
because I would die to gain your love!'

And so exclaiming, with tears in her eyes and in
her voice, she flung herself prone upon the floor at his
feet, even as Guinevere lay before the broken-hearted
king.

Then Harry spoke, very slowly and distinctly ; and as he spoke she gradually raised herself, and at the end of his sentence was standing before him.

'Get up, please. Making a scene can do no good. You are right in saying you have committed a crime. It is a crime as black as crime can be. You have, to gain your ends, played the part of a fiend! I can never forgive you. Your pretence of love is scarcely worth alluding to. I content myself with saying that I do not believe you. You have played your foul game for what you value, after your kind. You have a right to your title' (the scorn he threw into these words would have crushed a less strong woman than Amalia into dust, but from her it only evoked a glance of defiance) 'and to the settlement made upon you, and at my death to your jointure. But you have no right to *me*. From me you have earned only contempt and hatred. Now you may go. As to our compact, I shall take no heed of it now. No engagement of that kind is binding on me with such a woman as you are. You have secured a legal claim to certain things. Take them ; but you shall have not one jot more. Now go.'

But Amalia, after confronting him for fully a minute, as he surveyed her with a cold gaze full of loathing, sat down in the chair in which he had found her sleeping.

'You have not named my legal rights. I think there are such things as conjugal rights to which married women who have committed no fault are entitled.'

'Woman, do you presume to argue with me, or to force yourself any more upon me ? Go !'

'I will not go until——'

He interrupted her, with rising passion :

'Then I shall have you removed by my servants or a policeman.'

'Ring the bell, and when they come tell them to

turn your newly married wife into the street. See if they will obey you ! '

He made three steps forward and then checked himself; but before he could draw back she had seized his arm, which was outstretched for a moment as if to execute his threat of ejecting her, and she was covering his hand with kisses.

' Hurt me, do what you like with me ! To be touched by you, to be beaten by you, is better than to be caressed by another man. Turn me out, Harry ! Nay, I will go now, without another word. I will obey you without a murmur; I will go abroad, I will never assume your name; not a soul shall ever know we are man and wife; you shall be as free as you were a week ago—free to marry, and to keep your position in the world—only say that you forgive, that you do not hate me.'

It must be confessed that the pleading of her tearful eyes, upraised to his, was very eloquent; her arms were strong, too, and he could not shake her off so easily this time. At last he succeeded, and she threw herself into the armchair in a violent fit of hysterics.

Now a woman in hysterics is a very difficult animal to deal with. A man in *delirium tremens* is nothing to it. It must be confessed Harry's position was singularly perplexing. Here was he in his chambers at the dead of night alone with a wife who was shrieking, laughing, and crying by turns, and entirely beyond the pale of reason or control.

Burnt feathers he had heard of, but there were no feathers in the place. He had also heard of hand-slapping, and he slapped her trembling, convulsed hand. Cold water he had heard of, and eventually that cure had its effect, and she gradually calmed, lying in her chair and firing minute-guns of distress in the shape of sobs that shook her whole body, white as a sheet, and with closed eyes.

' Don't turn me out yet. Let me get strong enough

to walk,' she murmured, feeling for his hand feebly
with her own. ' I feel so ill; I think I shall die.
Say you don't hate me—say so only once, and let me
go!'

To ask to be allowed to go and to stay in the same
breath was scarcely logical; and it was this fact probably
that made her remark so difficult to answer. At any
rate he said nothing; he only sat in a chair at her side,
and watched the colour slowly return to the soft cheeks;
watched so that he was scarcely conscious of it when he
found her eyes fixed on his with an expression of con-
trition that touched him despite himself. Then she
kissed his hand again, tried to raise herself, failed, and
with fresh access of weeping, fell back in her chair.

' Oh, Harry!' she sobbed, ' if I could only die now
that you have looked kindly on me : before your hatred,
your looks of scorn, come back! I wish you would
take me by the throat and strangle me. My last thought
would be my love for you, my repentance for what
that love has tempted me to do.'

There was a long pause. She had his hand in hers,
and now and again raised it to her white and qui-
vering lips. She was one of those women[1] who are
not disfigured by weeping, and she looked more lovely
than ever as she lay there in her repentant distress, all
dishevelled and helpless.

She had conquered, and she knew it. There would
be no more talk now of policemen, and turning out of
doors, and strict legal rights. After trying all other
weapons, she had taken advantage of that strongest one
pertaining to her sex—its weakness; and with that she
had won the battle. But her victory was not to re-
semble those modern British victories in strange lands,
which generally end in the speedy retreat of the British
forces, so that the general may have leisure to send a
masterly despatch home describing the advantages of

[1] Most heroines in novels are like this.—AUTHOR.

his tactics. She was determined to hold the position
she had taken.

'I think I am strong enough to go now—I can
easily walk till I find a cab,' she said, after another
long pause, during which Harry still watched her; and
rising with much difficulty, she tottered to the table
where lay her cloak and hat, and began, with trembling
hands, to attempt the donning of those articles.

'You are not well enough to go,' said her husband,
coming up to her.

'Oh, yes,' she answered, with a miserable attempt
at a laugh, choked by a sob. 'I am not such a weak
fool as that. I can get a cab somehow.' But her action
belied her words. She dropped the cloak on the floor
and would have followed it had not Harry caught her
in his arms.

'I shall be better in a moment,' she murmured, her
head resting on his shoulder. 'It is only faintness.
Don't trouble about me.'

'You cannot go,' repeated he; and this time she
detected some tenderness in his tone.

Then she fainted in downright earnest (people say
some women can really faint at will), and all question
of her going was suspended till she came to again.

The decorous body-servant was somewhat astonished when he came into the room at eight o'clock to
find a lady lying on the sofa—a lady with a white wan
face and a profusion of dark brown hair straying about
her shoulders, and his master in full evening dress
sitting by her side.

'Get some breakfast at once, and order the
brougham in half an hour,' said Harry, with the
unaccustomed peremptoriness occasioned by the consciousness of being caught in a false position. Then
as the servant left the room he said to Amalia—and
there were no remains of hatred in his face or voice:

'You must have something to eat, and then get

home and go to bed. You are not well enough to talk
over things now. I will come and see you in the
evening.'

Amalia's only answer was to possess herself of his
hand and to convey it to her lips.

'Give me one little kiss to say you forgive me,'
she whispered.

He hesitated.

'No—I do not deserve it. But it would have made
me so happy.'

Then the lips of husband and wife met; and one
more was added to the monstrous list of proofs that a
man is wax in the hands of a clever woman, provided
she be beautiful.

. . . .

'What does this paragraph mean?' asked Mrs. St.
James of Lord Scobell, handing him across the table a
copy of that same number of *The Spy* which had so
distressed Nellie Erdmore.

Lord Scobell put on his glasses, and read it through
twice over.

'Good gracious! It seems to point to—I'll go and
make inquiries at once, my dear lady—at once! But
Dirtell so often gets hold of the inventions of his
enemies.' And the Whip left Belgrave Square, wondering whether the glory of retailing such a story would
give him more pleasure than the grief brought upon
his friend Mrs. St. James by its truth would cause him
sorrow.

His inquiries made those who had not seen the
paragraph, and those who had seen but paid no attention to it, set about finding out its truth; and
before a week had passed all London was ringing with
the fact of Harry's *mésalliance*. There were many
different stories as to Amalia's origin. The publican
version was discarded by those who always amend
every story. Some said she was daughter of a Fenian

head-centre ; others of the clown of the Surrey Theatre; others of a Nihilist who was in the Siberian mines for life ; others that Harry found her serving a term of imprisonment in Coldbath Fields, bribed her way out, and married her ; while the most popular story was that he had got into a scrape during those disreputable days when he was earning his own living, and that this marriage was the price he had to pay some father for holding his tongue. On one thing only were all agreed—that the woman he had made Lady Piccadilly was something very low, very vulgar, very bold, and probably very bad.

And Society was much exercised in its mighty mind as to what should be done to his Lordship if he appeared in it. For he was too great a man to be given the cold shoulder without much consideration.

In the meanwhile the objects of all this talk were spending their autumn in a cottage called Winterbourne, in the Isle of Wight, and Harry was trying to accustom himself to the occasional glimpses of vulgarity that showed through the veneer Amalia had managed to pick up by the art of imitation; while Amalia herself struggled hard to obtain that mastery over her husband through his heart which she had determined on. He scarcely knew whether he hated or liked the woman to whom he had tied himself for life. At times her beauty, her vivacity, her ready wit and anxiety to please conquered him ; at others her ill-repressed selfishness, her innate vulgarity, and her animal nature repelled and disgusted him. It certainly was a strange union, the characteristics of which were all summed up by the cook they had hired out of the neighbouring island-town: 'Why, it's just as if you served up a dish of tripe garnished with truffles.' How the human dish agreed with the great world of diners, and how its ingredients mixed together, we have yet to see.

CHAPTER XL.

WHEN the Duke of Ulster gave a ball at Granderly House, to which festivity the heir to our throne himself was certain to go, the newspapers—even the most serious daily newspapers—were accustomed to make much mention of it, and to devote many precious lines of space to a description of its glories, its beauties and its social importance. His Grace did not often honour Society in this manner; but now and then, when the stable with which he was connected had done an especial good stroke; or when some new money-lending toady came within his lure, he burst forth in a grand ball—as distinguished from the select little dances which could be done cheaply. And the grand balls were very grand. The house was large, and the reception-rooms well arranged; the Corps Diplomatique made a point of wearing all their Orders on these occasions; and beauties vied with one another as to the splendour and harmony of their auxiliary weapons. Of course it was 'the thing' to go to Granderly House, and it has been whispered that, when a fancy ball there had taken place, men have appeared attired in fanciful costumes at Clubs when morning hours were striking, who were not in the list of the invited as published in the papers.

One of these fancy balls is in full swing: and the Duke of Ulster, looking superb as King Henry the Eighth, had done his duties of host with courtesy, tempered by discrimination; just as, according to some historians and politicians, landlordism in Ireland is mercifully tempered by assassination. Poor Lord de Videbourcy had received a bow according to the position he held in Society, and with no snobbish regard for his six centuries of ancestors; while Lord Abchurch (the banker, with a peerage three weeks old)

had been taken in to supper with the Royalties
and Ambassadors. The host had even so far con-
descended as to admit to this honour Mr. Isaac Solomon,
that philanthropist who had come to the rescue of so
many of the aristocracy, and who had only lately been
permitted to make one of the Granderly House set.
But amid his duties, so nobly performed, his Grace
found time for the beautiful desires of his heart, and
envious fair ones remarked, with asperity, that his
attentions to Mrs. Maintenong fell not far short of
being disgraceful. That they were ungraceful no one
averred, and the disgrace—by that sweet feminine logic
which almost reconciles us to the continued exclusion
of women from Parliament—seemed to be considered
to belong entirely to Mrs. Maintenong.

But Mrs. Maintenong's triumph did not last all the
evening. It did last until the Royal Personages who
had honoured the ball by their presence departed; it
did last until Mr. Scorchall Windsor (the Society wit)
had said that to those assembled there could be no
morrow, because all was 'Maintenong' (maintenant);
it did last until Mr. Clemmy Diddler, having had his
usual supper, began his usual tricks and antics, to the
delight of his usual admirers; it did last until the
band began to play false and to interpolate visions of
too much champagne into Strauss's harmonies; and
then it collapsed with a crack.

But before we recount this almost tragical occurrence, it is worth while listening to a conversation
between Mr. Kelt and his partner, Lady Gloriana Lane
(Lord Abchurch's second daughter), as they sat toying
with aspic jelly and ortolans at a little round table in
the supper-room.

'And so they have really come to town?' said the
lady, wishing she could, without loss of refinement,
give her magnificent appetite free scope and verge
enough.

' Yes,' answered Mr. Kelt, trying a languishing look but failing, his partner's eyes being inclined to look into each other, and consequently difficult to understand.

' Yes, and I hear that Piccadilly House has been done up from floor to ceiling. Of course the position is very difficult, and I feel for poor old Mrs. St. James.'

' Why do you feel for her ? ' questioned the young lady, looking or seeming to look lovingly at a contiguous dish of cutlets.

' Well, of course, you see, the woman was a rope-dancer—and——'

' You think she won't know how to keep her balance in Society.'

' I don't see how she can be received.'

' Don't you? She will, though. How much is Lord Piccadilly's income ? '

' Oh ! that don't matter.'

' Doesn't it ? Papa was made a peer because he was rich. He never danced on a rope, because he couldn't ; but he could keep other people's balances ; and he cannot pronounce his *h*'s.'

' *H*'s are a matter of prejudice, my dear Lady Gloriana,' sighed Harry Kelt, softy wondering how much Lord Abchurch would put down on the wedding-day, and whether that sum would be disagreeably tied up.

' I daresay most things are. But to return to the new Lady Piccadilly. I don't believe she was a rope-dancer ; and I don't think it much matters what she was. My maid tells me she gets her frocks from Paris, and is very lady-like.'

' Maids are not the best judges, Lady Gloriana.'

' Ain't they ? My maid is far more ladylike than I am, and never drops an *h*. One of our footmen, she told me the other day, really left us because of the

want of refinement in the drawing-room, though he
pretended to leave to go to a country situation; and
I always have to be very careful while I am being
dressed, lest I should shock Eglantine by any indige-
nous vulgarity.'

'High life below stairs,' sighed Mr. Kelt, making
a determined attempt to discover what object it was on
which Lady Gloriana's eyes really rested.

'Low life above stairs, you mean. But tell me
about the Piccadillys. I heard that they were asked
here to-night; but I suppose they won't come. Indeed, it's much too late now, people are beginning to
go. But I do so want to see her. How desperately
in love he must have been!'

'Marriage does not always mean love,' said the
cynical little man; and at that moment Lord Scobell
approached them.

'Oh, Lord Scobell!' cried the irrepressible
banker's daughter, 'do tell me!—is it true that Lady
Piccadilly is beautiful, and well-dressed, and so witty
and fresh?'

'She may be all that,' replied the statesman, sinking into a chair beside the lady, much to Kelt's disgust; 'but she is new, you see.'

'You mustn't say sarcastic things about *us*, Lord
Scobell.'

'Sarcastic! No. But there are degrees of newness.
I mean to go and call to-morrow, and bring your Ladyship a report, if I may.'

'Certainly. You have been very dull at tea-time
lately; and as to Mr. Kelt, I think he must be either
preparing a great speech or in love.'

'People in love,' said Lord Scobell, smiling with the
consciousness of being about to say a good thing,
'very often do make one great speech and afterwards
wish that they had moved the previous question.'

'Well!' said Lady Gloriana, rising, 'I have

finished, and I want to go back to the other room.
I'm going to dance with little Dupuis, the French
attaché, next, and turn round and round on one spot in
the middle of the floor like a top, while he does the
humming in the shape of absurd compliments. Oh!
how I wish I didn't squint; I cannot disconcert a
donkey, as other women can, by looking him full in
the face.'

The couple moved off, and Lord Scobell gained
quite a reputation as a wit by remarking to the next
person he met: 'How impartial Lady Gloriana is
about her oddly-shaped nose! She is always trying
to see both sides.'

The Duke of Ulster had just finished a valse with
Mrs. Maintenong, whose cheeks glowed with the exer-
tion of keeping him from falling—for he was courageous on some occasions, and knew well how to tackle
his own champagne—while her eyes flashed with the
consciousness of having had what gamblers call a 'good
night.' There was no doubt of it. She had been the
queen of the revels; and even Tom, before he went off
to smoke at Martha's, had owned that there was some
excuse for the passionate love of admiration that made
his life so hard to bear. The music had just ceased;
in leisurely fashion the couples sought refreshment, or
corners for flirtation, or chaperons; and the brigade of
male wallflowers and shy youths moved away from the
doorways they had blocked, and plunged courageously
into the throng in mid-room. The leader of the
band looked round upon his little army, and wondered
how soon the second violin would become obstreperous,
whether he himself saw two chandeliers hanging from
the ceiling because of their real existence, or whether
his memory, that told him of only one an hour ago,
was correct after all. Chaperons struck one more
dance off the list of their torture, and looked round
uneasily for the lambs they had brought to market;

and all betokened the beginning of the end of the entertainment.

Then, just as the host was whispering to Mrs. Maintenong that the little arbour in the garden would be a charming place for them to go and get cool in, there was a slight stir in the doorway, a fat dowager was seen to rise and apply her double glasses to her portly nose with a gesture of astonishment; Mr. Kelt was observed to rush forward almost indecorously, and then, right through the throng and straight up the room to where the host was standing, came a tall stately figure, marvellously clothed, with a grace of movement that all acknowledged as they looked, and surmounted by a face of surpassing loveliness. With dark bright eyes flashing, half from excitement, half from self-contained defiance, with masses of brown hair coiled carelessly on a shapely head, ornamented with a string of pearls that set its colour off with good effect, Amalia, Lady Piccadilly, advanced to the Duke, who, seeing Harry behind her, at once understood the situation, and shook her warmly by the hand.

'I am glad to make your acquaintance, Lady Piccadilly. You come late; but better late than never. How are you, Harry?'

'My husband only came back from the country to-night late, and I did not like to come without him,' said Amalia, with much composure; and then, turning towards the Duke's partner, who still stood near him,—

'This is Mrs. Maintenong, I am sure. I have often seen her pictures and longed to know her. Harry, will you present me?'

He bit his lip, but did as he was bid; and in a few moments the two ladies were engaged in animated converse on a neighbouring sofa, while Harry and the Duke stood exchanging occasional words, watching them ; both, I think, wondering which was the more beautiful. And, in half-an-hour, all 'the best men in London' had been presented to John Heckthorpe's daughter.

CHAPTER XLI.

THE dignity of history, as is well known by that eminent true story-teller, Mr. Thucydides Clarendon McCabby, requires us to go into all kind of queer things, reporting them, as members of a court-martial vote, without fear, favour, or affection. And so I offer no apology to my myriads of readers for taking them into the holy of holies, that sweet mysterious precinct 'behind the veil,' where Mrs. Maintenong, after the fatigues of her day and the victories of her night, did lie down 'in her loveliness.'

She was not alone on the present occasion. I hasten to add that her companion was her husband, who sate up (with a pipe) to do duty as a maid when she returned.

'Enjoyed yourself, Flossie?' said Tom, struggling manfully with a string at the back of her 'body,' which refused to yield to his clumsy attempts.

'No—how stupid you are ! Marie is twice as quick.'

'You see, she was educated for the profession,' humbly remarked the poor man, still fumbling.

'She's bad enough, but you're—— There ! You've broken it ! Never mind, Tom. You're a brick, after all, to sit up. I wonder how many pipes you have smoked ! Do you know, I sometimes wonder why you don't run away.'

'Run away !' said Tom, looking at her in vague astonishment.

'Yes. If I were a man and married to what they used to call a P B. I should, I know.'

'You could never have been that. I hate the term!'

'Do you mean to say that I'm not a beauty?'

'No, but——'

'And do you suppose, sir—there, put my frock carefully on that chair—do you suppose I would do anything in an amateurish fashion? If you act on a small stage, surely you want to appear as professional as you can! And it's the same on the big stage, Life.'

'I don't know about that,' said Tom, helplessly. 'I only know I hate the idea.'

'Do you? I'm not sure myself. How do you think I look to-night?' She asked the question suddenly, and taking both her husband's hands, drew him closer to her that he might more conveniently criticise.

'Lovely, dear.'

'Ah, but you're prejudiced. I thought so until——'

'Until what? Did you look into a cracked glass? Or did old Lady Marabout make one of her nice speeches to you?'

'I don't care twopence for Lady Marabout's speeches, and I'm not afraid of any glass—except that third B. and S. of yours, you naughty boy. No; but just as I was thinking of coming home and preventing you drinking it, I was eclipsed! Everyone seemed to be looking at me as if I were an astronomical curiosity, and I wondered at last whether they'd sent for telescopes.'

'How do you mean, Flossie?' asked Tom, taking the opportunity and drawing her on his knee.

'Don't. You make me blush for you, Tom. Who knows but Daddles' (Daddles was their pug) 'is in the room and can see us? Well, I'll tell you, only I can't if you put your stupid old lips in the

way. Be good! I was eclipsed by a paragon of
beauty. Paragon sounds like an umbrella, but I
can't help it; that's the word. I was just like a
candle beside the sun when she stood near me—and
a very little candle, too.'

'And who's the paragon?'

'You'd never guess. Oh, it's all very well for
you to think me nice, but it don't really matter; we
are one, you know; and it's like one's praising oneself.
All the men were at her feet. The Duke (and he
really kept nearly sober all the evening, too; I put
water in his champagne twice when he wasn't looking)
—the Duke is lost!'

'Dear me!'

'Lost to me, at any rate. Fancy its being Harry
Piccadilly's wife!'

'Why, she was a greengrocer's daughter!'

'I don't care whose daughter she was. She is the
loveliest woman I ever saw; and so calm and collected,
and dignified; with poor dear Harry following her
like a lap-dog! He of all men too!'

'You didn't think he would have dropped easily
into a position like—like mine?'

'No, Tom,' said Mrs. Maintenong, with ready
frankness, 'I didn't. I thought his was rather a fine
character.'

'And you think mine——'

'I think you are a duck,' and she kissed him.

'A drake, my dear,' he said, when he had recovered
from the joy occasioned by this rare incident; 'the
husband of the——'

'Oh, Tom!' she interrupted; 'and her diamonds,
and her frock—Paris, of course—and the way she
moved, and the way she snubbed Teddy Dirtell, and
Lord Scobell, and little Kelt, and even his fat Grace!
You would have thought she had lived all her life in

X

houses like Granderly House. I thought, when I heard of Harry's marriage, that I——'

Then it struck her to whom she was speaking, and she stopped.

'You thought what?'

'Oh! Only that he would want consolation from—from somebody, and now he—he doesn't seem to want any consolation at all.'

'Is that all?'

'Not quite all. She is coming here to lunch to-morrow. We have become great friends. You see, you must either be one thing or the other with a woman like that, and perhaps friendship is best—at any rate at first.'

'What a philosopher!'

'I don't know about philosophers. Do they often cry, Tom?'

'Not as a rule, I believe.'

'Then I am afraid I am not one. For I am going to cry.'

'Poor little Flossie! Is it jealous?'

'Jealous! I never heard such nonsense. But to think that Harry should have gone and done such a thing!'

'I don't see how that matters, my dear.'

'Don't you?'

Then she rose from his knee with an air of deep resentment.

'But you never do see anything. That's the worst of it. He was the one man who understood me, and he——'

'I won't have such things said, Flossie,' said the husband, angrily.

Then the little lady, who only wanted an excuse for her tears, declared that he was cruel and harsh, and didn't love her, and that she was lonely and persecuted; and it was quite late in the morning before poor Tom had obtained forgiveness.

In the meanwhile another very different scene had been enacted in Piccadilly House, when its owners returned from the ball.

'I shall do, Harry,' said Amalia, surveying herself in the cheval-glass of her room.

'Do what?' answered he, somewhat sulkily.

'Do for Lady Piccadilly.'

'Will you? Perhaps. Impudence is the great quality needed nowadays for success.'

'Say, rather, looks and tact,' she replied, very calmly, still with her eyes fixed on her presentment in the mirror; 'and I have both. Where are you going?'

'It is too late for bed. I shall write some letters, and then have a ride. You won't appear till luncheon, I suppose?'

'No. Oh, by the way, we lunch with the Maintenongs. I promised her.'

'I always make my own engagements,' said Harry, with some haughtiness; 'and I shall lunch at the Ravellers.'

'As you please,' she answered, as she took off her sparkling necklace. 'As you please. I think I can get on alone.'

Then he left her; and probably, as he sat trying to collect his thoughts for his letter-writing, spent as bitter an hour as ever had fallen to the lot of man. The glamour of her beauty had fallen from his eyes; he saw through her acting; he penetrated the recesses of what seemed to him an ignoble ambition. He even resented her love for himself, while he inwardly rebelled against the success he saw she had cleverness enough to make.

And Amalia, Lady Piccadilly went to bed and dreamed of London's greatest and proudest bending their necks for her embroidered shoe to rest upon.

CHAPTER XLII.

IF it be true, as a great statesman is reputed to have said, that the man who can succeed in 'Society' could succeed in any position, then assuredly Amalia was intended by Nature to be a great woman. For she fairly took the town by storm. Her little vulgarities, it was decided, were charming instances of *naïveté* and freshness ; her crude mixtures of colour in costume were revelations to those weary of monotonous good taste ; her outspoken delight at her new position, and frank amazement at having reached it, pleased those who would otherwise have been her bitterest rivals and foes.

'It does seem so absurd,' she would say to Mrs. Maintenong, with whom she had struck up a friendship, 'that I should be going about into swell houses, and be "hail-fellow-well-met" with Royalties and such like ! I, who once drew beer for all the snobs of Ilborough, and used to think it a great honour to be allowed to mix a glass of whisky-and-water for the leading solicitor ! '

But behind all her outspokenness on this subject there was a distinct view and object. She had seen at once that success could only be attained by striking out a totally new line. The old, worn path of exclusiveness and reserve would avail her not. So she disarmed criticism by laughing at herself, and closed the mouths of the wits by saying sharper things of her victory than they themselves could concoct.

Then, it must be confessed that an enormous income, and one of the finest houses in London, are great aids to popularity, and Amalia took care that nothing of their assistance should be thrown away.

The grave, handsome St. Jameses of days gone by looked upon revelry such as had not been seen in those

lordly halls since Geoffrey, Lord Piccadilly had feasted
Charles II. and vied with Rochester in prurient wit.
All that was most fashionable was collected at least
once a week in the big house overlooking Green Park,
and a sort of perpetual party-giving went on there in
the shape of general invitations to luncheon and tea,
while the dinner-party seldom consisted of less than a
dozen.　At first Harry revolted against living in such
a whirl, but he soon became accustomed to it, and
after a time he discovered that the less he and his wife
were left alone together the better for his peace of
mind.　Politics made an amusement for him, and
there was perhaps in his mind a feeling which he
scarcely himself was aware of—a certain liking for the
position in Society which Amalia had forced him to
assume.　A cottage in the country with Nellie
Erdmore would have been far better, or a villa on
some Italian lake with Flossie Maintenong; but
with Amalia this certainly was the proper life to
live—a life of show, of dazzlement, of splendour, of
everything but thought, and the repose which brings
thought.

'Take care,' said an old friend of his one day; 'take
care that you do not become only Lady Piccadilly's
husband.'

'I am not afraid of that,' answered he; and, to
do him justice, there was no need for him to fear such
a contingency.　He was not one of those men who sink
easily into adjuncts of their dashing wives, such as was
poor Tom Maintenong; for he was a man with a will,
which could be exercised, if he deemed the occasion of
sufficient importance to call for its exercise, with
relentless severity.　His mother scarcely knew whether
to be pleased or the reverse at the turn events had
taken.　An interview with Amalia had been sufficient
to show her — for she was shrewd enough — that
snubbing was impossible and patronage out of the

question. There only remained enmity or friendship; and, like a wise woman, she chose the easier and pleasanter course. Within two months of Amalia's appearance the Dowager found herself actually listening to complaints from the ex-innkeeper's daughter of the shortcomings of Harry, and listening to them with accord and sympathy.

Amalia scarcely knew what it was she wanted of her husband. She knew that there was something to which she should be entitled, and which she did not get.

'Why bother me to come to tea,' he said, 'when you have all the others? I never was a five-o'clock-tea man.'

'But I never see you now,' she complained, stamping her foot.

'It wouldn't be seeing me in the sense, I suppose, you mean, when half-a-dozen other men were in the room. If you like to give up this party to-night I don't mind staying at home after dinner. There's nothing on in the House, and my clubs bore me one more than the other.'

'Oh, I couldn't give up my party; it's one of the best of the season.'

'I wonder how you know,' he said, looking at her curiously, for he had not yet got over his wonder at the victory she had gained over Society.

'By the way, is that odious Lacroix coming to dinner again?'

'Yes. Why do you call him odious?'

'Because—because he is not a gentleman.'

Then Harry fairly burst out laughing; and, not wishing for a quarrel, prudently left the room as he laughed; bethinking himself the while of a certain adage concerning a beggar on horseback.

There were, however, times when the woman's excessive beauty—excessive is exactly the right word

for it—did fascinate his senses.   He had always been
a great lover of beauty of form, and in her there was
not a shape that was not perfect.   He knew, too, that
he had the power, when he chose to exercise it, of
calling into those large, bold eyes a softness that no
one but himself had ever seen ; he knew, too, that
were he to throw aside his coldness and his easy,
sarcastic manner, and adopt a lover's tone, she would
have given up everything for his sake without a pang,
and that she in her heart valued one loving glance
from him more than all her successes in the world
of fashion.   In short, he knew—and he was not
guilty here of self-flattery—that she was in love with
him.

   But in the man there was something that absolutely
forbade him to act a part, or to make to seem a thing
that was not.   So every day Amalia saw more clearly
that she was nothing to him, and she fiercely resented
her inability to gain from the one man from whom it
had any value one of those expressive glances that were
extracted in such easy profusion from her many admirers.

   These admirers could not quite make her out.   She
was such glorious company, 'such good fun,' such a
cheery companion, so natural, genial, and unconventional—up to a certain point.   Then she became
rather alarming, and many a professor of fliration
had gone away from Piccadilly House with a puzzled
hang-dog expression upon his regular features.

   Report even had it that one poor beauty had been
seen walking down Pall Mall with the distinct impression of a human hand marked upon his cheek ; but this
I believe to be a calumny, as a box on the ear would
scarcely have left a mark as far as from Piccadilly to
the end of Pall Mall, and no one in St. James's Street
seems to have noticed it.

   One story that was true created some amusement

in the town; and I may as well tell it here, as it is characteristic of the manner in which Amalia managed her affairs.

The Duke of Ulster, Lady Burlington, Mrs. Maintenong, Lord Scobell, Mr. Kelt, Mr. Teddy Dirtell, and two or three other men were gossiping over tea and bread-and-butter in her drawing-room one afternoon, when the butler announced Mrs. Fitz-Jones.

'Mrs. Fitz-Jones!' repeated Amalia. 'Let me see —oh, yes, show her into the library;' and, apologising for her absence for a few moments, she proceeded to confront her whilom teacher of etiquette.

In a moment she comprehended the situation— comprehended it from one glance into the genteel lady's half-nervous, half-defiant expression.

'Take a seat, Mrs. Fitz-Jones,' she said, with a certain haughty affability which was very well done indeed, and which poor Mrs. Fitz-Jones could never have taught.

'Thank you, my Lady. I took the liberty of calling on your Ladyship——'

'No liberty at all, my dear creature; only just now I have some people in the next room. If you could call again——'

'Oh, I won't detain your Ladyship a moment. I only wished to ask your advice about—about a little literary matter.'

'A literary matter? Have you written a novel?'

'No, your Ladyship. But a gentleman—the editor of *The Aristocrat*, a weekly paper I daresay your Ladyship has seen—he suggested to me that, as I have had so much to do with the aristocracy, some of my reminiscences, thrown into the form of weekly articles, might amuse the public.'

'Dear me! Yes, I daresay they would,' answered Amalia, with languid interest.

' But,' went on the genteel lady, her lips seeming to get thinner as she spoke, ' I am delicate about putting anything in print that might hurt the feelings of any persons who—who were not exactly born to the position they have acquired, and who have had recourse to my knowledge of etiquette to fit them for that position. At the same time, as your Ladyship knows, my circumstances are very, very straitened, and sometimes one's sense of delicacy has to give way to necessity.'

' Indeed !' and Amalia suppressed a yawn. ' If I were you I shouldn't bother so much about the sense of delicacy. By the way, I should like to show you the drawing-room ; and perhaps you'd take a cup of tea ? '

And before Mrs. Fitz-Jones could put on her best company manners she found herself in the presence of the great Duke of Ulster, whom she knew at once by the photographs she had seen of him in the shop-windows, and being contemplated through the gold-rimmed eye-glass of the terrible Lady Burlington.

' Let me present Mrs. Fitz-Jones,' said Amalia with a wave of her hand, and a glance of amusement at the nervously curtseying woman. ' What do you think, Duke—it will interest you at any rate, Mr. Dirtell— she is thinking of bringing out a series of reminiscences of the aristocracy she has known, in *The Aristocrat*. It will be great fun for me.'

' And why for you ? ' asked Mr. Dirtell, eyeing Mrs. Fitz-Jones as if she were a canister of dynamite.

' I'll tell you. When I was horribly frightened at the thought of the awful things I might do to shock all of you correct people, I sent for dear Mrs. Fitz-Jones to teach me better. You would have laughed to see us. She did the Queen on a footstool, and I used to come and curtsey till my back ached. Then we had dinner-parties, and talked pretty to imaginary grandees ; and I used to send the chairs and tables in to dinner with strict regard for precedence — Chippendales coming first and modern Maples last. Dear me! if you describe all that properly, it ought to be capital, Mrs. Fitz-Jones. Really, Mr. Dirtell, you ought not to let *The Aristocrat* get it. Make a bid now for it for *The Spy.*'

Then, amid a shower of chaff and laughter, poor Mrs. Fitz-Jones slipped out of the room; and, as she climbed into an omnibus on the road home, acknowledged to herself that her quondam pupil was a little too much for her.

Next day there came to her a note which was some slight consolation:

'Dear Mrs. Fitz-Jones,—As in the interval, while you are preparing your interesting memoir for the press, you may perhaps be incommoded by want of money, I enclose you 5*l.*, which I hope may be useful to you. I have no objection to appearing in print, but, as Lord Piccadilly has some prejudices on the subject, I should be glad to hear that you had found it possible to avoid any mention of me in that memoir. In such a case I shall hope to be able to be of further assistance to you.—Yours truly,

'AMALIA PICCADILLY.'

The statement with regard to Harry contained in this letter was perfectly true. He had been horror-struck at the idea of his wife's name appearing in a gossiping paper, and her being made the mark of clumsy satire for all gossip-mongers to grin at; and had Mrs. Fitz-Jones only been a little more adroit in the levying of black mail, she might have very much augmented the 5*l.* and small subsequent donations which were the price of her silence on the subject of the lessons in etiquette. Publicity Harry had a holy horror of, and his anger when, walking down Regent Street one day, he came upon a shop-window full of photographs of his wife in various attitudes and costumes, was quite comical.

The shopkeeper gladly sold him the whole of his stock, and told where he thought more of them might be obtained, but politely refused to make any engagement as to procuring and selling more of them. So Harry went raging to the photographer whose name was on the back of the pictures. By the time he had mounted to the studio he had arrived at the point of smiling at his own heat, and feeling a little ashamed of the scene he had made in the shop.

'Look here,' he said, when the artist appeared, 'there has been some mistake. Lady Piccadilly never gave you permission to sell her portrait, and I have just come upon all these displayed in a shop-window. I am Lord Piccadilly.'

The man was obsequious, but firm. Her Ladyship, he said, on being informed of the invariable custom nowadays, had distinctly given him the required permission.

'You were mistaken,' said Harry; 'and the custom nowadays is an odious one. Give me the negatives at once.'

After about half-an-hour's argument, during the course of which Harry was sorely tempted more than once to lay his cane over the man's back, an agreement was come to, and he had the satisfaction of breaking the negatives to fragments, and of leaving the house a poorer man by 50*l.*

'Amalia,' he said, entering her room abruptly, and disturbing her pre-prandial slumber (for Amalia thought wisely of her looks and digestion), 'this will not do. I found a lot of your photographs stuck up for sale. No doubt the man was mistaken in think-ing you gave him leave to sell them. But be more careful, please, in future.'

'There was no mistake,' said she, sitting up, and at once accepting the challenge contained in the tone of his voice. 'I told him he might sell them if he liked. Everyone does it now.'

'I don't care what other people do. My wife shall not do it.'

'Shall not?'

'Shall not. Do you refuse to obey me?'

'Yes.'

'Then my course is clear. I shall advertise in all the London papers that I intend to prosecute any photographer doing so without my permission.'

'And make yourself a laughing-stock?'

'Perhaps. Anything is better than the indecent hawking about of your face, for every snob to criticise or buy. Make me the promise I require before to-morrow morning, or I shall at once take the step I have mentioned.'

By the advice of Mrs. Maintenong, Amalia struck her colours next day; but as Mrs. Maintenong observed feelingly, it was one of the worst instances of domestic tyranny and marital barbarity on record.

'Are not our faces our own, my dear?' said the beauty. 'I should like to see Tom daring to interfere with me in such a manner!'

'But if he did?'

'Dear Tom! I suppose I should give in. But he never would, you know.'

And the wayward little woman sighed, perhaps rather wishing that he would.

CHAPTER XLIII.

I MUST ask the gentle reader[1] to cross the Channel
again with me, and see what is happening at Castle
Erdmore.   Changes have taken place since last we
were there.   The old man is dead, Mr. Barry Delancy
deposed, and King Humphrey reigns over all.   The
will had been more satisfactory than was expected,
for Nellie had to a certain extent counteracted Mr.
Delancy's influence, and they were comparatively well
off.   A greed for wealth, however, had seized upon
Humphrey Erdmore, and having made up his mind
that his rents should be doubled, he had engaged as
agent a member of a firm of solicitors in Dublin, and
had begun a warfare—of not an unusual kind in
Ireland—with his tenantry.   At first they were, although surprised and alarmed, not at all inclined to
accept the challenge, except with memorials, pleadings,
and every imaginable weapon of delay; but at about
that time had arisen a conspiracy which, aiming at the
separation of Ireland from England, proposed to strike
at first through the land hunger of the Irish peasantry.

A letter from the Ballydrum solicitor, to whom
some of the Castle Erdmore tenants appealed, soon
brought down a brace of professional agitators from
Dublin ; and, to the excessive annoyance of Humphrey, he found one morning affixed to his own gate
the following notice, printed on green paper in enormous capitals :

'MEN OF BALLYDRUM !

'Assemble in your thousands on Sunday next to
protest against the extermination threatened against
some of your number on the Castle Erdmore estate by
their landlord.   Are the people of Ireland to starve,

---

[1] This is a courtesy title : many readers are not gentle.—AUTHOR.

while an alien army of landlords, sharks, and robbers
fatten on their blood?　Will you tamely see your
wives and daughters turned out on the roadside to
rot?　Or will you awake in your myriads and demand
justice and blood for blood!　The land for the people
must be your watchword—the death of landlordism
your object.

'GOD SAVE IRELAND!'

Angrily tearing down the placard, Humphrey re-
entered his house in no amiable mood, and his equanimity was scarcely restored by the receipt of a letter
from his agent in Dublin, saying that he thought it
would be as well to postpone the evictions contemplated, and to wait for quieter times.　But Humphrey Erdmore was possessed of that obstinacy which
is born of ill-temper and stupidity, and vowed by all
the gods that he was not going to be frightened
out of his just rights by all the Leaguers and placards
in the universe.　So a sharp and decisive letter was
written to the agent to proceed at once with his instructions, or to hand over the agency to some person
who would do so.　A friendly or quasi-friendly visit
from the parish priest produced no effect whatever,
save that the reverend gentleman went away smarting
from the rudeness with which he had been treated,
and determined in his mind to stir no finger in
defence of the 'black Protestant' who was courting
danger.　Irishmen are governed nearly altogether by
their feelings.　Old Mr. Erdmore, who was very popular, might probably have raised his rents without
incurring more than a certain amount of low-voiced
abuse; but Humphrey had taken no pains to know
the people about him, and had done as much as possible, whenever he interfered with the management of
his cousin's estate, to give rise to a feeling of bitterness against his hardness and absence of sympathy

for misfortune. Nellie, certainly, those that knew her
adored; but she seemed such a different order of
being from her husband that they looked upon the
two as wholly apart, and scarcely thought that any
harm befalling the one would greatly affect the other.

Now that these troubles had begun, too, she rarely
paid those visits to the farms about that had gained
her so much popularity; for while she could scarcely
listen with approval to the loud complaints against
Humphrey, on the other hand she could not in her
heart declare they had no reason in them. So the
ponies got fat, and the pony carriage remained in the
coach-house.

Nellie at this time had grown very sad. Her
boy was her only consolation, her only amusement.
Harry's marriage had hurt her more than she dared
to acknowledge even to herself; and when bits of
news from London of his splendour, his hospitality;
his wife's beauty and dresses, came across the sea, she
sighed to think that the ideal she had formed of
a strong good man making his position and power
blessings to those around him had been so utterly
false.

Then came the day of the great meeting. Ballydrum was alive at an early hour of the Sunday morning with flags, and bands and processions, and for
miles around flocked in the country folk in their best
clothes, seated mostly in their little 'ass cars,' and
all mightily cheerful and good-humoured; looking
more like people on a holiday excursion than down-
trodden slaves coming to protest against their chains.

'The drink' was strangely absent that day. Father
Mahoney took care of that, and dire would have been
the ecclesiastical penalties of the wretch who had
disgraced the seriousness of the occasion, and brought
discredit on 'The Cause,' by any dereliction from the
paths of sobriety.

The constables chaffed the crowd, and the crowd chaffed the constables, as the market-place gradually filled; and patiently they all awaited the arrival of the train which was to bring their orators, with lungs of brass and rhetoric of fire.

Then cheers arose, the band played, vastly out of tune, ' See the Conquering Hero Comes,' and slowly a waggonette came along, surrounded by enthusiastic processionists, and bearing in it two seedy-looking individuals, one of whom was no less a person than Patrick O'Gory the mighty agitator, who, having been pardoned and let out of gaol by a confiding Government, had never forgiven such an indignity, and had come back to bring fire and sword upon that Government.

What pen could do justice to his impassioned oration! He told the people that the time had come when the ægis of landlordism could no longer trample in the mire of eviction, starvation, or enforced expatriation, the rights and destinies of a united people. He declared amid wild cheering that the upas tree of coercion would soon cease to fawn upon a bloody-minded oligarchy; that the hour had struck when a squealing Government would have to kneel at the spurning feet of a justice which had been too long delayed.

' Let the garrison of England,' he cried, ' who have through the long centuries feasted their ghouls' souls on the murder of Irish women and Irish children; who have danced, and feasted, and revelled in their luxurious halls of vice while the owners of the soil died of starvation in the keen light of heaven and the workhouse, who have made robbery a fine art and torture a profession—let them eat their fill now for the last time; their death-knell has been set to a glorious tune by the all-pervading angel of Revenge!'

And then he went on to tell the excited multitude what they must not do, much after the fashion of the adviser concerning the pump and the nailing of the ear thereto. They were not to exceed the law; they were not even to take that 'wild justice' to which they were justly entitled; they were not to band together, as they might so easily do, and defy all the process-servers that were ever enrolled; they were not to teach the brutal landlord, who now threatened some of them with eviction, a lesson that should make the name of the people of Ballydrum an honoured name for ever in the history of Ireland. No, none of these things, of course, were they to do; and the allusions to shooting and ounces of lead, which frequently interrupted him, the speaker declared to be more or less wrong in intention. 'What's the use of lead unless the powder's dry?' he asked in an undertone. Then, descending from the loftier heights of declamation and denunciation, Mr. O'Gory came to the details of the Castle Erdmore property, and after describing the atrocity of the contemplated evictions, he wound up as follows:

'There is only one charitable construction that can be placed upon this Erdmore's conduct. He is mad. He is a dangerous lunatic at large. What is the proper course to pursue with such a person? Why, to lock him up, of course. And what prevents you doing this right and sensible thing? I will tell you. The law! (Groans.) The law, made by Englishmen for the purpose of keeping Ireland down, says that these dangerous lunatics shall not only go at large, but shall actually be aided by magistrates, by police, and sheriffs, and bailiffs, and all the strength of the red-coated army, to play their mad pranks amongst us. A mad Englishman is at all events better than a sane Irishman—that is their creed. Now let us see what defence we have. The landlord's power is strong; he can and will evict, and you may be, at a nod from him, houseless, homeless, ruined. What can you do? Fellow-countrymen, you can do nothing! You may

Y

not lock the lunatic up; the law would set him free. You may not combine and prevent his barbarities from being carried out; you would be shot down with buckshot; you would be punished by hireling judges and packed juries. As long as a madman landlord is alive—I say, as long as an evictor lives—his evictions may take place. Far be it from me to say one word that should tempt you to do anything beyond the law. I only say that you have no remedy save one which——'

Here he paused, and a yell of intelligence and approval filled up the gap.

'You may submit to be cast out of your homes; to see your wives and little ones starving on the roadside, eating grass as our poor people did in '46. But no, the grass is the property of the landlord. You would be imprisoned for that! You may tamely bow your necks beneath the yoke of the alien oppressor for some years, until the old spirit of Erin is broken for ever; but if you do you are not the men I take you for—the descendants of the heroes that have fought through all the past ages of penal laws and oppression against the brutal, base, and cowardly tyranny of that Judas amongst nations, England; whose every step forward has been a foul robbery in the name of religion; whose name is a by-word for deceit and cowardice amongst the peoples of the world; whose proud boast is that the sun can never set upon her blood-guilty rule.

' "Who would be free themselves must strike the blow." Remember that across the sea you are now being eagerly watched by tens of thousands of your expatriated fellow-countrymen, who only await the favourable moment for flying to your help, and, with one great and resistless movement, realising the dream for which every true Celt would gladly die—Ireland for the Irish!'

Then, when the orator had gone into the inn to partake of whisky-and-water, shouts arose in the crowd of ' To Castle Erdmore!' 'To hell with Black Humphrey!' (a name that had been lately given to him), and others of a more sanguinary nature. Eventually, however, by the exertions of the more peaceably inclined, any excursion of the sort indicated was abandoned; and after a few more speeches had been delivered by local orators, the meeting gradually dispersed. But Mr. Patrick O'Gory, bombastical as his language was, understood his audience. No refined and practised orator could have worked more skilfully on their feelings than he had done in the speech of which I have given a few extracts. Cupidity, class and sectarian hatred, longing for revenge—all were roused in their bosoms, to bear fruit anon.

And the first fruit they bore was in the shape of a letter received by Humphrey Erdmore a few days after, ornamented at the top by the usual emblem of a coffin and at the bottom signed by the mysterious and ubiquitous ' Rory of the Hills.' He placed it in the hands of the police, in whose custody it remained (he might about as usefully have given it to one of his dogs to eat), and then forgot it, and urged on the evictions with extra activity.

The neighbourhood had for many years been celebrated for its freedom from outrage of an agrarian nature; and Humphrey, although much annoyed by the meeting and the visit of Mr. O'Gory, and a little alarmed at the moment by the receipt of the threatening letter, did not in the least believe that he stood in any danger.

The people he met in the roads touched their hats to him as of yore, and if they scowled, well, they had generally looked at him in a far from friendly way. To give in, too, now would be put down to cowardice on his part after all his braggings at meetings of magistrates and county gatherings; and, like all cowards, he had a horror of an imputation of cowardice. So the notices to quit were served with but slight difficulty, and life at Castle Erdmore resumed its wonted quiet. Nellie heard scarcely anything of the matter; her husband had given up consulting her in affairs of business, and indeed they saw but little of each other now. He was out most of the day looking after his farm, and immediately after dinner he was wont to retire to look through accounts, to smoke and to sleep. She had at first gone with him, but after a few glasses of whisky he was scarcely a pleasant companion; and, besides, he had shown a decided dislike to her presence when he got to his third tumbler, and met her reproachful eyes fixed upon him as he drained it.

So in the lonely house in Ireland, as in the gorgeous house by the Green Park, dwelt a couple estranged in heart and feeling, and bound together by bonds of law. Over one house there lurked a shadow, growing darker and more threatening each moment; while all the radiance of fashion and gaiety scarcely served to relieve the gloom gathering in the other. And, divided by a chasm far deeper and wider than the Irish Channel, there dwelt two human beings whose lives were intended to run together—there slowly broke two hearts that might have been so happy.

It is always so. When Jack does get his Jill, as that legend that appeals to our earliest sense of romance tells us, even then the only result is a cropper and a broken crown.

Yet surely it was happier for Jack that he should have fallen while incautiously looking round to ogle Jill, than that, with steady step and undeviating straightness, he should have drawn that pail of water for his solitary drinking. Remember, too, that pathetic moral of the little story—' Jill came tumbling after.'

CHAPTER XLIV.

THE great ball at Piccadilly House was, by common consent, to be not only *the* event of, but the brilliant wind-up to, a brilliant season. It was to be of that order of ball which is called fancy; and the Court milliners with French christian-names contravened the law against night-work with praiseworthy boldness in their determination to keep faith with their clients. London talked of nothing else; and even politics and the last new divorce case gave way before the question as to who was to wear what on the grand occasion.

The Duke of Ulster and six other noblemen of much fashion had banded themselves into a kind of Amateur Ball Committee, and dashed in and out of Piccadilly House in much excitement at short intervals. Lady Burlington volunteered to get up one quadrille, all the characters to be from Rubens' best known pictures; and Mr. Kelt was sent over to the Louvre to make sketches of the costumes, which were said to be cheap; and Mrs. Maintenong was to head the arrangements for another—personages from the 'Tales of Boccaccio,' which the little lady had only just read, and which had deeply impressed her, through a translation. Her first idea was Zola, and when Tom interposed she pleaded hard for Dumas the younger.

'Think how nice I should look as the Camellia lady,' she said.

'Bother the Camellia lady!' was his response.

So she resigned herself to the inevitable, and set to work to discover, from the plates attached to her version of the Tales, a dress which should be what those respectable fossils who still lingered in Society would call decent. It is to be hoped that none of my readers will be able to appreciate the difficulties that the poor beauty had to encounter in her zeal for prudery.

The Amateur Ball Committee, after a few days' purposeless bustling, got tired of thinking of anything beyond their own dresses, and so they appointed a secretary, or, as he insisted on calling himself, an *honorary* secretary, who had some experience in managing quasi-public affairs, having indeed secretarised himself into his position of Adviser-General to the fashionable world.

This gentleman, Mr. John Braysey, was of real assistance to Amalia, and without him many of the effects that made the entertainment famous for ever would have been missed. The spirit of Barnum is often wanted in things of this kind; for, after all, a big show in the entertaining line is but an advertisement of the giver's grandeur, or power, or wealth, or ingenuity. No one gives parties merely to amuse friends nowadays. That style of extravagance has long passed.

Secretly, Amalia was much more at her ease with Mr. Braysey than with any of her fine-born friends. He, like herself, had sprung from nothing, and he, like her, was not using Society as an amusement of leisure, but as the work of life. Besides, he treated her with an easy brusqueness that reminded her of the happy days when, as she drew down the ivory beer-handles, she had parried the clumsy compliments of thirsty bagmen, and had smiled saucily as she kept an unappreciative customer asking many a time vainly for 'A pint of bitter, please, miss.' Braysey did not consider that when alone with her he need keep up the rather ostentatious reverence with which he treated her in public, and the mixture of outward adulation with secret dig-in-the-ribs-with-the-elbow-ism was especially pleasant to her.

She, like the Peer who danced alone among his cabbages with his coronet on, liked to dance now and again without quite putting off the dignity she had acquired, and yet without allowing it to restrain her gambollings. And with Braysey she knew that, whatever length she might go in the one way, a word from her was sufficient to bring him back to her feet as no longer the 'pal' of the ex-barmaid, but the fashionable admirer of the great lady.

I have often wondered whether splendid people, such as kings and prime ministers, and town councillors, and editors of daily papers, ever have a longing to make fun of their greatness, and, as it were, turn their crowns, or portfolios, or journals, into foolscaps for them to wear; whether the comicality of the whole business does not sometimes become almost too serious to be borne; and the continual sight of the practical joke of themselves humbugging themselves grow as painful as never-ending laughter would be. Every one of them cannot be so foolish as to believe in himself; at least, I suppose not. Yet I have met dignitaries—bishops, lord mayors, and masters of workhouses—who never seem to have seen the humour of the thing, and who go on just as if they had really been intended by Providence to make prayers, and city obstructions, and refractory paupers, until the end of time.

These reflections arise from a consideration of the conduct of my Baroness Piccadilly, who, while appreciating her grandeur to the full, could not quite subdue the humorous ideas to which it gave rise. And Braysey, who had a sense of fun, was always ready to laugh with her, and yet was possessed of sufficient tact to cease laughing the moment he saw that the lady's sense of dignity was coming back.

'The ball will make a splash,' said he.

'Yes,' replied Amalia, whose attitude on the sofa, if comfortable, was scarcely elegant, and would not have pleased the fastidious taste of the Duke of Ulster. 'Yes, but I don't see much good in it at all. We are pretty fashionable now, eh, Braysey?'

'Well, you see with these beggars—I mean these swells—you never can tell. Get 'em down, that's what I say; get 'em down, and then you can be sure they won't trample on you in the end. Now you know, my Lady, with all the flourishing, they're all ready enough to talk against you.'

'What do they say?' asked Amalia, sitting up so suddenly that Braysey thought he might have gone too far.

'Oh, the usual thing,' he replied, with a wave of his jewelled hand.

'You mean they say I am not a lady?'

'Well—more or less; though a good many of 'em shouldn't talk too much of their pedigrees. But you must always remember, my dear Lady P.'—he waited to see the effect of this little familiarity, and proceeded with more confidence—'you must remember that they construe gratitude t'other way up. The more you do for them, the more they at heart despise you. Now, with all your parties, with this affair coming off, with everything you can do, you are not of so much account in what is called the " social scale " as Lady Pendragon, for instance, with her lot of seedy ancestors and her dirty little house in Ebury Street.'

'Power,' said Amalia, lying down again, and showing the neatest ankle in the world; 'that's the thing! Get that, and the rest may go hang.'

'Exactly what I say. But to get power you must always keep on the right side. Never give 'em a chance. You know how I got on. I've never accepted a snub, but I've never made a mistake. And I go pegging away. They can't stand pegging away. They used to say, " Who the devil is Braysey ? "; then they began to exclaim against that infernal fellow coming here and going there ; then they began to allow him to make their acquaintance ; and soon after began to ask to make his, and to speak of him as a social conundrum

that was worth guessing. There are men now, Lady P.,
men with handles to their names, who a year ago
wouldn't have introduced me to their wives and
daughters, and who now ask me to get invitations for
those same wives and daughters to this house!'

'I daresay,' said Amalia, languidly. 'They're a
mean lot, and I almost wish I had never come among
'em. But there are exceptions.'

'Oh, yes! There are some stuck-up brutes that
can't be conquered, and you won't do it any more than
I shall. However, as things go nowadays, those people
don't count. They haven't got a market to take their
pigs to, and so they stay at home. Of course, they
may be the cream of the cream, but so long as they're
only a small lot it don't much matter.'

'They are whipped cream, thick and not inclined
to move,' put in Amalia.

'Publicity is the thing. Now I've arranged that
there shall be column after column in all the papers about
your ball, and we'll see whether these exclusive people
won't be on their knees to be asked for the next. The
Duchess of Surrey, for instance, who said the other day,
when someone asked whether she was going, " No, no !
I know one oughtn't to be too particular now, but I do
draw the line at barmaids." '

'I should like her to ask for an invitation,' said
Amalia, again sitting up, her eyes flashing.

'If she did,' remarked Braysey, rising as a servant
came in and announced Mrs. Maintenong, 'you would
at once welcome her with open arms.'

'Never!'

'Yes—that is the way to fight them. Their contempt is open, their koo-tooing is private. Let your
contempt be concealed, and your friendship public.
That is the way.'

'Oh, bother moralising! How d'ye do, Flossie?'
and the two lovely creatures' faces met in that kiss

which, as an eminent lady novelist has mournfully told us, is so much of a good thing absolutely wasted.

Flossie Maintenong, to her credit be it said, had a holy horror of Mr. Braysey, and her unconcealed aversion soon drove him away.

'Why do you snub him so?' asked Amalia, when he had gone.

'My dear, he makes my flesh creep. I never, when he comes fawning and grinning up to me, can help thinking of how it would be were I to go to smash— moral smash, I mean—and were to ask him to bow to me in public. You remember Kate Chantry? Well, after she had her little misadventure, he happened to meet her in the street, and he cut her dead. Yet hers was the first decent house he ever went to, and she was the person who persuaded the Cannibal to know him.'

'And now he's the Cannibal's dearest friend.'

'Oh, yes. He's a useful creature; I don't deny that. I like my especial crossing-sweeper in Curzon Street, but I don't give pennies to sweepers in Belgravia. We all have our especial toadies. I've got lots, and they have to run pretty quick, too, on my behalf. I remember your little Braysey once, in a veiled sort of a way, hinting that he could keep Tom handily absent; that was when I—when Count du Bouillon was so assiduous. Oh, what an ass he was! He told me at last that he had fathomed my feelings and respected them; and that he would go, and not allow my heart to be torn any longer in the struggle between my duty to Tom and my inclination for him—a black thing with tiny hands, and greasy hair, and little square-toed boots.'

'But what did you say to Braysey?'

'I told him that flirting with Tom was the only real excitement I had in life. And I declare it's nearly true. How do you manage about Harry?'

'How do you mean?'

'Do you ever get a chance of seeing him?'

'Yes; as often as we wish.'

'*As we!* Both seldom wish it. Tom does, and I do, very often. Not always. Men are so stupid. You no more want the man you care for most to be always by your side than you want always to be eating beef or mutton. And yet, if you prefer, for the moment, truffles, or mushrooms, or larks, they will have that you never will care for wholesome food again.'

'I declare I am persecuted with moralising to-day.'

'Somebody said that people only moralise when they contemplate something wicked, and I don't think I do at present. Where's Harry?'

'Harry? Oh, I don't know. He got a telegram this morning that seemed to put him out very much. But he did not tell me about it. He tells me very little.' And Amalia sighed—a genuine sigh.

Mrs. Maintenong looked at her narrowly, and smiled to herself.

'How does he like all this business?' she asked.

'You mean the ball? He hates it.'

'I wonder he allows it. I wouldn't if I hated it.'

'Wouldn't you? I thought that Mr. Maintenong——'

'Oh, Tom's different. Tom's a dear good old thing, but he isn't Harry.'

Amalia assented to the latter self-evident proposition, and Mrs. Maintenong, whose tongue was as active as an inventor of a Jubilee Celebration, went on:

'There are such a lot of different men, my dear, that I shall soon despair of classifying them. I treat Tom, for instance, horribly; but it makes me furious when the very position I put him in makes him the subject

of my men-friends' sneers.   Harry, if he were my
husband, would make me throw the fire-irons at his
head ; but if he boxed my ears for doing so I should
simply ask his leave to black his boots next morning.
Do you ever feel a wish to black his boots ? '

'Never ; although many people would say that
would be my proper place.'

'Would they ?   I'm sure you look fit to be
anything.'

'And yet the Duchess of Surrey says she can't come
here because she draws the line at barmaids.'

'I'm not sure I shouldn't like to be a barmaid. You
have a lot of chaff, don't you ? And the parlour of an
inn always looks so cosy and nice.   But you don't mean
to say you mind that old cat?   She tried to stop
my flirting with that red-headed cub of hers, Lord
Shepperton, and I simply sent her a message to say
that if she interfered in my affairs I'd make the price
to young men of knowing me the promise never to
dance with one of her hideous girls.   And she caved
in at once.   She'll be on her knees for a card soon.'

'I hope she may,' said Amalia, gravely.   'But now
let us talk about the quadrille. Have you quite settled
the couples ? '

And then they fell a-talking *chiffons* until
interrupted by the usual flow of afternoon visitors.

.   .   .   .   .   .

The carriage was at the door to take Lord and
Lady Piccadilly out to dinner, when Harry entered
his wife's room.

'Not dressed !' she exclaimed. 'It is really too
bad.   I promised to be punctual, as we want to see as
much of the play as we can.   Do hurry !'

'I can't go, Amalia,' he answered. 'I have to run
over to Ireland on business.'

'To Ireland ! Now ! What is this sudden business,
pray ?'

'It is enough that I have to go.'

'And am I not to be told? No need! I can guess. You want to go and see your lovley Mrs. Erdmore?'

'Yes.'

'And you think I will stand it?'

'I think you will. Her husband has been wounded to death, and wants to see me before he dies. Now go to your dinner. I shall be back in a week at furthest. Write, if you have anything to say, to Kilhorty. Good-bye.'

CHAPTER XLV.

'My Dear Lady Piccadilly,—I trust you will not think me guilty of any impertinence if I venture to ask you to let me come and see your ball next Tuesday. I hear it is to be splendid, and quite mark an era in London entertainment. My girls, Ænone and Algitha, are as ambitious as I am of being present on such an occasion. I am obliged to go first to dear Lady Macdougintosh's Scotch party—which is *not* amusing—but shall try and be in your lovely house as early as possible. I remain, dear Lady Piccadilly, yours very truly,

'Cecilia Surrey.'

This was the note that gladdened the eyes of Amalia when she woke the morning after Harry's departure, and hurriedly, lest Braysey or Mrs. Maintenong should come and give her prudent advice, she penned a reply in her large, bold, masculine handwriting:

'Lady Piccadilly presents her compliments to the Duchess of Surrey. Lady Piccadilly has received

many requests for invitations to her ball from persons
with whom she is far better acquainted than with the
Duchess, and therefore must deprive herself of the
pleasure of the Duchess's company. Although large,
Piccadilly House will not hold all the world, and
H.S.H. the Grand Duke of Spitzbuberei especially
wished that the ball should not be too crowded for the
fancy quadrille to be seen.'

Then Amalia took a copy of this precious epistle
and showed it about, with all the pride of an angry
woman and an author rolled into one. Braysey shook
his head regretfully, and Mrs. Maintenong, who,
despite her rebellious words, still cherished a secret
awe of Dukes and Duchesses, prophesied evil.

'She has the tongue of—the unmentionable party,
my dear.'

'Who cares?' said Amalia. 'She'll swallow that,
and come again for more.'

'That throwing in of the Duke of Spitzbuberei
was very clever,' remarked Braysey, reflectively; 'but it's
always better to accept an alliance with a strong power.'

'We shall see,' sagely said the hostess; and the
subject was dropped with an alacrity worthy of the
House of Lords at dinner-time.

The Duchess, when she received Amalia's answer,
first wept, then 'gave it' to her daughters in such
style as to make them weep too; then dashed off to
Mr. Loddy, who was a cousin of hers, and implored
him to enlist his chief Mr. Dashleigh's sympathies on
her behalf; which Mr. Loddy promised to do, and
took care to say nothing to the Prime Minister on
the subject, as he valued that gentleman's good
opinion of his tact and seriousness. Then her Grace
determined that she would say nothing of the letter;
but she had already said enough to make people talk.
Amalia showed her copy to everyone who called on her,

and in twenty-four hours it became a settled thing
that the *entrée* to Piccadilly House was the crowning
point of social eminence. A good many persons thought
Amalia's letter both insolent and vulgar, but one person respected her from that hour, and that was the
Duchess of Surrey herself, whose feelings the morning
after the ball, when she read the account thereof in *The
Morning Post*, could only have been described by the
bard who sang of the Peri at the Gate of Paradise.
And it certainly was enough to make a poor Society-
going woman's mouth water. First there was the
dinner-party, of which royalties, ambassadors, dukes,
and intensely fashionable people partook; then a
French play, acted by a company brought over ex-
pressly from Paris, at which a set of people only a
little less intensely fashionable assisted; and then at
eleven o'clock, the ball, to which came everybody who
was anybody (bar the Duchess of Surrey) in London
Society.

The romantically-shadowed shrubbery walks for
lovers; the equally useful summer-houses scattered
about the gardens; the electric-lighted lake, with its
gondolas, and its singers on the island; the tea-room
in the centre of waving tropical plants, with fountains
plashing and rivulets murmuring around; the flower-
covered walls; the show of plate in the supper-room;
the acres of canvas for picture-loving non-dancers to
study—it all seemed so exquisite; and the reporters
revelled in its account.

But to Amalia it must be confessed there were a
few drops of bitter in the cup. First, the absence of
Harry; for she knew that no woman is strong enough
to shine without the outward sanction of her husband.
Then the Duke of Ulster overstepped even his usual
limits, and would, had he been an ordinary mortal,
have been forcibly removed from the supper-room as
tipsy and incapable. His attentions to herself, too,

were (before he had reached this stage) too marked
and familiar to be agreeable ; and it was in vain that
she attempted to turn his eyes to Mrs. Maintenong,
who was always ready to relieve her of her duties in
his regard.

'Mrs. Maintenong!' he said, scoffingly and
thickly; 'let her go to the deuce. I don't care a
brass farthing for all the Mrs. Maintenongs in existence while I can look at your bright eyes. Oh,
Amalia!' Then his Grace's feelings became too deep
for utterance, he essayed to seize her hand, and narrowly escaped falling on his face as he missed it.

'You forget, Duke,' she said, biting her lips; 'I
have duties as hostess to perform.'

'D—— your duties! The people 'll get on all
right without you. And, I say, it's too comic your
talking of duties of that kind, eh? I wish I'd
known you when you were a jolly little barmaid.
Would you have given me a——'

But what the thing hypothetically asked for was
never came out, for at that moment Amalia suddenly
left the Duke and crossed the room to welcome some
new comer ; leaving his Grace open-mouthed and in-
dignant, but not quite sure enough of his balance to
follow her until he had, as he would have put it, 'pulled
himself together' a little.

And Amalia thought to herself how gladly she
would have gone back for a moment to the time he
alluded to, simply for the pleasure of giving him the
box on the ear which in those days was the reward of
too precipitate gallantry.

The Duke of Spitzbuberei, who in his now renounced
country had been content with meat three times a week,
was good enough to compliment his hostess on the
supper, although he confidentially remarked to his
aide-de-camp that the ortolans were a trifle small ; and
expressed his opinion that not even in the Schloss of

Spitzbubeberg could things have been better done;
which, considering that the revenues of his princely
father's domains amounted to about a month's income
of the Piccadilly estates, is not unlikely; and was very
grand and patronising, although his evening was a
little spoiled for him by the circumstance of one of
the linkmen at the door (who was afterwards alleged to
be short-sighted) not having removed his hat as he, the
Duke, entered his carriage. However, it did not take
more than a year for the Foreign Office to arrange
this little matter.

'You are the Queen of hostesses,' said Mr. Dashleigh, as he said good-bye to Amalia at the top of the
grand staircase. 'But where is Piccadilly?'

'He was obliged to go over suddenly to Ireland.'

'Ah! by the way, I forgot that the outrage on a
landlord must have been close to your place. I hope
you have good accounts of the wounded man's health?'

'Oh, yes,' said Amalia, who had heard nothing
whatever, and had, indeed, scarcely taken the trouble
to read what there was in the newspapers concerning
the attack on Humphrey Erdmore.

But these words of Mr. Dashleigh's now called up
bitter thoughts concerning Nellie; and, as soon as the
tardiest guest was gone, she sent for the last few days'
papers, and carefully read through all that pertained
to what was called the 'Ballydrum Outrage.' It
appeared that Erdmore had been to a magistrates'
meeting in the county town, had then remained on for
some time looking at horses and transacting other business, and eventually set out in his dogcart, accompanied
by a groom, to return home in the evening. About
two miles outside the town, as the groom testified, a
man with a black veil over his face jumped out of the
hedge in front of the mare, and caused her to stop and
shy violently, and a moment afterwards two shots were
fired from the hedge. All the groom knew was that

z

the mare set off at a gallop, that he caught the reins just as his master was dropping them, and that, when he managed to stop the animal's speed and look round, he saw that Erdmore was insensible, and had fallen on to the floor of the carriage. Arrived at Castle Erdmore, a man on horseback was sent for a doctor, who pronounced the wounds—for there were two—very dangerous, although not, as far as he could yet tell, mortal. The police were communicated with; but, up to the last account, no clue had been obtained as to the perpetrators of the outrage. Nobody—although the road where it occurred was much frequented—had seen any suspicious characters about. Oddly enough, the inhabitants of a cottage not a hundred yards off, although their windows and door were wide open (for it was a warm evening), had not even heard a shot. A reward of 200*l*. had been offered by the Government, and this had been supplemented by an additional 200*l*. offered by Mrs. Erdmore, for the discovery of the miscreants; and the League, at a meeting held soon after the occurrence, had repudiated all sympathy with them, Mr. O'Gory especially denouncing murder as 'unnecessary.' Meanwhile Erdmore lay at his house, still unconscious, and one of the bullets had not yet been extracted.

'He will die, and she will be free,' said Amalia to herself, as she laid her throbbing head upon her pillow that morning. 'And then——'

CHAPTER XLVI.

IN the room at Castle Erdmore which went by the name of the 'Boudoir' sat Mrs. Erdmore and Harry, expectantly, starting at every noise and evidently awaiting something of importance. The door opened, and a fussy little man, looking, with his shooting-coat and gaiters, more like a gamekeeper than the doctor that he was, entered.

'Well?' said both the others in a breath.

'Well, Sir George will be here in a moment. He is having a glass of wine in the dining-room. Likes good wine, does Sir George. He thinks badly of him.'

'Does he think there is no hope?' asked Nellie, standing up. Her face was very pale, and there were black rings round her eyes.

'No; he does not exactly say that—but here he is.'

'A bad case,' said Sir George Linden, the great Dublin surgeon, entering the room; 'a bad case. I don't despair. But—well, we are in the hands of Providence.'

This was so obvious a truism—although useful to persons in Sir George's profession on occasion—that no one replied; and there was a pause.

'The question is,' said the surgeon, looking at Nellie, and thinking how pretty she would look with a widow's cap on, 'whether he can survive the extraction of the bullet. He certainly cannot live unless it is extracted.'

'And when do you propose to perform the operation?' said Harry, speaking for the first time.

Sir George turned to him with marked deference.

'To-morrow, my Lord. It cannot be postponed any later.'

'If—if,' faltered Nellie—'if he should not survive it—do you think he will recover consciousness before——'

Here she stopped, but the doctor understood her. It was not by any means the first time such a question had been put to him by a weeping wife.

'Yes, I think he will—I feel sure he will. Will you kindly'—this to the local practitioner—'see that all is prepared for to-morrow at eleven?'

Then Sir George, with many bows, and a muttered sentence of hope and condolence for Mrs. Erdmore, took his leave, accompanied by the little doctor.

Thoughts are unruly things, and, despite himself, the possibility of Nellie becoming free, and of what might have happened in such a case were he not bound, would obtrude itself into Harry's mind. His old love had come back in all its force at the sight of her gentle face, at the sight of her tender devotion to her husband; and he felt that to be tended by her hands, to have the right to call her his own even for one brief moment of consciousness before death, he would willingly have taken the place of that husband.

'Shall you stay till—till after to-morrow?' she asked, not looking at him.

'If you will let me. It is so far to Kilhorty, and I cannot bear to think of you all alone in this fearful suspense.'

'Thank you. I suppose I am foolish, but I own it is a comfort to me to think a friend is near. It was very good of you to come over—all the better of you because you have so much to do in London; and besides, it often seemed to me when last you were here that you and Humphrey were scarcely on good terms.'

'No, we were not—I may say so frankly. But, of course, all our differences are forgotten now.'

'I am glad of that,' she said, gently, raising her eyes for a moment to his. 'I know Humphrey has his faults, but he has much—much that is good in him. He has always been a kind husband to me. If—if—when he becomes conscious, will you say something to tell him you are reconciled to him, that you forgive anything he may have done to anger you. I know the estrangement with you preyed upon his mind.'

'I will do so. Nellie, I will forgive him as you would forgive him.'

'I have nothing to forgive,' she said. 'But it is time I relieved the nurse. There is no knowing when he may recover consciousness, and I shouldn't like him to find a stranger at his side.'

'You will kill yourself with watching, Nellie.'

'Would that matter much?'

'Yes. There are others to think of besides him.'

'You are right. There is my boy. But I am strong yet. You do not know how strong women are in such things as these.'

'I know they are angels.'

Then she left him, and he sat down to read a letter he had that morning received from Amalia.

'I do not think,' she said, 'that there can be any necessity for your staying in Ireland. Humphrey Erdmore is not such a friend of yours that you need sham all this humbug about him. If he is to die, your being there cannot save him. If he is to live, do you think he will care to know that while he was lying ill his wife was philandering with you? I know the sympathetic, brotherly dodge. Your absence from the ball was much remarked; indeed, Mr. Dashleigh hinted that he thought your going to Ireland quite unnecessary. Considering what you said to me about what you called my flirting one night with Charlie Despard, I must say that your conduct now is pretty cool. At any rate, I could not be hypocrite enough to make your being desperately ill an excuse for a flirtation. Ask your conscience whether it is only friendship for this man that has taken you over. You know it is not. And what am I to do? The season is over, and I can absolutely make no plans. Unless you come home immediately, I shall go to Homburg with Mrs. Maintenong and a lot of her set. But don't suppose that I shall easily pardon your neglect of me for this

woman, and don't suppose I am one to let the neglect
and the *peculiar conduct* be all on one side. What's
sauce for the gander is sauce for the goose, my dear
Harry. Remember that.'

'And to think this woman is my wife!' thought
Harry, as he put down the letter. Then he hastily
wrote a few words:

' I am sorry that you should send me such a letter
as that I have just received. Mrs. Erdmore is, as you
know, a very old and dear friend of mine, and she is
in great distress. Whatever you may say, you are
perfectly aware that the infamies you hint at are quite
impossible for me or for her. I cannot precisely say
when I shall return. It must depend upon Erdmore's
health. As you are aware, Mall is quite ready for you
if you choose to go there, but if you insist upon
Homburg I will make no objection, although I would
rather you went to Mall.'

When Amalia received this, her eyes glittered
with rage, and she wrote another letter.

CHAPTER XLVII.

THE recovery of Humphrey Erdmore was very slow—
if, indeed, it could be called a recovery at all. He
became a hopeless cripple, one side being paralysed ;
and, moreover, his mind was affected by the wound in
the head, and he entirely lost his memory. It was
sad to see the strong man of so short a time ago sitting
helpless in his chair, a vacant smile upon his face—
dead to all interests and purposes, yet doomed to
perhaps many years of this miserable, useless existence.

' It is too terrible,' said Harry one day, soon after
the truth had at length been put before them by the

doctors. 'Terrible indeed for him—though he cannot feel it—and doubly terrible for you.'

'Providence must have some good reason for thus punishing us,' said Nellie. It was the day decided upon for Harry's departure, and her heart was very full.

'Providence! Well—perhaps. But can any possible good come from such a thing either to him, to you—or to me?'

He said the last words almost to himself, under his breath; but she heard them.

'I have long ago found out that life, for some people, is only a struggle towards the end—a disagreeable journey. This is only one more of the trials. But it is terrible to think of poor Humphrey—always to be like that!'

There was a pause, and then Harry spoke:

'Nellie, we are going to part to-day, you know. Will you promise me one thing—that you will appeal to me in any difficulty, or trouble, or danger, as you would appeal to a brother who loves you?'

She did not answer, but all her force of will could not keep the tears from her eyes.

'You will promise this?' he repeated, taking her hand and gently touching it with his lips.

Then she started up away from him.

'I cannot.'

'You cannot?'

'No. I will give you no reason. But I cannot promise. We must be nothing to each other. I hope it has not been very wicked, but your presence here has been much to me. The knowledge that I have your friendship has helped me through all my troubles. But it must end now. Even friendship between us is wrong.'

'Wrong?'

'Yes. We both have our plain duties, and our

ways of life lie far apart. I have my duty here—by his side. You have chosen yours.'

He tried to take her hand again, but she evaded him.

'Nellie,' he said gravely, 'you speak in riddles. There is nothing wrong in our friendship. If—if —things had been otherwise—if an unworthy trick had not been played, you know—it is useless to disguise it from each other—we should have been united by the holiest of ties. We cannot ask for each other's love; but your friendship is as necessary to me as mine is to you. Are you in earnest in refusing it?'

'Yes.'

'And your reason?'

'Do not ask me. It may be that I am weak— and——'

'No. It cannot be that reason. You are not weak, and moreover you trust me—in your heart you trust me; at least, I thought so. Tell me your reason, or else I must believe that you have withdrawn that confidence; in which case the friendship had better go too.'

He spoke with some bitterness, as he saw the firm expression of her face and anticipated another refusal.

'You insist?' she asked.

'No; I have no right to insist. You can choose your own friends. But I shall know what construction to put on a refusal.'

Then she unlocked her desk and drew out a letter which she silently gave to him. It was in a feigned hand, but not so well disguised but that Harry at once recognised it; and thus it ran:

'People here know all about what is going on at Castle Erdmore: the sick husband, and the lover who takes advantage of his sickness. Even if you have no respect for yourself, do you think it is to Lord P——'s advantage that he should neglect his wife and proceed with his old disgraceful intrigues? If you have no feeling for your husband, you should have some for the man you profess to love. You may have no character to lose, but he has, and the world—in which you pretend to wish him success—is not tolerant of such heartless behaviour as his. Let him go, Mrs. Erdmore. Let him go, or one who has the power may take such revenge on him as will make you rue the day—if you care for him—that you ever tried to seduce him from his duty.

'A FRIEND OF HIS.'

She watched his face of growing scorn as he read this, and when he had finished, and dashed it down to the ground, she asked :

'Can you guess from whom it comes?'

He hesitated.

'Yes, I can guess.'

She did not pursue the subject, but she understood.

'You see now why we cannot be together?'

'No.'

'Yes, Harry, you must. That is a cruel, coarse, vindictive letter ; but it expresses, to a certain extent, what the world would say.'

'It does not. It expresses only what one worthless, wretched woman could dare to say.'

'Harry—I—it is hard to say the words—I *cannot* in my heart look upon you only as a friend—a brother. There is enough truth about that letter to prove to me that the reasoning is right. You are—I dare tell you now that I have made up my mind to see you no more—the brightness of my life ; still, as at first at Richlake, my only love.'

She stood before him, blushing as she made this

confession, and with a strange light of love, and pride, and half shame in her eyes.

'I cannot be ashamed of it, Harry. You, to me, are as far above all other men as the stars are above the earth. To see you at a distance from time to time would make my life happy. But it must not be. I have been all these years wronging him'—she indicated her husband by a gesture towards the door of his room—'in my thoughts; and, my heart being as it is, every moment we have spent together has wronged him still more. I have prayed so hard for strength to say this, dear, and then to part; and it did not come to me till I read that letter.'

'And you will permit that villainous scrawl——'

'No,' she interrupted, with gentle firmness; 'no; it is not the letter itself. But it is the truth, as I know it to be, which the letter confirms. In love, Harry, there are no half-measures, that is, if the love be real. Do you think I could see you often, or seldom, or even live knowing that I should before long see you, without thinking always of you? While Humphrey was well it did not seem quite so bad that I should love you in my thoughts; but now, while he is helpless and dependent on me for everything—on me, his wife! Oh, Harry! Do you not see that I am right?'

Then my hero—if I may use that much-abused word in these unheroic days—behaved like a scoundrel for, I hope and trust, the only time in his life. He met her beseeching gaze with a look of love before which she quailed, and, ere she could prevent him, he had seized her two hands in his, and held them while he spoke:

'No; you are not right. Life is not the narrow-grooved thing we are taught in our nurseries. We are not bound to throw everything away at the pleasure of a few dead-and-gone inventors of dogmas and rules for our guidance. We love one another.

See how we are situated. On the one hand, you are practically free—morally free. The doctors have told us that there is no hope whatever of your husband recovering his senses. Do you think it matters to him by whom his meals are brought or his pillow smoothed? Would not a hired nurse do it as well or better than you? And what do you owe him? Listen to me. When he married you he thought he was already married. He thought he was—for the sake of your 20,000*l.*—committing bigamy; he thought until not long ago that you were his mistress, and your boy a bastard. I thought it also.'

'What do you mean?'

'Let me finish. By an accident I discovered that a vindictive, clever woman, sister of his first wife, was on his track, had discovered him, and was about to disclose his shame. Do you understand me? —his shame—that is, yours and that of your boy.'

'Yes,' said Nellie, who had released her hands, and fallen back into a chair, while he stood before her watching the expression of her face.

'Not for his sake, but because I loved you, I determined to prevent this; but my whole fortune would not suffice. Only one thing could do it, and I did that thing. I made the woman who would have proclaimed your ruin my wife.'

'Your wife!'

'Yes—I, the man you think it wrong to speak to because of your duty to the man whom I saved from a prison. I married this woman to save you. And then, when she was Lady Piccadilly—after you had refused me your sympathy, I remember—then I discovered that I had been tricked; that his first wife had died, unknown to him, the very day before he married you. He was none the less a scoundrel, but you were his legal wife, and your son his legal heir; and I —I was the husband of the writer of that interesting epistle that lies under my foot, and because of the receipt of which you forbid me ever to see you again.'

It never occurred to Nellie Erdmore to doubt for a moment the truth of this statement. It stunned her for the moment, and when he paused she could not reply; she could only look at him in dumb love, with a world of hopeless gratitude in her eyes.

Then he went on, his voice hoarse with passion:

'I would have borne my life of hell—for such it has been—cheerfully, knowing I was suffering for your sake; but when I knew that it was all in vain, Nellie, I nearly went mad sometimes. Do you think I can go back from you, knowing that you love me still, to her? Do you think that I can leave my darling to end her life as the nurse of a man who can be as well tended by others—the man who had made her his mistress but for an accident of which he knew nothing? To which do you owe most? Have I no claim upon you—I, who sacrificed everything for your sake? And whom should we wrong? Are not there countries, away from the jargon of what we call "the world," where we could lead a life—pure—yes, pure as life can be—a life of happiness and love? That woman in London—well, you can judge of her by that letter. Humphrey—he will never know of anything again. Whom, I say, do we wrong?'

'My son.'

'Your son! How had his father wronged him?'

'You forget—Harry, I cannot bear to say it, but you force me to—you forget that you now would ask me, with my eyes open, to do what I might then have done not knowing. You forget that when my boy grows up he will have the right to judge me. He will grow up to know what I am!'

'There are occasions,' said Harry, trying to speak calmly and to subdue his emotion, 'when the narrow rules of life can be—and can rightly be—abrogated.

It sounds a hackneyed phrase, but I say that in the sight of God we are man and wife. I ask of you for my sake to make a sacrifice, but not so great as that I made for you.'

'Oh, Harry!' cried the tortured woman, 'you know I love you.'

'Prove it.'

'But I am a mother. Could I bear that he should be, as it were, implicated in my guilt?'

'Let him stay here, then. There are relations who will bring him up. Leave him.'

'Leave him!'

'Yes. Choose—choose now between him and me.'

She did not reply for some moments, and he stood like a figure of stone before her, waiting. Then she spoke, in a low voice:

'You tempt me more almost than I can bear; you are cruel.'

'Oh, love!' he cried, throwing himself at her feet and kissing passionately the hands he had again seized; 'do not talk of cruelty! We will go away together and be forgotten by the world and forget the world, and be all in all to each other, and live only for each other, and at last know happiness unmeasurable. Of this world that has been so bitter we will make a paradise of love. Even now our hearts beat as one. Nature has ordained that we should love. Shall we rebel against that holy law? The very strength of our mutual love hallows it—to stifle it would be a crime before Him who raised that feeling in our hearts. Look into my eyes, my love, my Nellie, my own one! What do you read there? Crime? Guilt? Shame? No! love—happiness! Shall we not be good when we are together? Could anyone, so happy as we shall be, be aught but good? Oh, my love! do not let the prejudice of a narrow world destroy it all. Trust to me. If you have doubts now, I will remove

them.   Give me but the time to do it.   *Can* you send
me from you?   Can you bear to think of me living
in misery and daily torture?   No! you cannot be so
inhuman, so atrociously cruel to one who loves you.
Nellie, by every law, human and divine, you are mine
as I am yours.   Can you say no?   I dare not live
longer as I have been living; I dare not live without
you.   Speak!'

He rose to his feet and again stood before her,
watching.

He saw her lips move, as in prayer.   She too rose,
and her trembling limbs almost refused to keep her
upright.   Then she held out her hands to him, her
lips quivered, and twice she essayed in vain to speak.

They stood thus hand in hand, while you might
have counted twenty, and then at last she forced out a
sound.

'I must do my duty.   It is hard—bitterly hard.
But—good-bye!'

He dropped her hands and said hoarsely:

'This is your decision?'

'I must do my duty!' she repeated, as if she had
learned the words by rote; and then she staggered and
clung to the table for support.

He never stirred; his hungry, maddened eyes never
left her white face.

'And we part like this?'

Again came the words, this time as a faint wail of
anguish:

'I must do my duty!'

'Then, good-bye,' he said, holding out his hand.

She only looked piteously into his face, and did not
take it.

'You will not even take my hand?   Am I so
vile?'

'We——'

She broke down for a moment, and then recovering

herself, went on, in a voice so weak that he could barely catch her words :

'We are parting for the last time. You will, for my sake, go back and try to forget me. God will make your life easier, and I will pray for you—and for myself—and for myself. We will forget all—all this. Good-bye.'

'Good-bye.' His voice was stern, almost fierce; and she shuddered at the expression of his face.

'You will forgive,' she murmured, 'and—give me one—our last—kiss, Harry !'

He took a step towards the door, and then stopped, attracted by a cry, as of acute pain, that had escaped her. The agony in her sweet eyes would have melted a heart of stone. He caught her to him, and their lips met in one passionate kiss, in which, indeed, their 'whole hearts' were 'wasted.'

And in a few hours Harry was on his way back to London.

CHAPTER XLVIII.

'So you have left that woman at last !' remarked Amalia when her husband walked into the drawing-room of Mall Castle. 'Just in time to see me,' she went on, when they had gone through the ceremony that husbands and wives call a kiss. 'I start to-morrow for town—you might as well have waited there for me by the by—and then go straight on to Homburg. The Cannibal is coming, and the Arcades, and dear Harry Kelt, and old Abchurch, and Lady Gloriana Lane, and Brayscy, and, let me see—that must be all.'

She paused for a moment, and then for the first time looked at Harry's face. He was deadly pale, and there were traces of suffering about his eyes which maddened her.

' You are almost a large enough party,' he said.

' Yes—I like big parties.   But fancy my forgetting Flossie Maintenong is coming too !   We have taken most of the Hôtel des Quatre Saisons, and we shall have great fun—that is, unless——'

' Unless what ? '

' Unless you take it into your head to come too.'

He stared.

' Well, really——'

' Well, really ! ' she repeated, mocking him.   ' You have been away having your fun—now I am going away to have mine.   You must look upon the Cannibal as my Mrs. Erdmore.'

' I do not understand the comparison.'

' No,' said Amalia quickly, her eyes flashing.   ' She is all purity and perfection, whilst I——'

Then he remembered the anonymous letter, and interrupted her.

' You are a woman incapable of a generous thought.'

' Thank you, my Lord.'

And she got up, and made him an elaborate curtsey that would have delighted Mrs. Fitz-Jones.

' What a pity it is that I happen to be your wife.'

' Yes,' replied he sternly ; ' it is a pity.   I never thought I could be married to a woman capable of this.'

And from his pocket he extracted the anonymous letter and showed it to her.

' You think I wrote that ? ' she said, after perusing it with apparent interest.

' I know you did.'

' Well—we won't argue the point.   Anyhow, it's true enough.'

' It is the basest thing on this earth to do.'

' Is it ?   I should have thought that to leave your

wife and make love to your friend's while he, your friend, is at the point of death, was baser still.'

'Amalia,' said Harry sternly, 'I have had enough of this. It is easy to understand why you are incapable of realising what a pure woman should be. But I have had enough of your insinuations, the falseness of which you know as well as I do. Let me never hear the subject mentioned by you again.'

'Oh! I'm not good enough to mention Mrs. Erdmore, am I?'

'As to your journey,' he went on, without taking any notice of her angry words, 'you can do as you please. I will not interfere, and I will not spoil your party by coming. As you know, Mr. Dashleigh has promised to come here about the 15th; so I beg you will be back by then to receive my guests.'

Then he turned to leave the room.

'You will come as far as London with me?' she asked, catching hold of his arm to detain him.

'For what purpose? I have only just left it.'

'To—to—— Harry, I won't go abroad if you'd rather I didn't!'

'I have no objection.'

'You don't care a bit what becomes of me. If you would only say you do care—just a tiny bit—for me! I am very sorry about the letter, if it hurt you; and I'll only believe exactly what you want me to believe. Only don't be so cold and stern. Can't you understand how lonely my life is?'

'Lonely!'

'Yes. People round one don't prevent that. I want you, and if I can't get you, of course I must put up with Ulsters, and Brayseys, and Kelts, and people. But I had rather be alone with you than anywhere. Do you believe me?'

He paused for a moment, and then made answer, sternly and decisively:

'It is time to put an end to all this, Amalia. You
know how you became my wife—how by a shameful
trick you led me to believe that I had but one way of
saving from humiliation and undeserved shame the
woman I love best on earth.'

'Ah!'

'But who can never be anything to me now.'

A curious smile passed over the face of his wife
when he said these words; not a pleasant one.

'Where is the good of keeping up appearances when
we are alone together?' he went on. 'Before the
world I hope my treatment of you gives you no cause
of complaint. If we are much apart, we are not very
different from many other married people in that.
There is plenty of room for us to go our own way without disturbing each other. I have tried to let it be
otherwise, and might have succeeded, but this letter
decided me. You and I must hereafter live lives
totally apart; husband and wife but in name. I will
not conceal from you that all my heart is with the poor
woman to whom you dared deal this cruel blow.'

As he spoke he threw the anonymous letter into
the fireplace, having torn it in pieces.

'But you can trust to my honour and to hers—
and you know that.'

'I know nothing of her honour.'

'Then let your knowledge of mine suffice. Let
there never be a renewal of this painful scene between
us. It may be unavoidable that we sometimes have to
be alone together, but there is no necessity for us ever
to renew any discussion of the kind. I will not insult
you by saying anything as to your future conduct,
except that it would be well to remember that the world
is not very charitable, and that the Duke of Ulster
is not very reticent.'

Amalia gave a splendid gesture of contempt.

'You need not be afraid of me,' she said, 'or of a

million Dukes of Ulster. Well, I accept the terms—
as I suppose I must. It might have been otherwise,
and I think we both should have been happy if it were.
But I'm not going to whimper. I suppose the way I
got you was not quite fair; and I can scarcely expect
you to believe that it was far more—a thousand times
more—to be your wife, Harry, than to be Lady Piccadilly. I told you that you should not be disgraced by
your wife in any way, and I think I am keeping that
promise. Of course, the smartest set in London may not
be a very *nice* set; but I can't pretend to be a judge of
that sort of thing. I have taken the Society you put
me in as I found it; and, thanks to your money and
to my—what shall I call it?—my tact and observation,
mimicry, perhaps—I have got Society pretty well at
my feet. Of course, any open rupture between us
would do me harm; but you say you don't wish that.
Very well; I accept the terms.' And she held out her
hand.

He took it for a moment; and then she threw herself suddenly at his feet, and her enforced calmness
vanished.

'Oh, Harry, my darling!' she sobbed, 'must it be
so? Won't you let me be your true wife? I will be
anything—second to Mrs. Erdmore, even—only let me
love you.'

But Harry could think of nothing but the dumb
misery he had lately read in Nellie's eyes after that
cruel letter had been sent her.

'Please get up, Amalia,' he said, coldly. 'These
scenes are painful and—ridiculous. You will perhaps
let me know the exact time of your departure, so that
proper arrangements may be made.'

And he left the room, leaving Amalia seated on
the floor, weeping bitterly.

From that day forth no word of affection ever
passed between them; the barrier set up on purpose

by the husband increased day by day, until they were as separate as China from Peru.

. . . . . .

When Amalia reached London she found that the expedition to Homburg had been put off for a week to suit Mrs. Maintenong's convenience, she having a London flirtation that she wished to finish off for good before commencing a new one elsewhere; and Amalia therefore had to kill her time as best she might by visiting the theatres and partaking of such somewhat dismal revelries as are afforded when 'the season' proper is at an end.

Harry remained at Mall Castle; and a few days after his wife's departure he received a letter from Nellie Erdmore:

'I promised to let you know, dear Harry, how poor Humphrey gets on. He is now much as you left him; but it has occurred to me that I should not be doing my duty if I left anything undone on the chance of curing him, or at least of doing him some good. So I have made up my mind to start at once with him for London. They say the journey will do him no harm; and possibly the doctors there may find out some remedy. Perhaps we had better not meet, dear. I am not quite courageous enough yet. Give me a little more time.

'NELLIE.'

CHAPTER XLIX

'A LADY wishes to see you, ma'am,' said the waiter, entering the room which Nellie had taken at Buckridge's Hotel in London.

'A lady? Did she give her name?'

'No, ma'am; but she said she knew you'd see her.'

'Oh, it must be the new nurse. Show her up.'

But it was not the new nurse. It was a very smart, handsome woman, looking somewhat excited—a woman that Nellie had never seen before.

'To what do I owe the honour——' she began.

'I am Lady Piccadilly!' said the other.

The two women looked at each other as two duellists before engaging.

Then the visitor opened fire.

'You are surprised to see me?'

Nellie, usually so meek and gentle, seemed another being as she stood haughtily in front of her rival, and answered:

'I am much surprised.'

'And yet it is not so very extraordinary that I should wish to see one of whom I have heard so much from my husband—his old friend.'

'Under ordinary circumstances it would not be so, Lady Piccadilly. Under these it is. I may as well tell you at once that I know the whole story.'

'That is what I came to know. Is your visit to London to make it public?'

'It was told me in confidence.'

'And why?'

'I really do not see why I should reply to that question.'

'No; for the answer is plain enough. Lovers have no secrets from each other.'

Nellie made a step towards the bell, her cheeks flushing, but checked herself.

'I can scarcely suppose,' she said, with creditable calmness, 'that you have come here for the purpose of insulting me.'

'No,' replied Amalia, with an overdone assumption of carelessness that was intensely insolent. 'No: I came to look at you—perhaps to give you a triumph.

I don't know why—a whim. I have a sort of wish to tell you that you have won after all.'

'Won?'

'Yes. If it's any satisfaction to you to know that my husband and I are nothing more than acquaintances, and never are to be more, you can know it.'

'It is not a satisfaction to me.'

'Yes, Mrs. Erdmore, you've about spoiled it all, and that should please you.'

'It does not please me, Lady Piccadilly.'

'What! You don't care for him, after all?'

'You forget that I am married, as he is.'

'Do I? I think not. If I were you, though, I should forget it. If Harry only——'

Then Nellie interrupted imperiously:

'Excuse me, but I do not care to enter into such a subject with—a stranger. I am engaged now, and——'

'You mean you want me to go?'

'Lady Piccadilly, I think your visit to me very ill-timed. I do not want to hurt your feelings, but I have no wish for your acquaintance.'

'You think me too low—a barmaid—eh? And yet I'm fashionable, too.'

'I express no opinion whatever. But I claim the right to receive whom I choose.'

'And I'm not chosen. Well, I've seen you, and that's what I wanted. Harry has good taste. I think you and I are about the two best-looking women in London.'

Nellie stood still, waiting for her to go; but some fascination riveted her to the spot, and she chattered on, still looking at Nellie with admiring eyes:

'How you must hate me, to be sure! Own that you hate me! Well, it's a pity, for I like you. I feel that I should be very fond of you, and you would do me good. I always like pretty people, and plucky

people; and I can see you're that. Look here, Mrs.
Erdmore——'

'Really, Lady Piccadilly.'

'Don't kick me out for a few minutes. I'm not
quite so bad as you think me. Of course my scheme
was wicked enough, but you can sympathise with its
object. I would die for Harry, Mrs. Erdmore.'

The coldness in Nellie's eyes gave place to a look
of pity. There was no mistaking the honesty of the
other's accents.

'Yes, he is all in all to me; and he hates me
because of you. He says it is because of my tricking
him. But I could have made him forget that. It is
because of you, and I can never make him forget you
—unless perhaps you would help me. See here: I
throw myself on your mercy. Help me with him!'

'What can I do?'

'If he thought it was hopeless, he might——'

Nellie interrupted her.

'He and I are, and can be, nothing to one another.
We may possibly meet, as it is hard to avoid people in
the world, but we shall always henceforth meet only as
acquaintances. I do not see how I could help you. I
would do so if I could.'

'If Harry knew that you had forgiven me, perhaps
he would.'

'What have I to forgive?'

'Haven't I taken him?'

'Lady Piccadilly,' said Nellie with a half smile at
the other's bluntness, 'you really must permit me to
say that I don't understand you.'

'Yet it's clear enough.'

'I am very sorry that you and your husband—as
you tell me—are not on terms such as a husband and
wife should be on. If I could do anything to put
matters straight I would do so, for both your sakes.'

'Write and tell him that you have forgiven me,

and ask him to give up his cruel scheme of estrangement.'

'You forget. By what right——'

'Good gracious!' exclaimed Amalia, losing patience.
'By the right of being the woman he loves!'

'Lady Piccadilly!'

'Yes. Where's the use of mincing matters?
Don't you know? And do you dare tell me you
don't care for him in return?'

'You have no right to interrogate me, and I
request——'

'Oh, yes, I know—I have no right. But I ask you,
as one woman pleading to another for mercy, to use
your influence to help me. Don't think I want to
offend you—all my suspicions have gone. I see how
base and unjust those suspicions have been. Help
me!'

'But how?'

'Write and ask him to reconsider his determination.
Tell him what you think.'

'His determination?'

'Yes—that we should be nothing to each other,
only outwardly husband and wife. I love him with all
my heart.'

Then Amalia suddenly went down to her carriage,
and soon after Harry received the following letter:

'Dear Harry,—I have seen your wife. She came to
my hotel and asked me to intercede with you on her
behalf. I believe she repents certain acts of hers. I
believe she is really desirous of making you a good wife.
As to that wretched letter, if I forgive and forget, so
may you. Whatever may have brought it about, you
are husband and wife, and you owe her the duty, the
love (yes, even that) of a husband. Your idea of your
future life is miserable—it is even wicked. Do not be
angry with me for writing so plainly. I do so because

I want you to be happy, and I am sure that you are
going the way to be wretched. You used, long ago, to
say that my advice was always good. Take it for this
once.

'NELLIE.'

Men are strange animals. The only effect of this
epistle was to shift on to the shoulders of Mrs. Erdmore
some of the fierce resentment Harry felt against his
wife.

CHAPTER L.

I HAVE seen two convicts painfully trudging to their
work united by a hateful chain; I have watched, in an
Irish *boreen*, an adventurous goat dragging after him,
to the height of a steep bank, his less adventurous
companion; I have on one occasion been startled by a
madly careering dog pursued by the tin-kettle attached
wickedly to his tail; and I have seen the vain
struggles of a pickpocket in the grasp of a policeman.
I have pitied the convicts, the goats, the dog, and the
pickpocket; but my pity for all these has been weak
indeed compared to what I have felt for many married
couples in Society.

Watch that pretty woman yonder: how bright and
gay she seems; how prettily she turns the compliments
of her admiring cavaliers; how deftly she throws her
little barbed arrows at her sisters around her! In her
heart she is thinking of the inevitable moment when
her carriage will come, and the brightness and the
compliments be exchanged for the usual weary
grumbling and reproaches of an unadmiring and
unsympathetic husband.

Let them feast and caress her as they will, that

dark shadow is always over her : a grinding misery that at last becomes almost unsupportable.

Look at the whilom jolly dog, Jack So-and-So, who married for love a few years ago. He has taken to his Club again, and for a few hours now and then quite blooms out the cheery companion of old days. But there is a shamefaced look about him, as he glances at the clock and hurries home to dress for dinner, that reveals easily enough to his sarcastic friends how gladly —did he dare—he would stay and dine at the Club.

Like gout and sea-sickness, marital infelicity gets no pity; worse than that, it may not be mentioned by the sufferer. You think a man a bore who retails to you his sufferings between Dover and Calais, or explains the exact nature of the shooting pains in his great toe; but you would think him something worse than a bore did he take you aside to tell of his wife's flirtations, of her jealousy, or of the terrors of her tongue. So with man and woman alike, unsuitableness repressed, and growing on its own growth, warps the nature and deteriorates the moral character.

My hero's life, after the events of the last chapters, was simply one long effort to forget himself. He did not take to drinking, because drinking was abhorrent to him. He did not take to other kinds of dissipation, because Nellie Erdmore was a woman. But he plunged recklessly into every form of gambling, and into every fashionable folly of the moment. He allowed no portion of his day and but little of his night to pass without some fresh excitement; and at his extravagance—notwithstanding his great wealth—knowing ones shook their heads.

'No fortune would stand it,' said Lord Scobell, as he sipped his tea in Mrs. St. James's drawing-room.

'Why, what has he done *now*?' asked the lady, who, truth to tell, rather liked the sort of fame her son was achieving.

'Only given his friend, Jim Dacourt, who happened to complain the other night of living in lodgings as uncomfortable, a house in Curzon Street, beautifully furnished, cellar stocked, a stable full of horses, two carriages, and all the necessary servants, with their wages paid for a year.'

'Good gracious!'

'Yes, indeed; you may well be surprised. Monte Cristo was nothing to him. They even say that he went to all Jim's tradespeople and paid their accounts; and that Jim found the wardrobes full of new clothes, and boots, and hats, and everything. The way they managed the thing, too, was extraordinary. Jim, as I daresay you have heard, is not the soberest of mortals. Well, they made him very tipsy one night last week, took him to this house, and put him in bed. When he woke in the morning, he rang the bell to know where he was. "Why, in your own house," said the servant who answered. "And who are you?" "Your butler, sir." Jim's a queer creature, takes everything very coolly; and I'm told he didn't give himself the trouble to inquire about the thing, but lived several days in the house before he knew that Harry had done it all.'

'He must have been very grateful.'

'Well, he didn't show it. He merely went up to your son at the Sward Club, and said, " 'Pon my soul, Harry, it's too bad. You accustom me to luxury like this, and when I go back to my lodgings I shall be wretched. Besides, what the deuce is the good of a house and a French cook if you haven't a wife?" '

'And what did Harry say?'

'He went straight to the *Matrimonial News* office and inserted an advertisement in Jim's name, which brought twenty or thirty eligible females to Curzon Street a few days after; and there was very nearly being a riot when he refused to see them.'

'It is so curious all this,' said Mrs. St. James

musingly; 'for I always thought Harry rather serious than otherwise.'

'Well, I don't think he gets any fun out of it all. He always seems to be trying, and trying vainly, to amuse himself so as to forget something.'

'Amalia came back from Homburg yesterday.'

'Yes, and I hear they are going to have all the world and his wife at Mall. Shall you go?'

'I'm not asked.'

'Not asked, my dear lady?'

'No, I'm not fashionable enough for my daughter-in-law. She says she will invite me to their less smart party later. *This* one, I fancy, is asked entirely by the Cannibal.'

'That is going on still?'

'Oh dear, yes.'

'I wonder Harry——'

'Oh, he takes no notice at all. He lets his wife do just as she pleases, so long as she does not interfere with him.'

'And he?'

Here Lord Scobell looked very sly indeed.

'He *seems* to be a good deal with Mrs. Maintenong. She went a cruise with him in his yacht the other day.'

'But Maintenong was there.'

'I daresay,' said the lady, carelessly; 'but he doesn't count, you see.'

'But he makes a kind of chaperon.'

'Perhaps. Still, it was rather audacious; and I wrote to Harry about it.'

'What did he say?'

'Not much. I have his letter somewhere. Yes, here it is. You may read it.'

Lord Scobell adjusted his glasses and read:

'My dear Mother,—You state a fact—that Mrs.

Maintenong has been a cruise in my ship; and you draw an inference—that I have been making love to her. Against your inference I place two other facts—my wife and Mrs. M.'s husband. If what you seem to imagine could be true, it would be your duty to close your door in my face as a scoundrel unworthy to enter honest folks' houses. Unless I am denied admission when I next come to Belgrave Square, I shall believe that your letter was intended only as a joke.

'Your affectionate Son.'

'Very haughty,' said Lord Scobell, putting the note down.

'That's better than being naughty, perhaps,' said Mrs. St. James, with a half sigh. 'But, then, he's not like anybody else.'

'There's no doubt that he drove the Cannibal mad taking her away from him.'

'And he is trying to revenge himself? I don't think Harry need fear any man's rivalry, somehow.'

'You forget what you said about Maintenong. A husband don't count.'

'Oh! That depends on what sort of a husband. Harry counts a great deal.'

It was quite true that Harry had allowed himself to drift back into his dangerous friendship with Flossie Maintenong, much to the silent agony of Tom, her husband. And indeed any husband might well quail before the task of appearing in better colours before his wife than this gay young lord, with his noble figure, his expressive face, his gentle manners, and his reputation for generosity and for that recklessness which women love. Tom was not the only person to whom this flirtation was gall and wormwood. Amalia was driven nearly wild by it, and the Duke of Ulster, deserted by Flossie, was outdoing all his previous achievements in the same direction in his efforts to be revenged. It was a curious game of four, with poor Tom vainly hoping to be allowed to cut in.

The party at Mall Castle was as grand as predicted. Never had guests been entertained in so royal a fashion. For those who shot there were pheasants innumerable to sacrifice. Those who hunted could pursue the fox on five successive days, and each sportsman had two hunters and a hack assigned him each day as a matter of course. There were two balls, one for the home party only, and the other for the county at large ; there was a cross-country race meeting in the park on the one non-hunting day ; there were theatricals one night, a concert another ; and indeed there was everything that could be desired by the heart of Society-loving animals. Even his Highness of Spitzbuberei expressed himself as delighted, and the Duke of Ulster drank enough champagne to have floated a canoe.

But the week was not to pass off without incident of another sort. On the last night of the party, when a move had been made from the drawing-room—the ladies to go to bed, to each other's rooms to talk, or to the billiard, or smoking, or card room to join the men ; and the men to attire themselves in strange garments of violent hues, supposed to be necessary to the proper consumption of tobacco—two of the party remained behind.

One, a man, seemed a trifle incommoded by a tendency to topple forward, which caused a pendulum-like motion from his toes to his heels ; the other, a woman, radiant, bold, her great eyes sparkling with excitement and a kind of soft defiance.

' You will come then ? ' said the Duke of Ulster · for it was no other than that great man—resisting a tremendous lurch forward which threatened immediate destruction on Amalia as she stood before him. ' No one need know ; and I want to show you over my house. Come up to town—you can't want to stay here

when we're all gone. If it's necessary, say you're going
to—to a party—anywhere ; and then we shall be so
happy together, Amalia.'

He accompanied the enunciation of her name
with a dive for her hand which very nearly brought
him to grief.

Then she spoke, in very composed tones :

'What you ask would compromise me. You know
that.'

'No woman can be compromised if she wears a veil.'

'Nonsense ! You know you would talk.'

'Amalia, I give you my word of honour as a gentleman——'

'Then what good would it do you ?'

'I love you—you know I love you.'

'Do you ?' she said, looking at him with a contempt
that even he would have seen had he taken one glass of
wine less that night. 'Do you? And so you want to
ruin me ?'

'Ruin you ! What does your husband care? I'm
not asking you to run away.'

'No,' and her lip curled in bitter scorn ; '*that*
would compromise *you.*'

'I don't care about myself !' cried his Grace, wildly.

'You shouldn't ask me to care about what you
don't, then.'

'Don't laugh at me, Amalia. I'm in earnest !'

'And you want me to come to Granderly House
next Tuesday evening ?'

'Yes—at least, no—is that someone in the next
room ?'

They stopped and listened, but the noise was not
repeated.

'Granderly House wouldn't quite do. But I've
such a pretty little place down in Kensington. I'll
write down the exact address. I should so like you to
see it.'

' You're a very wicked man, I'm afraid.'

' It can't be wicked to love you.'

' And is that why you took the little house in Kensington ? ' asked she, knowing the house's history well.

' Of course,' lied he readily and sturdily. This especial lie he had told so often that it came very easy to him.

' Well, we mustn't stay here any longer. I'll think it over—I won't promise. Perhaps I may come.'

' And you'll say no more ? '

' That is enough, surely.' And she escaped his clumsy effort to detain her and left the room.

The play that night was not as late as usual. The Duke was in bad luck and left after about an hour of it, and the others soon followed. Just after his Grace had taken off his coat and waistcoat, and was indulging in the long look in the glass with which he always wound up his day's amusements, there was a knock at his door.

' Come in,' said he ; and, to his astonishment, there entered his host. This astonishment was not lessened, and was incorporated with another feeling, that of terror, when Harry, without speaking, locked the door and pocketed the key, and when the Duke observed that he carried in his hand a cutting whip.

' Come to have a chat ? ' he began feebly, not knowing what to say.

' Yes. At least, scarcely a chat. I happened to pass the door of the inner drawing-room this evening, and I heard what you said to my wife.'

' I'm sure—my dear fellow—I——'

' Don't make any excuses. The invitation you honoured her with was plain enough. I don't ask for any explanation. I come to offer you alternative terms. Your behaviour does away with all obligations on my part towards you as my guest. Now, the proper thing would be for me to call you out and shoot you. But I will forego that privilege on one condition.'

'And what is that?'

'That you consent now, without any opposition, to a sound thrashing. I might do both, you know, but I claim only one of the two. Choose. I give you one minute.'

The poor Duke's teeth chattered. Harry looked so terribly strong and resolute. The immediate horrors of chastisement were very terrible—but then had he not heard of Harry's prowess with a pistol? Death would be far more terrible.

'The minute is past. What is your choice?'

'Look here, Piccadilly, I give you my word——'

'I will not argue with you. Unless you choose at once, I will flog you now and shoot you afterwards. Choose!'

'I choose—I choose—the——'

'The thrashing?'

'Yes,' whimpered the Duke, his knees knocking together.

'If you do not stay quiet I shall double your punishment. At present it is my intention to give you twenty strokes.'

'But if I swear to you——'

'Now I shall give you twenty-five, and add to the number every moment of delay.'

'But my health, the doctor says——'

'Thirty strokes!'

Then Lothario gave himself up in terrified silence to the executioner.

Harry took up the cutting whip, grasping it firmly in his right hand, and raised it in the air.

.   .   .   .

'Is there a ghost here?' asked Mrs. Maintenong at breakfast next morning.

'Not that I know of,' returned Amalia. 'Why?'

B B

'I heard such strange noises down at the end of my passage last night, or rather early this morning.'

'Well, there oughtn't to be a ghost there, as it's the newest part of the house.'

'That's where the Duke is, isn't it?'

'Yes. He had the far end of it all to himself, as the other rooms are not quite finished. He likes a big bed-room, and it's the biggest in the house; with a sitting-room off it that looks out on the mountain side.'

'A magnificent view that is,' said Mr. Kelt.

'Well,' went on Mrs. Maintenong, 'I heard all sorts of curious sounds—like muffled cries. It quite frightened me, but I went to sleep just as I was thinking of rousing the house. Good morning, Lord Piccadilly. Where's the Duke? He's generally down before you.'

'I've just had a message to say that he is ill and won't come down yet,' said Harry, going to the side-board and helping himself. 'And he won't go in the train with you all. I'm to get him a special later on.'

'Poor dear Duke!' said Amalia. 'He *has* exerted himself so much all the week.'

Whereat sundry of the company did covertly smile, and Mr. Kelt observed *sotto voce* to his neighbour that he had never heard drinking too much called by that name before.

Before Amalia left the Castle, which she did with her guests, she had a short interview with her husband. He came into her room when she was dressing, and sent her maid away.

'Amalia,' he said sternly, 'I heard the Duke of Ulster's proposition to you last night. I have administered a flogging to him. If I do not see that this—flirtation—is entirely dropped at once, I shall——'

'Flog me too?' asked she defiantly.

He made a slight bow, still very grave:

'Exactly.'

CHAPTER LI.

ALTHOUGH Harry wrote in such a haughty manner when his mother hinted at his flirtation with Mrs. Maintenong, her words nevertheless did cause him to reflect. Hating his own home, and being naturally inclined towards the conversation and pleasantnesses of a pretty woman determined to please, he had drifted almost unconsciously into this friendship. It was very agreeable to escape from the unhomelike grandeur and distasteful display of Piccadilly House to the cosy drawing-room where Flossie received her many worshippers, and reigned a lovely little queen amid her blue china and photographs of the worshippers themselves. Decidedly agreeable, too, was it to know that none of these gentry would be admitted while he was good enough to stay, and be petted and amused. Mrs. Maintenong thoroughly understood the art of making a man comfortable and putting him at his ease. Even Jack Bumbledom of the Blues, who blushed and lost the power of speech when addressed by a lady, declared that 'one feels in Mrs. M.'s room just as one does in the ante-room ; except that one is more comfortable, and has a feeling one oughtn't to swear. But then there is also the feeling that one might swear if one liked.' On only one occasion had Harry been annoyed by an attempt to sit him out, and this attempt was perhaps to some slight degree excusable, seeing that it was made by Mr. Maintenong. Tom had nerved himself to the task one afternoon, and, fortified by an extra glass of sherry at luncheon, began pretty creditably. Unmoved by the hints and frowns of his wife, he sat stolidly on, now reading the paper, now cutting into the conversation with some vague remark.

At last to him, Flossie—

'When are you going, Tom ?'

'I don't think I shall go out this afternoon, my
dear. It looks rather like rain.'

'Then are you not going downstairs to smoke?'

'No. I don't want to smoke.'

'Good gracious, Tom!'

This was accompanied by a resolute stamp of the
little foot upon the carpet.

'Good gracious! How on earth *can* I talk to
Harry if you stay there listening to every word, like
a cross between an owl and a gaoler? If you don't go
I declare I'll ask him to make love to me before your
eyes!'

'But, my dear——' began poor Tom, rising in
desperation.

'Oh, it's no use "butting" or "my dearing." Two
is company: three is horrid!'

'Perhaps I'd better go,' said Harry, half laughing,
half embarrassed.

'If you do I'll never speak to you again!' cried
Flossie, her eyes flashing at her mutinous husband.
'Do you want to lose me a friend, Tom? Do get out,
that's a dear,' she continued, in softer tones; 'I have a
lot of things to say you oughtn't to hear. Go to your
Club at once; and mind you come back with plenty of
gossip for me. I want particularly to know the exact
truth about the Y.'s. Do you hear? Come back in
good time to dress, as we dine out, you know. Ta, ta!'

And the husband, not knowing whether to admire
or to be angry with his petulant little wife, did forth-
with depart, and never again attempted to interfere
with her afternoon receptions.

Some little time after this Harry turned in as usual
at about six o'clock, and after that kind of casual and
fitful converse which is only possible between people who
know each other well enough to be silent when they
have nothing to say, he entered upon his subject, which
it must be confessed, was scarcely an easy one to

manage; for it was no other than his determination to
give up his dangerous intimacy with her.

'Why do you say "not at home" to the others when
I am here?' he began, hoping that her answer might
guide him a little on his track.

She opened her eyes wide.

'Why? Because I like you better than the others,
to be sure.'

'Do you?'

'Don't be silly, Harry. We are great—pals, are we
not?'

There was a gravity about him that frightened her:
and the shadow of a fearful possibility—perhaps that
he had fallen madly in love with someone else, even his
own wife—caused her to turn pale.

'Yes—great pals. I wonder why the world won't
allow of such friendship.'

'What does the world matter? You always say
you don't care for it.'

'Yes, I have said that; but I spoke as a fool,
Flossie.'

'That's better. You called me Mrs. Maintenong just
now; and I began wondering what I had done to offend
you. Let us both be fools, Harry. It's much pleasanter.
What are you thinking of, that you look so solemn?
Has her Ladyship done anything terrible lately? Oh,
I beg pardon! I forget you forbade my ever talking
about that sacred person. But what *are* you thinking
of?'

'I was thinking of Tom.'

'Of Tom! What an extraordinary thing to think
of—with me.'

'Is it? I don't quite see that. He is your husband.'

'Yes, so he is. Well, let us think of him, if you
like. How shall we consider him? You begin.'

'I'm serious, Flossie. You remember the other day,
when you sent him away?'

'Perfectly. How silly he looked—dear old Tom!'

'I did not notice that he looked particularly silly. I did notice one expression in his face, though.'

'What—viciousness? Oh, no. He's as tame as—a Radical in office.'

'No. Pain.'

'Pain!'

'Yes. Has it ever struck you that what is fun to you may be torture to him? He bears it very bravely because he is so fond of you.'

'He is that,' murmured the lady, her eyes fixed in amazement on the young preacher before her.

'But that very fondness must aggravate the torture. Do you think that when you flirt with——'

'With you,' again put in Flossie.

'With anyone. Do you think he doesn't suffer although he says nothing?'

'Doesn't he? He talks a great deal sometimes, particularly when we've dined where the champagne is strong. But I don't understand——

'You don't understand why I, of all people, should talk like this. Will you believe one thing, my dear Flossie—that I say what I am going to say because I am your "pal?"'

He had taken her willing hand, half without knowing it, and held it as he went on, she still looking at him in dumb amazement.

'I am older than you are a good deal; and I have seen more of life than most men of my age. Besides, I have now the wisdom of misery. Knowing what misery which has to be borne patiently and in silence can be, I know what Tom suffers. I know—as you do not—that life is not all beer and skittles; that duty is something more than a mere name. To me, God knows, it is pleasant beyond my describing to come here to you, and to be welcomed by your sweet words and your exquisite beauty.' (Even the compliment, much as she loved compliments, did not serve to allay the growing consternation in her heart.) 'But such pleasures can be bought at too dear a price. You know I speak the truth, Flossie. I am now speaking like this for your sake, and not at all for my own.'

'I don't care for my sake,' she said, with a half-sob, 'and I think you are going to be cruel.'

'We—both of us—are skating on ice that will hardly bear us. Our names are coupled together, and——'

'What do I care? The idiots must have somebody to couple together. As long as we know there is no harm.'

Then he was crafty and diplomatic.

'No harm! No harm to you with your hundreds of adorers, and your true love for Tom—for I know you do at heart care more for his little finger than for all of us—no harm to you, you wicked little man-killer! But no harm to me? Do you think I am made of adamant? Do you think I can sit every day before the fire of those eyes and never melt?'

'You never do melt,' said Flossie, with a smile on her lip and a tear in her eye.

'But I might go all of a sudden.'

'But you said just now that you were talking like this—in this horrid way, just like Tom's mother—for my sake.'

'Yes, that was because I didn't want to confess to my weakness. Say it is for my own sake, if you like. Say it is a little—just a little—for the sake of your name; say it is a great deal for the sake of your husband.'

'Do keep Tom's name out of it.'

'How can I? Tell me now, Flossie, and tell me the exact truth. Are you not very fond of him?'

'Yes, of course I am—as a husband.'

'Well, you are making life one long misery to him.'

'He shouldn't have married me ; then he wouldn't have been my husband. I told him ages ago, when we first thought of marrying each other, that he had much better let me marry old Lord Slopergore, who asked me, and then we might never hate each other, or grow tired of looking and holding hands and saying pretty things ; but he would rush on his fate. It is his own fault.'

'I want you to be serious, Flossie.'

'But I never can be serious. It is not my nature.'

Then she disengaged her hand from his, and stood up, and looked very serious indeed and intensely in earnest.

'Of course I see what it all means. You have heard some wretched gossip, or perhaps Lady Piccadilly has heard it, and you, like all men, want a quiet life at any price ; and so you come to me with all this specious goody talk about Tom, and my name, and your weakness, or else—let me finish *please*, you've had your say—you are tired of me, and want to go and have tea every afternoon, and tell your secrets, and ask for advice which you don't take, somewhere else. Oh, Harry!' Here she with difficulty repressed a rising storm of sobs. 'Tell me it isn't that!'

Then Harry rose too, and leant against the mantelpiece, while she moved restlessly about the room, looking very pretty in her mingled anger, and grief, and wonder.

'I always speak the truth, Flossie. We shall always be great friends ; but perhaps, considering Tom and—and my wife—we have been rather too great friends. I have a sort of feeling—you won't think me a conceited ass, for you know I am not quite that—but I have a kind of notion that if I were out of the way you——' He stopped. It certainly was a hard thing to say. But she was quick-witted enough, and helped him generously, considering the circumstances, out of his difficulty.

'I know what you mean. Yes, it is quite true, Harry. Shall I tell you? I must; for I feel this is our last talk alone for a long time. Well, I care more for you than anything—much more than Tom. And next to you comes Tom—only Tom. All the others are——' and she snapped her fingers expressively. 'They all say the same things and wear the same clothes. I keep all their photographs with names underneath to prevent my forgetting which is which. It is all you—and Tom.'

'And it mustn't be me.'

'Mustn't it?'

Perhaps Harry had never been in any real danger till that moment. There was something so touching in her pretty humility and the utter absence of any natural resentment.

But he was obstinate when he had made up his mind; and he put aside an inclination to take her in his arms, and went on:

'No, I'm not a man, like Braysey or Kelt, who can go on dangling after a woman and playing at love. With me it is all or nothing; and I could contemplate nothing so terrible as for me to fall hopelessly in love with my friend Tom Maintenong's wife.'

'It would have been very nice, though,' said Flossie, half to herself.

'One proof how much I trust you, how I esteem you above ordinary women, is my daring to come to you to-day and talk like this. I really don't believe there is another woman in England who would have taken it as you have.'

'I've no proper pride,' said she, in a tearful voice. 'Tom's mother—oh, how I hate her!—says that. And she says something else now much more dreadful. She told Tom the other night that she was so sorry that I was losing my looks. Oh, Harry, can that be true? Can it be the reason for your—your talking like this?'

'You are,' said he slowly and deliberately, looking at her imploring, upturned child's face, 'you are the loveliest woman I have ever seen, and you are more lovely than last year. You cannot improve any more —that is the worst of it—because you are perfect now.'

'Thank you, Harry,' said the little woman quite humbly, as if she were a beggar who had received alms. 'I hope you mean that, because you don't often pay me compliments. I am glad you think me as pretty as your wife.'

Harry frowned. To speak of his wife with anyone was distasteful to him; to speak of her with Flossie Maintenong especially so.

There was a short pause, during which he contemplated, without seeing it, a photograph of a gorgeous Hussar Lieutenant in full uniform which lay on the table (one of Flossie's very latest conquests from Hounslow), and then he said:

'I am going away soon.'

'Away? To Mall or Ireland?'

'No; a long journey—round the world, I think. My ship wants a little exercise.'

'Round the world! How I should like to go! It's a great pity you should have taken these ideas. Will— will Lady Piccadilly go too?'

'She hates the sea.'

'And I love it. What a pity that is!'

'I probably shall stay away a year or more.'

'Will you? How dreadful! But——'

'But what?'

'Will that be exactly doing your duty?'

He sat down opposite to her, and only just checked himself as he was about to possess himself of her hand.

'I don't think, Flossie, that a man is bound to be

tortured beyond a certain point.   My affairs will get
on quite well without me for a year; and I am not
wanted at what I call, for the want of a better word,
home.   It would be absurd for me to pretend to you
that I am happy.   But even you cannot guess the full
extent of my misery.   To go on without a break would
drive me mad.   Virtually my wife and I are separated
—you will, of course, never breathe a hint of this to anyone—and never shall be together again.   Outwardly
all will go on as it did.   If anyone is blamed it will be
me, and I had rather it were so.   Thank heaven there
are no children; that, indeed, would have complicated
matters.   Now that you and I must, to some extent,
cease to be the same to each other as we have been ;
now that I can no longer run away from my troubles
each day for an hour or two, and forget them all while
with you, I must change my life for a time.   If I stay
in England I am bound to assist in all the duties and
so-called pleasures that Lady Piccadilly is so determined
to do and enjoy.   But there is nothing strange in my
going for a long cruise, or in her being sea-sick and
therefore staying at home.'

'And whom shall you take with you?'

'I shall go quite alone.'

'That'll be dreadful!'

'My friends all bore me now on shore.   Think what
they would be at sea!   I might manage with Tom,
though.   Shall I take him?'

'No, no!   Fancy poor me left without you or Tom !
I should take arsenic.'

'You forget the others;' and he pointed to the
picture-gallery.

'Pooh!   But you don't go yet awhile?'

'Directly the ship is ready.   Can I do anything for
you in China—or the South Sea Islands?'

'Oh, Harry!' she exclaimed, as she put her hand in
his to say good-bye, while the tears flowed freely down

her cheeks. 'Don't think of me as a bad woman—only as a woman who loved you very dearly, and whom you have made better than she otherwise would have been. Good-bye; I want to go and cry, and then let Tom try to console me. I shall tell him all about it—everything. I may? How I wish I were a South Sea Islander! I hear they wear such pretty clothes, and have such nice notions about propriety and husbands. Good-bye! You won't forget me—I—I——'

Then she burst into an agony of weeping; and he, after a moment of hesitation, fled hastily from the house.

CHAPTER LII.

ANOTHER London summer's sun has opened afresh the leaves of the party-givers' visiting-books, and tinted anew the coronets of desirable elder sons; again the sweet-voiced harbingers of spring—the linkmen—have carolled outside of the houses of those who give entertainments; once more the tender budding maidens have blushed before the Queen; and once more the full-blown damsels have coloured and expanded vainly for the benefit of careless cavaliers. Charwomen have disappeared with snow, and fog has been exchanged—thanks to intelligent vestries!—for the block occasioned by taking up a few principal West-End thoroughfares. Hunting men who dislike jumping look desperately valiant, for the red coats and top-boots are put away; and country gentlemen, leaving their wives at home, are in town doing business—during the Derby week. All is bustle, and dust, and hand-shaking, and hat taking-off, and retailing of country-house scandals —in short, not to put too fine a point on it, the London season has again commenced. And still Piccadilly

House is the great place of entertainment. For a week or so, until the will of a mighty personage could be ascertained, it was just a little doubtful whether the absence of the husband would make any difference; but when cards were issued of the largest size, coronetted and glazed, bearing at the top the mystic words 'To have the honour of meeting '—the aforesaid personage, no doubt remained but that, when Lady Piccadilly said that she was dancing at home, she would not be allowed to dance at home alone. So the Piccadilly House affairs, which generally began by being dinners and ended in dances, were 'the thing' again ; and no one thought anything about that eccentric Lord who preferred yachting on distant seas to doing the honours of his house and of his handsome wife.

Mr. Braysey was triumphant in the new order of things. He had the same kind of dislike for Harry as a rabbit has for a ferret, though the ferret be muzzled, and was intensely relieved by the absence of the master of the house in which he ate such good dinners. To the Duke of Ulster, too, Harry's absence afforded unmitigated joy. No inkling of what had happened between them at Mall Castle ever came out; and although there was a twinkle in Amalia's eyes when his Grace first called upon her in London, she had too much tact and respect for her guest's position to breathe a word of her knowledge of the painful incident. Shame is the exact reverse of a secret in one respect: for the former—for philosophers like our Duke—does not exist while only one person knows of the fact ; and the Duke resumed gaily his old position of first favourite in Piccadilly House.

Mrs. Maintenong, oddly enough, did not now respond to Amalia's advances, and this was a source of some annoyance to the latter, seeing that it was the fashion nowadays to bury the hatchet of jealousy, and to invite as many pretty women as possible to smoke the

pipe of peaceful flirtation beneath your ceiling.   But
Mrs. Maintenong, after all, as Amalia argued to herself
and her intimate friends, was already passed by as a
beauty.   Her photographs had vanished from the shop-
windows; no one could rightly fix upon a new flirtation
of hers; and she had actually been seen on two
occasions—*mirabile dictu*!—at theatres *alone* with her
husband.   A student of human nature might have
marvelled at the amount of bitterness which was caused
by these two apparently simple acts on her part.
Was she trying to make domesticity fashionable?   It
was horrible.

And so all the dear creatures wagged their nice
little tongues at her, and it was industriously rumoured
that she had commenced an intrigue so low and base
that hypocrisy had to be called in to hide it.

'She'll turn religious next,' said Amalia, scornfully,
as she drove away from the Maintenongs' door, after
having had tea with Flossie and Tom; and Mr. Kelt,
to whom she was giving a lift, said that he feared the
very worst from her apparent quietude.

It is sad to have to record that Flossie Maintenong
cared not at all for this talk, but went her way—now it
was the right way—just as fearlessly as she had gone
her way when it was perhaps scarcely in the most correct
direction.

'Do you know what I am losing for you, Tom?'
she said on that very occasion when Amalia had clat-
tered away in her smart barouche.   'I am losing my
position.'

'All the better, darling.'

'And you'll like me just as well now, although you
know why I—I am good?'

Tom did not reply.   His feelings were so mixed
that nothing but a German sentence of fifty lines with
the governing verb at the end could have expressed
them.

'But I mean to be good—oh, so good! Can't you give me something to do, Tom dear? I did the house-books this morning, and your stockings; and you know what they say about idle hands.'

'Give me them.'

And her husband restrained for a moment any independent action on the part of the little hands, which as a rule were almost as eloquent as her tongue, so much did she rely upon them to elucidate her meaning.

'Can you ever forget *him*?' he asked, almost piteously.

All the woman in her was stirred by the look in his sad eyes. She met their gaze for a moment, and then her own filled, and she threw herself upon his breast.

'Oh, Tom! Tom! how good you have been to me! and what a brute I have been to you! Of course I can —of course I can. I was mad, I think. He is noble and good, but I love you, Tom—you! Do you understand that? I am sane again at last.'

'My darling!' That was all he said, but there was no need of words. He was happy.

Let our curtain fall now on these two. We need them no longer in our little comedy. They have played their part, and may go. But before saying farewell to Tom Maintenong and his wife, the whilom professional beauty, might we, even in this age of blind belief in disbelief, ask our readers to pardon her the faults which arose more from Society's laws than from her own nature; and him the lack of that austerity which should of course mark every husband's conduct? He was weak in one way—she in another; and the end should have been utter ruin. Punishment and shame to her: loneliness and misery to him. But, you see, the end was otherwise, and the moral is all wrong. I —(the stilts are off again now)—I would not make it otherwise an I could. The labelling principle is very pretty and comprehensive and clear, but it has one little defect. It does not act. Human nature refuses to be all good or all bad, and rebels against the clerical ethics of some critical authorities, who are incensed to find the villain turn only half a villain in the third volume.

Let the Maintenongs go now. I don't pretend that reading of such is particularly good or wholesome. It may be that one should never mention any who are not both good and wholesome, except when one introduces a transpontine scoundrel to scowl and scheme, and help the plot along. All I do pretend to say is that such like are the actual folk that live and eat and drink and do many things they should not amongst us, and that it requires more skill than I can compass to describe ' the world ' without them.

CHAPTER LIII.

When Humphrey Erdmore died it would be untrue to say that no one mourned. Nellie was oppressed by the sense that in her heart she had never quite done him justice, for she never fathomed the poor wretch's meanness of heart. And the boy wept—not at the loss of the parent he had first feared as a gloomy tyrant, and then thought of with awe as a strange, gibbering, uncanny creature in an upper room—but at the awsome presence of death in the house; and the housekeeper mourned, for she was only left a small sum to buy a mourning-ring ; and the resident doctor mourned, for his occupation was gone. But not by the greatest stretch of the meaning of language could his death be said to have created a gap; nor, indeed, could any unprejudiced person say that he was wanted any longer in the land of the living. His case had long ago been given up as hopeless, and when, about six months after their

vain journey to London, Nellie was summoned in haste
to his chair-side only to find him gone, even she could
scarcely feel that it would have been for anyone's
benefit that his death in life should have still continued.
She was left fairly well off, with the guardianship of
her son, and the use of Castle Erdmore until that son
came of age ; and she at once accepted her duty in
life, and determined to devote every energy she possessed to making the boy worthy of his heritage of
manhood.

The wild dreams of happiness that she had once
cherished were now succeeded by a calm vision of content ; and I question whether, when the blow of her
widowhood had somewhat passed, and she was able to
view her married life justly and calmly, she was not
happier by far than she had ever been since that day,
now so long ago, when Harry and she had confessed
their young love in the Richlake garden.

That, of course, stood apart; round the head of her
Harry—not the Harry that had married Amalia, but
the Harry she had known—her imagination had formed
a halo of glory ; and often, with secret misgivings
of unfaithfulness to the dead, of wronging her boy, she
would take out of her desk the well-known letters that
he had written her in those happy days.

The love of a good woman is a solemn thing, for
it endures with her life, let the object thereof be what
it may.

It must not be supposed that Nellie Erdmore shut
herself up and moped. It was necessary that her son's
life should be made bright, and she could scarcely open
her house only when he came home for the holidays.
So she let visitors come and go, and among the most
constant was that mysterious, quaint, but alway devoted
Mr. Lacroix, who asked no better than to fetch and
carry for her and hers.

He had refused Harry's offer of a berth in the

Banshee, much to the delight of the owner of that vessel, saying that he was growing old, and that he could not bear the thought of dying far away from his child. Harry's only motive for asking him was that he thought Lacroix might feel lost without him; and he was glad to know that near the woman he loved he should leave someone at least ready to defend her with his heart's blood.

Rumours came to Nellie from time to time of the mad life that Lady Piccadilly was living in London, of the way her name was coupled with that of the Duke of Ulster, and, in a minor degree, with that of a Mr. Braysey, who, it was reported, had owed his seat in Parliament to her purse. She heard in a vague way of some quarrel between Amalia and the Dowager, her mother-in-law, and of the commencement of a reaction of feeling against the former.

Those of the county who went to the capital came back with queer stories of the equivocal position into which she was drifting, and of the havoc late hours and the excitement of gambling (to which she had taken) were playing with the beauty's looks; and one day, as Nellie laid down a letter from Lacroix, in which he told her things that almost made her innocent blood run cold with horror, her eyes happened to fall upon a telegram in the Dublin paper that lay upon her table.

'Rumoured loss of a yacht and crew.—A report has reached Southampton of the total loss of the schooner-yacht *Banshee*, off Newfoundland, with all hands. It is not yet known whether the owner, Lord Piccadilly, was on board, nor has any confirmation as yet been received.'

'Why, mamma,' cried a handsome boy, running into the room, 'what's the matter? You look as you did when papa died! Is anyone dead now?'

'I—run to Mr. Lacroix—he is in the garden!'

cried Mrs. Erdmore, gasping for breath ; ' tell him I want to see him at once !'

In a few hours Lacroix was on his way to London, leaving her praying for strength and help.

CHAPTER LIV.

A YEAR, which passes so quickly for the novelist or for the unfortunate wight who is accustomed to negotiate three months' bills, must be supposed by the reader to have passed since the events recorded in the last chapter. Although all the characters in my story are thus necessarily twelve months older, they have not materially changed. If Lady Piccadilly has developed any wrinkles, she has the skill to hide them ; and indeed, in view of the gigantic strides made of late in the art of ' getting up the face and eyes ' (as the advertisements in papers for the fair sex have it), a woman may be said, for a certain portion of her fashionable existence, to grow younger instead of older as she becomes initiated in the great art's mysteries.

For some time after the terrible news of the loss of the *Banshee* had been received, she wore widows' weeds so becomingly that even the dressmakers pitied her ; and it must be owned that her conduct was quite free from reproach. At first her grief was very great—was very real; for she did love her husband in her animal, brutal, selfish fashion ; and she did, in a kind of angry way, reproach herself with many items of her conduct towards him. But even with her regret—she being ignorant of Latin and of the ' de mortuis ' theory— there mingled much fury with the dead man for his refusal to reciprocate her love, or what she called her love. With the spirit of a barmaid Amalia combined

the sentimentalism of a French novelist; and even
though Harry's affection had been only of the kind
which is half hate, so pathetically depicted by Messrs.
Belot and Zola, she would have preferred it by much to
his semi-disdainful fits of admiration for her person and
indifference to all else about her.   To be inferior and
to be too stupid to recognise your inferiority is nothing.
The man or woman who knows where the *h's* ought to
be and cannot always insert them is to be pitied; while
your *h*-less plebeian knows no trouble on the subject.
Amalia was clever enough to know exactly how unsuitable she was to the man she had adroitly inveigled into
marriage with her, and she fiercely resented the fact.
No amount of lessons in etiquette, though they enable
people to shine easily enough in the lax society of the
day—which loves gold so much as to care nothing for
its form and shape—could have served to bridge over
the chasm that divided her from a ' lady,' as Harry
esteemed a lady.   And she knew it—that was her
curse.   Look at that gaudy damsel, out on Easter
Monday for a well-earned holiday, attired in all the
colours of the rainbow, and glittering with chains and
gew-gaws.   She is perfectly happy in her horrible
splendour.   But observe the poor struggling waif of
gentility driving round the park in her hired victoria.
How conscious *she* is of the little defects in her dress,
of the subtle difference between her turn-out and that
of Lady Gloriana Slyward, who has just passed by!
Gnashing her teeth, she goes back to the dingy street
in South Belgravia, where she lives for six weeks in the
season, and almost vows to fight the battle of poverty
versus fashion no longer.   So Amalia, not being content with the vulgar mind that she could not escape
from, had gnashed her white teeth at intervals; and,
while exclaiming against the absurdity that her husband
should refuse to take her, as others took her, at her own
valuation, confessed to her own self that he, and not

'Society,' was right. Had she been as methodical as
Robinson Crusoe, she would, when the news of the
yacht's total loss was confirmed, have set down her
accounts somewhat in this way.

Loss.—1. Harry. 2. The chance of making him
fond of me. 3. The position his being alive ensured
to me. 4. My opportunity for repairing the past.
5. The difference between the income we enjoyed and
my jointure.

Gain.—1. Freedom. 2. The uninterrupted enjoyment of the society of Braysey, or anyone else I like.
3. Power of making my own plans. 4. Sympathy
for my widowhood. 5. Becomingness to me of mourning. 6. Power of marrying again. 7. Annihilation of
any chance, with regard to Harry, that Mrs. Erdmore
may have had.

The odds were seven to five; and, as one versed in
Turf matters, Amalia was after a time decently contented with her lot.

And it was, to speak vulgarly, a good lot. Harry
had been generous enough in the matter of settlement,
and his widow was rich. She had a charming dower
house in Grosvenor Place, bought with money vested
in trustees for that purpose; she had a nice income;
she had all the carriages and horses, and some of the
plate; and she had all the money that happened to be
lying in the banker's hands at the time of the catastrophe.

And so, after an interval, she was contented, until
one dreadful day, when his Grace of Ulster ventured
to hint that she was wrong in her ideas as to the suit-
ability to her style of beauty of the widows' caps. With
all his faults, the Duke was a real connoisseur in female
beauty; and his word was law as to looks and dress.

So Amalia pondered and asked advice. Braysey,
who had projects with reference to the jointure and to
the ease with which the fair Baroness could insure her
life, fell in at once with the great man's views.

The abolition of the cap would, he thought, be a great stride towards his ambitious realisation.

'You've worn it long enough,' he said, smoking a cigarette in her boudoir, 'and it's beastly ugly. Besides, no one believes you cared a d——I mean a bit—for him, and people hate hypocrisy nowadays.'

Amalia, to do her justice, held a very just estimate of this gentleman; but his words had some effect nevertheless; and when, some five months after the loss of the *Banshee*, the Dowager called, annoying with her ostentatious trappings of woe—which, poor lady, did not in the least belie the sorrow that 'passeth show' within her—Amalia was in a very doubtful mood on the great question.

The catastrophe had brought these two ladies together again to a certain extent, though neither forgot, nor would ever forget, certain things that had been said when they had quarrelled.

'I am thinking of giving up my cap,' said Amalia.

'Good gracious! Surely you are not serious? Give up your cap? Now?'

'Why not?'

'Why not!' said the Dowager, who was a little afraid of her dashing daughter-in-law. 'Why, it wouldn't be decent.'

'What does that matter?'

'It matters, my dear Amalia, a very great deal. It would be an insult to Society.'

'I don't care about Society.'

'And an insult to my poor son's memory.'

'That's nothing.'

'Nothing!'

'No. It could do him no harm, poor fellow! And he never cared much about all these observances. I remember his telling me so once. And I hate the thing; it's so ugly.'

'Ugly or pretty, it is considered correct.'

'My dear Mrs. St. James, do try and remember that I am—as I believe you once called me—an uneducated, vulgar upstart, and I can't therefore be expected to care very much about correctness.'

'You have become one of us.'

'No! For you never received me. I made my own way in this world you call fashionable, not by your help, but in spite of you. You would, no doubt, have helped me on in a condescending, useless kind of way, and by this time I should perhaps have been acquainted with a few of the second-rate people who have tea in your house. No, I have never been one of you in the sense of belonging to the family. You repudiated me when I was weak, and you cringed to me when I was strong; and now I repudiate you!'

'Amalia!'

'Yes, I am sick of the business. Even your son, though I was his wife, always kept a line drawn between us—always made me feel that he was a great gentleman and I was not a great lady. I could beat the world—such as they are—but I could never break down the barrier of his pride. Yours was pitiful and weak enough, I admit; but I could do nothing with his, for it was real and grand. And now you come to me and talk of what I owe to his memory and to the Society which would have kicked me if it hadn't been afraid I could kick hardest. Bah!'

The concentrated anger of her broodings came out now in violent passion, as she declaimed before the affrighted and trembling Dowager; and as she finished the sentence and gave vent to the exclamation of mingled rage and contempt, she tore her widow's cap from off her head and flung it violently upon the fire.

Then her mother-in-law started up:

'You are not a lady!'

Amalia, immediately after the action, had become

calm, and had sat down to watch the fragile stuff burn up brightly on the coals.

'Who said I was?'

The Dowager was conquered. She did not dare meet the other's mocking smile lest she should burst into tears.

'Will you let me have my carriage?'

'With pleasure,' said Amalia, stretching out an indolent hand and ringing the bell. 'I will let you have anything—except the right to lecture me—or any of my money.'

There was a silence till the carriage came round from the stable, where it had been sent, in view of a long interview; and then, as she was going, the elder lady turned round at the door, having motioned the butler to precede her downstairs.

'You are aware, I suppose, that Mr. Bury St. James is shortly about to claim the peerage as the nearest of kin, although, I suppose, there may be said to be some doubt still as to my son's death?'

'I daresay,' said Amalia, carelessly. 'What does it matter to me?'

'Not much, perhaps,' remarked the Dowager, pursing up her lips; 'but of course you will have to give up the family diamonds.'

'I am ready to do that.'

'And there will be some accounts to go through.'

'I like business.'

Then she stood up.

'Look here, you said something just now about there being a chance of Harry not being dead. What did you mean by that?'

'I meant,' replied the other, with her hand on the door handle, 'I meant that it is impossible to be certain. The yacht was seen to be in difficulties in a gale of wind. It is as certain, I suppose, as anything can be that when she struck on those rocks she sank in deep water, and that all on board were drowned. But who knows that some did not escape in some marvellous way?'

'If they did should we not have heard of them before this? Do you think that Harry or any of the crew would remain quietly at Newfoundland without making a sign for five months?'

'Wonderful things happen sometimes.'

'And will you explain to me, please,' went on Amalia, to whom the subject seemed to have great attraction, 'how any of the survivors, if there were such, would have lived meanwhile? Where would their money come from?'

'I don't say it's likely,' said the Dowager, opening the door.

'And I say it's impossible and ridiculous and absolutely wicked to talk in such a way. I believe you wish me to remain unmarried all my life, and have invented the doubt to spite me.'

Then the old lady managed to assert some of the dignity which the other's ferocity had sadly disconcerted.

'You are unworthy to speak to a lady,' she said, and went down to her carriage.

.   .   .   .   .   .

All Amalia's bosom friends roared with laughter that night when she told them the story of her throwing her cap on the fire; but it would have been better for her to have foregone the joke, good as it was. For in a few hours it had gone the round of the clubs; the next day it was the talk of tea-tables; and Society began seriously to ask itself whether this woman should not know that she could no longer be a power amongst them; should not be dethroned from this false eminence on which she had been placed. But the Duke of Ulster remained true to his fealty, knowing as he did how few women there were who could be so kind to his frailties, in the matter of champagne at dinner and other libations after, as she was; and, the change of residence having been effected, he found the drawing-rooms of the house in Grosvenor Place far too pleasant a retreat to be lightly abandoned.

Amalia—although very fond of him, as she averred and he believed—was not of a jealous temperament. Nay, more; she would ask those ladies of whom he expressed his admiration to meet him at the little dinners she now affected ; and she would even go so far as to condole with him on the reverses that not even the great ones of the earth are free from when dealing with capricious womankind, and would tender him sage advice as to his next move.

More·than this ; when, the full year having passed since her widowhood, she was enabled to throw her door a little wider open to the world, she would allow him to meet—of course accidentally—the wives of some of his friends at her house, while she—equally accidentally—was called away on urgent and irresistible business.

Braysey approved in a way of her goings on, but not altogether.

'You'll get yourself into trouble with that Cannibal,' he remarked one day.

'Mind your own business,' was the reply.

And he, being a wise man, and knowing when to speak and when to be silent, held his tongue.

But only then. Abroad he talked much and adroitly, deploring Lady Piccadilly's infatuation, and kindly hinting at her utter want of all proper caution and reticence ; for, argued the social diplomat to himself, 'if she finds the ground slipping from under her feet she will naturally turn to me to help her ; and—and six thousand a year, even though she won't insure her life, would be very nice.'

Meanwhile, as Society forgets its favourites easily enough, it was not long before Harry's name· ceased to be mentioned in those houses and clubs where he had ever been most welcome. The vast estates were broken up among members of the St. James family, one second cousin taking the title of Baron St. James, and the Barony of Piccadilly becoming extinct. There was a great sale at Christie's of the wonderful and beautiful things in Piccadilly House, with the exception of those which indulgent trustees allowed the widow to keep to herself—and she took a good share—and then, horrible to relate, the house itself was purchased by the West-End Hotel Company, Limited, and ruined many hundred confiding shareholders before a twelvemonth was over.

Amalia, although a very great lady still, was much less of a great lady than when she had reigned in her palace, and sometimes, even though the Duke was her slave and Braysey her *laquais de place,* was sorry that the *Banshee* had not contrived to escape the treacherous Newfoundland rocks. Poor Lacroix was inconsolable, and never left Nellie Erdmore's side for months after the dreadful news had come.

There is something of hope always while there is life; and although Nellie had long ago put aside as unworthy all thought of Harry and herself being anything to each other, she could not bear to think that now inexorable Death stood between them; that what she would have done of her own free will she was compelled now to do by Fate.

CHAPTER LV.

As the years rolled by Lady Piccadilly found it more and more difficult to procure for herself sufficient excitement—even flirting will pall after a time if there

is no heart in it—and looked eagerly round for something to divert the current of her life from its course.
She was far too sensible a woman to spoil her fine
health by dram-drinking, or by doing too much of what
the world calls dissipation. Amalia liked her night's
rest, and knew well that out-of-door exercise was
necessary towards the enjoyment of her hearty meals.
She had just enough real religion left to keep her from
any of the hysterical forms in which utterly creedless
women often take refuge from the monotony of naughti-
ness: and the kind of philanthropy prevalent then—
' slumming,' singing songs and reciting before East End
audiences, or attending meetings and wearing pretty
clothes on platforms, all seemed to her provincial mind
more hypocritical than the religious dodge. Politics
her keen shrewdness and sense of humour told her were
impossible for women at present, the political *salon* of
to-day being merely a place where politicians invent, to
please their hostess, something which resembles political
talk just as much as a horse chestnut resembles a
chestnut horse. And Amalia hated to be made a fool
of, be it never so nicely. That she could act, the reader
is aware, if he remembers how she stormed the inner
citadel of Society armed only with the weapon of
mimicry ; but going on the stage struck her as being only
a last resource : the confession of either inability to procure admiration with no footlights to hide the paint,
or else of an impecuniosity which was shameful when
there were so many rich young men about. Braysey,
like so many men without money, was thoroughly
conversant with the ways of investing it : and soon our
lady was able to talk fluently of bulls and bears, and
Brighton A's, and syndicates, and other such mysterious
articles. Conversing of them soon led to dabbling in
them—at least, not in the bulls and bears, but the
stock they manipulate—and her neat brougham might
then often be seen taking her down eastward to con-

sult with Baron This and Millionaire That on the changing of her various ventures.

At first she floated gaily on the dark deep waters, like a dry sponge ; but soon, as with that sponge when imbued with moisture, so with her, the sinking began. And quickly indeed she realised the meaning of Bathos. Down, down, clutching, not at straws, but at men of straw, as the capitalists eluded her grasp, fighting desperately for retrievement ; but all to no purpose.

Then, one fine day (it was a foggy December after-noon, but I like the old formula) she, like a brave lady, looked the matter in the face, and very ugly she found it. All her latest investments had 'turned up crabs,' as a young friend of hers in the Guards called it ; her jointure, together with her house and other property, was mortgaged to its full extent, and she was reduced to an income which, as the butler observed, when offered a salary unworthy of him, was not larger than that received by one of the inferior clergy.

Of course all this took time ; but it is best to tell such a sad tale as quickly as may be.

Then, having ascertained for certain this terrible truth, her ladyship rang the bell, ordered her carriage, and drove to see a friend of hers who amused herself by imagining she patronised men of letters, actors, and such folk, never dreaming that they thought her highly honoured by their company, and went away abusing her wines, her cook, and sometimes herself. A little dinner to meet an eminent manager of theatres was speedily arranged ; the Duke of Ulster was per-suaded to attend it ; and in a week's time it became known to society that Lady Piccadilly, merely from a passing whim, was about to exhibit her talents and figure for so much money at the Theatre Royal ——. Her beginning was not good ; but it showed promise. However, Londoners care little for promise ; and soon the last nights were announced ; and in provincial papers appeared the announcement : ' On such and such a date will arrive the celebrated " Lady Piccadilly Company " from London.   Principal parts by the Right Honorable Baroness Piccadilly.'   This took.   The provincials flocked to see a live Baroness on the stage.   She gradually learned her art, for which she had a distinct genius, till at length her desire was fulfilled—she could make almost as much money as she pleased, and she could carry her audience with her—could make them admire and applaud the actress, and not the ' Lady.'

Ungrateful London saw little of her now.   She did not care to be a ' sight ' to those of whom she had been the leader ; and, besides, she was possessed of the demon of restlessness, and could scarcely stay in one town for the short periods of her several engagements. Youth began to leave her : but the art to conceal its departure became more cunning.

Her name stood high among the actresses of the world (for had she not taken the gold of the Californians, the dollars of the New Yorkers, the francs of the Parisians, and even the thalers of the Berliners ?) when I take up the thread of my story, the scene being a room in the Shelbourne Hotel, Dublin : the persons present, our noble actress herself and a young fair man, or boy, for he was scarcely eighteen, with a pretty face and a pleading voice.

' Then you *will* let me come to New York ?   It *is* so good of you.'

' Is it ? ' said Amalia languidly, stopping in the writing of a note.   ' I don't see why.   You can make yourself useful, and you are not unornamental.   A pity you're so young.'

' But I shall get better of that.'

' Yes—but then I can't wait for you.'

' Oh, Amalia, what do I care ! If only you knew——'

She jumped up with the note in her hand, and rang the bell.

' I do know.   But it is not worth talking about.'

' My love not worth talking about ! '

' You can't marry your grandmother, my dear.' (To the waiter who now entered): ' Take this note to the theatre at once. Now, Jack, don't let's bother any more about such fooleries ; you can come to New York if dear mamma will let you, and that is enough for you.'

Jack, who had in his pocket a letter from dear mamma imploring him in agonised tones to come back and not be deluded any longer by that odious woman, ' old enough to be your mother,' and reminding him that he had already spent about four times his year's allowance since leaving his tutor's, turned rather red ; but contented himself with following his enchantress downstairs, and placing himself by her side on the car which was to take them the inevitable drive in that park where Thackeray, or, rather Mr. Molony, liked

> for to see the young haroes
> All shoining with sthripes and with stars,
> A horsing about in the Phaynix,
> And winking the girls in the Cyars,
>   Like Mars,
> A smokin' their poipes and cigyars.

CHAPTER LVI.

When Nellie Erdmore realised that her young hopeful—who was, let us hasten to confess, no other than the Jack we have seen in the Shelbourne Hotel— had actually, despite her entreaties, prayers, and commands, sailed across the broad Atlantic in the *suite* of Amalia the actress, that gentle lady for once showed the bit of temper there must be somewhere in all high-spirited natures.

'I will follow him,' she cried, with her eyes flashing, 'and I will drag him from this shameless woman! I will have her hunted from her theatre with execrations. The world shall know her as she is! To extort money from my poor boy—to delude—to——'

'Well,' interrupted Lacroix, as she paused for a word strong enough, 'well, I don't think money is part of her game; at least, not with Jack. You see, she has plenty of money.'

'Then why does she take him?'

'He is a gentleman—good-looking—and useful, I suppose, to fetch and carry.'

'My son fetch and carry for Amalia Heckthorpe!'

'It *is* strange. But wait a little—he will soon come back to your feet.'

'No, I won't wait. The woman has defied me. I will accept her challenge and I will rescue my son. Is she to pursue me through all my life? First Harry, and now Jack! No. Lacroix, you want something to do, ride or drive into town and get a Bradshaw—the sailings of the Atlantic boats are there. I'll go to New York at once. Will you come?'

'I would go to the end of the world for you, as you know,' said the old man fervently.

So it was arranged, and Master Jack, feverishly passing backwards and forwards from his stall in the front of the theatre to the smart dressing-room where Lady Piccadilly received between the acts and the changes of her toilettes, little dreamed that speeding towards him at the rate of eighteen knots per hour came his mother, fully determined to tear him from the companionship of the woman who to his boyish and impressionable mind represented all that was most brilliant and most lovable in female human nature. *Si jeunesse savait!*

   ·   ·   ·   ·   ·   ·

The theatrical society of New York city was in

commotion: even the magnates dwelling in brown stone mansions *on* Fifth Avenue were stirred from their ordinary 'dollar-first-everything-else-nowhere' state of mind, and the enterprising gentlemen who interview other gentlemen and ladies for their own profit and the glorification of the latter, were full of work. A new play written by a German individual of Hebraic extraction, who was a naturalised Englishman and who resided in the United States, had been accepted at the 'Bird o' Freedom Sawin Theatre;' and no less a company than the 'Lady Piccadilly Company,' then domiciled in New York, was to enact the same for the first time on any boards. Critics were feasted, newspaper editors and owners were petted, paragraphs flew about like rain, twenty thousand copies of a life of 'The Most Noble The Lady Baroness Amalia of Piccadilly' were distributed, and photographs were exhibited in the windows of the *parure* given by H.I.M. the Czar of all the Russias, the pearl necklace laid at her feet by no less a person than Prince Bismarck, the ormolu writing-case presented by the Prince of Wales, and the promissory note sent her by an illustriously obscure Prince who aspired to the throne of Bulgaria.

It was a 'boom;' and the first night was awaited with feverish anxiety even by those of whom an ill-natured Eurōpĕăn once said, or is reported to have said, 'No more feelings than fish! A fish may have some sentiment about spawning, but *they* feel nothing until they are crimped.' Amalia could scarcely stir out of the Brevoort House Hotel—whither she went because it was so respectable—without a mob collecting; and the excitement when she rode in Central Park on an animal reputed to be able to trot a mile quicker than any other animal, placed at her disposal by one of the foremost citizens of the city (who had a wife and seven daughters and never gave them a mount) was unequalled in the 'boom' annals of New York.

Mr. Vanderackay had four of the best boxes thrown into one for the performance, and 'planked down' an incredible sum for the same.   The Duke of Ulster, who had come over in his steam yacht in order to see his cutter attempt to wrest the coveted 'America' Cup from the Yankee sloops, had announced his intention of attending in his mightiness: and it was indeed rumoured that a select circle of profound people from the 'hub of the universe' were coming to sit in judgment on the new play and the titled player.   Everything comes at last to them who know how to wait, as the *garçon* at the restaurant said when he pocketed his *douceur*; and at last the long-expected evening came.   Those concerned in the production were nervous, because the American public is very apt to spurn a good thing for the sake of showing American independence and originality; but the leading lady was far above such feelings, and reclined in her dressing-room ready dressed, with the air of a Cleopatra to whom all dudes are Antonys.

'A lady to see you,' said the maid, after a moment's whispering with a servant of the theatre at the door.

'Who?'

'She says she won't detain you a moment, and that it is important.'

'Well—has Mr. Erdmore been behind yet?'

'No, my Lady.'

'Then show her in.'

In another moment Nellie Erdmore, Harry's first love, and Amalia, his widow, were face to face.

'My son is not here,' said the former, advancing into the middle of the room; 'but perhaps I can take his place.'

Amalia started, but regained her composure almost immediately.   Then rising slowly, with that dignity she knew so well how to assume:

'Mrs. Erdmore!   May I ask you to be seated? To what do I owe the honour——'

'You may well call it an honour for any honest woman to exchange words with you.'

You see the little woman had kept up her spirit bravely, even over all those miles of sea; but we know what even a timid hen will do for its offspring. Amalia's fine eyes flashed dangerously. She was dressed in a rich Eastern garment, covered with barbaric gems, her splendid arms were bare, and on her brow glittered a coronal on which shone stones almost beyond price; at least for ordinary mortals.

'You are insulting. This is a free country, but yet there are limits to freedom. I shall have you removed.' And she rose and went slowly towards the electric button in the wall.

'One moment,' said Nellie, stepping in front of her. 'I am sorry I insulted you; but—one moment——'

Amalia stood still, haughty, but willing to hear.

'I have a few words to say.'

'Say them, then.'

'Lady Piccadilly, years ago you took from me the man I cared for: I had done you no harm. Since then much has happened; but still I have never harmed you. Will you take my boy from me too?'

Alas! all the fiery spirit had gone; only the pleading humble mother remained.

'What do I care for your boy?'

'He follows you everywhere; he is giving up all that his life promises; he——'

'I don't want him—take him back with you, if you can.'

The satirical venom of the last words cannot be described. They roused the other woman again.

'You mean that you will keep him! Woman, your look is infectious, your touch is shame: yet you cannot be altogether a devil. Are there not others—why must you ruin that poor boy?'

'It is you only who speak of ruin. On the contrary,

I keep him from harm. He is foolish and wants looking after.'

'He has his mother.'

'Apparently he wants somebody else.'

'Then you refuse my request?' The cool insolence of the last of Amalia's speeches had made the situation unbearable for the other.

'Yes,' answered the actress with infinite coolness, 'I refuse to let your silly son go because—because——'

'Because?'

Amalia paused a moment; her bold eyes flashed, and a hard look came over all her face such as she seldom allowed there—for it was not pretty—and she suddenly said, her calm manner changing to a kind of subdued ferocity:

'Because I hate you. Because he is the only weapon chance has put into my hands with which to punish you.'

'To punish me!'

'Yes, I loved Harry. Ah, you may believe I can't love; but I did—I loved him—and between him and me there always was the recollection of you.'

'Of me!'

'Yes! Do you think I don't know why he got to hate me, why I so soon lost all his affection—for I had it once—it was all you.'

'Lady Piccadilly, I never——'

'You never did anything a perfect woman should not do—oh no! But you ruined my life—ruined the only chance I ever had of being a good woman. *Now* do you understand why I will not give up your son?'

'Surely,' gasped Nellie, scarcely knowing what she said—'surely it is hard on me that——'

'Hard on you! Why not? Do you think in this world we are punished for our own sins? I cared so for Harry that all other men were then, and are still, so many cabbage-heads to me; and the ruin, as you call it, of your cub, or the fooling of the Cannibal, only please me because they go to prove that all other men are merely baboons compared with him.'

'I loved him too!' cried Nellie, off her guard, and moved by the recollections the other had called up.

Amalia had suddenly resumed her calm disdainful manner.

'More fool you,' she said, putting a cigarette between her lips and lighting it at a candle. 'The more fool you. I married him—and he is dead.'

The door opened and the manager entered, profuse in his compliments to Amalia on her attire ; a call-boy was summoned to show 'the lady' out, and in a few moments Nellie found herself in the street, being jostled by the crowd arriving to take their seats to see the grand performance.

And it was a grand performance.

All the aristocracy of New York and its vicinity was there—all the 'dudes,' all the critics, all the millionaires, all the celebrities, and—crowning triumph!—the ladies with the red shawls from Boston Amalia's success in the first act was complete. Bouquets showered upon her—the 'floral offerings' handed from the orchestra were larger than the big drum—and the applause might have been heard in Wall Street. The privileged hurried to the back to express their delighted admiration, and foremost among these was the young Englishman whose mother had just gone back to her hotel with a breaking heart.

Nellie Erdmore had only arrived that afternoon in the steamer, and had hurried straight to the theatre, sending Lacroix off to the hotels, to discover where Jack was lodging.

The second act had in its first part a strong situation, which involved a struggle between the heroine and one of the villains of the piece: a struggle which the author fondly thought would prove the arch-success of the play. And well indeed it went. Amalia's deep voice echoed round the house as she denounced the traitor—her shriek as he seized her by her white arm caused a shiver among the more impressionable of the audience, and with breathless interest all watched her marvellous reality of acting as she fought him inch by inch towards the side. Suddenly there was a crash—no one could quite see what had occurred—but a sudden light shot out from the wing, and in a moment, before it was possible to realise the catastrophe, the actress was enveloped in a sheet of flame. The actor with her lost his head, the audience shrieked and fainted, men shouted out contradictory orders and suggestions—all was hubbub and confusion—when suddenly a tall man leaped across the orchestra on to the stage, and, divesting himself as he went of a heavy overcoat, threw it over the shoulders of the mad, shrieking, running woman.

Then the curtain fell. There was silence for a brief space, broken by the appearance before it of the stage-manager, to tell them with a grave face that the Baroness had received very severe injuries, but that there was some hope.

But there was no hope. In that little room where she had so lately insulted and defied Nellie Erdmore, Amalia died. A man—the man who had attempted to save her life—sat with her to the last, doing all he could to alleviate her agony. Once she opened her eyes and looked into his, and then turned away with a shudder and a groan.

Once again, when a fussy doctor had asked him to leave the room, as having no business there, her hand had closed on his and held it, to forbid his going; and once again, at the very last, when the spirit was about to go, she looked up into his face and murmured ' If it is real—not a vision—forgive me, Harry—forgive——'

These were her last words. The last words of Baroness Piccadilly, leader of fashion, actress, and once Amalia Heckthorpe, daughter of the Ilborough publican.

> Soft is her skin,
>   Bright were her eyes,
> Will they get her in
>   To Paradise ?

CHAPTER LVII.

AT the counter of the office of one of the less fashionable of the New York hotels, a week after the events of the last chapter, stood Jack Erdmore, trying to possess his British soul in patience as the clerk, totally disregarding the work for which he presumably received a salary, proved his American independence by neglecting a Britisher. At length his patience was rewarded, and he learned that Mr. Jameson was now able to receive visitors and doubtless would see him if he walked up to No. 27.

' He has been pretty bad,' said the clerk, picking his teeth thoughtfully, ' and the doctor told me his burns were about as bad as a man could have without going to kingdom come.'

Arrived at No. 27, Jack knocked, and on receiving permission from the inside, entered. Lying on a sofa, with both his arms wrapped in bandages, and with another bandage about his neck and the right shoulder, was a tall handsome man with regular features, a pair of kind blue eyes, and curly hair beginning to show signs of grey. He started as he saw Jack, and then winced with pain, as the motion disturbed a bandage.

' You are the writer of this ? ' he asked, pointing to

an open note that lay on the table by his side. Jack nodded.

'Sit down. I can't shake hands, as you see ; but you are welcome. So you are Jack Erdmore.'

He looked hard at Jack as he said this—a concentrated, critical, yet kind look—and the boy blushed and fidgeted.

'I wanted to say—you know—to thank you—about poor Amalia——'

The man stopped him with some sternness.

'I require no thanks — certainly none from you. I only did what anyone would have done to save a human life.'

'But you must let me thank you,' pleaded Jack, with tears in his eyes. 'You don't know what she was to me—how I—I cared for her—and how good and beautiful and clever she was—and now——' And the lad fairly broke down and, turning away to the window, burst into tears.

'I don't know !' muttered Harry to himself grimly. Then aloud : 'My dear boy, you needn't be ashamed of being sorry. The sudden death of any friend is always sad——'

'She was more than a friend,' sobbed Jack.

Again Harry's tone became somewhat hard, as he interrupted him.

'She is gone, and I will not judge her ; but there is one who *is* your friend—whose love is worth more to you than the love of all other women on earth, and whose heart you must have been breaking by all this folly. Where is your mother ? '

'My mother, Mr. Jameson? Even she is sorry now she thought so hardly of Amalia.'

'She has cabled to you ? ' asked Harry, lifting his eyebrows ; or, to be accurate, lifting the place where his eyebrows had been before they were burnt off.

'Cabled? Oh, no ; she is here.'

'Here, in New York?'

'Yes.   She'—Jack looked rather shamefaced now—
'she came to—to——'

'To try and save you.   I understand.'

Then Harry was silent for a long time, till the other
thought his visit had tired the sick man, and rose to go.

'I *must* say what I wanted to, Mr. Jameson,' he exclaimed, standing before the sofa, hat in hand—'that
your trying to save her life at the expense of your own
was noble—and——'

'Pish!' said Harry impatiently, 'that's enough.   You
shall show me her grave when I can get about; and I
will make arrangements about its being looked after.'

Jack looked surprised.   'You?'

Harry changed the subject abruptly.

'Will you give me that bottle on the chimney-
piece—the blue one?   Thanks.   These infernal lotions
get dry in no time.   Can you give me a hand?   Thanks.
Now unwind it gently.   Bravo!'

Jack helped with much gentleness at the re-wetting
process; and when it was finished inquired, hesitatingly,

'Will you come and see my mother, sir?'

Harry looked at him at first suspiciously, and then
kindly enough, as he answered:

'I am only a rough Canadian farmer, my boy, and
know nothing now of ladies' ways.'

'But, Mr. Jameson, that's just what we are going to
be—I mean I am—and old Lacroix.'

'Farmers!'

'Yes.   You see the Government have been keeping
order in Ireland in such a funny way that no rent is
paid at all—at least, none of our rents; and the mort-
gages really can't be kept up.   So my mother, who has
some money of her own, has determined to buy some
property out here—either in America or Canada—and
then when I come of age I can either go back to
Ireland or I can sell my interest—such as it is—in the

Castle Erdmore estates and settle over here with her.
I shall know by then whether I like the life. So,
you see, you are speaking to another farmer, Mr.
Jameson.'

Harry thought a little, and then said in a low
trembling tone which caused the boy to think he was
in pain: 'I will call upon Mrs. Erdmore, if she will
receive me. Tell her an old friend of hers wishes to see
her—an old, old friend.'

.   .   .   .   .

One word of explanation.

When the *Banshee* ran on those cruel Newfoundland
rocks after a week of fog that would have baffled better
navigators than Harry or his skipper, all were lost
save the owner and the cook, who had preferred sticking
to the ship to trusting themselves to the boats. Picked
off half dead by a fishing-smack next day, they had
been taken to a small fishing port, and the idea had at
once struck Harry of abandoning for ever both his
name and his miserable existence as Amalia's husband.
It was not difficult to invent a plausible story to
deceive the honest fisher folk: and the cook, who worshipped his master, entered, if with dismay and wonder,
still with loyalty, into the plot. Harry had not forgotten his early commercial training, and it was not long
before he was earning a comfortable living at St. John's.
Men with brains, muscles, and industry can always
make their way in that country.

As the years rolled on he made money, rose to a
partnership in a small shipping house, and, when he
paid his visit to New York, just in time to see his
wife burnt to death before his eyes, he had come for
the purpose of winding up some business there, pre-
paratory to resigning his partnership and retiring to a
farm in Upper Canada that he had purchased a year
before.

Such was the position of affairs when he said to

Jack, Nellie's son : ' Tell your mother that an old friend wishes to see her.'

' An old friend!' repeated Mrs. Erdmore, when her son gave her the message. ' What is he like?'

' Very tall and good-looking, with a fair beard and blue eyes, and a bit grey about the head. He says he's a Canadian farmer; but he looks and speaks like a gentleman. He reminds me of some one too.'

Nellie looked at her son inquiringly and blushed, she knew not why, as she met his gaze.

' An old friend,' she repeated again, dreamingly.

' I have it, mother!' exclaimed the boy, starting to his feet. ' It's that photograph you have—the one you always carry about with you——'

Jack stopped suddenly at the look in his mother's face—a look that seemed like that of one who has seen a ghost.

' Why, mother, you look as if——' he was beginning, when there came in suddenly Lacroix, his white hair standing up on his head in ludicrous disorder, his eyes full of tears, but trembling with indescribable joy, his tie under one ear and his dress showing signs of a wrestling-match; while his manner was that of the most intense and ungovernable excitement.

He threw himself into a chair which creaked under the onslaught, and exclaimed, in a voice that was between crying and laughing :

' I am quite calm ! There is nothing to excite you, my dear. Look at me, I am quite calm!'

' What the deuce——' began Jack, but stopped as he saw his mother, still with that stony look of wonder on her face, approach the old man.

' Lacroix,' she said, and her pretty soft voice sounded almost sepulchral, ' Lacroix, tell me all.'

' Ah! parbleu! I am calm. I am quite calm : he told me to——'

' He? Who?'

'Why, my dear Mrs. Erdmore, I——'

'Tell me all.'

She put her hand on his shoulder with a gesture of authority.

'I *will* know all.'

'There are no ghosts nowadays,' almost screamed Lacroix, beside himself with excitement. 'There are no ghosts! Prepare yourself, Nellie—my Nellie—for a shock—one cannot die of joy, though!'

She did not notice his familiar and unwonted address, she was trembling in every limb, and only steadied herself by holding him still by the shoulder.

'What do you mean? Who?' she gasped.

'Mother,' said Jack, approaching her; but she waved him back.

'Make him speak!' she cried, indicating the old man, who sat feebly gesticulating in the chair.

'Look here, you know, Mr. Lacroix,' said the boy. 'Out with it.'

'I am to break it to her! I am to break it to her!' cried he. 'Mon Dieu, don't I long to say the words!'

'You torture me!' cried Nellie, in a voice in which horror mingled with hope. 'What is it that you would break to me? Speak!'

'He cannot,' said a deep voice at the door, 'and so I must!'

Nellie Erdmore turned with a shriek, in which joy was the predominant note, took two steps forward towards the man who stood there with outstretched bandaged hands, and, tottering, fell into his arms.

.   .   .   .   .   .

'Some pains are pleasant?' said Mr. Jameson the Canadian farmer one summer evening, as he sat in the verandah of his house: on one side of him his wife with a child in her arms, and on the other a sturdy young man, who liked to argue now and then.

'Some pains are pleasant, you say, Jack. Well, I'll

tell you the only really pleasant physical pain I ever felt : and that was when that inconsiderate mother of yours would faint and oblige me to catch her with arms that were only incarnated burns two years ago at the Brunswick Hotel in New York.'

So Joseph Lord Piccadilly's advice to his nephew bore fruit, notwithstanding its cynicism.

'Goodness,' as Joseph wrote in the letter Harry received after his death, 'the only thing I never tried, is possibly the only thing that leads to that grand desideratum, happiness.'

And Harry Jameson was quite content to be good, when he had always with him the great incentive to virtue, Love.